HARD DRIVE

HARD DRIVE

J. MARK COLLINS

iUniverse®

HARD DRIVE

iUniverse books may be ordered through booksellers or by contacting:

iUniverse
1663 Liberty Drive
Bloomington, IN 47403
www.iuniverse.com
1-800-Authors (1-800-288-4677)

ISBN: 978-1-4917-8041-1 (sc)
ISBN: 978-1-4917-8042-8 (e)

Library of Congress Control Number: 2015917214

Printed in USA.

iUniverse rev. date: 1/7/2016

To Allan,

All the best!

Mark

PROLOGUE

The young man held the titanium attaché case in a loose grip, trusting the chain locked to his wrist to keep it safe. He showed little emotion and wasn't the least bit nervous. He'd made the trip twice before without incident. He'd been warned to be careful, but what the hell. Nothing even close to exciting had happened so far, and it wasn't like he was risking a real career. He had plans. *Big plans.* This was just a part-time gig. He wasn't planning on being a freelance courier for the rest of his life.

As he walked the length of the jetway leading away from the Aeroflot Airbus A350, his eyes raked the long, sexy legs of a flight attendant walking ahead of him. He let his gaze travel up to the tailored skirt that hugged her fine ass. *Yes sir, big plans.*

The chain jangled conspicuously against the side of the case with a rhythm that matched the swaying of her hips. The young man didn't try to hide the significance of his assignment. He enjoyed the feeling of importance it gave him. He hoped the young woman walking ahead of him might take notice. Maybe turn around and flash him a smile. She didn't.

Oh well, her loss.

He was too tired anyway. The long flight left him feeling worn thin. His body ached, and he was looking forward to a hot shower before falling into his own bed. Although he enjoyed the travel, it always felt good to come home. But first he had to get rid of the damned case.

Stepping through the arrivals gate, he was surprised to see a driver with a placard bearing his name, obviously sent by his employer. *Too bad the flight attendant couldn't see this.*

He'd barely taken two steps in the direction of the waiting car when a man behind him snaked out a hand and grabbed him by the collar. He was yanked backward with a vicious jerk that swept him off his feet. He crashed to the ground with a bone-jarring thump. Shocked, he tried to catch his breath as he stared up at a face only a few years older than his own—thin mouth, gray eyes, tanned complexion, close cropped sandy hair. The stranger pulled him to his feet as if he weighed nothing. It was only then he noticed the retreating taillights of the limousine that narrowly missed hitting him as it roared through the passenger pick up area of Pearson International Airport.

"You've got to watch them. Always in a hurry," the stranger said, dusting off the back of the courier's jacket. "You okay?"

"Yeah. Thanks. Shit, I didn't even see that guy."

"You should be more careful."

"I guess. Man, thanks again. I owe you one."

"Don't worry about it," the stranger said.

"No, seriously. If there's anything—"

"Wouldn't happen to be going downtown, would you?" The stranger interjected, indicating the courier's waiting limo with a tilt of his head. "My ride blew me off."

"Uh …" The courier faltered, suddenly apprehensive.

"Don't worry. I'm sure it's against the rules." The stranger said, looking pointedly at the case.

"Probably, but …" The courier hesitated another second before making a snap decision. It was the wrong one. "I'm sure it will be okay."

"Hey, don't worry about it. I can grab a cab," the stranger said.

The courier ignored the protest and moved towards the limo, followed closely by the stranger.

"Don't mind me. It's been a long day. I'll feel better when I get rid of this thing."

"You sure? I don't want you to get in any trouble."

"What can they do? Fire me?"

The courier nodded politely to the driver who was holding the rear door open. He ducked his head and bent to step into the stretch Lincoln, saying over his shoulder as he did, "My name's Peter, by the—"

His words ended abruptly when he noticed the plastic on the floor of the limo and felt a sharp push from behind. His brain didn't have a chance to register the blade of the stiletto the stranger thrust between his ribs. The courier was dead before his head hit the plastic sheet covering the plush carpet.

As the stranger stepped into the back seat and pulled the door closed behind him, the driver moved in behind the wheel and started the car. The limo cleared the passenger pick-up and moved out along the pretzel twist of highways that surround the airport. Highway 409 snaked around until it merged onto Highway 401, 16 lanes of blacktop that slash across the top of Toronto like a great wound.

In the back, the thin chain holding the attaché case proved much stronger than it looked. Like the case, it was titanium.

"Problem?" The driver spoke over his shoulder, his eyes flicking to the mirror.

"Pay attention to your driving," the stranger said, pulling a hacksaw out of a small duffle bag.

He quickly cut off the courier's hand at the wrist.

"You've got a spot picked out?" The stranger asked, nudging the lifeless body with his foot. "I don't want this found too soon."

"Don't worry."

"I always worry."

The driver didn't respond.

The back of the limousine became a mobile workshop. The stranger, who called himself Wolfe, opened a duffle bag again and extracted a leather pouch containing an array of jeweler's tools. He selected a nickel-plated screwdriver and tested it for balance. Ignoring the locks on the attaché case he began to work on the exposed hinges, managing to spring them in a matter of a minute. The alarm in the attaché gave a brief scream of disapproval before being quickly silenced. The driver kept his eyes glued to the road ahead.

Wolfe exhaled a slow breath, an uneasy feeling starting to grow in the pit of his stomach. He'd been ready to take the case elsewhere if he had to, but apparently it wouldn't be necessary. *Is it really going to be this easy?* He slowly began to lift the lid, shaking his head at his own insecurities. *Of course it is … she's an amateur.* He opened the case carefully and smiled, anticipation pushing aside the doubt. The smile didn't last long. *Empty!*

Wolfe struggled to remain in control, his face a frozen mask. *Okay, think! Did she know or did she get lucky? Bitch!* After a minute, Wolfe broke the silence.

"Can you make it so this is *never* found?" He kicked the body again.

Wolfe caught the driver's furtive glance in the rearview mirror. The man hesitated a fraction of a second too long.

"Answer me, damn it!" Wolfe's calm tone was replaced by menacing snarl.

"Can you make this disappear or not? I want it buried deep. Understand?"

The driver nodded. "Yeah. Sure. But …"

Wolfe waited for what he knew was coming.

"It'll be much more difficult … and expensi—"

"How much?" Wolfe snapped.

"Two grand … on top."

"Done."

Wolfe peeled off a number of large bills from a stack he pulled from his pocket and handed them to the driver.

"Make sure I get my money's worth. No trace."

The driver smiled, apparently forgetting Wolfe could see him in the mirror.

Good. Wolfe thought, knowing the man would never live to spend a dime of it.

"Stop at the next corner."

The driver pulled to the curb. By the time the rear door slammed shut Wolfe was lost from view in a crowd of businessmen scurrying to make luncheon meetings. The driver licked his thumb and began counting the extra cash, totally oblivious to the lifeless body in the back of his limousine, the severed hand pointing accusingly in his direction.

CHAPTER ONE

Ricco sat in an over-stuffed chair with its back placed carefully in a corner. He had a clear view of both the front door and the fire escape. His eyes darted from left to right and back again. The corded muscles of his forearm, covered with intricate tattoos, tapped the armrest with nervous energy. He rubbed a hand over his goatee as he looked around the room. Everything in view had to be labeled as either a help or a hindrance—something that could save his life or end it. Avenues of attack, a means of retreat, areas of cover and concealment, all were cataloged without a conscious thought. It was an old habit for such a young man, more suited to a theater of war than to a four-story walk up, but Ricco had been at war for years. The street was no place to be complacent. His instincts kept him alive. He was a survivor.

His companion, bent over a cheap melamine table in the small kitchen, was organizing an extraordinary array of weapons and explosives. The two men said nothing to each other.

Ricco's gaze slid across the heavy steel door that led to the hallway outside the apartment. The lock was set and the chain in place. He fingered the trigger of the Smith & Wesson .50 caliber Magnum in his lap, a nickel-plated five shot revolver with a nine-inch barrel. Not his weapon of choice on a daily basis, but at a time like this, when he had nothing to do but wait, it felt good to hold something so lethal.

Ricco eyed his new companion. They were an unlikely team, to say the least. The slightly stooped, middle-aged man showed no sign that he had a care in the world, quietly going about the business of preparation as he waited for the final set of instructions. Dressed in a rumpled suit and white shirt, a cheap tie pulled askew to one side, Tinker looked more like an accountant than one of the best demolitions men in the business. The only sound he made was a resigned sigh whenever he brushed a strand of rapidly thinning hair back into place. That and a distant telephone ringing insistently were the only sounds that disturbed the peace of the dingy little room.

Ricco watched the back of the man's head, trying to get a feel for him. People had to be categorized in the same manner as objects. Asset or liability? Survival or extinction. It was a cold approach to life, but it had been a damned cold life. He looked at the revolver in his hand, swung out the cylinder, and checked the cartridges for the hundredth time.

Satisfied, he leaned further into the floral print of the armchair and tried to shake off an increasing sense of urgency. His surroundings were as secure as they'd ever been in his 27 years and yet something was pushing him to move. He listened carefully to the world around him. He could hear Tinker humming a nameless tune as he cleaned and loaded the Uzi machine pistols and arranged the other military ordnance in neat lines, like a general inspecting his troops. He could still hear the persistent ringing of a telephone in the distance. Otherwise, it was a quiet night in the heart of the city.

What am I missing?

Six members of the Emergency Task Force (ETF) crouched along the east wall of the fourth floor hallway. All of them wore black military style fatigues and Kevlar body armor over bodies hardened by years of intense training. Three of them held fully automatic MP5 sub-machine guns. Two more waited impatiently, white knuckled, gripping the handles of a heavy iron battering ram known as *The Key*. The sixth listened silently at the door with a small audio amplifier. The apartment was too small to risk inserting a camera.

The ETF is an elite squad of highly trained officers who provide specialized support to all units within the Toronto Police Service. Using high-tech equipment, special tactics, and an impressive array of weapons, the ETF takes on the unusual, the unexpected, and the unwanted. Described by some as 'big boys with big toys', tonight's game was a tactical entry. Intel said they'd be going into a hot zone. None of them thought of this as play.

All eyes focused on the team leader, Sergeant Karski, standing some fifty feet away talking quietly into the microphone of a state-of-the-art headset. He was listening to a report by two other members of the team—a sniper and an observer—stationed in a fifth floor apartment of the building directly across from the target.

The final member of the team, crouched on the fire escape two floors below the target, began moving with remarkable stealth towards the window above.

The rooms to either side of the target had already been cleared, as had the room directly below. There was a man stationed in each of the end stairwells to stop anyone from entering the "zone," and two more on the roof above. Karski was a man who didn't like to leave anything to chance.

He looked at the six men in the hall, making sure all eyes were on him before giving one final whispered instruction.

"Stay ready. Go on my signal."

Darcy Caldwell crouched on the landing of the fire escape, now only one floor below the target. She checked the safety on her Glock 17, a high-powered 9 mm semi-automatic pistol. Her dark shoulder length hair was carefully tucked beneath an even darker stocking cap, her face and neck blackened with camo grease. Only someone watching very carefully could pick out her graceful climb as she started to move farther up the outside of the building. No one did.

Darcy moved across the landing onto the second step and stopped. While she tried to listen for any noise from above, she focused most of her attention on the receiver buzzing softly in her left ear as the Observer relayed information to Karski. This would be the final report before they were ordered to move. Every second they waited increased the danger. Despite the tension, her thoughts began to wander as she waited for the final signal.

Next time, Karski, you can stick someone else on the goddamn fire escape. Outside looking in. I'm always getting shafted with shit like this.

She unconsciously rubbed the sweat off her forehead leaving a lighter smudge of camo, her nerves making her shake in the mild spring air. She brought herself fully back into the present and released a slow breath. Eyes locked on the target window, she took another step up.

CHAPTER TWO

Ricco shifted to the edge of his chair, unable to resist the impulse to move any longer. Something was definitely wrong … something didn't fit. He looked around the room again, scanning frantically for anything out of place. Tinker continued to hum under his breath as he wiped the excess gun oil from the weapons he had so carefully cleaned and loaded. He seemed totally oblivious to the mounting sense of urgency that pervaded the room. Ricco continued to scan. His eyes fell on the sliding steel gate that covered the window leading to the fire escape, only partially visible through ancient curtains. It was unlocked, an inch gap separating the leading edge from the locking plate.

Ricco swore as he shot off the chair. "I told you to keep the fucking gate locked. You want people walking in off the fucking street?"

Tinker didn't react.

Ricco slid the gate back and slammed it home, locking it in place. The report of steel on steel echoed between the buildings. He stood to the left of the window and moved the curtain to one side.

Darcy Caldwell crouched three steps below the landing, her face tucked into the crook of her elbow to hide her eyes, unable to breathe, her heart pounding like a trip hammer. Every nerve ending in her body screamed *Run*, but she sat motionless as the seconds ticked by. Her earpiece buzzed with the voice of the Observer.

"He locked the gate. He's at the window right now. Jesus, he's carrying a fucking cannon. Don't move Darcy."

Darcy took a slow breath, but didn't respond with the '*No shit!*' that was on the tip of her tongue.

Another voice crackled in her ear-the sniper half of the Sierra Team. "He's just standing there. Do I have a green light?"

Yes! Thought Darcy.

"No!" Karski's order was firm. "Not until he moves. The second he raises that cannon, take him out."

Karski looked at the men in the hall. He didn't have to say another word. Talbot and Jenkins stood slowly, lifting the heavy iron ram.

Ricco swayed slightly as he stood to the side of the window, the Smith & Wesson at his side, his eyes trying to pierce the inky blackness. But it wasn't the darkness that was playing on his nerves, and it wasn't the unlocked gate. There was something else … something more …

The ringing of the telephone shattered the stillness of the apartment like a scream. Ricco jumped. Tinker only sighed and brushed another uncooperative strand of hair across his bald pate. Ricco moved quickly back to his chair in the corner and picked up the handset before the third ring.

"Yeah?"

Knowing who should be on the other end, his mind concentrated on the problem at hand as the solution slowly began to surface. The telephone. The telephone next door had been ringing constantly. Why hadn't the old lady who lives there answered it? She was *always* home.

"Vince?"

Ricco answered instinctively before realizing he didn't recognize the voice on the other end of the line. With that, the steel door of the apartment exploded inward as the cheap wooden frame gave way under the first violent impact of the heavy steel battering ram.

CHAPTER THREE

"GO! GO! GO!"

Darcy moved before her brain had time to register the command ringing in her ear. She slammed her back against the weathered brick, almost knocking the wind out of herself trying to get into position. She risked a quick peek through the gap between the curtains. She couldn't see either of the targets. Swearing at the locked gate, she moved to her left to gain a better view. She could see most of the main room and the opening to the hall where the heavy steel door lay canted against the wall. Members of her squad were moving into position, weapons extended, eyes scanning side to side. When the first shot rang out Darcy felt like the greatest drama of her life was being played out and she was about to miss it.

Before the door slammed against the far wall, the men stepped back to make room for Karski, throwing the battering ram to the right as they moved. Each man now held a Glock 17, light-duty compared to the MP 5's carried by the rest of the team and the .50 caliber Magnum Ricco held in his hand.

Karski was the first one through the door. Exploding forward, he all but flew the length of the short hall and into the bedroom straight ahead. It was a calculated risk, but he had no choice. He slammed his full weight against the door and swept his MP5 across the room. The doorknob punched through the plaster behind and Karski could feel without looking that no one was hiding behind it. The room held a cheap metal office desk with a computer on it and a drafting table. Nothing large enough to conceal a person. He turned his attention to the main room as a burst of automatic fire bisected the bathroom door.

Karski could hear Asher shouting at one of the suspects, his baritone an octave higher than normal. "Police! Don't move! Drop It!"

"It's down. It's down!" An unknown voice.

Ragins lay in a crumpled heap across the metal door. Karski dragged his teammate into the relative safety of the bedroom as another round of gunfire splintered the doorframe above his head. He couldn't tell if the man was alive or dead.

Giving Talbot and Jenkins the 'hold' sign, Karski extended a small convex mirror on a telescoping handle. It gave him a fish-eye view of the rest of the apartment. Through it Karski could see Asher standing with his back to a wall, his MP 5 pointed at a man cowering in the corner. The doorway to the kitchen was empty except for smoke from the expended rounds and the cavernous barrel of an M72 rocket launcher. Karski looked at Talbot as he exhaled a barely audible,

"Oh shit!"

Darcy barely flinched when the first burst of gunfire exploded, even though she was only six feet away from the gunman and moving across in front of the window at the time. Her breathing became extremely shallow and the ordinary noises of the city ceased to register. Time and space seemed to exist on a different plane. Her peripheral vision disappeared. She found herself staring down a narrow tunnel in a dense fog.

The second salvo of gunfire shattered the air around her as she pushed her left shoulder against the brick and raised her Glock. Through the gap in the curtain she caught a glimpse of a man moving around the kitchen. Even through a pane of glass, she could hear the metallic click of his weapon going dry. She moved to a better position and found herself staring at the back of the suspect as he dropped what looked like an Uzi sub-machine gun on the dingy linoleum floor. She watched as the man calmly reached for an already extended M72 rocket launcher and raised it into firing position.

Darcy hesitated. The man seemed to change his mind. He raised his left hand and let the weapon fall from his shoulder. She could hear Karski shouting orders. The man bent to place the weapon gingerly on the floor in front of him. As he struggled to straighten back up, Darcy caught a glimpse of something she knew instinctively the other members of the team couldn't see—a pistol in his right hand. She had no idea where it came from, but she had no doubt what he meant to do with it. This time she didn't hesitate. She double-tapped the man in the back of the head.

Karski watched in disbelief as the head of the man who was surrendering to him suddenly exploded before his eyes. For a split second there was complete silence inside the apartment and out on the street. No one moved. Then, as reality began to sink in, noise and motion exploded in the apartment. Karski moved into the main room barking orders into the microphone of his headset.

"Shots fired. Officer down. I need paramedics. Now! Jenkins with Asher. Talbot with me."

A sense of organized chaos gripped the whole area and it was impossible to tell who was shouting the orders and who was following them.

"Hands out to the side!"

"Get the paramedics in here!"

"Turn around. Slowly. Slowly!"

"Stairway's clear. Roof clear."

"On your knees! Cross your right foot over your left."

"In the bedroom. One down. Shit!"

"Keep your hands out. Palms facing me."

"Kitchen clear. Talbot, get the window grill."

"Hands on your head. Interlace your fingers. Palms up."

"Cuffed and clear."

"Bring in the board. Somebody get this fuckin' door out of the way!"

"Caldwell— what the fuck?!"

When the scene was secure Karski looked out the window in time to see Darcy slump against the wall, her back creating a small shower of soot and brick dust as she slid into a sitting position on the landing of the fire escape. The pistol, held loosely between her knees, pointed carelessly at the emergency vehicles converging on the street four floors below. There was no need for stealth. Sirens wailed and lights rotated across the buildings again and again as curious neighbors looked on.

Darcy sat staring out into nothing. Karski could tell time and space hadn't realigned for her yet. He knew she was still somewhere in the middle of what's known as a 'tache psyche episode'. He knew from personal experience that she couldn't make her fingers work the safety on the semi-automatic in her hand, couldn't trust herself to stand, and probably couldn't even hear her own name being called.

Karski stepped out on to the fire escape, squatted down beside her, and very gingerly removed the pistol from Darcy's grasp. Expertly locking the breach open and dropping the clip, he set the weapon on the steel slats beside him.

"It's gonna be okay."

"Yeah?" Darcy said.

"Yeah."

"He had a piece … a back-up." She sounded like an automaton.

"I know. We got it."

"I almost didn't see it."

Karski only nodded, thinking about what could have happened

"Anybody else hit? I mean besides …" Darcy inclined her head toward the window.

"Rags."

Darcy's head snapped up.

"Relax. He'll live. He took two in the vest and one in the arm."

"Shit."

"Would've been worse if it wasn't for you."

"Yeah?"

Karski waited until she spoke again.

"You ever have to shoot anybody?"

Karski responded quietly, "Yeah."

"It's not like in training."

"I know."

"And it sure as hell isn't like on TV."

"I know."

"It sucks."

When it was obvious she wasn't going to say anything else, Karski said the only thing he could think of under the circumstances.

"You did what you had to Darcy."

"It still sucks."

"I know … and it's probably only gonna get worse."

Darcy finally looked up at him. "SIU?"

Karski nodded. "And an internal. I have to take your kit."

Darcy's eyes seemed to regain a little fire. "Fucking wonderful."

"Standard procedure. You know that."

"Doesn't make me feel any better."

"I know," Karski said again.

They sat in silence for a few minutes as the night cooled and the revolving lights created a theater of grotesque shadows around them. When it seemed like enough time had passed Karski hauled them both to their feet. They rejoined the subsiding confusion in the apartment. The one suspect, the one not in the body bag, had been formally arrested and removed to the station to wait the inevitable question and bullshit session that was sure to follow. Ident was busy taking video and thousands of pictures. The coroner's office was just removing the other suspect's body from the scene.

Karski surveyed the kitchen. Spent shell casings, discarded Uzis, and bricks of C4 lay scattered on the floor. The unused M72's had rolled harmlessly off the upended table into the far corner and lay tangled in a web of brightly colored wires and timers. Asher's voice brought Karski back from another place.

"Would you look at this shit! What the hell was going on here?"

"I don't know," Karski said.

"I sure wish the informant told us there was going to be rocket launchers in this fucking deal. I would have booked off sick."

Karski smiled, but didn't respond.

"Seriously. This isn't your normal gun running operation. These guys were playing for keeps. At least that guy was." Asher motioned to the outline on the kitchen floor. "This shit just doesn't happen here. Not in Toronto."

"I know," Karski said, "But somebody better find out what the fuck's going on before it happens again."

CHAPTER FOUR

Less than a mile away, Jack realized he was in trouble. His assailant was pressing forward rather than tiring, gathering strength and momentum with each kick delivered on target, with each punch that broke through his defense.

"Give it up, old man," his opponent said, landing another well-placed jab to the solar plexus, causing Jack to double over. "You haven't got a chance." A wicked ax kick missed him by a fraction.

Jack didn't need this. Holding his arms up to protect himself he tried to gain some time by creating a little distance, but it was too late. His feet shuffled like a man doing a poor imitation of the old soft-shoe. A slow left followed by a lightning quick right to the nose made Jack's eyes water and his head spin. Desperate to save himself, he dropped to his left knee, spinning his right leg in a back kick designed to sweep his opponent's feet. A roundhouse kick caught him squarely on the jaw and sent him sprawling on his back. His assailant held him down with a knee on his chest, fist poised to strike a death blow, palm down, fingers pulled back.

"If you're going to sweep a girl off her feet, try flowers and dinner out." His opponent smiled and increased the pressure on Jack's chest.

Cocky, Jack thought to himself. *Cocky son-of-a—*

Light applause and a few chuckles from the students who had remained after class echoed off the walls of the spartan Karate *dojo*. Jack's adversary stepped back, exerting a little pressure with her knee to remind him that he had been beaten ... again. He accepted the slender hand extended down to him and stood with some difficulty. His ears were still ringing and he had the strangest sensation that the world had somehow canted to the left.

Regaining his composure along with his equilibrium, Jack bowed formally to the beautiful young woman standing opposite him.

"Thank you, Sensei. Next time dinner and roses it is." Jack's smile was genuine, if a little chagrined.

Nina Mariko, Jack's Karate Instructor for the past four years, smiled and returned the bow. "Dinner would be nice." Her smile said she meant it.." But seriously Jack, forget the fancy stuff. Never works. Stick with the basics. Low kicks. Jab, jab, punch. And forget about a backward spinning anything. This is real life, not a movie. You've tried that move on me a dozen times and it hasn't worked yet."

Jack bowed again, lower this time. "Someday it may just surprise you," he replied, although he was pretty sure he was wrong.

"When are you going to grade for your black belt Jack? You're ready and I'm getting tired of beating up a brown belt."

Jack had been expecting the question. She'd been asking it after every class for the past six months.

"Sorry Sensei." He offered an exaggerated bow and continued in a very bad imitation of a Japanese accent, "I must humbly disagree. I am not yet worthy of the honor."

"You, Detective Sergeant Jack Wright, are a coward."

After some light stretching, Jack grabbed a quick shower. Catching a glimpse of himself in the mirror, he stopped to take stock, hoping no one would walk in at that point. He still didn't like what he saw, but he had to admit it was a lot better than before he started training. *Not quite a six-pack,* he thought to himself, *but not bad for a guy who use to walk around with a keg.* "Keep working, buddy. You still have a long way to go."

Jack left the dojo and stepped into a quiet side street in the Annex, an older neighborhood in downtown Toronto. The moon was rising in the early June sky and the evening was cool. His .40 caliber semi-automatic Glock 27 rested in a pancake holster on his right hip covered by a light windbreaker. The weight of it was comfortable and reassuring. He smiled at the thought that if he couldn't beat Sensei Mariko on the mats, he might have to shoot her.

He reached back to rub the knotted muscles in his neck and right shoulder. Nina was probably right. It *was* time for him to grade for his black belt. But that thought brought up memories of gradings he'd attended in the past. They lasted hours and students were forced to continue past the point of exhaustion and required to defend themselves against the attack of three, four, or even five assailants. It was an awesome tribute to the human spirit. It was also legalized torture. It was something he had no intention of doing in the foreseeable future.

"You, Detective Sergeant Jack Wright, are a coward!" Nina's words brought a wry smile to his face as he circled around his unmarked Chevy Impala, performing a cruiser check, a practice left over from his very early days as a uniformed traffic cop. Seeing no obvious signs of tampering, he slid behind the wheel. The road-weary dark blue departmental didn't explode or fall apart when he started the engine, so he reached over to locate his pager amongst the cafeteria, office, and bedroom clutter on the front seat.

He smiled at the empty LCD screen. He was free to go home and enjoy something he cooked rather than something he unwrapped. Out of necessity he'd become pretty good in the kitchen over the years. Before that thought could drag him down into a familiar depression, his beeper emitted a series of raucous squeals, dispelling both the aroma of home cooking and the weight of past mistakes.

CHAPTER FIVE

Being summoned to the station at all hours of the day and night wasn't new for Jack. That was life on the Hold-up Squad. He parked the dark blue Chev in a space marked 'Inspector Only'. To hell with formalities. He entered the four story dung-colored brick building 30 minutes after answering the page. It was from Detective Richard Turpin, a dinosaur in the unit, two years past retirement and about ten years past useful.

"Evening Dick, you're looking svelte."

Turpin dusted icing sugar from a jelly donut off his expanse of stomach and swung his feet off a desk with some difficulty.

"It's all the women in my life. Can't help but stay in shape with them chasing me all the time."

"Lawyers or bill collectors?"

"Fuck you, Wright."

"What have you got?" Jack said.

"ETF capped some guy over on Vaughan Road about two hours ago. Gun running operation. Now they want us to clean up their shit. Got one in custody. Think one of us should talk to him."

"And?"

"And I'm off in an hour."

"So?" Jack asked, incredulous.

"You're on call. Besides, it's right up your alley."

"How so?"

"Guy's name is Vincent Ricco, a street punk. When they brought him in he started talking about a robbery that's going down in the next two weeks—guns, diamonds, alarms. That's why they called us. They need a backhoe to dig through his bullshit. That's your department. You're the human lie detector. I need to take a dump and go home."

"Most productive thing you've done all night," Jack said, not quite under his breath.

"Like I said before Wright … fuck you."

Jack shook his head. "Who's in charge of the investigation?"

"Guy named Dempster from Guns and Gangs. He's upstairs talking to the CI who started the whole thing. Waste of time if you ask me. Her story's full of shit too. Enjoy."

The second floor of the station looked like it had been cobbled together from a police yard sale. The main room was crowded with an eclectic mix of mismatched furniture. Desks were stacked with filing trays overflowing with court briefs, dope sheets, and unassigned cases. Battered institutional gray filing cabinets stood sentinel along every wall. Small offices along one wall were reserved for the shift supervisors.

Jack found Calvin Dempster in a small interview room in the back. He was seated very close to a young woman. Jack didn't interrupt right away, but watched through a small window in the door. It didn't take any special skill to tell the woman had seen her share of hard times.

There were the obvious signs – a black eye melting into yellow with age, a split lip somewhat healed, bruises on the back of her hands – but there was something else. The way she was sitting. The downward tilt of her head. The protective way she hugged herself.

Although much of his ability was natural – a kind of sixth sense for detecting deception – Jack had studied body language for years. He was a people watcher, always had been, even as a kid. It was a hobby that became a habit, something that stood him in good stead as a cop. It gave him the uncanny ability to see the truth in most situations, and complemented his later training in statement analysis and polygraph.

He became an expert on detecting deception, and was often asked to lecture on the topic, although he hadn't done any teaching for a long time. Even so, he was still considered to be in a league of his own when it came to getting at the truth, and many investigations had turned on

Jack's talent for freeing fact from fiction. Now Jack waited and watched until Calvin Dempster made a move for the door.

"Sorry to interrupt. Can I talk to you when you get a second? Nothing urgent."

"Sure. We're just finishing up. Rita Alvarez, Detective Sergeant Wright. Ms. Alvarez has been very helpful over the last few days, but I think she'd like to go home."

"Nice to meet you, Ms. Alvarez."

Rita said nothing.

"I'm going to arrange for a ride," Calvin said to Jack, as the young woman scuttled past him. "I'll be right back."

He was back in ten minutes with two cups of coffee that smelled like it had been brewed in an old sock.

"Thought maybe you could use a cup of coffee, but all I could find was this," Calvin said, handing Jack mug. "I put cream and sugar in to mask the taste."

"Works for me."

"I've heard your name around, but I don't think we've ever met," Jack said, extending his hand. "Jack."

"Cal. Not officially, but your reputation precedes you." Dempster spread his hands palms up. "What can I say?"

"Don't believe everything you hear."

"I don't, but I caught a few of your lectures," Calvin Dempster continued. "Interesting stuff. I use a lot of your techniques—mostly on my wife—but they seem to work."

Jack smiled. "I'm glad you got your money's worth."

"Definitely. So what can I do for you? I told Turpin not to bother you on this one. I think our boy is just trying to sell hot air."

"No worries. Dick Turpin and I have a history that goes way back. This is just his latest volley." Jack took a sip of his coffee and grimaced. "So, what's the latest on Mr. Ricco?"

"He's talking to his lawyer right now. If he's got something to trade I think it will cost us, but I think it's probably smoke and mirrors. Ricco is small time at best."

"What makes you think it will cost us if he does have something?"

"His lawyer. Italian suit, fancy shoes, perfect smile. He's got Osgoode Hall written all over him. If Ricco has something to sell, he's got a very expensive agent."

"How does a small time hood get connected with talent like that?"

"Couldn't tell you," Calvin said.

"I'd love to know that before I talk to him." Jack's mind was starting to spin with possibilities.

"You still want to talk to him? Seriously, I think you're wasting your time."

"It's all pensionable, right?"

"God, I hope so," Calvin said, with a smile. "Your call. Can't say I mind the help."

"Good. I'll wait till morning, though. Let him spend some time in a cell. That usually has a way making them more talkative. Besides, the brass hate paying overtime."

"I hear that," Calvin said.

"You have time to fill me in on the details? I hate going in cold."

"I'm off as of now, but if we can go somewhere to get something a little better than this," Calvin said, holding up his mug. "I'll tell you what I know."

"Why don't we make this unofficial," Jack said. "That way I'm off the big clock and we can get something with a bit more kick."

"Sounds good. You know a place called Stats?"

Jack only smiled in reply.

CHAPTER SIX

"What the hell are you doing here?" She exploded, after the door to the outer office clicked shut. "If someone sees—"

"We need to talk."

"I told you, no more face to face. We use the link. I was very clear on that—"

"I'm not talking to you about this on a god damned computer. I don't care how secure you say it is."

"What's wrong?!"

The air conditioning hissed quietly, barely audible in the spacious office. 'Oscar' stood behind her large burled walnut desk. She watched her unwanted visitor from across the room, a feeling of dread spreading through the pit of her stomach. He was facing the diplomas and degrees displayed on her wall.

"One of my team was killed tonight … by the police."

"What?! Who?

"Tinker."

Oscar's hand shook as she reached for a cigarette. She had to concentrate to work the thin gold lighter. "How?"

"ETF takedown. Apparently Tinker tried to start World War III."

"With what?!"

"Guns," Wolfe said simply.

"I said no violence!" There was a tinge of panic in her voice. "What the hell was *he* doing with a gun?"

"I didn't say gun, I said guns. And the *guns* were supposed to be just for show. We want the cops to think this is an actual robbery, right? People involved in that kind of business carry guns. Tinker fucked up."

'Oscar's' mind worked frantically. This wasn't part of The Plan.

Wolfe continued, "By the time I found out what was going down it was too late."

She wasn't listening. *Damn it! What happened? How did the police get involved?*

"Nothing's broken that can't be fixed," Wolfe said. "The police took care of one loose end. I'll take care of the other."

She drew on her cigarette and exhaled a cloud of smoke at the ceiling before the full meaning of his words sunk in. "What other? What do you mean?"

Wolfe didn't answer.

"What loose end?!"

"Ricco. Don't worry about it. It's not your concern."

"What do you mean, *it's not my concern*? I hired you to steal something, not to— this has gone too far. We have to stop ... or delay." Her mind was spinning

"No!" Wolfe barked the word out.

Oscar felt like she'd been slapped.

"There can't be any delay. You told me that yourself," he reminded her.

He was right and she knew it, but this was more than she'd bargained for.

"We can still make it work." There was a sudden venom in his words. "We stick to the plan, *your plan*. No delay."

She backed away from him as if stepping back from a spreading fire. "But how—"

She fought to control her voice and her emotions. She was having a hard time concentrating on the problem at hand. Her mind was reeling.

"Exactly as planned. No delay. No problem."

"You can't be serious. We can't go through with it now. It's too risky. There's too much at stake." She could feel a cold fear start to clear her mind.

She heard him exhale slowly before answering.

"Nothing changes," he said. "Nothing."

"And what about Ricco and Tinker?"

"Tinker's dead," he said flatly. "He can be replaced. Ricco will play by the rules or he can join Tinker."

The coldness in his voice sent a shiver down her spine, and she could feel a fine sheen of perspiration break out on her forehead.

"It's gotten out of hand," she said. "I need time to think."

"Time's the one thing we don't have."

"I'm not—"

He cut her off. "It goes ahead as planned … unless you want to pay me my share right now to walk away."

"I can't do that," she said. "You know I can't."

She watched a smile play at the corner of his mouth. He was bluffing and she knew it, but she'd told him too much at the start, too much about her own desperation. He was playing a game with the cards she'd given him, subtly pointing out she had no choice. But they were traveling down a road she hadn't foreseen. It was time to take back control … if she could.

"Listen to me," she said, staring into his dead gray eyes without blinking. "I've got the codes, I've got the pass, and I've got the information you need to pull this off. Without me you haven't got a chance. So far we've lost two members of your so-called team. One's in jail and one's dead. Now we have a courier who's disappeared off the face of the earth. If Pavel wasn't paranoid enough to do a dry run, there wouldn't be anything to steal in the first place."

She watched for a reaction, but if Wolfe knew anything about the fate of the courier he didn't let on.

"You hired an amateur instead of a professional," Wolfe covered. "Your courier friend probably thought he was set for life and skipped. If what he was carrying was bogus, I'll bet he's just as pissed at you as you are at him."

"He shouldn't have known he was carrying anything that valuable in the first place and the police shouldn't have known what was in that apartment. Your *Team* has a leak. Nothing goes ahead until you find it and do whatever you have to do to plug it."

"Are you suggesting violence?" he asked. She could hear the mock surprise in his voice.

"I'm suggesting you do what I'm paying you to do. I want to know what happened to the courier and I want to know what happened at the apartment. Until then, nothing goes ahead. Do I make myself clear?"

Her eyes remained locked on his, but she had to jam her hands in her pockets to keep them from shaking. She could see him trying hard not to let a smile climb back onto his arrogant face. He turned to leave without a word.

"And from now on we do everything via the computer. Do you understand?"

"You got it … boss." The sarcasm hung in the room long after Wolfe left.

'Oscar' played with her cigarette lighter and thought about her plan. It started out as a chance remark, a joke that grew into a game. But the game had become an obsession born out of desperation. Now her obsession had turned deadly.

She closed her eyes and leaned her head against her office window. A picture leapt into her mind's eye unbidden. She saw herself tumbling downhill, rolling out of control, heading straight for the opening to a lair. A wolf's den. She opened her eyes and looked out the window at a sliver of the moon just disappearing behind a bank of dark clouds.

CHAPTER SEVEN

"Get me the fuck outta here!"

Originally designed as a storage closet, the air was oppressive in the small drab interview room in the basement of the 56th. Ricco stared at his lawyer and waited for a reaction. The man sitting across from him didn't say a word. A wooden table, scarred by a thousand forgotten cigarettes, separated the two men.

Ricco's lawyer was a surprise ... even to Ricco. They'd never met. He stared hard at the man across from him and allowed a small sneer to curl the corners of his mouth. The man smelled of old money. Ricco was unimpressed with the snotty accent, the perfect teeth, and the country club tan.

"I'm not fuckin around here. If you're really connected with Oscar, you tell him I'll sing like a fucking canary if he doesn't get me out ... now!"

Ricco leaned back in his chair feeling more in control.

His lawyer smoothed his silk club tie as he stood to face Ricco. He stepped quietly towards his client and smashed a backhand across the side of Ricco's head. The force of the blow dropped Ricco to the floor and sent the chair clattering. The door opened almost immediately.

"Everything okay, Counselor?"

"Certainly, officer. Mr. Ricco leaned back a little too far. Are you all right, Vincent?" The man's voice was full of sincerity and concern.

Ricco looked from the lawyer to the officer and back to his lawyer again, too stunned to move.

"Can you get up?" The lawyer moved around to assist him.

Ricco came back to life quickly and scrambled to his feet, backing away from both men.

"Yeah. Yeah, fine. Just leaned back …"

The officer closed the door behind him. Ricco stared at the lawyer. The Ivy League manners were gone, as was the cultured inflection in the man's voice.

"Time to listen, Vince. Pick up your chair, sit your ass down, and shut your fucking mouth."

Ricco did as he was told.

"Listen carefully, Vince, because I won't say it again. I don't *tell* Oscar anything … I listen. I suggest you do the same. Okay so far?"

Ricco nodded. He was all ears.

"If you so much as breathe out of turn, you're dead. Here's what's going to happen. A deal's going to be offered before trial. You're going to take it. You behave yourself and I guarantee you won't do more than six months. When you get out you'll get your cut and a bonus for keeping your mouth shut. Play your cards right and you'll do okay."

Ricco stared straight ahead without speaking.

"Or … I walk away, Oscar's unhappy, and you're dead before breakfast."

Ricco glanced at the door but there was no help for him in that direction. He watched his lawyer check the shine on his oxfords and brush some non-existent lint from the razor-sharp crease in his pants. Ricco was afraid to speak or look away.

"What do I tell Oscar?"

Ricco sat on the edge of his chair in the airless room. He tried to think but Ricco's survival on the street had always been instinctual. His strengths were intuitive, not cognitive. He listened to his internal alarms and acted accordingly. It was when he stopped to think that he got himself in trouble, so he stopped trying and went with what worked in the past.. Vincent Ricco was a survivor. His instincts told him to nod and not say a word.

Wolfe stepped onto the sidewalk and picked up his pace as he headed away from the police station. Streetlights cast eerie shadows across his path and painted strange portraits on the walls. His eyes scanned the dark recesses of buildings up and down the street in a furtive manner. He stepped lightly among bits of litter like a native avoiding dried branches and the rustle of long dead leaves. His haste and wariness had nothing to do with fear. His contempt for the police was total. He was merely following his training. Good habits make good soldiers.

He'd joined the military at 18. With few friends and a violent temper, his parents thought strict discipline might make something of him. It did. In the army he found an outlet for his temper and learned to control his emotions. He excelled in the physical aspects of training and practiced the skills he was taught with a zeal few recruits demonstrated. His lean six-foot frame never really filled out, but hardened to a muscular, sinewy 185 pounds.

In Special Forces training he learned to kill with precision. When at all possible, he used only his hands. He found it strangely calming to take a life using nothing more than his strength and skill. He was proficient with edged weapons and a garrote, but there was something about using his bare hands that was so personal, so intimate, so … erotic. His least favorite method, despite a honed skill that most Olympian marksmen would envy, was the pistol and rifle. It was a necessary evil that he found far too removed and impersonal. As for explosives … they could be fun.

His practical and academic training also taught him about the importance of intelligence and counter-intelligence. His instructors taught him to hone his instincts and how to never let down his guard. He learned how to blend in and how to disappear. At the end of an exhaustive four years the government had what it wanted – a highly-trained talented, educated, and capable assassin. And S/F Private First Class John Niles had what he wanted – a marketable skill that suited his less than conventional nature. Cheaper than college and a hell of a lot more fun. Be all that you can be. The day after graduating from the program he did what they trained him to do. He disappeared.

As he put some distance between himself and the police station, Wolfe changed direction several times without warning, twice stopping abruptly to look at something in a store window. When he didn't catch sight of a tail, he felt safe in walking the three blocks to where he'd parked. The car, battered and dirty, was exactly where he'd left it in an underground parking garage, with the wheels turned fully away from the curb and the windshield wipers left exactly halfway through their motion. A tiny piece of paper trapped, seemingly by accident, between the frame and the driver's door was undisturbed. Nobody had touched the car. Wolfe quickly slid behind the wheel and left the area without looking back. His thoughts raced far ahead of the vehicle.

The car moved through the streets in much the same manner that Wolfe did, without attracting attention. As he drove along, his mind began to examine his present situation from different angles.

Given a choice he'd prefer to kill Ricco. Death was a much more permanent solution. The problem was Oscar. Killing Ricco would mean the end of the operation. She'd end it before he had a chance to find out the rest of the plan. He wasn't worried about her pass or the security codes, but without the actual location and schematics he couldn't pull it off. He controlled his breathing and worked through the alternatives.

Her plan was workable, even brilliant, and the payoff would be huge. The opportunity was too good to let pass, even if it meant working to her rules … for now. Which means Ricco lives … for now.

CHAPTER EIGHT

Stats Bar & Grill was a police hang out long before the owner's favorite niece, Darcy, decided to join the Toronto Police Service. A stone above the front door recorded the date of the building as 1924, which was about the same year that Stats Caldwell was born. Both the building and proprietor had seen better days.

The best word to describe the bar would be familiar, especially if you knew the owner well. The walls were decorated with the memories of a life well lived; antique beer steins from his father, framed tintypes of his ancestors, and fading photographs of both the famous and infamous who'd wandered into the bar over the years. The only mirror in the place lined the wall behind the time-worn oak bar. There wasn't a neon light to be found anywhere, and the music was kept low.

Jack and Calvin sat in one of the booths at the back after stopping at the bar to order drinks from the lone waitress. The pub was surprisingly busy. In the past smoke would have clung to the ceiling rafters in a diaphanous cloud, but smoking in bars had been banned in Toronto for years. Calvin looked around the room as if lost in his own world for a few seconds. Jack watched him intently out of habit.

"I haven't spent much time in here, but I know a few who have. What about you?" Calvin asked.

Jack almost laughed out loud. "I've been here once or twice." And then after a pause. "A few years ago this place was like my second home. I think I still own stock in it."

Calvin cocked his head, waiting for Jack to continue.

"You ever work Homicide?" Jack asked.

Calvin shook his head. "Never had the pleasure."

"It tends to wear on you," Jack said. "Changes you, whether you realize it or not. You see so many lives cut short, you tend to put more into your own. For some guys that means spending more time with their families. For others, it's an excuse to push the envelope—wild parties, affairs, bullshit heroics, that sort of thing."

"Which group did you fit in to?"

"Neither. I formed my own club. I took on way too many cases. It was like my own personal addiction. Solve more puzzles, catch more bad guys. It was like a game. If I didn't catch them, I lost. I spent my days talking to witnesses and my nights staking out suspects. When I wasn't doing that, I was working on those lectures you slept through."

"You were single?"

"Not at the time. But …" Jack hesitated. "Shit happens … at least it did to me." Jack shrugged. "I shut down for a while. Spent a lot of time here. Took me a while to get back on track, but when I did McAllister offered me the Hold-up Squad."

"The Chief?"

"Long story. I'll save it for another time. But he wasn't the Chief back then, just a Superintendent … and a friend. He threw me a lifeline. I still get to solve puzzles, but there's a lot less blood involved … usually."

Jack went quiet, lost in thought about the 'shit' that ended his marriage, not something he felt like sharing over his first beer with a new acquaintance. The silence grew from uncomfortable to downright awkward, and probably would have continued for a while if not for a voice that boomed above the cacophony of other conversations.

"You're not drinking on duty are you, Detective Wright? What if Superintendent Casson finds out?"

Jack turned to see his old partner in Homicide, Ken Kotwa, squeezing his great bulk past a few patrons leaning against the bar, a broad smile on his round face.

"Screw Casson … and screw you, you great pile of—"

"Ken Kotwa," Ken said, ignoring Jack and extending a hand the size of a dinner plate to Calvin Dempster. "You're Dempster. Guns and

Gangs? We met on that Montgomery thing, right?. Two years ago. Bad business. You were new in the unit."

"Good memory," Calvin said. "Cal."

Jack smiled as Calvin's hand was almost swallowed by Ken's meaty paw.

"So what's the skinny? You breaking Regs or not?"

"Not," Jack said. "I live and breathe for the Regulations. Calvin here declined any official help, so I am *officially* off duty."

"Help with what?"

"You coming or going?"

"Passing through. A little bird told me you were heading over here. Just wanted to say Hi."

Jack knew Ken was checking up on him to make sure he was being good, but he didn't mind. Ken was one of the few who had stood by Jack when things went to hell in a hand basket.

"I'll fill you in later if Cal says it's alright."

Calvin nodded, and Ken stood up, eclipsing the light from the front half of the bar.

"Right. Then I'll leave you two lovebirds to your date. Nice to see you again, Cal. Don't let him stay out too late. Bad for the complexion."

Before either of them could respond, Ken Kotwa turned his back and headed out, bumping the same patrons he'd pushed past on his way in.

"Jesus!" Calvin said when he was sure Ken was out of earshot. "What the hell do you feed a guy like that to make him so … big?!"

Jack laughed, "In here, suicide wings. Anything milder and he'd eat them out of house and home."

Calvin's smile broadened, "Hot?"

"Want to try a plate? My treat."

"Well, I have to use the can but when I return I just might take you up on that offer. My Momma didn't raise no coward."

Waiting for Calvin to get back Jack casually scanned the faces in the bar. Studying people in everyday situations was one way that Jack sharpened his skills as an investigator. He watched the way people sat, the way they moved, how they gestured, the direction their eyes looked when they spoke, and dozens of other signs.

He watched as an attractive young woman entered the front door of the bar and walked to a table for two. He'd seen her before, but couldn't place her. Her steps were leaden and her shoulders slouched like she was carrying the weight of the world. It seemed to Jack she was wading through waist-deep water, like she had to fight her way through to the table before falling into a chair. To anyone else watching she was simply a young lady tired after a long day. To Jack, there was something much more interesting at hand. Before he could form a theory, however, Calvin and the wings arrived at the table at the same time.

"Thanks. Those would be for my friend here," Jack said as he winked at the waitress.

She returned his wink like any good accomplice before saying, "If you need anything else like another drink, water, 911, just whistle."

"What did she mean by that?" Calvin asked.

"I have no idea." Jack raised his right hand. "Swear to God."

Darcy sat at the small table in an alcove of her uncle's restaurant, physically and emotionally drained. She leaned into the wall for support. Her whole body ached.

Darcy was sure her uncle would have heard about the shooting by now. If she was lucky he might have taken the night off and be miles away from here enjoying a playoff game of some kind. If she wasn't, he'd corner her and lay on some well-intentioned sympathy, about the last thing she wanted. What she needed was a stiff drink and someone to talk to who had absolutely nothing to do with police work, or guns, or rocket launchers, or bad guys. She looked around the room, and laughed.

"Well you certainly picked the wrong place," she said to no one in particular.

Calvin stripped the meat from his first chicken wing in a single bite and licked the sauce from his fingers.

"I thought you said these things were hot?"

Jack said nothing, but watched the beads of sweat start to form on Calvin's forehead. Calvin gamely picked up a second and then a third wing without breaking stride, looking around the room as if he didn't have a care in the world. Even if Jack hadn't been a student of human nature, it would have taken a much better actor than Calvin Dempster to pull off the deception. After another minute Calvin threw up his hands in mock surrender.

"I give up."

Jack laughed. "I'm impressed."

"Impressed, shit! Give me some water or something. My God, are these legal?"

Jack passed him a bread basket and said, "Here. It's your only hope."

Calvin stuffed a great chunk of fresh bread in his mouth and washed it down with a swallow of beer. After a minute both the breadbasket and his beer were empty. When the fire in his mouth subsided Calvin looked at Jack and said, "Thanks for dinner. We'll have to do this again some time."

Over coffee Jack kept glancing at the attractive brunette at the table in the alcove, intrigued by her unusual body language. When the coffees were finished, however, the two men finally got down to business. The girl with the gorgeous hair and vacant eyes was forgotten. Jack had a real puzzle to solve.

"So what do you have on Mr. Ricco," He asked.

"The Reader's Digest version?"

Jack nodded.

"Four days ago Rita Alvarez came into the Station with a problem. Her boyfriend's selling guns—big ones."

Jack didn't interrupt.

"After two days of background and surveillance we got a warrant and brought in the ETF to take down the apartment."

"Any interesting Intel prior to going in?"

"Not really. As far as we can tell Ricco is strictly small time. He's been in and out of trouble since he was a kid, but he's never done any serious time."

"What about juvey?"

"Negative. He didn't get pinched for anything until he was an adult, and even then it was chicken shit stuff. Assault, possession, theft, that kind of thing. Nothing even close to what they got him with this time."

Calvin briefly ran down what happened at the apartment, and what they'd learned since, which wasn't much.

"So with M72's and C4 we're talking military ordnance, right?"

"Right," Calvin confirmed.

"And Uzis? Are they common on the street?" Jack asked.

"Not common. Available if you have connections and a lot of coin, but …"

"So you want to know who's financing this thing."

"Right."

"And?"

"So far … zip. It seems Ricco's only loyalty is to Ricco."

"OC?" Jack asked, using the abbreviation for Organized Crime.

"I don't think so. Nobody on that side of the house has heard shit."

"What about somebody selling him the hardware as a one shot deal? Would any of the bikers or one of the families do that?"

"That depends on the organization," Calvin mused. "If he was known to them as a player, maybe. But the kind of equipment they scooped in that apartment would have cost a small fortune. From what we've found so far, Ricco didn't have the connections and couldn't afford it on his own."

"So he's not just running guns to make a profit."

"Highly unlikely," Calvin answered.

"What about the other guy. Could he be the money?"

"I don't know. We're trying to do a background on him right now, but so far zip. Not even a name. Couldn't match his prints through AFIS. When we get some more on him I should have a few more answers for you."

The two men sat in silence for a few minutes. Jack took a second to study the other man's face surreptitiously, a habit that was hard to break.

Calvin Dempster looked to be in his mid to late thirties, although Jack was sure he must be at least forty-five. Obviously kept himself in good shape. A strong, determined face the color of walnut. Bright eyes and an easy smile. He sat straight, leaning a little forward when he spoke to Jack, and when he gestured his movements were large and free. To Jack, the proverbial open book.

"So what about the robbery angle that Ricco's spouting? Anything to that?" Jack finally asked.

"Honestly?" Calvin continued. "I'm not sure what to make of it. Most guys cough up something or somebody from their past. Ricco's talking about the future. At first, I thought he was trying to knock a gun running charge down to simple possession."

Jack looked at Calvin quizzically, not really sure where he was going.

"By claiming he had them for personal use only. A great big sign that reads 'Not for Sale'," Calvin said.

"But by claiming to have them for an armed robbery he's supposed to be part of in the future, he's leaving himself open to a charge of 'Conspiracy-to-Commit' …"

"Which, in the absence of any corroborating evidence or a co-conspirator …"

"…could be dealt away in a plea bargain by a sharp defense lawyer," Jack finished.

Calvin nodded.

"It fits the facts," Calvin said, after a long pause.

"Maybe … but is your boy smart enough to come up with something like that on his own?"

Calvin could only shrug.

"What about the computer and the drafting table and the filing cabinets?"

"The computer's a laptop. Maybe stolen. Why? What are you thinking?"

"I'm thinking I still want to talk to Mr. Ricco," Jack replied, "but in the morning."

Calvin nodded. "What do you have? A Blackberrry or an iPhone?"

Jack hesitated. It was the same thing every time he told someone he didn't own a television or a CD player.

"Neither. Page me if you want to talk, or call my cell." Jack held up his phone.

"Jesus! Does the museum know they're missing that?"

Jack just smiled.

"Does it fit in a shoe, or do you have to carry it in a briefcase?"

"I don't do technology. Not my thing."

"No shit. I'd never guess. What do you do your reports on? An Underwood?"

"I wish," Jack said.

Calvin slid from the bench and straightened his coat. "Okay Mr. Edison. I'm heading home to a hot shower and a warm bed ... and if these wings have any effect on my bodily functions, you can expect to get paged ... repeatedly."

Jack laughed. "I'll expect your call around four in the morning."

Calvin grimaced. "Next time it'll be my treat. I know this little place that serves catfish that's spiced ... just right."

On the way out of the bar Jack nodded at Stats who was sitting with the young woman he'd noticed earlier. Her eyes were no longer vacant, but red and swollen from crying. Jack's interest was piqued. Stats sat holding her hands in his, looking lost and out of place.

The two detectives stepped on to the street a little before two in the morning and felt the fine mist of a light rain. Jack had a puzzle to solve. Two if you included the gorgeous brunette with Stats. Maybe they could keep his mind from dwelling on an empty house and, unlike Calvin, a cold bed.

CHAPTER NINE

Darcy needed sleep. She needed a week-long shower. What she didn't need was another drink. Bad idea. She set her beer on the floor next to the couch and looked around blankly. A cocktail of emotions was rolling around inside of her, turning her stomach and giving her the start of what promised to be a massive headache. Fear and disbelief and sadness played into it, but it was anger that seemed to be most prevalent. Anger at being stripped of her gear and left alone to write a report, anger at the SIU investigator who seemed intent on finding her at fault than in finding the truth, and anger at the rumor that was already flying around the office—that she'd double tapped a guy just as he was about to surrender.

Her cat, Miro, sat watching her from across the room. His head cocked from one side to the other every minute or so, like a metronome set on dead slow.

"What are you looking at?"

Miro sat up as if to beat a hasty retreat.

"Sorry, baby. Been a long night."

She reached down and gently lifted the cat onto her knees. He settled in with a contented purr as she gently stroked his back. She'd gotten him for company after a bad break-up six months earlier and named him after the Spanish surrealist, Joan Miro. His calico coat reminded her of some of the artist's more whimsical paintings. After getting him home and seeing how well they got along, she'd made herself a promise that he would be the only man in her life. So far, she'd managed to keep her word.

"Want to hear about it?"

Miro was her confidante and sounding board. He never interrupted and never told her she was being stupid. The perfect man … almost. Miro stretched and yawned

"Alright. Maybe in the morning. I could use some sleep too. They've given me a few days off to get my shit together. We'll have time."

After feeding Miro, Darcy drew a deep bath. She eased herself into hot water scented with lavender, and closed the shower curtain that dangled from plastic rings on a brass hoop—a poor man's steam bath. She rested her head back, closed her eyes, and stretched out her long, sinewy legs so that her feet rested just out of the water on the edge of the old claw foot tub. She was asleep almost immediately, waking about an hour later when the water cooled to an uncomfortable temperature. With just enough energy to towel dry, she tumbled into bed and was asleep in minutes.

About four in the morning Darcy heard the sound of breaking glass. A sense of déjà vu enveloped her as once again she found herself staring down the barrel of a weapon. This time it was a Glock 17, like the one she carried on duty. It was held in a gloved hand that extended into her bedroom through the broken window. Everything moved in slow motion. A pale moon face grinned at her through the shards of glass that hung from the upper portion of the window frame. She could see the ribbing on the back of the black leather gloves tighten and stretch as the hand began to squeeze the trigger. She instinctively turned away and tried to roll to the floor, but the sheets and blankets tangled around her legs wouldn't let her move. The first shot went wild and thudded into the bureau across the room. She kicked frantically at the bed linen and lunged for the off duty revolver she kept in her bedside table.

The second shot was preceded by a peel of maniacal laughter that made her heart beat even faster. The bullet caught her in the right shoulder blade just as she grabbed the butt of her Smith & Wesson .38. She marveled that she felt no pain at all, only a sharp push from behind. She swung the revolver up in her left hand, her right arm hanging uselessly at her side. She tried to snap off a quick shot, but the hammer fell on the cylinder with a heart-wrenching metallic *click*. She kicked at the covers but her legs were trapped in a cocoon of cotton. She pulled the trigger again. This time the cylinder fell out and rolled towards the window. A gloved hand picked it up and held it out towards her as a voice said, "You missed."

The other hand raised the pistol, which suddenly changed into the capacious barrel of an M72 rocket launcher. She tried to scream but the sound caught somewhere low in her throat.

Darcy bolted upright and kicked the sheets and blankets onto the floor. She was bathed in a sheen of sweat. The thin white tank top she wore was almost transparent. Her breathing was rapid, her chest rising and falling to keep pace with her racing heart. She knew before looking at the window that it would be intact, but she looked anyway. *God, that seemed so real.*

It took her a few minutes to get her breathing back to normal and even longer for her heart to stop its trip-hammer cadence. After checking the doors and windows twice, she crawled back into bed and tried not to fall back to sleep, afraid that if she did the dream would come again.

Emotionally wasted, she finally dozed off at about 5:00 AM. She slept through until 10, waking only when Miro, sitting at the window, started yowling at the world outside.

"Shut up, butt-head! It's not too late to send you back to the shelter."

Darcy threw off the one blanket she'd dragged back onto the bed and stumbled to the bathroom. As she passed the window she unconsciously let her fingers brush the unbroken pane of glass. *Just a dream.*

Twenty minutes later she was sitting at her kitchen table blowing the steam off her first cup of coffee and wondering what the hell she was going to do with herself. She'd become used to living her life around the ETF, working, training and waiting for the next call-out. She began to wonder if she was in danger of becoming one of those types who identified a little *too* much with the job. The kind who kept working long past retirement because without the job they had nothing to live for except a good pension and bad dreams.

Darcy shook her head. "Too young to start thinking about that shit," she said to Miro.

She began to feel a little better after her second cup of coffee. The sun streamed in through the windows of her breakfast nook and made her feel warm and a little more human. What she needed was a workout. A long run and an hour or two at the gym. Everything else could wait. That included Karski, the SIU, and a session with the force shrink, something she'd been told was mandatory.

There are a thousand things experienced in the line of duty that can scar an officer. Killing someone is at the top of the list. Despite what's portrayed on television and in the movies, taking a life, no matter how justified, is never easy. Even so, Darcy would have scoffed at the idea of needing help until she opened up her morning paper and found the man from her nightmare staring back at her from the front page. His pale moon face seemed to mock her with an arrogant grin. Darcy gave up trying to read the accompanying story after a paragraph, folded the paper and tried not to cry.

CHAPTER TEN

Jack turned the lights off as he rolled to a stop in the mutual driveway that ran beside a three storey Victorian. The driveway ended near the rear of the property in front of a carriage house that had been turned into a guest cottage. It was a beautiful limestone building trimmed in a shade of green so dark as to be almost black. The gabled roof with three small dormers in front was sheathed in cedar shingles. A latticed wooden fence separated the lane from a tiny English garden, lovingly tended. Both the house and the cottage were immaculate, something right out of House and Home. Unfortunately, neither of them belonged to Jack. They belonged to his neighbor, Mrs. Leishman.

His house, although similar in size and style, was what polite company might describe as a 'fixer-upper'. He'd lived in the house almost twenty years. Caroline inherited it when her parents passed away shortly after she and Jack were married. It had been in her family for three generations. Now it belonged to Jack.

At one time, the house had been something to behold, equally as beautiful as Mrs. Leishman's. Caroline spent hours in the garden planting and weeding, and still more hours pouring over decorating magazines and turning her favorite pictures into reality. But that was before Jack's life went unexpectedly sideways-before Ricker.

Jack kicked the bottom of the heavy wooden door that opened on to a small mudroom at the back of the house. It always stuck. He keyed the alarm and walked through the kitchen without turning on a light. Hobbs and Flynn, two stray sisters Jack had allowed temporary residence three and a half years ago, rushed into the living room, meowed once, and then proceeded to ignore him. The greeting from Charlie, a Shih Tzu rescued from a dumpster up in 32 Division, was much more enthusiastic. Jack headed upstairs with the little dog close at his heels, still wagging his whole back end. After a quick shower, with the alarm set for 6:00 AM, Jack fell into bed beneath a down duvet, a remnant from his previous life as a married man. Charlie waited an appropriate amount of time and then leapt effortlessly on to the foot of the bed, burrowing a warm little lair into the folds of the comforter.

Jack awoke, ten minutes before the alarm was set to go off. Sleep didn't come easily to him, and when it did, it didn't last. After a shave, he dressed and headed downstairs to kitchen. Charlie sat at his feet waiting for the last bite of toast. Hobbs and Flynn sat like porcelain statues on a deep windowsill, staring out at what was left of Caroline's beautiful garden. The phone rang as it did almost every morning about this time. Jack knew who it would be.

"You a good boy last night?"

"Yes, Mother."

Ken Kotwa ignored him. "Just making sure, Boyo. Old habits die hard."

"That was four years ago, Ken."

"Yeah? So was the last time Mary and I had sex ... but I still get the urge."

"Then you have more of a problem than I do."

"Just kidding."

"I know."

"About the urge, I mean. The sex thing is absolutely true."

"Bullshit! You and Mary are like a couple of horny school kids. That's why I stopped hanging around you in the first place."

"You stopped hanging around because you were too drunk to find the house."

"Whatever. How was your night?"

"Dandy. I'll tell you about it when I'm not so damned tired. You hear about the shooting on Vaughan?"

"The ETF thing? Yeah. That's what Calvin and I were working on at Stats last night."

"I figured. Unofficially, of course."

"Of course. I don't need to get involved in anything else."

"What's your take on it?" Ken asked.

"Don't know. I'll have a better idea after I talk to the guy that *didn't* get blown away."

"I thought you weren't getting involved."

"I'm not. Just giving Calvin a hand."

"Because …?"

"Because it's a puzzle."

"You and your fucking puzzles."

"And because the guy I'm going to talk to is telling anybody who'll listen about a robbery. Something coming up. Something big."

"Something involving lots of firepower?"

"Right."

"Brings it into your bailiwick."

"Maybe," Jack said.

"So that part's true."

"What part?"

"What they found in the apartment. The guns and shit."

"So I'm told."

"God damn."

"What?'

"Maybe the other part is too." Before Jack could ask, Ken continued. "Word is our guy tapped the other asshole – the one they carried out in a body bag – when he was about to give up. Shot him in the back."

"Credible source?'

"What do you think?"

"Bullshit rumor and wishful thinking," Jack said.

"Probably," Ken agreed.

"Who pulled the trigger?"

"Nobody's saying. Very hush-hush until SIU gets through with the poor bastard."

Jack just grunted.

"So what's your guess? Guns R Us or is the asshole telling the truth?" Ken asked.

Jack smiled into the phone. Ken certainly knew how to turn a phrase.

"Calvin said there was a lot of military equipment," Jack said. "High grade. Specialized. Very expensive."

"Hard to sell on the street," Ken offered.

"You got that right," Jack agreed.

"So you're thinking robbery?"

"I'm thinking I'll let you know after I talk to the guy behind door number 2. Why don't you get some sleep, Mom, now that you know I've been good."

Ken gave up. "Right. Let the master work his magic."

"Night, Mom. Give my love to Mary."

"Later."

"Later."

Vincent Ricco's day started out much the same as Jack's, with breakfast and a conversation. Although the breakfast was less than tasty and the setting somewhat confining, the conversation was riveting.

A portly guard in an ill-fitting uniform set a tray of juice, cold cereal, milk, and a Styrofoam container of coffee across the stainless steel sink attached to one wall of the cell. He stepped back and smiled at Ricco, thin strands of black hair neatly plastered to his scalp with sweat and Brylcream. His eyes, set in a puffy face and rimmed in red from a binge the night before, seemed impossibly small and held no warmth whatsoever. He smelled of Zest and stale scotch. He stared at Ricco and rubbed his chubby hands together like a man about to devour a steak.

Ricco said nothing. Laying on the thin mattress with his feet crossed and his hands behind his head he stared at the wall.

"Whatsa' matter, Vince? Not hungry?"

"Fuck you."

The guard didn't bat an eye. "Yeah? Oscar sends his regards."

Ricco shot off the cot like he'd been stung. He stood with his back against the cold painted brick, eyes wide.

"I thought that might get your attention."

"Who are you?"

The guard smiled but didn't answer.

"What do you want?"

"Just need to pass on a message, Vince."

Ricco waited, his back to the wall, palms at his sides pressing into the brick.

"Keep your mouth shut. Understand?" The guard stepped closer and leaned in. "Keep your fucking mouth shut … and enjoy your breakfast."

The guard laughed as he slammed the bars behind him and turned the key in the heavy lock.

When Jack entered the cell about an hour later, the tray with Ricco's breakfast was still on the sink, the food and drink untouched.

CHAPTER ELEVEN

In nature, communication is conducted on a non-verbal level. Happiness, anger, aggression, and a thousand other thoughts and feelings are communicated in the wild without the use of a single word. What Jack knew instinctively and developed through training was that man, stripped of the trappings of civilization, was essentially an animal. Words are the primary medium people use to hide their true intentions and practice deceit. Truth is in action. Jack learned to detect dominance, insecurity, acceptance, and the signs of deception, but Jack took it further. It was a pastime he enjoyed and one that he found essential in his work. It was what made him such a popular speaker, but that was all in the past. Ricker took that away too.

When he entered the cramped and uncomfortable interview room at the Don Jail to interrogate Ricco, he felt fairly confident that he could learn the truth. An hour later, he wasn't so sure. He made his way back to the room where Calvin Dempster waited

"So?" Calvin asked.

"Well, for one thing," Jack replied, "he doesn't like you very much."

"No!" Calvin feigned deep anguish. "Tell me it ain't so."

"That's about the only thing he said that *is* true."

"What do you mean?"

"He's lying about everything else, in particular the robbery. He says it was a gun running operation, plain and simple."

"And that's a lie? There is going to be a robbery?'

Jack nodded.

"You sure?"

"I wouldn't bet my pension on it, but … yes."

"How do you know? I mean … that wasn't exactly a long interview."

Jack frowned. Sometimes it was harder to explain how he did it than to actually do it.

"When you go to a crime scene, what do you look for?"

"Evidence. Clues. Something that doesn't fit," Calvin replied.

"Same thing when you're trying to detect deception," Jack agreed. "You look for something that doesn't add up—missing words, added qualifiers, misplaced anger, that sort of thing. Mix in body language and you start to get a picture of what's fact and what's fiction. But you have to have a base line."

"A baseline?"

"I thought you've heard this lecture before?"

"I think I must have dozed off."

"Nice."

"Anyway …"

"If you try to read somebody without knowing what they're like when they're telling the truth, you're going to get it wrong. And sometimes you just have to go with your gut."

"You believe in hunches? I thought you were a man of science."

"Sometimes a hunch is all you have."

"Okay, Professor," Calvin said, "but you're not relying on a hunch this time. What makes you so sure he's lying?"

"A combination of things, Cal. It's hard to explain."

"Try me."

"The way he sat. The way he held his hands. His eyes. Then I started listening to his words."

"And?"

"You were listening, right?" Jack countered. "You heard what he said about his lawyer and the advice he was given. What do you think?"

"It's possible, I guess, but …"

"But what?"

"But something definitely doesn't feel right."

"A hunch?" Jack asked.

"Yeah, I guess so."

"Well, I'd say you're right. How many lawyers do you know who admit the police have an open and shut case? And how many tell their clients to plead guilty on the first appearance?"

Calvin nodded, a look of recognition on his face. "None. Adjourn, adjourn, adjourn, Ca-ching, ca-ching, ca-ching."

"Right. Time is money. And besides, most lawyers love publicity and a chance to spout off in court. Why miss the opportunity on a case like this?"

"Maybe he's afraid we'll add assault charges for Rita Alvarez," Calvin suggested.

"Bullshit," Jack said. "Every time I mentioned her name he relaxed. He's definitely not worried about her."

Calvin's features hardened into a scowl as he muttered, "Son of a bitch"

Jack ignored the comment. "On the other hand, when I mentioned the name Oscar, he just about shit a brick."

"Who's Oscar?"

"I have no idea. I made a call on a ..."

"Hunch?"

Jack nodded, a smiling playing at the corner of his mouth.

"I spoke to the super of the building on Vaughan. He said a guy named Oscar rented the apartment. Took a year's lease and paid in cash."

"In advance?"

"Yep."

"Who the hell does that?"

"Someone with a lot of cash. Someone who doesn't want the landlord knocking on the door looking for next months rent. Someone who likes his privacy."

"So, where does that leave us?" Calvin asked.

"You tell me," Jack said. "It's your case."

"Like shit. As far as my unit's concerned, this thing's a done deal. We'll do our best to source the weapons, but I'm not gonna hold my breath on that one."

"So that's it?" Jack asked.

"As far as my boss is concerned … yes. Too many other fish to fry. What about you? Can you run with this?"

"Officially? Not a chance. Given the budget cuts and manpower issues, we're spread too thin. I'd never get the brass to give me the go ahead … officially."

"You keep using that word."

"What word?" Jack asked, even though he knew full well where Calvin was headed.

"Officially. Does that mean you're thinking of doing a little 'unofficial' investigation?"

Jack smiled. "I thought I might poke around, see what I can find. I hate leaving a puzzle unsolved. Bugs the hell out of me."

"You looking for company on this one?" Calvin asked.

"You offering?"

"Two heads..," Calvin said with a shrug.

"Can get in more shit than one," Jack said.

Calvin paused for a moment before saying. "Sounds good. Where do we go from here?"

"South," Jack said.

"South?" Calvin asked, missing the joke.

"Yeah," Jack replied. "Might as well start in that direction. These things always go south sooner or later."

Jack had no idea how right he could be.

CHAPTER TWELVE

Twelve hours after the ETF smashed Ricco's heavy steel door out of its cheap wooden frame, Katherine Sharpe sat behind her large walnut desk, the surface polished to a mirror finish. She stared blankly at a reflection of the modern buildings that lined the boulevard across the street from her office. The grid pattern of glass and steel warped in the grain of the wood and became a surrealist painting. With the contract, fully as thick as a Bible, placed precisely in the middle, the whole thing reminded her of an abstract by the French mixed media artist Tapiezo. Ironically, she had one of his works in her rather extensive collection, a collection she would lose, along with everything else she'd worked for, if things didn't go exactly to plan.

The contract, the one she'd signed with Sumner against the advice of her own lawyer, was to be her salvation. It was meant to ensure the growth and success of her upstart company. Now, however, it seemed an evil thing. Its pages, and the words they contained, threatened her very existence and mocked her own arrogance and overconfidence. How could she have been so sure of herself, so absolutely certain of her success, to make the promises she'd made? Promises that now bound her to Sumner, a man she hated with a passion. Promises that—if not fulfilled—would cost her everything. Promises that forced her to set in motion a desperate plan.

She tried to tell herself it was for her employees and the company itself that she'd signed the contract in the first place. That she'd handed over a controlling interest in her company to raise the funds she needed for research and development. Looking back, however, she had to admit that it hadn't been for them at all. It had always been about her, about her need to succeed. A need to prove her 'daddy' wrong, that she wasn't *good for but one thing*. A need that wouldn't let her be happy with just being good. She had to be the best.

The sizable investment from Sumner and his backers was meant to place her where she needed to be, where she deserved to be, on the cutting edge of technological advancement, an industry leader. And now it was all in danger of coming apart.

Staring at the contract, iron clad and without loopholes, Katherine let her mind wander back in time to conversation she'd had with her lawyer just prior to signing the damned thing almost five years earlier.

"Katherine, let me be blunt. If you sign this thing, you're a fool … and I don't think you're a fool."

"Sumner and his people hold all the cards," he continued. "I can't believe they have the audacity to ask what they're asking. It's ludicrous. And if you sign it, you're being just as ludicrous. I don't care how much money they're willing to invest."

"Bernie—"

"They call these demands … what … performance guarantees?" He asked, angrily flipping pages on the contract.

"Yes Bernie, but—"

"Performance guarantees! Crap! They're nothing short of blackmail, and you know it."

"Bernie, they're just trying to protect their interests. They want a high tech company that can give them high tech results, a product they can hold on to, something they can turn over for a profit. They want to get in on the ground floor of the next Microsoft."

"And if you can't deliver they take what little of the company you have left and leave you with nothing!"

"I'll still own 49 percent of the stock if I sign."

"And right now you own 100 percent of a very successful little company if you don't."

"Exactly," Katherine said

"Exactly what?"

"It's not good enough."

"Excuse me? I don't under—"

"You said it yourself, Bernie. I own a successful *little* company, but that's not what I want. I want to own a successful *big* company. If I do what I know I can, I'll own 49 percent of a Fortune 500 company worth billions."

"Right, and if for any reason you fail to meet even one of these *performance guarantees,* that's what they'll take away from you. That, and everything else you own. For heaven sake, Katherine, they want you to put up your condominium, the cottage and everything else you have in this world as collateral. You can't do that. You need a safety net, something to hold back."

"Sumner and his people won't have it any other way. They want me 100 percent committed, or they won't sign."

"If you sign this contract, you should be committed. For God sake, you can't see into the future. You need an escape clause."

"The contract is for five years, Bernie. As long as you've known me, have I ever not done what I said I was going to do? Why would I start now? What do you think's going to happen?"

"Oh, I don't know," Bernard Schultz said, a little sarcasm to color his words. "Economic collapse, a strong competitor, industrial espionage, global warming, a tsunami, the end of the world. You name it, you're not protected against any of it."

"Well if it's the end of the world, I won't have to worry about losing everything I own, will I?"

"Don't joke, Katherine. You can't, you just can't sign this thing."

"Yes, I can. I know what I'm doing."

Katherine Sharpe smiled. She knew something her lawyer didn't. It was her little secret, hers and Pavel's, and not even the sanctity of attorney-client privilege would make her feel comfortable in letting that cat out of the bag.

"It's insane. I can't let you agree to this. I won't let you sign it."

It was the wrong thing to say. Suddenly Katherine felt like she was ten again and standing in front of 'Daddy', a man who spent most of her life telling her why she'd never be good enough. Until the day he died, he tried to project his weaknesses onto her. He blamed her for everything that was wrong in his life, and predicted her future as one gigantic failure in the making. The color rose in her cheeks. She controlled her voice, but not the shaking in her hands as she reached for a pen.

"I appreciate your advice, but I know what I'm doing."

The intercom on her desk buzzed and broke into her reverie. It was almost five years later. She was still the president of ComTech Dynamic Industries, but she was no longer the only shareholder. That ended the moment she signed the contract – the same damned contract that now sat in the middle of her desk.

She was also no longer the CEO of the company. Sumner had snagged that title as part of the deal. He also used his controlling interest in the company to establish a Board of Directors made up exclusively of the major investors of his hedge fund. Of course, he'd also appointed himself Chairman of the Board before the ink on the contract was dry.

Katherine didn't object then and didn't care now. Sumner was a moneyman with little knowledge of, or interest in, the field of advanced computer technology. Katherine didn't care what he called himself, as long as he stayed out of her way and provided the funds she and Pavel needed to complete the work they'd started so long ago.

"You asked me to give you a warning," her secretary said. "Mr. Sumner's expecting you in his office in five minutes."

"Thanks, Jane. Buzz me in ten."

The meeting with Sumner didn't go well, but that was to be expected. Sumner was an officious prick, a prissy little man with good manners, better connections, and a Napoleon complex that kept him hungry for power and control.

He used most of the fifteen minutes they spent together to politely remind her of the looming deadline, the expectations of the investors he represented, and the consequences of failing to meet those expectations. In the past she'd simply assured him that she and Pavel were on schedule and making tremendous progress. This time she took a different approach. *The best defense is a strong offense.*

"Don't threaten me, Ted. It's counterproductive and quite frankly, I'm sick of it."

Sumner started to get up, but Katherine waved him back to his seat. "Don't bother."

"I've listened to your bullshit for five years," she continued, "because I had to. You held all the cards. But none of that matters anymore, because I've done what I said I would do. And in two weeks when we make the announcement, you'll know you should have believed in me from the start. I'm only sorry you and your friends will be the ones to benefit from it."

Sumner smiled, his fingers steepled below his chin. Katherine ignored the smug look that was beginning to creep onto his face. She'd been planning this speech for some time, and she wasn't about to let him steal her thunder.

"You can't begin to understand what it's taken to make this project a reality. You sit in your office all day and plan how to spend your profits without knowing one iota about what we do here, or about the people who make it happen. You throw money at people and hope they throw it back with interest."

"That's what investing is all about."

Sumner sounded almost bored. Katherine needed to up the stakes.

"No, that's what being a parasite is all about."

"How dare you!" Sumner sputtered.

"It's the truth," Katherine said. "If you were a real investor, if you shared any of the hopes and dreams of the people who work here, instead of weaving your webs and planning what to do if I failed—"

"You didn't ask me to share your hopes and dreams when you signed that contract," Sumner shot back. "All you asked for was my money, so don't act like a wounded prima donna. And hedging your bet is just common sense. If you fail to deliver and I have to sell this company at a loss, your 49% will ensure my investors still make a profit. That's good business, plain and simple."

"I'm not a prima donna and I'm not going to fail."

"So you say," Sumner said. "But I want to see the specs on this thing and a demonstration … prior to your presentation to The Board."

"Not possible," she said simply.

Sumner's face flushed with anger. "As the CEO of this company I have a right to be privy to—"

"You may have the right," Katherine interjected, "But you don't have the expertise to understand the schematics, and I don't have the CPUs."

Sumner didn't interrupt.

"Pavel still has them, and without them a demonstration is impossible. You and The Board will have to wait. But I'm glad you brought up selling the company."

Katherine let the comment hang in the air between them. This was what she'd been working towards since their meeting began. She knew Sumner would never be able to let it pass. She was counting on it. She was right.

"What do you mean?" Sumner's eyes narrowed, but he didn't seem surprised.

Thank you, Michael. I knew I could count on you to do the wrong thing. That was one St. Patrick's Day that was worth a fake hangover.

"Oh, you know what it's like, Ted." She smiled. "You may not know about technology, but you certainly know about business and competition and … rumors."

She let her words sink in for effect.

"This business generates a lot of rumors. People talk. Secrets get leaked. It happens all the time."

Sumner was no longer smug and his smile was long gone.

"I've been approached by some people, much like you and your investors, but with deeper pockets and a better grasp of the world of high tech."

"You had no right to disclose—"

"I didn't disclose anything, Ted." Katherine feigned shock. "You know me better than that. I signed a non-disclosure clause as part of the contract, and I was the one who insisted on the security measures we put in place, remember? But the rumors, Ted. You can't fight the rumors."

Before he could gather the thoughts Katherine saw racing around behind his beady eyes, she continued.

"I'm sure I could arrange for the sale of your share of the company prior to the announcement. We've been holding our own since you bought in and the figure they mentioned would ensure a fair return for your investors based on what's on the table. They'd have to forget about the future of the company but if, as you suggested, I can't be trusted … better safe than sorry, right Ted? Good business, plain and simple?"

"You bitch."

Their meeting ended a few minutes later, with Sumner telling her in no uncertain terms that he was not about to sell his majority share of the company, rumors or no rumors. He didn't make any more threats and, more importantly, he didn't press for a demonstration. That was all she needed, what she'd been working for all these months, and essential to The Plan. A little more time.

At first Katherine was relieved her bluff worked, but as she thought about it later, an alarm in the back of her mind started to sound very softly. Was it really that easy to manipulate Sumner? Had he given in too quickly? Was he planning something? Although she tried to dismiss it as paranoia, the thought sent a chill racing down her spine.

Later that evening, Katherine sat in front of a computer in the spacious den of her luxury downtown condo. Her shoulders and neck ached from the tension of the day. As she stared at her screen saver, Van Gogh's Wheat Field with Crows, the enormity of the challenges she faced began to overwhelm her. It was 'Daddy' all over again. She could hear his derisive laugh in the deep recesses of her mind. *Ain't good for but one thing.* As she had so many times in the past, she found strength in her hatred of the man. She found thinking about him made it easier to rationalize what she was about to do.

Even so, her touch on the keyboard of her computer was light, as if striking the keys too hard might wake up something dangerous. She tapped out her message like a sorceress whispering an incantation. The latest instructions to Wolfe and his team. When she hit send, the encryption software on her laptop made it impossible for anyone without the codes to read the message. Because of her confidence in the software, software that she had written, she didn't bother to edit her list of recipients. She forgot that one of those recipients was a laptop sitting on a dusty shelf in a Toronto Police Service property vault. It was a mistake that would cost her a life.

CHAPTER THIRTEEN

Calvin didn't have much luck running down information on the two men from the apartment. His favorite snitches had little to add to what he already knew. Ricco was small time. Nothing special. The second guy on the other hand was a different story. Nobody had heard of him. He was a complete mystery. That alone made him special. Nobody's a blank slate.

Calvin leaned into the worn leather seat of the shoe shine stand and looked at the dirty blond dreads of the man with the rag in his hand. He looked to be about 45, but Calvin knew from his rap sheet he was closer to 30. He'd cleaned up his act as far anyone knew, but his early life had left an indelible mark. If there was any information to be had on the street, this was the man to have it. He was Calvin's best and last chance.

"What da ya say, Nick?"

"Nothing anyone 'ud listen to, Boss. How 'bout you?"

"S.S.D.D., Nick. Same shit different day."

"You oughta' see the world from where I'm sitting. What'll it be today? Quick buff or a deep shine?"

"Just a quick buff, Nick. Shine's worth more than the shoes."

The man gave a sharp bark of a laugh and started to meticulously buff a pair of shoes that didn't need the attention. Calvin stopped in once a week. The shine was good, but the information was usually better.

"So, what do you hear, Nick, about this?" Calvin said, tapping the newspaper on the seat beside him. The photograph of Tinker was grainy but distinguishable.

"He the smart one or the dead one?"

"The dead one. The smart one's in The Don."

"Too bad."

"Why's that?" Calvin asked.

"Word on the street is pretty thin about your boy here," Nick said. "He's not local for sure, but nobody seems to know where he came from. Guy's a ghost."

Calvin grunted.

"Sammy says he's an import from Nevada. Mob connections."

"Yeah?"

"Yeah. Sammy aslo says Elvis runs a sandwich shop on Grosvenor. Wears a turbin to hide his hair."

Calvin laughed. "Thanks anyway, Nick. You hear anything …"

"I'll let you know.

"What do I owe you?"

The young man held up his hand in protest. "Same as usual, Boss. But you make Chief and I'm gonna double the price."

Calvin smiled and dropped a folded ten dollar bill in the tip jar by the foot rest. "In case you decide to get a hair cut."

Calvin shook his head as he walked away. It seemed Tinker was determined to stay as anonymous in death as he had been in life. It was time to try a different angle.

CHAPTER FOURTEEN

Calvin watched Jerry Stein rest a meaty hand on the wrist pad that he used to keep from developing carpal tunnel syndrome. With the other he reached for the last Twinkie in a six-pack, bought that morning to cover the stretch between breakfast and lunch.

"Man you gotta' lay off the health food. Stuff's gonna kill you one of these days," Calvin chided.

"What? This?" Jerry asked. "Just a snack." He sailed the cellophane and cardboard at a wastebasket on the far side of the room, missing by two feet.

"What I'm really worried about is the UV from these terminals. And now they tell me these machines will start to give off radon gas as they get older. Can you imagine what that would do to your system?"

Calvin looked around the windowless room and took in the junk food wrappers and the unmistakable dusting of cigarette ash on a number of Coke cans within easy reach.

"Man, you gotta be kidding."

"What?"

"Radon gas wouldn't stand a chance in this hole. If the Twinkies don't absorb it, the smoke will choke it out."

"What are you talking about, Detective Dempster?" Jerry looked at Calvin, his face a picture of innocence. "It's against regulations to smoke in the station. You know that, sir."

"Of course. Silly me. What could I have been thinking?"

"I don't know."

"A paragon of health like you wouldn't defile your body by smoking anyway, would you?"

"Of course not. My body's a temple."

"You mean—" Calvin caught himself and laughed. "Nope. Too easy. What have you got for me Jerry?"

Jerry Stein leaned back and the material at the front of his shirt pulled tighter against the buttons as it stretched across his remarkable belly.

"Sorry, Cal, but I got diddly. The square root of diddly, to be honest."

"What do you mean?"

"Exactly that. I got nothing. I can't get into the secure part of the hard drive. Hell, I can't even get to the front door."

"Passwords?" Calvin offered.

"I wish," Jerry snorted. "Passwords are my bread and butter. Easy-peasy."

"Okay," Calvin said. "So what are we up against here?"

"I don't know. That's the problem. If it was just a matter of hacking an access code there'd be no issue. Security codes get breached on a regular basis. Just ask Ashley Maddison."

Calvin just shook his head.

"The problem is most of the security programs are written using languages that are based on fairly standard binary codes. Once you get to the front door, it's just a matter of time and patience. Most hackers write programs to try a zillion different combinations until the right sequence pops up. As long as the original programmer hasn't built in an attempt maximum, eventually the odds win."

"An attempt maximum?" Calvin asked.

"Yeah. Just what it sounds like. After a certain number of attempts the connection is broken. The computer hangs up or shuts down. But there are a million ways to defeat that."

"You're not making anything clearer for me. What have we got here?"

"A failure to communicate."

"No jokes, Jerry, it's almost four and I haven't had a straight answer all day."

Jerry Stein shifted his 310 pounds forward again and became serious. His florid face looked more flushed than usual. "No joke. I can't seem to communicate with any of these programs. I can't get to the front door. I can't get them to ask me for a password."

"That's a major problem?" Calvin was looking even more bewildered.

"Let me try to explain this in laymen's terms. Let's say you had something valuable stored in a lock box – jewels let's say."

That's apropos, Calvin thought.

"Any lock pick in the city could get into that box given enough time, no matter how good the lock, right?"

"Right," Calvin answered, becoming more interested.

"Now let's say the lock box was in a room with only one door and no windows. Good lock on the door."

"No problem. Pick the lock on the door and then spring the lock on the box," Calvin replied.

"Simple," Jerry agreed. "But … what if you can't find the door? It's hidden. It looks just like the rest of the walls."

"Problem." Calvin was beginning to see the light.

"Big problem." Jerry nodded. "But it gets better. What if the box is in a room that's in another room? What if you don't know how many rooms there are, one inside the other? And all of them have only one door, and all the doors look like walls."

"Is that what we're up against?"

"Something like that … only really fucking complicated."

Calvin was starting to catch on. "What about a back way? Can you break through the walls?"

Jerry Stein's features darkened as he leaned close to Calvin Dempster and dropped his voice. "Those files are better protected than anything I've ever seen. There're only two people who can get through that security —God, and the guy who wrote them. And I wouldn't bet the house on God."

CHAPTER FIFTEEN

The next day, Jack and Calvin grabbed lunch so they could bring each other up to speed. It was a short conversation. They'd split up the tasks hoping to minimize duplication on their 'non-investigation'. So far, the sum total of what they'd found out added up to a big, fat zero. Fingerprints, ballistics, DNA, contacts in the military, CPIC checks, NCIC, Homeland Security, Interpol – all negative.

"Nada," Calvin confirmed.

Jack was thoughtful for a moment. "So, what about the computer?"

"Amazing machines," Calvin chided. "You should try one some day. Eliminate all that messy carbon paper. Modern technology is wonderful."

Jack shook his head. "I'm a dinosaur. Get over it. The computer?"

"Right. Business. Basic IBM Think Pad. Nothing special. Serial number's gone, so I assume it's stolen."

"No way to trace it?" Jack asked.

"Not the computer itself, but I'm checking the ISP to try and get a handle on the IP, see if it's static or shared. My guess is it was DHCP, and probably masked."

"Plain English?"

"The computer was hooked up to the internet so it could send and receive e-mails, downloads, whatever."

"Okay," Jack said. "That I can understand."

"I'm trying find out who registered the account. The ISP is the Internet Service Provider. I'm not sure if they're willing to cooperate, but even if they do, I'm guessing the address is probably masked. Makes it impossible to get a name or address."

"Why wouldn't the ESPN—"

"ISP."

"Whatever," Jack said. "Why wouldn't they cooperate? We're the good guys."

"No paper. Without an official investigation, I can't exactly write a warrant for their records. I'm pretty sure that would send up a red flag."

Jack nodded, beginning to understand.

"And the service providers are pretty good at protecting their client's identities. I mean, if this was a kiddie porn case they'd cooperate in a heart beat, with or without a warrant. But Jack, we're investigating something that hasn't happened and probably won't happen. A figment of someone's imagination. Hard to sell that one to anybody."

"So it's a dead end?" Jack asked.

"Not necessarily. I'll keep trying, but ..."

"This just keeps getting more and more fun," Jack said.

Calvin didn't disagree.

"So what makes you think the – IP? – would be masked?"

"Well, that's one thing I can tell you about the computer. I had a friend from E Crimes take a look at it ... unofficially."

"Of course. And?"

"And nothing. He can't get into the files at all."

"Jesus, Cal. That's not much help."

"I know. But actually, it tells me something pretty damned interesting. If Jerry Stein can't get into it, that says something."

Jack waited for an explanation.

"Jerry's the best hacker in the business ... at least on our side. He could hack into the Pentagon if he wanted to. But the only thing Jerry could tell me is the *size* of the files on the hard drive. The rest is just his educated guess."

"Which is?"

"There's a lot of information on that computer, Jack. A lot. The hard drive's almost completely full. Small files, big files, and one massive file."

Jack didn't interrupt.

"Jerry thinks the massive file is an encryption file, very sophisticated, designed to protect everything else on the computer."

"Which means?"

"Whatever's on that computer … somebody went to a hell of a lot of trouble to protect it."

Jack had a thought.

"You said Jerry's the best hacker on our side. What about on the dark side? You know anybody that does this sort of thing illegally?

Calvin was way ahead of him.

"There's one guy I can think of?" Calvin hesitated. "Might be a bit of a problem, though?"

"Jail?" Jack guessed.

"Homework," Calvin replied.

Before Jack could ask, the pager on his belt gave a nasty squeal.

"Blackberry's don't do that," Calvin said with a grin.

"Neither would this thing if I could figure out how to turn it off," Jack said in response.

"You're pathetic, Jack."

Jack shrugged, trying to read the number to see if he recognized it. He didn't.

"That's all right," Calvin said. "I'll leave you to build a fire so you can send back a smoke signal, or whatever the hell you do. I've got a few other leads to check out, then I've got to get back to work on some real cases … official ones."

Calvin was out the door of the coffee shop before Jack could fish his cell phone out of his coat pocket. He punched in the number from his pager and waited as the connection was made, all the while wondering, *what now?*

CHAPTER SIXTEEN

"Jack Wright."

Darcy hesitated, not really sure what to say. The call had been impulsive.

"Hello?" The impatience in his voice was unmistakable.

"Yes." Darcy cleared her throat. "Sorry. Sergeant Wright?"

"Can I help you?"

God, I hope so! Darcy thought, but said instead. "I'm sorry to bother you. My name's Darcy Caldwell. I'm—"

"No longer a waitress at my favorite bar," Jack finished for her.

Taken aback, Darcy hesitated again. Either this guy has a hell of a memory or someone filled him in on a few details about last night, including the name of the ETF officer who pulled the trigger. Darcy guessed it was the latter. Secrets don't stay secret too long in a police department.

"Last time I saw you, you were a skinny little girl with braces running off to join the circus."

"Army," Darcy countered, unsure why she was suddenly angry.

"Same difference."

"Only the clowns," she said, trying for comic relief. It didn't work.

"So I hear," said Jack. "What can I do for you?"

Darcy took a breath and jumped in with both feet. "I understand you're looking into … into what happened at the apartment last night. Is that true?"

"No. I'm with Hold-up. I'm sure IAD will want to talk to you, and I imagine SIU already has ... but not me."

She listened for any hesitation, but if she caught him off guard, he was pretty damned good at covering up. Even so, she wasn't about to let it go that easily.

"No, what I mean ..." God, why was she so nervous? She tried again, "What I mean is, I understand you're investigating what these guys were doing with the hardware."

This time she could hear him falter. He was probably wondering where she got her information. She steeled herself for a long-winded denial. She needn't have worried.

"Sorry. Not my department."

"But the rumor—"

"You believe every rumor you hear, Officer Caldwell?"

"No," she said.

"Good. Neither do I. Otherwise I'd have to believe you shot a suspect in the back when he was about to give up."

"I didn't," she said quietly. She was too taken aback to say anything else.

"I didn't think so. A word to the wise. Don't believe everything you hear."

CHAPTER SEVENTEEN

Jack knew immediately he'd gone too far. He didn't want to hurt the girl, given what she'd been through, but that's the thing about real life ... there's no rewind button.

"Sorry. I didn't mean to—"

"No. I got it. It's just that ..."

"You're looking for answers." It wasn't a question.

"Something like that," Darcy replied.

"I wish I could help."

Jack felt like a shit, but he didn't want to burn Calvin as a co-conspirator, and he didn't want to risk getting anyone else involved, especially this girl. Christ, she'd just capped one of the suspects. Not exactly a neutral party in the grand scheme of things.

"Listen," he said. "Guns and Gangs are tracing the weapons. That's all I know. Beyond that, there's nothing official."

"What about something unofficial?" Darcy countered.

"I'm sorry?" Jack said.

"You said there isn't anything *official*. What about something unofficial? These guys had a damned arsenal in that room. Isn't anyone curious?"

Jack couldn't help but grin. Feisty.

"I think everyone's curious, Officer Caldwell, but—"

"I know—*manpower and priorities.*"

"You got it," Jack said.

"That's bullshit. These guys were involved in a lot more than selling a few Saturday night specials, and we're supposed to just walk away because of the budget? Fuck that!"

Jack listened to her breathing and could almost feel the anger and frustration. He understood her need for answers all too well. He still had questions of his own from too many things that happened in what seemed like another life. He couldn't help but empathize. After a long silence Jack made a decision.

"Officer Caldwell—"

"Darcy."

"Darcy. What shift are you working right now?"

"I'm not."

Jack waited.

"They've given me two weeks off to make sure I don't snap," she said.

Jack chuckled. "And will you?"

"Maybe," Darcy said. "But only from boredom. Why?"

Jack took a deep breath, but he'd already made his decision. "I was just thinking that maybe we should get together and talk – unofficially. No promises. You have plans for lunch tomorrow?"

"Let me check my calendar," Darcy said, sarcastically. "Nope. Free as a bird."

"I'm pretty sure you know a place called Stats' … just off Spadina?"

This time Darcy didn't have to force a laugh. "I've seen the sign," she said.

"How about 12:30?"

"Would 12:00 be okay?" she replied. "I've got an appointment at 1:30."

"Sounds good."

"Thanks, Detective."

"It's Jack." He may have to disappoint her in the very near future but, what the hell, might as well do it on a first name basis.

"Jack."

"See you at 12:00."

When he got off the phone, Jack made a few calls. He liked what he heard. Tough, determined, and intelligent. At about the same time, Darcy was making a call of her own and learned a few things about Detective Sergeant Jack Wright. Stats Caldwell was a wealth of information.

CHAPTER EIGHTEEN

Jack got to Stats' about ten minutes before noon. He sat at a table near the front so he could watch the comings and goings. He was hoping to pick Darcy out of the crowd, but he wasn't exactly sure what to look for. He hadn't seen her since she was a waitress, and his vision was usually quite blurred at that time. He remembered her as a gangly tomboy with short hair and braces. The second she walked through the door, however, things started to fall into place. Jack had to laugh at himself. The conversation the other night between Stats and the upset young woman suddenly made perfect sense.

Jack sat back and watched as Darcy stopped for a quick chat with one of the staff. He was playing an old, familiar game. Trying to read people without actually meeting them. It was like trying to figure out characters in a play before they say their first lines.

Darcy looked better today. Her thick auburn hair was brushed back from her oval face in a short ponytail. There were still remnants of dark circles under her eyes, but the vacant stare of the previous evening was gone. When the waitress said something funny, Darcy's eyes flashed and her full lips pulled back to reveal dazzling white teeth in a perfect smile. Thank God for braces.

Jack had to admit there was nothing tomboyish about her anymore. She was definitely a woman now, beautiful in a very natural way. She wore little makeup, but had that fresh scrubbed, rosy look of someone who's just stepped out of the shower. Her eyes were captivating, pale blue, and didn't need any help from Mabeline to make them stand out. She wore faded jeans that matched her eyes, hugged her slim hips and accentuated her long legs. Her white blouse revealed just enough cleavage to show the upper swell of her firm breasts. The waitress said something else and turned to look in Jack's direction. The two women exchanged a conspiritorial glance and a quick laugh before parting ways.

As she made her way to his table through the lunch crowd, Jack was struck by a couple of things at once. She was tall, 5'9" at least, and there was a strength and confidence about her when she moved. She had an athletic build that reminded him of a dancer or a swimmer, probably from years of training with the ETF. She stopped in front of Jack's table and extended her right hand at the same time Jack stood.

"Detective Sergeant Wright, I'm Darcy Caldwell."

Jack shook her hand. "I thought we got that straight over the phone. It's Jack."

"Right. Sorry. Jack."

"I hope you don't mind the jeans thing," Darcy said with a nervous laugh. "I don't get dressed up much when I'm off duty and this is unofficial, right?"

Jack nodded, but didn't say anything else.

"I'm really not sure what I'm looking for but …" Darcy shrugged, as if to finish her sentence.

"No problem. Like I said on the phone, I doubt I can help, but I needed lunch anyway and I'm hoping you can get me the family discount."

Darcy smiled, but didn't make any promises.

"So how'd you pick me out so quickly?" Jack asked. "Do I just look like a cop?"

"I worked in this bar for years, remember? You were kind of a legend."

Jack could feel a slight burning in his cheeks. It had been a long time since someone made him blush.

"Should I apologize now for whatever I did then?" Jack asked.

"You don't stand out in my memory so you couldn't have been that bad."

"You must have taken a lot of nights off."

Darcy's smile was radiant and caught Jack off guard. She had just the hint of an overbite. Her pale blue eyes were like the tip of an iceberg, seeming to hide much more than they revealed. The contrast with her dark hair was stunning. After some small talk, Darcy got down to the subject that brought them to Stats'.

"You know about last night ... I mean my part?"

Jack tried to keep it light, although he could tell that she was hurting. "Like I told you last night, I've heard rumors I don't believe. You doing okay?"

Darcy ignored the question. "Part of what they say is true." She swallowed involuntarily, but squared her shoulders. "The suspect was shot in the back of the head ... by me. But he wasn't *about* to surrender, not with a pistol in his hand. I did what I had to do, and I'd do it again in a heart beat."

Jack knew she meant what she said, but he could also tell it was probably the last thing she'd want to have to do again. He watched her steady her trembling hand on the table before trying to continue.

"It's just that ..."

Jack waited.

"There are so many questions ... you know? I mean ... I don't care where the god damned guns came from. That's somebody else's problem. But what were they doing with them? And why did he ... he didn't ... he didn't have a fucking chance! Why didn't he fucking give up?"

Jack tried to make it easier on her by staring at his coffee until she was ready to continue.

"They weren't running guns," she said. It wasn't a question, so Jack let her carry through. "Gun runners don't have the balls this guy had."

"Some of them have more balls than you'd think. Some of them just get stupid."

Jack wasn't arguing. He was just playing devil's advocate.

"This guy wasn't stupid, Jack, he was just ... cold. He didn't flinch. His hands didn't shake. He was so ... professional."

Her voice trailed off and Jack watched her eyes. He could tell she was accessing the memory, running the whole scene through in her mind's eye. She shivered ever so slightly, as if trying to shake it off.

"What were they doing in that apartment?" She asked after a long pause.

Jack took a long look at Darcy. He thought about how people had described her. *Intelligent. Tough.* She looked directly into his eyes now. There was nothing imploring or needy about her gaze. She wasn't asking him to make it all better. She was just asking him to help it make sense.

Jack decided to throw her a bone, even though he still didn't want to get anyone else involved.

"The word that we got from the other one, Ricco, is that it was a prelim to a robbery of some kind. Probably bullshit, but I figure that's where the rumor got started I'm involved."

"But you're not?"

Jack didn't respond and Darcy didn't press.

"Must be some robbery they've got planned," she said, trying to draw him out. "We're not talking about hitting your local mom & pop."

"Not with C4 and rocket launchers," Jack agreed. "But like I said, it's probably bullshit."

"Did he give you a location?"

"No." Jack shook his head. "The next day he denied the whole thing. Said he was just blowing smoke. Then he lawyered-up. Hasn't said a word since."

"You believe him … that he was blowing smoke, I mean?"

"Probably," Jack said, looking anywhere but in her eyes.

"For a guy who's supposed to know all about lying, you're pretty bad at it."

"You sure?" Jack said.

"I know you don't believe they were just selling that stuff. I'm thinking the rumors I heard about you looking into it are true. If that's the case, I want in."

"I told you, don't believe everything you hear."

"Then convince me I'm wrong."

Jack didn't say anything. Darcy was right. He was a terrible liar.

"From what I hear you like puzzles. Once you get into one, you never give up. Not until you have all the answers."

It wasn't hard for Jack to guess where she'd gotten that little tidbit. For years he'd carried a crossword with him wherever he went. He had one in his jacket pocket now. Lots of people carry novels with them to fill in those small gaps of time when you can't do anything else. For Jack it was always a crossword. Stats Caldwell used to kid him about it.

"And how is your uncle? I haven't talked to him in a while."

Darcy pressed on.

"I'm guessing that kind of passion spills over into your work. Maybe even why you got on the job in the first place. I don't believe for a second you're going to walk away from this one."

"I have lots of other puzzles to solve," Jack said.

"Not like this one," Darcy countered.

"Who has the time?"

Darcy stared hard at Jack, and for once he felt what it was like to be under scrutiny. He didn't like the feeling at all. Finally she broke the silence.

"You may not remember, but I was in Police College when you were a guest lecturer. I was one of the few students who actually did the reading you suggested. I even read the article you wrote for the RCMP Gazette."

"I'm honored ... but a little surprised. I thought only my mother read that one."

Jack's attempt at humor to throw her off balance didn't work.

"Know what Jack.?"

Jack knew he wasn't going to like what she had to say next. He was right.

"Everything you taught me tells me you're full of shit. You've used qualifiers, you've changed the subject, and you've talked all around it, but you haven't once actually said the words '*I'm not investigating this case*'. So let's cut the shit. That fucker made me put two bullets into the back of his skull. I want to find out why. You can let me help you or I'll just go ahead and investigate it on my own. One way or another, I need to find out what the hell those guys were up to."

Tough. Intelligent. His sources forgot to add ballsy and stubborn. She had him, and Jack knew it. If he could run an unauthorized investigation, so could she. He didn't want to let anybody else know what he was doing, but for some reason, looking into her beautiful blue eyes, he wasn't all that upset about the decision he was about to make.

"What do you know about computers?"

CHAPTER NINETEEN

"So you think everything's in the computer?"

"It's the only thing that makes any sense."

Jack and Darcy had long since finished dessert and were sitting in the empty bar sipping on coffee. Jack studied Darcy closely as she spoke. Her lips were full and her smile, the few times that he'd seen it, seemed almost too big for her face. Jack watched her struggle with the events that brought them to this point.

"So they were using the computer to plan a robbery?"

"That's the theory I'm starting with given Ricco's statement. Why else would it be in the apartment?"

"Stolen?" Darcy offered.

"Probably. The serial number's gone."

"Then maybe they were dabbling in a few things. A little fencing, a little gun running."

"M72 rocket launchers puts this way beyond the realm of a *little* gun running."

"But the computer could just be stolen property."

"Could be," Jack admitted. "But we're looking into other possibilities."

"Who's we?"

Jack swallowed involuntarily and signaled for the waitress to freshen his coffee. When he faced Darcy again she was staring at him with a slight grin that accentuated her dimples. Her raised eyebrows begged the question.

"I'm following a hunch, and one of the guys is giving me a hand. That's it."

"Dempster?"

Jack ignored the question. "We'll probably have to drop this in a day or so anyway."

"So I give you a hand for a couple of days. What harm can it do? Karski made sure I'm off for the next eight, and I'll go crazy if I have to sit around the apartment and watch my plants."

"Like I said before, Darcy, it's probably all bullshit."

"But what if you're right? What if Ricco's telling the truth and there really is going to be a major heist of some kind?"

"If that's the case, you stopped them before it happened."

"Come on, Jack, you don't believe that. You told me yourself Ricco couldn't plan his own supper. Somebody else has to be involved."

"That doesn't mean they'll go through with it."

"If you're right and the computer's the key, then there has to be more people involved. They're not going to quit just because we got lucky. And with the fire power these guys are playing with somebody's going to get hurt, especially if it goes wrong. You know these things, Jack, they always go wrong. That's where the ETF comes in, and that means it'll probably be somebody from my team if—"

"All right. I give." Jack could see the determination in her eyes. It was obvious she wasn't going to be deterred.

"Let me check with Cal and see if he got anywhere. If he turned up anything, I'll give you a call at home and tear you away from your plants. If not, you've got an eight-day vacation. Either way, it's on your time and nobody hears one word about this investigation. Deal?"

"What investigation?"

"Smart girl. Give me your phone number."

"On the first date? What would the neighbors say?!"

Jack couldn't remember the last time he'd blushed twice in the same conversation. He tried a quick cover.

"Funny. Good. A sense of humor will probably come in handy."

"Trust me," Darcy sighed, "If you knew anything about my life you'd know a sense of humor is about all I've got left."

"Let's hope not," Jack said. "It's going to take more than that to figure out what we're dealing with here … and that's no joke."

CHAPTER TWENTY

The Plan was Katherine's baby, and like any parent she pinned all of her hopes for the future on how well her offspring developed and matured. The day she contacted Wolfe was the day *The Plan* was born but, like any child, for a birth to take place there first has to be a conception. Katherine could remember the moment it was conceived, which was, ironically, nine months earlier. Even more ironically, the person who planted the seed of something so outrageous and illegitimate was the most conservative and law-abiding person she knew, her lawyer, Bernard A. Schultz. Katherine let her mind wander back in time.

"I'm sorry Katherine, but I did try to warn you."

"Christ! Is that the best you have to offer, Bernie? *I told you so*? I'm not paying you to tell me what I should have done. I'm paying you to tell me what to do."

"Katherine, I— I don't know what to say. I've been over the contract a hundred times. It's ironclad. I told you—"

Katherine felt bad for snapping on her lawyer and her friend. He was right then and he was right now.

"I'm sorry, Bernie," she said. "You did tell me. It's not your fault. It's mine. I just didn't think it would take this long. I didn't think Pavel would have so many ... issues. I was wrong."

Katherine couldn't look at her old friend and advisor. His words were painful enough. They spelled her ruin. But the sympathy shining in his rheumy eyes, magnified by thick glasses, would be more than she could stand.

"You weren't wrong, Katherine. Just naive ... and maybe a little over-confident."

"I think you mean cocky, don't you?" It was meant as a joke, but neither of them laughed.

After a silence that stretched on far too long, Katherine finally spoke again.

"So what are my options?"

"Best case scenario? You and Pavel finish your project."

"We're working on it, but I can't just sit back and hope that we finish on time."

"Option two," Bernie said, holding up two stubby fingers, "Is to get an extension from Sumner, but—."

Katherine nodded, the wheels in her head spinning with different scenarios she'd been thinking about for some time.

"I've thought about that, and I think it may be possible."

She could see a quizzical look cross her lawyer's face, but it was mixed with sadness, or perhaps resignation. She couldn't be sure.

"If I explain to him how close we are, that all we need is another six months or maybe a year, and then our dream of ..."

Her words trailed off as she watched the old man shake his head more and more vigorously.

"You don't understand, Katherine."

"Understand what?"

"Sumner. His deadline. The Project. All of it."

"Then don't just stand there shaking your head. Explain it to me."

"It took me a while to understand, and for that I apologize. I should have seen it at the start, given you better advice—not that you would have listened—but I get it now."

Katherine was starting to get pissed. Bernie was coming dangerously close to saying 'I told you so' again.

"When you sold Sumner 51% of your company and he insisted on those performance guarantees, he wasn't buying your dream. He doesn't care if you succeed or fail. He just cares that you do one or the other, and on time."

"What are you talking about? Of course he cares. It's why he bought the company in the first place. It's why he invested all that money. He knows if we succeed he'll be rich beyond his wildest dreams."

"But that's my point," Bernie interjected. "Sumner doesn't dream. He schemes. He's a pragmatist. He plans his acquisitions based on solid information, not hype."

Now it was Katherine's turn to look quizzical. "Meaning?"

"What was the company worth when you sold a portion to Sumner?"

"Twenty million. You know that. You did the paperwork"

"Right. And now? Twenty-five?"

"Let's say thirty. We've had a few good years lately."

"Okay, thirty million. Ted Sumner bought his share of the company hoping you'd succeed but expecting you to fail. He never believed in you, Katherine, but he didn't need to. He and his investors bought 51% of a very successful company that was owned, in their opinion, by a ..." Bernie hesitated.

"By a what?"

"A nut," Bernie finished, a pained look on his face.

Katherine could feel the blood rush to her face, but she didn't respond.

"Katherine, I know what you're capable of. I have no doubt that you can do what you say you can do. But to someone like Sumner, someone with too much money and no imagination, it sounds like a fantasy. Oh sure, if you succeed he'd more than happy to reap the profits, but that's not what he's all about."

"So what *is* he about?" Katherine was becoming exasperated.

"He's a bargain hunter, Katherine. He wants the deadline to pass."

"Why? What does he get out of it?" Katherine asked shakily, starting to realize where Bernie was headed.

Bernie Schultz sighed heavily, "An incredible deal, Katherine. When he takes over your 49% of the company after the deadline passes, Sumner and his cronies will have bought a $30 million company for a little over $10 million. Add to that your condo, the cottage, and a nice art collection." Bernie shrugged. "Not a bad return over five years. He then sells everything, takes his cut to do it all over again, and leaves you with—"

"Nothing."

Bernard Schultz nodded

"There's got to be something I can do, Bernie, isn't there?"

Bernie shrugged. "I don't mean to rub salt in the wound, Katherine, I don't, but I did tell you we needed to build in some safeguards to protect you."

"I know."

"And the one we did manage to slip through doesn't have any teeth."

Katherine had all but forgotten their one codicil. "Right. What does it cover? Natural disasters, social collapse and alien invasions or something like that?'

"Something like that. Intentional interference in the project by any person or persons connected to it, or otherwise."

"Right," Katherine said, remembering the words her lawyer had insisted be inserted into the contract. "And why did we put that in?"

"To keep Sumner from intentionally sabotaging the project."

"Can we use that?"

Bernie shook his head. "No. I know now Sumner isn't about to stall the project. If you succeed he wins. The only way that codicil will help is if someone steals your invention before the deadline, and seeing as how you haven't invented it yet, I don't know how that could ever happen."

Katherine didn't notice the sympathy in her lawyer's eyes or the defeated little shrug he gave before excusing himself from the room to leave her alone with her thoughts. And what delicious thoughts they were! The seed had been planted. Her mind was racing ahead like it did when she was on the cusp of a breakthrough in her research. The nervous tingling in the pit of her stomach was the same, the sense of anticipation. The only thing different was the fear, but Katherine chose to ignore it. She shouldn't have.

CHAPTER TWENTY-ONE

The black cotton gei, heavy with sweat, clung to Jack's back as he went through the ten basic Shotokan *Kata,* a series of formal movements representing attacks and defenses in some long forgotten battle. When the moves were done just right, the sleeves of his gei cracked like a rifle shot.

Jack worked out for two hours, well aware that four years ago he wouldn't have lasted five minutes. A lot had changed over the years. A lot of fast water had gone under a very shaky bridge.

It was 8:30 by the time he returned home. Charlie greeted him at the door, but the cats were nowhere to be seen. The house was quiet except for the soft beep of the answering machine. Along with the usual hang-ups, there were two messages. The first was from Calvin.

'Jack, it's Cal. Give me a call when you get in. Not much luck today, but we should talk. I'll be up late."

The second was a bit more interesting.

"Jack, it's Darcy. Sorry to bother you. I just wanted to touch base, see if you've spoken to Detective Dempster. I don't mean to be pushy. Actually I do. I'm sick of talking to my plants. Give me a call. You have my number."

Before he could decide who to call back first he heard the back door open and shut quietly. His first instinct was to reach for his Glock. He couldn't remember if he locked the door or not. When Charlie didn't bark, however, Jack relaxed.

"Ken?"

"You expecting someone else?" Ken said, as he pushed open the heavy oak door that separated the small butler's pantry from the dining room. "Spencer Tracey maybe?"

"Just checking."

"Excellent security protocol. Door unlocked. Dog ready to lick anyone who walks in. Nobody could get by that. How was your day?"

"Routine. Yours?"

"The same." Ken had a silly grin on his face.

"What?"

"Oh, nothing," The Cheshire cat grin remained firmly in place.

"What?!" Jack demanded.

"Nothing, really. Just heard you had another date at Stats today. Hell of a lot better looking than your last date from what I hear."

"You have me under surveillance now, Mom? You know I hate it when you do that."

"So … who's your friend?"

"You don't already know?"

"Yeah. Darcy Caldwell. ETF. Nice, from what I hear, and damned good looking."

"Then why'd you ask?"

"I like to see you squirm," Ken said with a smile.

"I'm not squirming."

"Okay, I like to see you blush then. Stats know about you two?""

Jack shook his head. "For Christ's sake, Ken, I've got a car that's older than she is. It's strictly business."

"Too bad. I hear she's drop dead gorgeous. What kind of business?"

"She wants some information about the guy she shot," Jack said, giving Ken a partial truth. "She's looking for answers. Closure."

"What did you tell her?"

Jack gave Ken enough to satisfy his curiosity, but not enough to get either one of them charged under the Police Services Act.

Darcy, too, felt the need for a little exercise but, unlike Jack, she thought of martial arts as something you do for work, not fun. Her thing was running.

Warming up in front of the mirror in the foyer of her apartment, she checked the load on the Smith & Wesson snub nose .38 she carried in a fanny pack strapped around her waist. She pulled it snug so that it lay flush against her flat stomach. She wasn't allowed to carry the weapon off duty but, given the events of the previous evening, she really didn't care.

She set out for a five mile run shortly after leaving the message on Jack's machine. Staring at the phone for half an hour hadn't gotten her anywhere. She was pissed at Jack for not calling and needed blow off a little steam.

She was hoping by the time she got home there'd be a message from Jack, but when she got back her answering machine was dark and silent. Darcy adjusted the shower temperature before stepping into the tub and kneeling under the soothing water. She thought maybe the cascading water would wash away the few messed up images that were still tumbling around in her brain. She was wrong.

It's funny how lives that are connected by the thinnest of threads can have a synchronicity that would suggest an omnipresent control, like a master puppeteer pulling the strings of a thousand souls. This particular night was a night for intense physical exertion followed by quiet contemplation. Wolfe was naked from the waist up, bathed in a thin sheen of drying sweat. He sat cross-legged with his eyes closed and his mind focused on his breathing.

The rising moon softly illuminated the room. The light fought to shine through heavily screened windows covered with grime situated around the top of the high walls of the loft. The five-storey building in the east end of Toronto, once the home of heavy machinery and the rough male voices of unskilled laborers, sat in the middle of a mostly forgotten section of the city. Wolfe had rented the whole building for a year, although he planned on being long gone in a few weeks.

The shadows that hugged the walls and corners of the loft were deep, but when he opened his eyes Wolfe could make out everything with perfect clarity. The service elevator, the only unbarred access to the top floor of the five-story building, stood like a giant mouth in the north wall. The security gates that slid down from the top and up from the floor to meet in the middle, were only partially closed. The solid bottom portion of the gate had been removed completely years ago. The safety switches that were designed to prevent it from operating when open had long since been disconnected.

The top portion, a tubular steel grate, was missing the bottom plate and a number of the perpendicular bars. The rest hung as if welded in place, completing the picture of teeth in a mouth, badly in need of braces. Wolfe had to be careful not to catch one of the jagged spikes as he ducked in and out of the lift. The elevator was old, and slow, and loud, acting as an alarm if anyone attempted to reach his sanctuary. The motor, powerful enough to raise and lower the ten by twenty-foot platform, squealed with disapproval every time Wolfe swung the lever to activate its ancient coils.

The access doors to the fire escape and lone staircase were secured by large bolts. As an added measure of security Wolfe had lagged heavy hasps to the metal doors and installed case hardened padlocks at the top and bottom of each. The only obvious means of advance or retreat was by way of the service elevator, and the lone escape route was so simple as to be unrecognizable.

Wolfe looked around the large space. When he'd first taken up residence, after securing the doors, Wolfe spent the better part of a day cleaning two distinct areas of the warehouse, each to be used for a separate purpose. One was for living, the other to practice his craft.

He worked out in a thirty-foot circle he'd scrubbed in the center of an otherwise filthy area. Wearing only light khakis, his tanned body toned to the point of being severe, he moved through a series of muscle tearing isometrics similar in nature to the 'kata' that Jack practiced on a regular basis. The difference was that where Jack's movements were designed to be defensive, Wolfe's were strictly offensive. His actions were designed to kill.

Wolfe clapped his hands together violently to send a brief shock throughout his body, and unfolded his legs. After a quick shower in what used to be a locker room and some fresh clothes, Wolfe felt more in control and stronger, more like himself. He hated to admit it, but the recent debacle at the airport had shaken him just a little. He wasn't used to miscalculations. And the cramps that set in during his meditation reminded him that perhaps his retirement was a little overdue. He needed to score big on the next few jobs, and then disappear forever.

He brushed a few particles of dust from his bedroll and sat down to a light meal of bread, cheese, and fruit. A canteen of water rested on the trunk that served as his headboard and held a variety of expensive weapons and equipment. He allowed his thoughts to drift as he unconsciously peeled the apple in his lap with a razor-sharp throwing knife. When he finished eating he reached for a disposable cell phone, one of several he'd purchased recently, and dialed her number. It would be the first of several calls.

Dried off, a terry-cloth towel wrapped around her head, Darcy sat in the living room of her apartment and flipped through the channels. Finding nothing of interest, she tossed the remote control to Miro on the other end of the couch.

"Here, go nuts. See if you can find something."

Miro opened one eye and then buried his nose under a paw.

"What's the matter?" Darcy asked, as if she expected an answer.

Miro continued to ignore her.

"C'mon, fur ball," Darcy said patting the couch beside her. "I need some sage advice."

No response.

"Great, just when I need you the most, all of a sudden you turn into a cat."

Relenting a little, Miro rolled closer, stretched full length, and allowed her to rub his belly.

"Typical male ... needy and impossible to understand."

Miro replied with a deep rumbling purr.

"So what do you think? Is Jack serious about this case or is he just playing around? I mean, it's not a robbery ... yet."

She scratched behind Miro' ears and stared at the phone. "Ring, damn it!"

Darcy almost hit the ceiling when the telephone, set on high to reach her in the shower, obediently rang. She snatched up the handset hoping to hear Jack's voice.

"Officer Caldwell?" The voice belonged to a man, deep and gravelly, with a slight accent Darcy couldn't place.

"Yes." Darcy answered, before she could stop herself.

"Officer Darcy Caldwell?"

"How did you get this number?" Like most police officers, her number was unpublished.

"Not important. Listen carefully."

Darcy knew instinctively not to interrupt.

"The guy you shot last night isn't a gun runner, he's a professional hit man from Chicago."

Darcy punched a button on her answering machine to start it recording.

"His real name is Denis Brousseau, born in Montreal." And with that the line went dead.

Wolfe cleared his throat with a cough that started deep in his chest. It was the fourth call he'd made that night; each to a different person, each with a different objective.

Giving Tinker's real name to the police was a risk, but Wolfe hoped it would keep them busy for weeks tracking down the very real story of one Denis Brousseau, only find that the trail led nowhere. By the time the police stopped chasing their tails, the operation would be over and he'd be a puff of smoke on the wind. He knew it could backfire, but he had to do something.

His source in the TPS, along with giving him Darcy's name and telephone number, had already informed him that someone with really bad handwriting hand logged the computer out of the property vault that morning. He wasn't able to provide a name, but it was obvious that at least one person on the force didn't buy the gun-running explanation and was smart enough to take a run at the computer.

Not good. Oscar said it was impenetrable, but Wolfe didn't feel like betting his life on it. He didn't trust her or her security programs. He didn't trust anyone.

Giving them Tinker was his only option. If he was right, the police would spend days or even weeks running around in circles. If he was wrong, there were other ways of slowing the investigation – or bringing it to a dead stop.

CHAPTER TWENTY-TWO

"The computer's the key," Ken said, continuing their conversation after Jack hung up.

"If Ricco's telling the truth."

"Even if he isn't, it's worth following up. You don't have much else to go on."

Jack nodded. "That was Calvin. He spent most of the day chasing dead ends. Took the computer up to one of the techies from Data Processing."

"No luck?"

"No," Jack said. "Apparently the security's something else, which means there's something on that computer worth protecting."

"Worth dying for," Ken corrected.

The two men sat in silence for a minute.

"So what about Ricco?" Ken finally asked. "You think he knows how to get into the computer?"

"That depends on how important he is to the plan, if there is one," Jack replied. "Assuming there is, if they've got any brains at all, then only one or two people will know how to access the information on that hard drive."

"So who are *they*?" Ken asked.

"That's the big question, isn't it?" Jack replied, staring into his empty tea cup.

"So what's your next step? If you can't get into the files, where do you go from here?"

It was 10:45. The cats were still nowhere to be seen, but Charlie lay on the floor by Jack's feet. He was never far away if there was food close by.

They were in the kitchen, one of the few rooms in the house that didn't need help. It was Caroline's favorite, where she and Jack spent a good portion of their married life. It was where they talked and laughed, where they fought on occasion, and sometimes even where they made up. It was also where Jack spent a good deal of his time cursing Ricker, questioning God, and drinking himself into oblivion.

Thirty panes of glass formed a large picture window that looked south over the once beautiful garden. The cupboards and counters were Monterey White set against a background of sage green. The hardwood floors had that golden honeyed hue that only age and wear could produce. Crown molding along the ceiling gave the kitchen a regal air. The two men sat at either end of the harvest table Jack had made for Caroline for their third anniversary. Jack stared at the moon as it crested the gables of Mrs. Leishman's carriage house.

Sensing Jack was somewhere else, Ken pulled him back by repeating the question. "If you can't get into the hard drive, what's next?"

"Leg work. Run down the guns, find out who's missing some M72's and a whack of C4. Get a make on the people involved," Jack continued. "Tinker and Ricco."

"So that's your job, Tinker and Ricco?" Ken asked.

Jack shook his head. "Not Tinker. According to Calvin, he's a dead end."

"No pun intended," Ken offered.

Jack let it go. "Nobody's even heard of him on the street. It's like he just dropped in from another planet. I'm going to take another run at Ricco tomorrow before they move him. Calvin's going to continue with the computer. Says he may know a guy who can crack the hard drive if we give him enough time."

"Time may not be on your side," Ken said.

Jack nodded in agreement. Both men were quiet for a few minutes. The only sound in the kitchen was the constant hum of the refrigerator and the occasional 'hrumph' from Charlie.

"So what about the lovely Officer Caldwell?" Ken finally asked. "Does she get a vacation, or are you going to put her to work?"

"Not much sense in getting her involved at this point. Too many cooks …" Jack left the rest of the adage hanging. "We'd be tripping over each other."

Ken didn't say anything, but it was obvious something was on his mind.

"It's bad enough that I'm running this investigation without official sanction." Jack continued. "I can cover my own ass, but bringing her in would be impossible to explain. Besides, she probably needs the time to get her head straight. Can you imagine the strain that she's going through right now?"

"Yeah," Ken said, "I can. She's sitting at home wondering when you're going to call, feeling useless because she can't do anything. Why don't you let her give Calvin a hand with some of the leg work? You can never have too much help."

Jack wasn't convinced.

"At least give her a call and let her off the hook. You owe her that much," Ken said, heading for the back door. "Thanks for the tea. Get some rest. You look like shit."

Jack started to say something, but Ken was already out the door. Even though they no longer worked in the same unit, Ken helped on more than one of Jack's cases just by listening and adding the odd view from a different perspective. What he said usually made a lot of sense. Jack wondered if he was right about 'the lovely Officer Caldwell'.

In truth, Jack couldn't explain why he didn't want her involved. In fact, part of him did. It was a strange tug-o-war that he felt in the pit of his stomach. He wanted to spend more time with her, but he couldn't shake the feeling she was in danger somehow, although the thought seemed ridiculous. Even so …

He reached for the telephone.

Darcy was still staring at the handset after the last call when the phone rang again. She was beginning to wish she'd never yelled at the damned thing in the first place.

This time she didn't answer right away. She couldn't. The ringing of the telephone startled her so much she'd dropped it like a hot potato. The phone bounced off the edge of the couch and skittered across the hardwood floor scaring Miro so much he almost moved. When she managed to retrieve the handset and listen, there was nothing for a second … and then, "Officer Caldwell?"

She held her breath …

"Darcy?"

… and exhaled. The voice was a little more familiar.

"Jack?"

"Are you okay? What happened? Girls don't usually throw the phone when they hear my voice until after the third date."

This time it was Darcy's turn to blush, although she wasn't feeling particularly coy at the moment. "You scared the hell out of me!"

"Sorry. I didn't realize the time until after I dialed. Were you asleep?"

"No. No, it's not that. It's just that I— never mind. Listen, I just had a call from some guy who gave me some information, maybe Tinker's real name. I don't know."

"Who was it?"

"No idea. Male. Sounded like a smoker. I tried to listen for background noises but I didn't hear a thing."

"Could be a joke, somebody playing a game," Jack offered. "There are a lot of nuts out there who read the papers. You've been kind of a hot topic lately."

"This guy sounded pretty serious, Jack. I don't think it was a joke. He said Tinker's a professional hit man from Chicago named Denis something-or-other. I've got it on tape. Hang on. Let me play it back. God, I hope this thing's working."

The two listened to the clicks and clacks as the machine rewound, and then to a gravelly voice,

"…*he's a professional hit man from Chicago. Look into a guy named Denis Brousseau, born in Montreal.*"

"Did you get that, Jack? Brousseau. Denis Brousseau. He's supposed to be from Montreal."

"I got it," Jack said.

Darcy could hear the scritch of a pencil on paper.

"What else did this guy say? What did he want?"

"You heard most of it, Jack. It wasn't a long conversation. He didn't seem to want anything. The name ring any bells? Brousseau?"

"Not with me, but maybe Cal's heard of him. He worked Organized Crime before Guns and Gangs. I'm sure he's got a few contacts in Chicago."

"Contacts willing to help out an unofficial investigation into a non-crime?" Darcy asked, only half joking.

"You ever work OC?" Jack asked.

"No," she said.

"Well, that's the kind of investigation those guys like best. You free for breakfast?"

"Our second date? I think I'm free," Darcy said.

"Fran's at 8:00. I want to hear that tape for myself. Make sure you bring it with you. Night."

Darcy wasn't sure if she was pissed that he'd hung up in her ear, or hurt that he didn't tease back. After all, he'd started it. *Men!*

"Nice speaking with you too, Detective, and by the way ... you're welcome!"

Jack looked at the phone for a while before getting up from the table. He wasn't sure why he'd panicked. It was just a joke ... right? She didn't actually think of this as a date, did she? He reached down to rub Charlie under the chin.

"Seems like I'm always apologizing to one woman or another, eh Charlie?"

Charlie woofed softly as if agreeing.

"Well, apparently I look like shit and need my beauty rest. Any apology will have to wait until morning."

As it was, a rash of violent robberies that landed on Jack's desk meant it would be three days before he and Darcy could manage their second 'date', and by that time, things had changed, all because of another phone call.

CHAPTER TWENTY-THREE

"*What do I do with it now, Daddy?*"

Katherine is sitting on a stool next to her father's work bench in the basement of a house that has long since been demolished. She's six years old. Her father looks on curiously, a glint of pride showing in his eyes, as his only daughter holds up a contraption of undeniable genius ... and inexplicable use.

"Well that depends," he laughs. "What is it?"

"It's something I made. I invented it."

"What does it do? No ... let me guess. Is it for sharpening pencils?"

Katherine shakes her head, "Nope."

"Is it for peeling apples?"

Another shake. "Uh-uh."

"Is it for curling your eyelashes?'

Katherine gave her father a look of exasperation. "No."

"Is it for catching little elephants?"

Katherine giggles. "No."

"Big elephants?"

She giggles harder. "No!"

"Okay. I give up then, Angel. What's your invention do?"

"I don't know. I just invented it. I don't know what it does yet."

William Sharpe laughs heartily and gives his daughter a bear hug that seems appropriate considering the man's physical appearance. He's a giant. Larger than life. Katherine laughs too. She loves being close to her father. William sets her back down on the stool and picks up the little collection of springs, pipes, and metal wheels, held together by twisted wire and luck, and examines it more carefully. She can tell he's impressed.

"I think it might just be a widget cleaner," he says in a serious tone.

"Really?" Katherine's eyes are bright and full of wonder.

"Isn't that what it looks like to you?"

Katherine nods her head slowly. "I ... think so ... but—"

"Well, why don't we put it up here, just until we find a widget to clean?" He looks at her and winks his approval, waiting for a nod from his daughter before he places her latest pride and joy in a place of honor. He sets it on a shelf to the right of his workbench, just at eye level, amongst a strange and wonderful collection of Katherine's gadgets that defy explanation or description. He called it his 'shelf of dreams'.

Of all the memories Katherine had from her childhood, this was one of the happiest—just her and her father alone in a world of their own design, making something out of nothing. Her father often stared at her inventions with a broad smile on his kind face. He said they gave him hope for the future, his and, more importantly, hers. He said he'd keep it until the day he died ... and he did.

He kept them until the day a drunk driver brought Katherine's world crashing down around her. Her father was on his way back from the store with a carton of milk for her mother and a Popsicle for her. He never made it. She never ate a Popsicle again.

The man who eventually took William Sharpe's place, a man her mother insisted she call 'daddy', cleared the 'shelf of dreams' with one swipe of his calloused hands. He had no use for her inventions, no time for her dreams, and no desire to be a father. His desire, she found out a few years later, cast her in a much different role. His desire put an end to her childhood and left her with nothing but her dreams and inventions for solace.

She was sitting alone with the lights out in her Forest Hill home, a condo that could have been featured in any decorating magazine. She wished with all of her heart that her father— her real father—was there to help her figure out her latest invention.

The ivory colored floor to ceiling curtains were pulled back and the sliding glass doors that opened onto a small balcony were open to the night. If she looked down she could see the towers of Casaloma silhouetted against the lights of Toronto. She sat on the floor to the left of the doors so that the cool night air blew across her back. The short satin nightgown that she wore was the one she bought just before the latest break up. It plunged daringly in front revealing the inside swell of her breasts and barely covered her upper thighs.

It was the fourth night after the shooting. It was a night for reliving memories. She was thinking of Peter, the last man she'd been with, allowing herself to imagine that she was warm and in love. The satin negligee caressed her nipples when she rocked forward, and caused them to harden even more than the cold. She let her right hand drop into her lap to brush against the front of her silk panties, sending delicious sensations throughout her body. She slipped her hand gently inside them. It made the memories more real as she caressed herself towards orgasm and remembered the times that Peter tried to do the same. Before she could bring herself to climax, however, memories of the pain and shame of her step-father crowded out memories of excitement and tenderness, just as they did when she was with Peter and every other man she'd ever tried to love. Her climax slipped away into the darkness like her step-father used to, leaving behind the smell of cheap whisky and stale cigarettes, and a little girl broken beyond all hope.

Katherine got to her feet quickly and closed the door, suddenly feeling as if everyone in the neighborhood was watching. She pulled the curtains and wrapped her arms around her shoulders in the hug she so desperately needed. She made her way to the kitchen and placed a copper kettle on the front burner of the stainless steel gas stove. When the water boiled and her tea was steeping, Katherine pulled back the curtains once again. Wearing a robe now, she didn't care if anyone was watching or not.

Katherine pulled open the sliding glass door and walked to the short cement wall that ran along the edge of the balcony. Leaning against the cold steel of the top railing, she looked into the burnished yellow aura that hovers perpetually above the night sky in Toronto. She searched in vain for the Big Dipper and Orion's Belt, but couldn't find either. She remembered doing this a thousand times with her father in their back yard, where the stars winked like ice crystals scattered on navy velvet. Sometimes her mother would join the two dreamers and listen to her husband tell fabulous tales. These were the best of times, lying with her head in her mother's lap while her father described ancient battles between the gods and mythical creatures. Katherine's heart ached for a time when life was simple. A time before Wolfe. A time before The Plan.

She hugged herself tighter and tried to think things out, but the answers wouldn't come. She felt like she was riding a dizzying merry-go-round that was about to collapse around her. She'd planned so carefully, looked at the problem from every angle. She thought she'd hired the best, but now she wasn't sure. One man was dead, another in prison, and Wolfe was beginning to scare the hell out of her. She'd seen something in his eyes the other day, something predatory and dangerous.

Katherine looked down for the first time since she'd stepped to the balcony railing and began wonder if death was the answer. She pushed herself up on her toes and leaned heavier against the railing, tipping the balance in gravity's favor. She could feel her toes start to slip against the rough surface of the concrete, relinquishing the tenuous grip they had on the floor. She leaned a little further out and saw herself falling in her mind's eye. Spadina Road seemed to be pulling her forward.

Just as quickly, she felt her knees buckle and her body drop to the balcony floor with a dull thud. Her shoulder scraped the cement wall on the way down, but the tears in her eyes had nothing to do with the pain that she felt. They did, however, bring her back to the reality of living and breathing. She pulled the bottom of the robe around her feet and buried her face in her shoulder. She fought to control the tears. She'd created something that was growing beyond her control, but she wasn't about to give in. She wasn't going to let one man, any man, take away what she'd worked so hard to create. She was a survivor and she would do whatever she had to do to win. Her stepfather had found that out the hard way. Sumner and Wolfe would have to learn the same lesson. Even so, when she thought about what lay ahead, one small voice kept hammering away in the back of her mind …

What do I do with it now, Daddy? What do I do with it now?

CHAPTER TWENTY-FOUR

The green walls of the cell were all Ricco had to look at during the four days he'd spent on the inside, the stainless steel toilet and sink the only contrast in a very green existence.

He'd been moved from the relative quiet of 56th to a proper detention center, one of three in Toronto. The Don Jail was the oldest— ancient, in fact— having been built in 1863. It was dank and fetid, and anything but quiet. Ricco found himself assailed by noise around the clock. During the day it was a cacophony of voices and echoes. It began with the slamming of steel on steel as the gates unlocked and slid back in preparation for breakfast. The florescent lights hummed to life behind heavy steel mesh and cast an eerie, unnatural luminescence. Orders were shouted and threats made quietly.

During the night it was mostly the building itself, and Ricco's own imagination.

Water dripping somewhere in the distance sounded like footsteps creeping along the corridor. Pipes hissing and spitting sounded like someone whispering meaningless words in his ear. The groans and snaps of an old building held terrifying possibilities that made sleep next to impossible.

Ricco sat with his feet up on a thin mattress, his hands wrapped around his knees, his back pressed into the corner of the tiny cell. The dark circles under his eyes looked liked shadows on his ghost-pale face. The recycled air that flowed through the antiquated ductwork left a metallic taste in his mouth. Despite the short duration of his stay at the city's expense, Ricco found jail to be a learning experience ... and the main thing he'd learned was that he didn't want to be in jail. Already the six by eight foot cell was closing in on him. He couldn't imagine doing two years. Not a chance.

When he didn't 'face up' for the walk to breakfast, a burly guard moved to the open cell door, one hand resting on the padded handle of a collapsible baton. Ricco pressed further into the corner and looked into the guard's questioning eyes.

"I ain't going."

"Come on, Sunshine, it's only breakfast. Lots of tables, no waiting. Move it!"

Ricco shook his head and dropped his hands to the frame of the bed, hollow steel piping bolted to the floor and walls. The guard's eyes crinkled in a smile that didn't reach his mouth. He stepped back to signal the other correctional officers and slipped the baton from the holder on his belt.

"It's time for breakfast. Move. Now!"

Ricco got a better grip on the bed frame. The guard flicked his wrist and the baton snapped out and locked. The 'click-ching' echoed along the walls like a shotgun racking. Without being ordered, all of the other inmates stepped back into their cells and waited for the cell doors to be electronically slammed shut. They didn't have to wait long. Two other guards and a supervisor appeared behind the first.

"What's the problem, Mikey?" the older man asked.

"Mr. Ricco doesn't seem to want to join us for breakfast, Lou," the guard said, pointing his baton in Ricco's direction, "I was telling him that's just rude."

The two younger guards snickered, but the Supervisor just shook his head.

"What's the problem, son?"

Ricco felt like he was about to explode. He looked from one guard to the next, down to the batons they held, and then locked onto the eyes of the supervisor. Ricco shook his head back and forth slowly, and his hands white knuckled as he increased his grip on the pipes.

"Relax son," the older man said quietly. "Just relax and tell me what the problem is."

Ricco stared at him for a full minute, as if trying to make a decision. He could feel sweat bead on his forehead and his breathing become shallower. And then, like a switch being thrown, things changed. Ricco relaxed his grip on the bed frame and stopped trying to push himself through the bricks in the corner. He stopped shaking his head from side to side and, instead, nodded once.

"I want to talk to that cop."

The supervisor and smiled.

"What's his name son?"

"Wright. I want to talk to Wright."

The supervisor tapped the burly guard on the shoulder. "Mikey, why don't you put that thing away and make a quick call. I don't think Mr. Ricco's gonna be a problem any more, are you son?"

Ricco shook his head. Having made the decision he just wanted to get the ball rolling. He'd rather face Oscar than spend another minute in jail.

In the control office another guard slipped out of the room, ostensibly to use the washroom. Just inside the door of the staff lounge he dropped a quarter in the pay phone and dialed a number, smiling at the thought of being one step closer to debt-free.

CHAPTER TWENTY-FIVE

It was the fifth morning after the ETF raid. The last three days had been hectic. Nice weather always brings out the industrious nature in people, especially criminals. After a short run to make up for the karate classes he'd missed, Jack left for the precinct around 7:00.

Traffic was lighter than usual and Jack made it to work in less than fifteen minutes. He parked his car in a spot marked 'Chaplain' and blessed somebody on the way into the building, just for good measure.

Jack was pleased to see the night had been fairly quiet. With luck, he could catch up with Calvin and maybe finish some of his paperwork. His desk looked a lot like the inside of his car, just short of qualifying for disaster relief. He shuffled through a pile of messages left on his desk by the duty sergeant, and couldn't help but chuckle. Every second one was from Darcy. He wasn't sure why he was avoiding her, but a little voice in the back of his head kept repeating the same line. *Detective Sergeant Jack Wright ... you are a coward!*

The real problem, Jack told himself, was there really *wasn't* a case. Calvin wasn't having any luck coming up with anything on Denis Brousseau, other than a dishonorable discharge from a Canadian airborne regiment and a record for theft and assault. It didn't appear that Brousseau ever lived or worked in the United States and there wasn't anything to connect him to Chicago. Even the RCMP was having a hard time locating a mug shot or prints. Without them, a positive identification was impossible.

The weapons and C4 were part of a military shipment hijacked four years ago in New Mexico. The trail on that one had long since gone cold. In fact, the whole case was growing cold. Unless they could crack the hard drive, they were dead in the water, and Calvin's ace in the hole hadn't come up with anything yet.

Jack sat at his desk and debated whether to call Darcy or shoot himself in the foot. Either would be equally painful. Thankfully that decision never had to be made. Everything changed with one phone call.

"Detective Sergeant Wright? This is Harrison over at The Don …

After a quick shower and a cup of instant coffee, Wolfe dressed carefully—double-breasted suit of medium blue, off-white shirt, understated tie, black oxfords, no tie pin, no pocket ruffle. Nothing that would stand out. To beard the lion once in his own den took nerve. Trying it a second time took planning and a degree of arrogance.

He slicked his hair back with too much gel and donned a pair of tortoise-shell frames fitted with slightly tinted clear glass. The glasses hid the intensity of his gray eyes. They also hid two lethal doses of potassium cyanide, one capsule in each ear piece.

He checked his appearance in a small field mirror of polished steel and tested a British accent to make sure it sounded properly self-important. He thumbed the blade of a four-inch plastic knife before concealing it in the end of a custom-made leather belt. The knife was honed to a razor's edge and totally impervious to metal detectors. Satisfied, Wolfe ducked under the hanging steel teeth of the service elevator and pushed the handle towards the floor. The old copper coils of the heavy electric motor squealed as the platform started down.

Jack tried to call Calvin and Darcy, but gave up after getting no answer at either residence. He told Harrison at the Don Jail that he'd be over as soon as possible, but everything seemed to be working against him.

As Jack joined the rest of the commuters trying to fight their way through traffic, his sense of urgency grew. He wasn't sure why, but he knew it was very important that he talk to Ricco as soon as possible. He nosed the unmarked through traffic snarls, and used the cross streets whenever he missed a light. It didn't help his progress, but moving in any direction felt better than standing still. Jack couldn't shake the feeling that time was running out. He pressed the gas a little harder to pull the Chevy closer to the car in front. He growled at the little compact ahead of him to move faster, knowing he was wasting his time.

Wolfe didn't like traffic any more than Jack, but the two men had entirely different ways of handling the problem. Jack drove the Chevy on the edge of his seat. Wolfe reclined in the comfort of a Lincoln Towncar and scanned the paper for any bodies discovered in the past 24 hours. There were none. The delicious silence and comfort of the limousine allowed the mercenary to investigate something he'd never given much thought to before—the stock market. The ramifications of the success of his mission were not lost on Wolfe. *IBM's doing quite well I see … for now.* Wolfe leaned forward and ordered the driver to take a short cut, any short cut, if he wanted to earn his tip. He dropped a hundred-dollar bill on the front passenger seat and smiled to himself as the big car lurched to the left and accelerated hard, cutting off a cab and getting both the finger and a blast from the cabbie's horn in return.

Jack was gridlocked. Even his siren and dash light couldn't help clear the congestion. The delivery van, half a block ahead of the cruiser, was parked squarely on top of a Honda Civic. All the lights and noise in the world weren't going to make it go away. Traffic crawled around the accident while the hands on Jack's watch seemed to fly.

By the time Jack arrived at The Don, a trip that should have taken him fifteen minutes had taken well over an hour. All the way along he could feel the grip of something powerful that didn't want him to reach the jail. He felt it in the pit of his stomach, much like the unseen hand that pulled at his side when he tried to add distance onto his infrequent runs. Jack was sure, though, this was much more than a stitch.

He brushed past two women sharing a cigarette on the steps of the prison, and had to sidestep to avoid a man coming the other way. Wearing a blue business suit and tortoise-shell glasses, the gentleman was obviously in as much of a hurry to leave the prison as Jack was to enter.

"Sorry, old man."

Jack automatically categorized him as a lawyer—the cut of the suit, expensive oxfords, Ivy League accent. *Funny, you don't often see a lawyer without a briefcase.*

Jack took the steps two at a time and stopped just before reaching the heavy brass doors of the old building. As his hand reached out to pull on the ornate door handle he found himself turning for no reason and staring at the back of the gentleman walking quickly to a waiting limousine. The man's gait was purposeful, and his shoulders seemed to stretch the fabric of the expensive suit. Just before he stepped into the back of the Towncar he turned and the two men locked eyes for a brief second. It was enough to make the stitch in Jack's side flare.

Jack pulled on the heavy door and slipped inside quickly. He bypassed the administrative offices and ran the length of the main corridor. After checking his gun at the guard station and clearing the security gates Jack was shown to the supervisor's office. The young guard who escorted him must have thought the world outside of the prison was falling apart. Jack was relieved to see a familiar face when he stepped into the watch commander's office.

"Stan! Christ, am I glad to see you!"

"Well shit for glory, Jack Wright. It's been years. How you doing? What brings you up this—what the hell's going on, Jack? You look like you're about to shit a brick."

"Stan, you have to trust me on this. I can explain in a few minutes, but I have to see one of your inmates right now! Can we bypass the usual bullshit? I wouldn't ask if- I just have a feeling."

"What's his name? I'll take you up myself." Turning to the guard he said, "Steve, get me a set of keys and a security pass. Jack?"

"Ricco. Vincent Ricco. He was brought in three days ago on a weapons charge."

"Okay. Ricco, Vincent …" the Corrections Officer said, reading from a computer printout of the population. He fumbled with the clipboard and seemed flustered for a moment. Jack guessed that things usually moved a little slower around here.

"Block D, Tier 2, Cell 18. Steve, hold down the fort."

And then to Jack, "Let's go."

Jack explained as much as he could as the two men made their way to the west wing, commonly referred to as 'D Block'. When Jack started talking about one of his feelings, he knew Stan wouldn't ask for any clarification. Stan Jacobs had spent 12 years of his career with the police department at 56 Division, the last two as Jack's partner in Homicide. The two cops had spent a lot of time together walking a beat on duty, and a lot of time walking the line off, most of it at Stats. Jack's sixth sense had saved their asses more than once in their short, but tumultuous acquaintance.

Four years ago, after twenty years of service, Stan had pulled the pin and accepted a two-thirds pension. No one, including Jack, was really sure why. Rumors flew at the time of his retirement, but Stan was a closed book. Eventually the whispers died.

In short order Jack found himself standing in front of a cell clearly marked in foot tall letters; **D2-18**. Ricco lay on his side facing the wall. His body was rigid and unmoving. He was curled in the fetal position and Jack could just make out the sheets twisted cruelly around his clenched fists. Ricco didn't move when Stan Jacobs announced their presence by banging on the closed cell door.

"Ricco, you got a visitor. Rise and shine."

Jacobs signaled for the cell to be opened and stood back. Jack approached the cot as the slam-clank of steel on steel reverberated along the walls of D Block. He wasn't sure what to expect, but wasn't all that surprised to see Ricco's face twisted with pain. Stan Jacobs, on the other hand, was as white as a ghost.

CHAPTER TWENTY-SIX

Things hadn't gone exactly as intended. *The best laid plans of mice and men ...* Wolfe thought to himself. *Shit!*

Initially, it couldn't have gone better. The security wand beeped only once when it was passed over Wolfe from head to toe. The female officer and Wolfe exchanged a quick smile and a nod when he dropped a set of keys and a money clip in the tray on the desk to the left. When she passed the wand again the alarm didn't make a sound.

Wolfe was directed through a door that led into an oblong room with a high arched ceiling. Heavy wire mesh covered the short windows that ran the length of the room on one side. Shafts of sunlight slanted in through the windows and traced diamond shadows on the far wall. One long table, obviously old and misused, ran the length of the room with just enough space for a person to pass by at either end. The table was sectioned off like an egg carton with partitions of wood every three feet. More wire mesh in the center separated inmates from visitors. Ricco sat in the far cubicle and looked up like a cornered rabbit when the door banged open. The dark circles appeared to be painted on his pasty white face, his skin tinged green by the color of the walls.

Wolfe nodded at the guard and started down the room. He adjusted his tortoise-shell glasses and casually palmed one of the potassium cyanide capsules with the proficiency of a magician hiding a coin. When he got to Ricco he extended his right hand—the one without the pill. Ricco didn't move.

"Shake my hand," Wolfe said in a menacing voice.

Ricco raised his hand like a man responding to a hypnotic suggestion.

"Officer," Wolfe said, raising his voice and turning to the door with a smile, "do you think I could speak to my client in private?"

The guard didn't move. "Go ahead, Counselor. I can't hear a thing from here."

Wolfe studied the guard for a second and then turned back to Ricco. He raised his voice again, this time speaking over his shoulder.

"Right, well then, would it be too much to ask you to get my client a glass of water? I believe he has the right not to die of dehydration." Wolfe allowed just the right amount of disdain to color his request.

The guard opened the door without taking his eyes off Wolfe. He spoke quietly to someone standing just outside the door and then raised his voice.

"Can't do anything about a *glass* of water but I think I can swing something in a paper cup. Any objections?"

Wolfe didn't answer. The silence that followed was almost visible. The pause gave Wolfe a chance to watch Ricco sweat. When the guard brought the water, Wolfe took it from him and dropped the capsule in without the slightest indication. Just before sitting down he set the water on top of the right partition to give the gel-cap a chance to dissolve. He hiked his chair forward and looked at Ricco through the grill.

"What do you want?" Ricco asked.

Wolfe didn't answer. He watched sweat start to trickle down the side of Ricco's face. Ricco reached up to wipe it away with the sleeve of his prison-orange coveralls. Wolfe stared at the man across from him without saying a word. Ricco shifted in his chair and looked away. He looked at the guard. He looked at the door. He looked at the paper cup. His mouth was dry and he desperately wanted a drink.

"What do you want?!" Ricco hissed again.

Wolfe was pleased to hear a hint of quiet desperation. Wolfe smiled a broad grin, like a shark might just before it attacked. Ricco was shaking visibly now and tears started at the corners of his eyes.

"What the fuck do you want?" He asked a third time, his voice barely audible.

Wolfe stood and, without saying a word, walked the length of the room and out through the door. It was the last time the two men would meet.

Ricco stood when Wolfe did, in self-defense, and then watched unbelieving as his nightmare left the room. He stood like a statue for a full minute, leaning on the table with both hands before he trusted his legs to hold him. He stared at the door as if waiting for Wolfe to come back and finish whatever business had brought him there in the first place. Part of him wished he would.

His mouth felt like it was full of sawdust. He reached out for the cup, his hand shaking badly as he brought it to his lips. The tears in his eyes were half terror, half anger. He didn't feel much like a man at that point. He felt scared, and alone, and weak. The male ego is a terrible thing when it's crushed. He threw the cup in the direction of the door, not knowing that he'd just saved his own life, at least for now.

"Fucking bastard! You fucking god damned fucking bastard!" Ricco's words came out in a high-pitched squeak.

A faint odor of bitter almonds hung in the air after Ricco and the guard left the room. The smell of cyanide—the smell of Death being cheated.

CHAPTER TWENTY-SEVEN

When Jack rolled him over he could already tell from the shallow rise and fall of the chest that Ricco was still alive. The inmate's hands refused to unclench from the sheets and his body remained tightly coiled in the fetal position. His eyes were red from crying and his face was twisted in the pain of a man who was at the end of a very short rope. He untangled one hand from the bedclothes long enough to reach out to Jack. His voice was pleading, on the edge of hysteria.

"You gotta keep him away from me. I want your word. Keep him the fuck away from me ... pleeease."

Jack just nodded, and Ricco turned his face into the covers with a groan and began crying again. Ricco's hand dropped back to the bed and bunched the covers up over his head.

Four hours later the interview was over. Jack's hand ached from writing the free-flowing narrative down verbatim, but it was the only way to do a proper statement analysis. Jack had gone over the body of it several times, adjusting the questions, clarifying the discrepancies, and trying to catch Ricco in a lie. It took a tremendous amount of patience to work with someone like Ricco. Every 'uhm', 'ah', and 'oh ya' had significance and had to be included. In the end, he'd held back a few things, rationalized a few others and softened his own culpability, but as far as Jack could tell Ricco hadn't lied ... and stuck to his original story.

Later in the same office, having left Ricco with a force artist to work up a composite sketch of Wolfe, Jack and Stan Jacobs sat across from each other in quiet contemplation. Jack scanned the statement for the tenth time while Stan stared at a few framed photographs on the far wall.

"So what do you think?"

"I think nothing much is getting any clearer."

"Hmmph. I know what you mean." And then after a silence. "But is he telling the truth?"

"As best as he knows it, Stan, for whatever that's worth. He doesn't seem to have many answers." Both men became lost in their own thoughts as another silence filled the room. Jack broke it a few minutes later with a change of subject.

"What about this part about dirty guards, one at 56 Division and somebody here, Stan? Do you think it's possible?"

Stan Jacobs looked at Jack, sighed audibly, and looked back at the pictures on the wall.

"I was afraid you were going to ask me that, Jack, and the truth is I just don't know. I want to say no, but you know what it's like. These kids come in here with car payments and expensive girl friends, somebody offers them a little extra cash just for a few favors … the temptation's pretty strong when you're young and stupid. I just don't know Jack."

"But you've heard rumors?" Jack guessed correctly.

"Yeah, I've heard rumors, but then you know what that's like, too. Around here you can't take a shit without starting a new rumor."

"Anything specific?"

"The usual—contraband being brought in, special treatment, special assignments—that sort of thing."

"Anyone in particular?"

Stan looked old all of a sudden and Jack felt a pang of sympathy, his first of the day.

"There's a name that keeps coming up regularly, if that's what you mean, but I'd like to handle it myself if that's okay with you. The kid involved is pretty decent on the whole and I'm kind of responsible for getting him hired. He's the son of one of my wife's friends. Damn it, I knew I never should have gotten involved with that woman."

Something in the way Stan spoke, in the way he sat, made Jack think there was more to the story. Jack guessed that maybe the woman wasn't just a friend of Stan's wife.

"Sure Stan. Handle it however you see fit, but keep the kid away from Ricco. Like I said, I don't know if he has anything else to offer, but as a guest in your hotel I'd hate to see him check out without paying his bill."

"No problem, and … thanks Jack. I appreciate it. If I hear anything …"

The two men shook hands across the desk like the old friends they were.

"Great to see you, Jack."

"You too, Stan. What say we get together for a beer when this thing's over?"

"Sounds great. You ever get to Stats anymore?"

Jack smiled and put his hand on Stan's shoulder as they walked the corridor to the front door. "I make it in every once in a while, Stan, but I've got a two drink limit and I stay away from the wings."

Stan laughed, "You must be getting older, Detective."

"Nope," Jack said, pushing on the heavy brass doors, "just smarter."

Wolfe received a second call from The Don Jail about an hour after Jack left. It wasn't news he'd been expecting.

"Listen, there was a cop—"

"What about Ricco?"

There was a hesitation on the other end of the line. "That's what I'm trying to tell you. Ricco spent the last few hours talking to a cop. A detective named Wright. Jack Wright. He—"

Wolfe interrupted. "What do you know about him?"

"Wright? He's from the Five-Six. He works Robbery, and he's smart. You don't want to fuck with him."

"And what did Mr. Ricco have to say?"

"Enough. He was talking about a jewelry heist he was going to be part of … everything except the where and when."

"Anything else?"

"Yeah. That's why I called. Ricco just finished up with one of the sketch artists from the department. They've got a composite of you. I don't know how good it is. I couldn't get close enough to see it, but I thought you'd want to know."

"I'll need to see a copy of that."

"Well, I …"

"I'm sure you could get one if you tried."

"How am I—"

"Ask Wright. Tell him you need one in case I make another visit to see Ricco."

The guard thought for a second. "Yeah. Okay. That would work, but …"

Wolfe waited for the inevitable. Greed is one of the few things in life he could count on.

CHAPTER TWENTY-EIGHT

Darcy was furious. Who in the hell did he think he was? She sat fuming in her apartment and listened to the silence. She rested her head on her elbow and looked sideways at the telephone. *Stupid phone!*

In between visits to the force psychiatrist, she'd spent the last three days cleaning the apartment and denigrating Jack Wright. During the days she organized her closets, sorted her clothes, and cleaned her service pistol and her off duty revolver. During the nights she dreamed about Tinker.

She could still smell the cleaning solvent and gun oil on her hands. The smell reminded her of the hours spent on the range shooting at pieces of paper. She set the revolver aside and turned the pistol over in her hand examining it from different angles. When she slid in a magazine and thumbed the slide lock, the gun jumped. The pistol was ready to fire. She turned the gun again and sighted along the top of the action. With the lights in the apartment turned off the tritium sights glowed green. For a split second she was back on the fire escape. She aimed at a spot on the wall near the door to the kitchen.

Did the sights glow? I can't remember.

Darcy swallowed involuntarily.

I remember killing him. That wasn't a drill. That wasn't a paper target. What did he see just before …

She stood in the hall in front of the mirror above the antique wash stand and pointed the pistol at her reflection and tried to look down the barrel. When that didn't seem real she reversed the pistol in her hands

112

and stared down the gaping aperture without thinking. When she realized that the gun in her hands was loaded she began to shake and quickly pointed it away. *Well that was the stupidest fucking thing you've done in a long time!* Killing someone, despite what they show on TV, does strange things to your mind.

After securing her guns in a steel lock box, Darcy picked up the phone and dialed Jack's number. She listened to a busy signal repeat over and over in her ear.

"Stupid phone."

CHAPTER TWENTY-NINE

"He caved?" Jack could hear the excitement in Calvin's voice through the phone.

"He's scared shitless of this guy Oscar."

"The guy you saw on the steps?" Calvin suggested.

"I don't think so. That was a guy named Wolfe, the number two man. From what Ricco says, Tinker would get a call from Oscar whenever it was time for the next phase. He'd be given an access code, punch it into the computer and, bingo, a new file of information would open up. Apparently Oscar is taking this thing one step at a time. He's only dishing out information on a need to know basis."

"Okay, but hang on. If this whole thing is being run through the phone, why couldn't Oscar just e-mail the next phase?"

"Too dangerous," Jack said, "E-mail can be intercepted or misdirected. We know the security on the computer is exceptional. By loading the computer with everything, all Oscar had to do was call in new security codes to move on to the next phase of the plan. Much safer."

"So the whole thing's in the hard drive?"

"I think so," Jack said.

"Which means right now we're holding all the cards."

"We just can't read them. How's your friend making out on that end of things? Is he as good as you say?"

Calvin hesitated. "He's giving it the old college try, Jack, but so far … nada."

"College— Don't tell me this guy's a college kid, Cal. We need somebody who knows what he's doing. When you mentioned homework I thought—"

"Don't worry. He's not in college," Calvin interrupted. "So where does this guy Wolfe fit in?"

Jack knew Calvin was changing the subject, but let him.

"Ricco says he's hired muscle, but I don't know … he looked like a professor of economics."

"You know the old saying, 'Never judge a book by its cover'."

"Tell me about it," Jack said. "I get beat up regularly by a little bit of a girl with big brown eyes and a sweet smile."

"Listen, what's your time like?" Jack continued. "I want to meet your hacker buddy if he's up for it, but there's something I have to do first. Might give us a leg up."

"Give me a shout when you're clear," Calvin said. "I'll make sure he comes out of his cave long enough to shake hands. We can meet at my place if that works for you. Where are you off to?"

"The scene of the crime," Jack said, thinking of a line from every bad cop show he'd ever watched. "Ricco's apartment."

"What's at the apartment?"

"Hopefully the key to our problem. I have to make a stop first, but I should be clear in a couple of hours."

"This stop have anything to do with a cute brunette, about 5'9" with nice eyes and a great ass?"

"You've been talking to Ken behind my back? It was lunch."

Calvin just laughed.

"You and Kotwa need to get a life."

"Hey, I'm just going by what I hear on the street."

Jack ignored him. "I'll call you later."

"Later."

Jack hung up the phone and waited for a few seconds until he was sure the connection was broken. His next call wouldn't be so easy.

The phone rang just as Darcy slipped beneath the bubbles that were threatening to overflow the tub. *Perfect.* Cursing softly and dripping everywhere, she stepped gingerly into the living room. A trail of bubbles tracked down her legs. Water puddled on the hardwood floor at her feet.

"Hello?"

"Darcy, it's Jack Wrig—"

"Detective Sergeant Wright, how nice of you to call. And with such perfect timing."

"I'm sorry. Did I interrupt something?"

She thought about telling him she was naked and wet, but given their last conversation, she figured that would send him running for the hills again.

"Never mind. Where the hell have you been, and why haven't you returned any of my calls? I was starting to look for your obituary in the paper."

"Worried about it, or planning for it?" Jack asked.

"Planning for it. Why haven't you called?"

"Listen Darcy, you have every right to be angry and I owe you a huge apology but …"

Jack explained the past few days. He didn't mention the other night and Darcy figured he was exaggerating here and there to fill in a few blanks, but his apology was good enough to keep his name out of the papers, at least for now.

"So I take it your dialing finger has healed up nicely and you're just now able to use it?"

"Darcy, I—"

"Sorry. Still a little pissed." She changed gears quickly. "What about Denis Brousseau? Was that just a crank call?"

"I don't know, but I don't think so. Calvin spent the last couple of days tracking him down. Minor sheet, from about twenty years ago—assault, theft, violence. Trouble is, he disappeared shortly after being kicked out of the military. There's nothing connecting him to Chicago, and nothing to put him in Toronto last Monday."

"What about a photo?"

"The RCMP are faxing one down as soon as they can locate it, same thing with the military. Apparently both files are missing pictures."

Darcy hesitated for a second, unsure of what she was asking. "Kind of a strange coincidence, don't you think?"

"Yeah, I do."

"So where do we go from here? Have you turned up anything or are we dead in the water?"

"We were … until this morning."

"What happened this morning?" Darcy asked, her curiosity peaked.

"I got a call from The Don. It seems Ricco doesn't like prison."

Darcy's heart picked up a beat or two. "And?"

"And, I think maybe you and I should get together for this one. Are you up for a little drive? I've got to check on something you might find interesting. I can pick you up in, say, 30 minutes?"

Darcy looked at the puddle by her feet and caught a glimpse of herself in the mirror. She shrugged at her reflection and turned back to the phone.

"Make it 45. I want to look good for our second date."

Darcy hung up before Jack could.

It was almost an hour later when Jack buzzed for Darcy.

"Hang on. Down in a sec." Her voice crackled through the speaker.

Jack stood in the foyer and read some of the decotype nameplates on the intercom system. He ran his hand down the names until he got to 'Caldwell/Belair'. *Roommate? Boyfriend?*

Jack was surprised to find himself a little disappointed at the prospect that Darcy may have someone special in her life. *Christ, Jack, you must have ten years on her … at least … and this is business.*

He turned back to the door and found Darcy leaning against the wall watching him with a funny smile on her face. It was as if she could read his thoughts, and Jack felt like a kid caught reading his father's Playboy.

"Sorry to keep you waiting, Detective, I hope you weren't bored."

"Let's go," Jack said gruffly.

Darcy followed Jack out to the Impala and slid into the passenger's side. Jack slipped in behind the wheel.

"This is lovely. Decorate it yourself?"

"Actually, I had somebody come in," Jack replied, tossing some of the debris into the back seat, "I just picked out the colors and she did the rest. Stunning, don't you think?"

"Beautiful," Darcy agreed. "It could be featured in Road and Crap."

Jack laughed out loud.

"Sorry. I don't usually have a passenger in this car. The seatbelt's probably buried under the rubble somewhere. Here, let me."

He had to clear away some papers, about six coffee cups, and an old glove before he finally located the catch. He started the car and pulled away from the curb while Darcy continued to throw things into the back seat. When she got to a black banana and held it up for inspection Jack grinned, having regained some of his composure.

"Be careful with that, it's just about ripe. I've been saving it."

"God," Darcy laughed. "This car looks like it supports its own ecosystem."

Darcy's smile lasted exactly as long as it took Jack to answer her next question.

"So where to, and why all the secrecy?"

"Vaughan Road," Jack replied without thinking. "To the apartment. I've got to check out something and I thought this would give us a chance to get caught up. A lot's happened since we last talked, and I want to go over some of the details in person. I don't trust phones. I know how many wiretaps I've been involved with and I can't help wonder—"

Jack stopped talking when he realized that Darcy had stopped listening. She sat staring out the front windshield of the cruiser. It suddenly hit Jack like a slap in the face.

"God, Darcy, I'm sorry. I didn't—"

"It's okay Jack, really. I just wasn't thinking about *there* as the best place for our second date."

Jack felt like an idiot.

"Darcy, I should have known better. I wasn't thinking about— I've got to check out a few things, but I can do it later on my own. Why don't we—"

"No, Jack, it's all right. Really. It'll be good for me. I'm all right … honest."

Jack spent the next ten minutes watching Darcy out of the corner of his eye. He could tell that she was anything but all right.

CHAPTER THIRTY

When they got to the apartment Darcy stopped and leaned back against the car. Jack watched her blue eyes turn cold as her gaze traveled up the fire escape along the path she'd taken on the night of the shooting. It wasn't hard to imagine she was reliving every step she took, every sound she heard. Her hands tapped quietly against the side of the car as if ticking off the passing seconds. Darcy closed her eyes and Jack wished he'd brought her anywhere but here.

She looked at Jack with a sad smile.

"Don't worry," she said. "I'm all right. And hey, I get to go in through the front door this time. That's got to count for something, right?"

Jack reached out to put a hand on her shoulder, but she brushed past him and headed for the apartment. Jack used a penknife to slit through the small white seals used to secure the door. It took him a second to realize that somebody had re-hung it after the ETF had knocked it off its hinges. He only clued in when he noticed Darcy running her hand along the hinge side of the heavily reinforced sheeting.

"They must have re-hung," Jack said, searching for a light switch. He found one by the bathroom but heard only a loud 'click' when he tried the light.

"I guess they cut the power to the apartment, too," he suggested, and switched on a small Mag-Lite.

"Hmhmm," Darcy agreed.

Neither of them said a word for what seemed like an eternity. Jack was experiencing a good case of the creeps. Jack played his small penlight along the walls, following a path that was clearly marked by bullet holes. He almost jumped out of his skin when Darcy snapped on the 'D' cell Mag-Lite that she kept at the ready in her purse. The beam illuminated much of the small apartment.

"Jesus Christ! Give me some warning before you fire that thing up! What does it use? Car batteries?"

"What? You have flashlight envy?" Jack turned and shone his light towards her face and was relieved to see her smile.

"So what are we looking for?" she asked.

Jack swept his flashlight around the living room and moved to the door of the bedroom. The handle was still stuck securely in the plaster of the wall.

"I had another chat with Ricco this morning. Apparently Tinker was the demolitions expert for a job they were going to pull."

"What kind of a job?"

"Jewels, according to Ricco, but he didn't know where, when, or how much."

"That doesn't make sense. How do you plan a robbery and not know where and when? He's got to be pulling your chain. That's crazy."

"Wait for it, it gets better." Jack moved around the living room looking at the mess left by the lab boys.

"Ricco wasn't planning the robbery," he continued. "He's strictly hired help."

"So who *was* planning it? Tinker?"

"No. A guy named Oscar but—and here's the good part—Ricco's never seen him or spoken to him. Neither did Tinker."

"So how …"

"It's all in the computer." Jack let that sink in before continuing. "Supposedly, there's another guy involved named Wolfe. I don't know if that's a first or a last name, but I think I saw the guy at the Don this morning."

Darcy had a confused look on her face. The apartment, the surreal lighting, and the strange story all made it feel like they were living in a

Grimm's fairy tale. Jack saw the look and realized he wasn't being fair. Darcy deserved a full explanation, not a riddle.

"Okay, listen. Reader's Digest version. We've got to be somewhere by ten."

"Ricco gets hired by this guy Wolfe to help pull a job that's apparently going to net millions." Jack continued. "Ricco's cut is in the neighborhood of two hundred thousand."

Darcy let out a low whistle. "For hired muscle? Nice neighborhood."

"That's what I thought, but the job's no piece of cake. High security, armed guards, time locked vaults, the works. High pay for high risk, right?"

"Okay so far," Darcy nodded.

"Ricco's put into this apartment with Tinker. Ricco says Tinker's a demolitions expert with no zero personality, but heavy on talent."

"That fits with what I saw. This guy handled that Uzi like a pro. He just stood there with bullets flying everywhere and didn't flinch."

"That would fit with the background of Denis Brousseau, too. Ex-military. Ex-Special Forces."

"So what about the computer and this guy Oscar?"

"That's the kicker. No one but Wolfe deals with Oscar, and all of the codes for the computer are delivered one stage at a time. They all know the stakes, but no one gets to see the whole plan so no one can get greedy and jump the gun. No one gets to see the main guy so no one can turn him in."

"Clever," Darcy acknowledged.

"Beyond clever," Jack said. "Even if we break the computer and learn the whole plan all we've got is the computer. Nothing more. If the plan starts to go for the shits, all the head honcho has to do is break communications and leave the rest of these guys high and dry. No instructions, no game plan. No game plan, no job."

"But something goes wrong," Darcy offered.

"Right," Jack agreed. "Ricco is the weak link. He was recruited by Wolfe but obviously the guy didn't do his homework. Ricco took some of the hardware home, maybe thinking to sell it after the job, and you know the rest."

Jack moved into the bedroom and shone his flashlight along the walls. Yellow circles glowed on the walls where the Crime Scene technicians removed slugs and marked the spots. Most of the shots came through the drywall partition separating the kitchen from the bedroom and buried themselves in the far wall.

Jack continued, "I figure Wolfe never knew Ricco moved the hardware, otherwise he would have killed him. He doesn't seem like the forgiving type."

Jack watched Darcy traced her fingers along the bullet holes.

"They were lucky."

"Who?"

"Karski and the rest of my team. Ragins escaped with a few scars and a good story to tell at Stats. Could have been much worse."

"That wasn't luck," Jack said, looking at her pointedly. "That was all you."

Darcy was quiet for a minute, and then said, "You saw this guy Wolfe at The Don Jail, right? Why would he visit his hired muscle in prison?"

"To scare him into keeping his mouth shut."

"So what made Ricco decide to talk?"

"I guess he doesn't like the food or the company. He's scared out of his mind. Wants to cut a deal. A shorter sentence and safer facility for information and sworn testimony."

"Safer facility?"

"He says there's somebody on staff at the jail who's working for Wolfe. He could be right, too, but a friend of mine is handling that end of things."

"So, full circle. What are we looking for here? We have the computer and the lab boys have gone over this place with a fine toothed comb."

"Ricco said he wasn't allowed to touch the computer, but Tinker was. He had to have access to it to plan for the placement and timing of the C4 charges."

"Which means?"

"Which means, I suppose, Oscar isn't as good with explosives as he is with logistics." Jack moved around the room sweeping his small flashlight from floor to ceiling and back again. "It also means Tinker knew how to access the hard drive."

"So …?"

"Ricco said Tinker had to write everything down to remember how to access the computer. He complained about it all the time."

"And you think the code's here somewhere." It wasn't a question.

"It makes sense. There wasn't even a scrap of paper in the apartment aside from those newspapers," Jack shone his Mag-Lite at a short stack in the corner, "and Ident went over those. Nothing unusual, which means the security code, must be written on the walls or the furniture, maybe under the rug somewhere. Why don't you start checking along the edges of the carpet. Watch out for cockroaches."

"You really know how to show a girl a good time, don't you Detective?"

The two worked quickly and quietly. Jack checked along the walls and inspected the door and window frames, while Darcy peeled back the edges of the rug and uncovered about a decade's worth of filth. They were looking for anything that could pass as an access code for the hard drive. Except for a rotting back issue of Hustler hidden under one corner of the carpet, and a few choice selections of graffiti, they weren't having much luck.

"Did Ricco tell you what we were looking for?" Darcy asked, startling Jack.

"No, he didn't know. Just said Tinker bitched about having to use such an elaborate code to open the computer."

"They didn't have time to destroy anything," Darcy said.

"Which means it has to be here somewhere, close enough that it wasn't a pain in the ass to get to," Jack said, carefully peeling back the plastic molding on the edge of the desk with his penknife.

"If we do find the codes and access the hard drive, what makes you think the whole plan will be there? Maybe Oscar uses a modem to send the information just before he phones in the new access codes. Maybe Ricco already knows everything that's in the computer. If that's the case, he still doesn't know where, when, or what and we're just wasting … our … time!" she grunted as she pulled up a piece of carpet that had been glued down over the years by some unknown substance. "God, this place is disgusting."

"I thought about that," Jack admitted, "but I don't think so."

"This place isn't disgusting?"

"No," Jack laughed. "I agree with you there. I was talking about the computer only holding part of the plan. It doesn't make sense."

"How so?" Darcy stopped and shone her 'D' cell in Jack's general direction.

"Three reasons really," Jack said. "First, there's too much protected memory on the hard drive. Why protect it if it's just recipes or a mailing list. Whatever's in there has to be important. Second, Oscar's been pretty careful. He's been almost paranoid about security and it's paid off. I don't think he'd take a chance on using a modem to send the instructions. Modems operate on regular phone lines that can be traced."

"And third?'

"No phone jack in the bedroom. It's one of the reasons I wanted to come over here and see for myself. I had to check that out."

"What about wireless?"

"If it was me, I wouldn't trust anything but a secure hard line. I'm guessing Oscar's just as paranoid. What are you smiling about?""

"Sorry?"

"You've got a silly grin on your face. What's so funny?"

"Just thinking you know more about technology than you think. Not bad for a guy who carries a shoe phone. So what now?"

"Keep looking. It's got to be here somewhere. Ricco said Tinker never carried anything in with him. He just came in, shut the door and—"

"The door!" Darcy said.

"It's got to be. We've checked everywhere else. Let me see your light."

Jack pulled on the bedroom door with the hand not holding the big flashlight, but it didn't budge. The doorknob was jammed through the plaster and tangled with the wooden lath underneath. He used the flashlight to probe the darkness behind the door but couldn't make anything out.

"Here, take this back," he said, handing Darcy back her Mag-Lite.

"You want a hand?" she asked. "A little muscle?"

Jack gave her a sour look and braced one foot against the wall while he grabbed a hold of the door with both hands. He gave a tremendous yank and ended up flat on his butt up against the far wall. The door wasn't all that stuck. The light Darcy was holding bounced around the room casting wild shadows, her laughter echoing around the room.

"My hero," she managed to choke out, before doubling over in a fit of laughter.

"Are you through?" he asked, as he grabbed the flashlight out of her trembling hands and muttered under his breath "Smart ass!" A few seconds later he joined in the laughter.

When the moment had passed and his professionalism was restored, bruised but not beaten, Jack started to examine the back of the door and the wall.

He could hear Darcy leafing through the papers. He spoke over his shoulder without turning around.

"If you're looking at the Sunshine Boy, Caldwell, I could use a little help."

"Crossword," Darcy said.

"A girl after my own heart."

Jack continued to search behind the door for any writing.

"Jack?"

"It's hard to see right to the back where the grain—"

"Jack?"

"Just a second Darcy, I want to check—"

"Jack!"

"What?!"

"What's a six letter word for buoy or sea anchor?"

"Excuse me?" It was hard not to be a little annoyed.

"A six letter word for buoy or sea anchor."

"Darcy, we haven't got time for—"

"Just answer the question, Jack. A six letter—"

"Okay, okay." Jack thought for a second before answering. "Drogue."

"Really?"

Jack nodded.

"Then I take it 'B4M6HT' is the wrong answer."

"What are you talking about?" Jack asked, intrigued by her smile in the glow of the flashlight.

"And I take it seven down, a four letter word for potato, isn't 'P14Z'?" Jack started to clue in. "Let me see that."

"It's a crossword, Jack. The whole thing's filled in, but as far as I can see there isn't a right answer in the bunch."

Jack took the paper from her hands and cradled the big Mag-Lite under his chin. In a few seconds he was beaming from ear to ear, certain of what she'd found.

"This is it. Darcy you're beautiful!" He took a step towards her without thinking, but stopped when he saw the look on her face.

"Don't even think about it, Mister," she said, pushing a hand into his chest. He could feel the warmth of her fingertips on the bare skin of his open collar.

"Not on a second date," She continued, "And never in a place like this."

"I wasn't going to— I mean—" He could feel his ears burning and thanked the good Lord it was dark.

"Didn't you say we had to be somewhere before ten?" She asked, her hand still resting on his chest. She pushed him away for emphasis. "It's already nine thirty."

"Yes," Jack said, clearing his throat, relieved and a little confused. "Just caught up in the moment."

Too young, too complicated, and way too beautiful. Give your head a shake, Jack! So he did just that.

"C'mon," he said gruffly. "Time to find some answers."

"The what, where and when?" Darcy asked.

"I'm more interested in the *who*," Jack said. "I think it's time we find out a little bit more about Oscar."

CHAPTER THIRTY-ONE

Life's funny, Katherine thought. *An off the cuff remark, and everything changes. A whole new chance at life.*

It took time to work out the details, but the basic DNA of *The Plan* was set by the time Bernie Schultz's words stopped reverberating in Katherine's brain.. *Have someone steal it. Someone totally unconnected. Intentional delay. The deadline becomes null and void. Pavel and I have time to finish it in secret, and I still own 49 percent of a company that will change the world.*

Katherine spent the first trimester of The Plan's gestation period doing research. She created a world of code names, passwords, blue prints. She told herself she wasn't serious, but her game quickly became an obsession. As Sumner's deadline loomed closer and closer, her obsession became desperation and the game became a reality.

Katherine was smart enough to know that if *The Plan* was to succeed, she was going to have to lay some groundwork. The second trimester was all about preparation – nesting. Sumner and The Board would have to be finessed. Others would have to be manipulated, a skill she learned from 'Daddy' whether she wanted to or not. She needed an ally in the company, but one who didn't know he was actually playing the role of a pawn. That was where Michael came in.

Michael Thorogood, a researcher and aspiring star at ComTech, possessed certain attributes that made him useful. He was driven, conniving in his own right and a kiss ass of the highest order. He loved to gossip about people at the company, and was obviously using his newfound friendship with her—the boss—as a fast track to promotion. His ambition made him greedy and his greed made him predictable. He was also a direct pipeline to Sumner.

For months Katherine and Michael had been meeting for drinks once or twice a week after work, something she'd initiated at the office Christmas party. St. Patrick's Day seemed like an appropriate occasion to up the stakes. Katherine made sure to have enough Guinness to fit in, but not so much as to lose track of her purpose. At first she kept it light. Talking about potential sex partners usually worked to keep Michael distracted.

"How about him?" Katherine asked, indicating a young bartender wearing a sparkly green bowler and a shamrock tie.

"For you or me?"

"For you," Katherine said. "He's young enough to be my son."

"Nothing wrong with that," Michael responded. "In fact it's very much in vogue."

Katherine looked at him perplexed.

"Cougars," he said. "You're all the rage."

"So now I'm a cougar?" Katherine asked.

"Definitely. And a damned hot one."

Katherine was having a hard time concentrating on the conversation, partly because of the beer and partly because of her agenda. In the end, her distraction worked in her favor. Michael gave her the opening she needed to get serious.

"You okay? You're not your usual self. Trouble in the Ivory Tower?"

Katherine kept to her script. It started with a shrug and a well-practiced look of desperation.

"What's up?" Michael leaned. "Seriously, are you okay?"

"Yeah. It's just ... Sumner." Katherine finally exhaled.

Michael was smart enough to know when to keep quiet, but his eyes shone a little too brightly. With the bait taken, Katherine knew it was time to set the hook, but she couldn't do it with a jerk. It had to be subtle.

"I have a few issues to work out. Nothing to screw up St. Patrick's Day over! What do the Irish say? Slainte!"

"Slainte. What issues?"

Katherine smiled behind her Guinness and, stalling, looked around for another likely partner for Michael.

"What about him?"

Michael barely glanced in the direction Katherine was looking.

"Too short. What issues?" He said again.

Katherine sighed. It sounded fake to her, but Michael didn't seem to notice.

"Politics and bullshit," she said, slurring her words intentionally. "Nothing to worry about. You're not losing your job … yet."

"I'm all ears," Michael said. "Impress me with a view from the top."

"When I get there I'll let you know."

"What are you talking about? You're the boss. Can't get much more 'top' than that. You own the company."

"C'mon Michael. I *owned* the company. You know that. I'm sure everyone in the world knows that by now. The Board calls the shots and Sumner's the Board, or he might as well be."

The script called for her to let a little resentment show now and then. Not surprisingly, she found it very easy to do.

Maybe it was the beer, or maybe it was her uncanny ability to play the part of a bitter woman, but Katherine could see a battle raging behind Michael's eyes. She waited to see which path he would take. Friendship or advancement? She didn't have to wait long. In the end, as so often happens, greed overcame social conscience.

"You and our beloved CEO having a difference of opinion?"

"You might say that?"

"About?"

Katherine leveled an icy glare at Michael, hoping to convey all the hatred she truly felt for the man about to steal her company. "Everything. Sumner's a fucking parasite."

She took another long pull at her Guinness while Michael stared at her, his mouth slightly agape.

"Don't look so shocked. Sumner's piggybacking on the talents and hard work of a lot of gifted people, you and me included,' she said.

"So why'd you sell out to him in the first place?" Michael asked, obviously deciding to hell with social conventions and propriety.

Katherine let the question hang in between them. Finally, when the silence became almost unbearable, she continued on with her script.

"Arrogance," she said, allowing a little truth to color her words with sadness. "At least that's what my lawyer says."

"Is he right?" Michael asked.

"Hell, no!" Katherine said loudly, slapping her hand on the table, playing her part to perfection. No one in the bar seemed to notice. St. Patrick's Day. Go figure.

"I'm not arrogant. Do you think I'm arrogant?"

"No, of course not," Michael said quickly. "But –"

"I'm confident … and with good reason. I needed Sumner's money to get where we need to be, where we deserve to be. Right here. Right fucking here!" She said, slamming the table again.

Katherine waited to see if Michael would ask, but she could tell from the look on his face he was a bit unnerved.

"Listen, Michael, I'll let you in on a little secret," she said, swirling the last of the Guinness in her glass. "Sumner has no real idea what we do at the company, and he has no fucking idea about what I'm about to accomplish."

She swallowed the last of her beer. Michael swallowed the bait.

"To be honest Katherine, neither do I. From what I understand, nobody does. What are you working on?"

Katherine shrugged, giving him an *I can't tell* kind of smile.

"Seriously Katherine, nobody has a clue what's going on in your world, but you should hear the rumors."

"Do tell," Katherine said.

"With all the security around your lab, people keep expecting Frankenstein or Iron Man to come crashing through the wall."

"Here's to Iron Man," Katherine said with a giggle, raising her glass in a toast. "Much hotter than Frankenstein." She clinked Michael's glass.

"Seriously Katherine, you know what people are like. You don't let them in on a secret, they come up with their own wild conspiracy theories. You've given them a mystery without any clues."

"Bob Seger. Great song."

Michael didn't laugh.

"You've got to admit, Katherine, you've been pretty hush-hush about what you're working on."

Katherine kept to the script. She had to let him draw the information out of her one beer at a time.

"Had to be," Katherine said, sitting up straighter as if struggling to become serious. "Secrets have a way of slipping out in this business. Industrial espionage, corporate raiding, all that jazz. Next thing you know the competition has what you've just developed. Not this time. This one's too big."

Katherine signaled the waitress for another round. On the surface her words were becoming slurred, but underneath she remained focused and intense. Her green eyes were still bright, but she doubted Michael would notice. He hadn't even noticed he was drinking three beers to her one.

Michael sat across the deuce from her looking expectant but not saying a word.

"ComTech is mine, Michael, or at least it should be," she continued. "I built it up from nothing. It wouldn't exist if it wasn't for me."

"No question," Michael said..

"I wrote programs that earned this company more money in the first year than anyone thought possible, especially my short-sighted bankers. I designed the hardware that's kept us in the game."

"So what's the problem? What do Sumner and his friends have to complain about?"

"They want more," she said simply.

"They want to buy you out?"

"More like force me out."

Fifteen minutes later, Katherine had given Michael probably more details than he wanted to know about the sale of the company, the contract, and the deadline she'd been fighting against for almost five years. Most of the information had been delivered in a seemingly drunken tirade, while some of it she gave up between sobs and tears. All she needed to do now was pass on a few bits and pieces of information and one gigantic secret. Then she could drop the curtain on her one-woman play. For the final act, however, she needed audience participation. Michael Thorogood was more than willing to be a part of the show.

"So what you've been working on, what you promised Sumner …," Michael hesitated. "What is it? I mean, is it really that big?"

Katherine looked around the bar to make sure no one listening.. Michael was on the edge of his seat, literally, and almost salivating. She decided to make it quick before his head exploded in one giant ball of ambition.

"Bigger," she slurred. "Much bigger."

"I take it you're not talking about new tax software or a better mouse," Michael said.

Katherine smiled like the cat who swallowed the canary.

"What have we dreamed about for years, Michael, people in our business, I mean? What's the ultimate goal?"

The question mark on Michael's face was his only reply.

"Come one, Michael. It's rhetorical. What's *our* Holy Grail?'" Her voice was rising in tone and volume.

"Okay, okay," Michael said, holding up his hands. "I'm sorry. It's just that … I don't know what we're talking about here."

"I'm talking about history, Michael. I'm talking about carving out a huge piece of fucking history and laying it down at Sumner's feet. I'm talking about handing over something to that piece of shit that he couldn't even begin to understand!"

"I don't—"

"Artificial intelligence!" Katherine slammed her hand down on the table for a third and final time. Her voice was loud enough now to reach the back of the crowded bar. A few of the other patrons turned to look in her direction, but most continued on with their own inebriated conversations.

"Artificial intelligence," she said, her words now barely more than a whisper.

CHAPTER THIRTY-TWO

"Artificial intelligence," she said again, but her words were starting to take on the air of a little girl losing her doll. "I've done what they said couldn't be done, and now they're going to take it away from me."

"Hang on a second. Back the truck up. When you say artificial intelligence, you mean …"

"I mean just that. Artificial intelligence. A.I. A computer that can do what no other computer can do. Independent thought. Cognitive reasoning. Everything we've ever dreamed of, this computer can do."

"You mean it expands on what you've programmed in?" Michael asked uncertainly.

"Skeptical, Michael?" She challenged. "I didn't take you for a cynic. I'm saying this thing thinks. It's self-aware. It asks questions. For Christ's sake, Michael, the damned thing talks to me!"

"It what?! Katherine, you don't mean—"

"I do. It talks to me, Michael, like we're in our own private chat room."

Michael was stunned into silence. It was obvious he was having a hard time appreciating the magnitude of what Katherine was telling him.

"A little too George Lucas for you?"

"I didn't say that, but—"

"But that's what you're thinking."

"Katherine listen … it's just … I mean, come on! Artificial Intelligence is a pipe dream. It's a myth. It's like Big Foot or the Loch Ness Monster. I mean, anything's possible but no one expects to strap a Yeti to the hood of his truck. It can't be done, not with the computers we have today."

"Bingo." Katherine sat back with a knowing look on her beautiful face. She was finding it hard to stick to the script. A smile danced behind her eyes.

"It isn't a dream, Michael—it's reality. It's taken me years to write the program and a hell of a long time for Pavel to develop the hardware, but we've done it. We've developed a computer that can actually think for itself."

"Christ, I don't know if you're crazy or I am. Start from the beginning. Tell me exactly what you're talking about, and keep it simple. I get lost easily."

"Simple. Okay, I can do simple. But pay close attention because I may have to use big words."

Michael didn't offer a comeback.

"Think of the fastest CPU in existence. Do you know what it is? The AMD Bulldozer. Just under 8.5 Gigahertz. Fast by any standard, right?"

Michael nodded.

"But not fast enough. Not nearly fast enough to handle the programs I've written. You said it yourself. There's no way we can manage A.I. with the computers out there today. Imagine the speed it would take! You'd need a computer that— I mean, the algorithms are massive. I've done the math. The CPU would have to operate at fifteen to twenty thousand times faster than the best we have, and conventional materials don't allow for that kind of speed. We'd need some kind of a super-conductive relay."

"But with the amount of research being conducted eventually somebody—"

"Not eventually, Michael, and not somebody. I'm talking about right now."

Katherine could see Michael was reeling from the information she was giving him, but she couldn't tell if he was convinced. His next words answered that question.

"Seriously Katherine, come on! I'm not doubting your ability to write the program. I know you're brilliant, but ..."

Let the ass kissing begin.

"But the processor itself? Twenty thousand times faster? How in the hell is that even possible? You're talking science fiction."

"I've already given you the answer," she said.

"Sorry. I can't imagine how I missed it," Michael said. "Try me again?"

She ignored his sarcasm. "Super conductive relays."

"Super conductive …" Michael looked perplexed. "Are you talking about particle acceleration?"

Katherine shook her head. "That wouldn't work. Hypothetically possible, but the facilities needed to develop it would be astronomical. Not to mention the power needed to run it would melt standard silicon-based CPUs."

Katherine hesitated for another moment, but this time it had nothing to do with her script or pretending to be drunk. She was actually telling Michael exactly what she and Pavel had been working on and she was having a hard time finding the right words.

In truth, she was having a hard time finding any words at all. She'd spent so long intentionally *not* talking about the project that she was finding it difficult to articulate even the basics. She wanted to explain the project carefully without giving away too much, but she needed Michael to know enough to pass it on to the right people at the right time.

"Pavel—"

"Your friend—the physicist or whatever—from Russia?"

"He holds three or four degrees, two of them PhDs. Applied Physics and Chemistry. He specializes in silicon hydrogenic amalgamation."

"I thought you were going to stick to small words."

"I really don't understand it myself, but to Pavel it's like playing with a high tech Mechano set. He's brilliant. To him it's child's play."

The look on Michael's face told her he was through interrupting.

"He's developed a synthetic material, a combination of silicon and graphene," she continued. "He didn't add a new element to the periodic table but it's as close as anyone's come since Madame Curie discovered Radium. It allows electronic pulses to flow more freely—faster—than anything in use today. We've talked about it for years, a universal conductor that would allow for smart appliances, virtual telephones, that type of thing."

"But that's not what we're talking about now, right?" Michael asked.

Katherine shook her head, "We've gone way beyond that. We're talking about a machine that can actually think and reason and plan and … dream!

"So what exactly *did* he invent?"

"Think of it like the human brain," Katherine said, sounding like one of her old MIT professors. "Every process the human brain performs, from abstract thought to mathematical calculations, has one thing in common."

Michael stared at her blankly.

"Electrical impulses," she said. "The human brain is a series of incredibly fast circuits. Electrical impulses shoot along nerves, millions of neurons fire at once, and synaptic gaps open and close to produce the desired results. And isn't that exactly what a computer does? The difference is that in a computer the synaptic gaps are circuits carved into silicon chips. Binary code—zip, zip—open, close."

"I think my circuits are over-loaded."

Katherine ignored him. "The main difference between a computer and a human brain is that the human brain isn't dry. The electrical impulses flow along the body fluids that coat the surface of the various circuits of the brain, not through the solid matter that makes up the brain itself."

Michael nodded, beginning to understand.

"If the electrical impulses of the brain had to be conducted along solid circuits without the normal body fluids to act as a conductor, the resistance would slow down the process to a fraction of the speed. It would be like running an engine without any oil. The engine would run, but slower, with less efficiency, and for a shorter period of time than if it was properly lubricated."

"So what … we need to start oiling our CPUs?" Michael offered.

"No, that's not what I'm saying." Katherine was too excited to get angry. "But think about the problem and the possible solutions. Every substance has a certain amount of resistance to electricity. That's one of the given properties of any element, a characteristic that can't be changed. Rubber is totally resistant to electrical impulse. It's a bad conductor. Wood is another poor conductor depending on the amount of moisture it contains. That's why if you need to move a live wire you'd probably be safe with a piece of dry wood."

"But if the wood is wet ..." He offered.

"Exactly!" Katherine almost shouted. "If the wood is wet, or you coat it with a lubricating substance that's highly conductive ..."

"Zap!"

"In the blink of an eye," Katherine finished the thought.

Michael still sounded skeptical.

"And Pavel found a way to lubricate the silicon chips in a CPU?"

"Better, Michael, much better. Pavel developed a material ... the best way to describe it is ... it's part silicon, part gel. It can be lasered like silicon to form a chip, but the surface of the silicon retains moisture that allows the electrical impulses to travel at an unbelievable rate ... and it can be synthesized at a fraction of the cost of silicon."

"And it works? You've tested it?"

"In Pavel's lab in Russia. He's too paranoid to send one over here for me to play with."

Michael cocked his head to the side.

"He has ... issues," she said, in answer to his unasked question. "Nothing I can't handle."

"So, what kind of speed are we talking about?"

Katherine let the question hang in the air for a minute. She couldn't resist the chance to play showman. Finally she gave him an answer.

"After burning up a few dozen prototypes, Pavel finally came up with a working model. The first test of the new CPU put it at just over twelve thousand times faster than any CPU on the market. He's doubled the speed since then."

"Jesus Christ!" Michael said, a look of wonder on his face.

"I know," Katherine said, echoing the sentiment.

"Jesus Christ!" Michael said again. "You'll put Intel right out of business ... along with everyone else. This is fucking huge."

Katherine was afraid she might have to expand on the potential, but Michael was way ahead of her.

"Bigger than huge, Michael. It's fucking massive. Combined with my A.I. programs, nothing is beyond the capabilities of this computer."

"And it's real, Katherine?" Michael asked, obviously astounded. "This isn't just some kind of bad St. Patty's Day practical joke?"

"It's real, Michael, and we're only just scratching the surface."

"And you and Pavel worked on it? You're the only two people in the world who know about it?"

"And now you."

"And now me." Michael's voice seemed to fade.

"You're the first person I've told about this and I swear to God if you tell anyone ..."

"Whoa, slow down, I won't tell anyone. I promise."

Katherine, however, could see the wheels in Michael's brain start to turn faster. She'd just dropped a bombshell on him. A nuclear bombshell. She'd offered him the first glimpse of a revolution in the world of computer technology. Not an innovation or an improvement but a true revolution of epic proportions. She was talking about a computer processing unit capable of operating at twenty-four thousand times the speed of the fastest CPU on the market, and programs that would take artificial intelligence out of the pages of science fiction and put them into the real world. Someone with real insight would be thinking about what an invention of this magnitude would mean to the world. Katherine was sure, however, that Michael was thinking about what it could mean to him.

She was counting on it.

CHAPTER THIRTY-THREE

"The Holy Grail," Michael said.

"The Holy Grail," Katherine agreed.

"You're going to put the competition out of business. Bill Gates will be slinging hash at a Denny's."

"I doubt that," Katherine said, staring into an empty Guinness glass. "Besides, I'd rather they stay in business and license the technology from us at a ridiculous price. Make the competition our customers. Makes the profit margins bigger and saves us the hassle of setting up a whole new distribution network."

"Sounds good. So what's the problem? Why the long face? This is freaking amazing!"

"Sumner," Katherine said simply.

"Sumner? I don't understand. He—"

"Politics and bullshit," Katherine cut him off. "I've been promising him I could deliver this ever since he and his cronies put up the money to fund the research. He never believed I could do it. He still doesn't."

"So what? You *have* done it. Sumner should be ecstatic. You get to keep your share of the company and everybody's happy. You'll be worth millions. What am I saying? Billions. Where's the problem?"

"Sumner controls the company, which means he controls what we produce," she said, genuine anger mixing well with the beer to solidify her performance. "He's a moneyman with no vision. If I prove this thing works, he'll only be interested in the bottom line. He'll sell out to the highest bidder in a heartbeat. He won't stop to think about what happens next."

Michael's next words made Katherine realize she was right about him from the start. He was a kindred spirit to Sumner, not to her.

"So? I still don't see the problem. You'll be rich beyond your wildest dreams."

"Don't you see, Michael? The scientific applications for this kind of technology are incredible and a little scary, but the military applications are fucking terrifying. Compared to this computer the Star Wars project would seem like a child's toy. Advanced weaponry using the new CPUs and A.I. would be unstoppable. A superpower could become omnipotent. A dictator— A dictator crazy enough to use those weapons would mean Armageddon. I don't want to be responsible for the apocalypse, for Christ sake, but Sumner wouldn't give it a second thought."

Neither of them spoke for a long time, but with the St. Patrick's Day celebrations getting louder and the beer getting lower, Michael finally broke their silence.

"I don't see what choice you have, Katherine. If you don't deliver, you lose the company. If you try to introduce the CPU as your own in the future, he'll tie you up in court for years."

"Don't you think I know that, Michael? Christ! I've been over it a million times. The only solution I can think of is to get Sumner and his investors to sell prior to the deadline."

Michael seemed surprised. "Is that possible? Would he do that?"

Katherine shrugged. "If the money was right … maybe. He doesn't think I can do it anyway. As long as he has no idea we've succeeded …" Katherine shrugged again. "Maybe. I don't know."

"So what you need to do is find somebody with a better moral compass and a huge bank account."

"I've already found him."

Katherine snapped her head up as if she just realized what she said.

"You can't repeat that, Michael." She reached out and took his hand for effect. "I'm serious. You can't. You can't repeat anything I've said. I shouldn't have said anything. I should have—"

"Hey, relax. I swear to God, I won't say a word," he said. "I probably won't even remember what we talked about in the morning. Neither will you."

His smile seemed genuine, but Katherine knew better. Michael's moral compass had been malfunctioning for years. After eliciting more promises of confidentiality and changing the subject back to your run of the mill bar talk, Katherine finally made her excuses and headed for the door. Sticking to the role she'd been playing, she took a cab home instead of driving the few short blocks.

On the solitary ride home to her condo all those months ago Katherine was glad to get one of the few cabbies in Toronto who knew when to shut up. The silence gave her a chance to critique her performance. It had gone as well as could be expected. She'd had to share a few secrets, but that was necessary to make Michael believe everything she told him, and he did, she was sure of that. She'd given him a lot to think about, a lot of extremely exciting information to pass on to Sumner and The Board – and some of it was even true.

Katherine had no doubt that once he found out what Michael knew, or thought he knew, Sumner would be convinced she'd succeeded. Assurances from her – the proof that he'd demanded on so many occasions – would no longer be necessary. And she was right.

The first pawn had been played. The next move was to recruit a knight.

CHAPTER THIRTY-FOUR

"It takes a village to raise a child."

Truer words were never spoken. There was no way she could raise her baby, *The Plan*, alone. She needed help. Someone who could pull it off and make it look good. Someone with a very specific set of skills. And someone without even a tenuous connection to her. That was paramount. If there was even a suspicion she was involved the contract would hold up in court and she'd lose everything—her company, her personal assets, and her freedom. She turned to the one place she knew she could find whatever she needed—the Internet.

The only things not found on the Internet are perspective and a conscience. Luckily for Katherine Sharpe, she wasn't looking for either. She was looking for someone to help take *The Plan* from conception to reality.

The Web is a virtual mall for anything you want to know or need to acquire. Everything is up for grabs and it's completely anonymous if you know how to mask your steps. Given her expertise in the field of high tech, Katherine had no problem searching in complete anonymity. What she found, buried deep in a semi-legitimate site catering to those interested in private security, was a simple ad:

"Aramis Wolfe—*specializing in simple solutions for complex problems. Discretion assured.*

It was only later, after all of the planning and scheming and manipulating, that Katherine realized she should have paid more attention to her fears. When you play this kind of a game it's hard to tell if you're the queen or a pawn when the knights start jousting and the rooks begin to crumble.

She found herself simultaneously looking back in wonder and looking ahead with foreboding. How the hell did it all get so crazy? Where did she go wrong? Was it all for nothing?

She felt trapped and alone, with nowhere to hide. It was a familiar feeling. It was 'daddy' all over again. It was every relationship she'd ever been in since his timely demise. So she did the only thing she knew how to do. She fought back.

The first order of business was Pavel and the CPUs. If Sumner didn't think there was something in the vault to steal, The Plan had no basis. First, he had to believe the processors worked. That was what the last few months had been all about; everything from recruiting Michael as an unwitting accomplice to inventing a fictitious competitor willing to buy her dream. But Sumner also had to believe they were ready and waiting to be unveiled at the annual Board meeting in two weeks time—July 3rd—two days after Canada Day. That meant that Pavel have to come for a visit, whether he liked it or not.

She knew Pavel hated to leave the sanctity of his lab and the comfort of his small apartment. He had a fear of the outside world that bordered on agoraphobia. It was legendary in the industry, and it was both a blessing and a curse. On the one hand, it made it more than a little difficult to deal with him when he lived half a world away. The courier debacle was only the latest in a series of trials and tribulations Katherine had endured over the years.

On the other hand, however, it made him the perfect collaborator. It gave him the time and focus to fully develop his particular genius. He was the high tech version of hired muscle, only in his case, he was irreplaceable. He didn't know, nor did he want to know, anything about the business side of the creative process. He knew nothing of Katherine's deal with the devil, or that she was about to lose everything. He only knew there was a deadline on the horizon, and that if he didn't produce something concrete very soon, Katherine's company wouldn't be able to continue to fund his research.

Surprisingly, when she contacted him to insist he fly over with the prototypes himself, he didn't argue. In fact, he seemed almost eager to make the trip. Katherine wondered if it was some kind of new psychotropic drug he was testing, or if he was simply stepping up to the plate and doing what had to be done. Either way, she didn't have time to dwell on it. She needed to regain control of The Plan and Pavel was due to land at Pearson International Airport in less than an hour.

CHAPTER THIRTY-FIVE

Gillian Dempster stood in the entrance of her modest three-bedroom side split on Firth Crescent in Scarborough, a smile on her face and a dishtowel in her hand.

"Cal said you'd be by," she said, leaning against the door frame. "The conquering hero got a call twenty minutes ago and went tearing out of here like his ass was on fire. Some tip about an arsenal in the basement of a Chinese food restaurant. It'll probably turn out to be a B-B gun or a Luke Skywalker blaster." She shrugged. "Said he'd be back later, but I never know." Her smile broadened.

"As usual, he left me to clean up after the kids and tuck myself into bed alone … again. God knows I love the man, but I'd replace him with the pool boy in a heartbeat … if we had a pool."

Jack stood with his foot on the bottom step and waited for her to run out of steam. Darcy was obviously trying not to laugh.

"I swear to God, one of these days if the bad guys don't kill that man, I may just have to do it myself."

Jack didn't buy a word of it. The woman had love written all over her face, especially behind her soft brown eyes. She was shorter than Jack had pictured when Cal talked about her—no less formidable—and a lot more curvaceous. She reminded Jack of what Betty Boop would look like if she were dipped in milk chocolate.

"In case you haven't guessed, I'm Cal's neglected wife, Gill," she said.

"Mrs. Dempster, I'm Jack Wri—"

"Gill. I know who you are, Sergeant Wright," she said. "Hmhmm. You're the man who keeps my husband out all hours of the night drinking beer and eating some sort of toxic bar food that makes him smell like a buffalo and fart like a mastodon."

Jack almost choked on his gum. "Oh, he told you about the wings, did he?"

"Told me about them?! He didn't have to." Her laugh was tinged with a touch of awe. "I couldn't sleep in the same bed with the man. Kids wouldn't come out of their rooms for two days. First time in ten years he didn't have to fight to use the bathroom."

Darcy, unable to hold it together, choked out a laugh.

"You must be Officer Caldwell," Gillian said, letting go of Jack's hand and turning to Darcy.

"Darcy. Nice to meet you."

"Nice to meet you too, Hon. Hopefully you listen better than the eye candy here," she said, indicating Jack with a tilt of her head. "It's Gill. Not Gillian and certainly not Mrs. Dempster. And if he throws in a ma'am, I may have to kill him too. The lord and master may not be home, but I don't think you came to see him anyway, am I right?"

"Yes ma'am," Jack said, intentionally.

"See what I mean?" She said to Darcy. "Cute as hell, but he doesn't listen." She gave Jack a playful punch on the shoulder.

"Cal said he'd have somebody here we should meet," Jack said, and left it at that. He didn't know how much Cal would have shared with his wife.

"Hhmm. Andrew. I know all about it," she said, as if reading Jack's mind. The expression on her face suddenly became serious.

"But before you talk to him, Jack, I have to tell you I'm not all that thrilled."

Jack waited for her to go on. He didn't have to wait long.

"Andrew's ... special. I've known him his whole life, and I still don't know what to make of him sometimes. He's gifted, to be sure, but sometimes it seems more like a curse than a blessing. It's lead him into a world of trouble, all of his high tech shenanigans. He's been arrested three times, but every time they drop the charges. I've been trying to help him, push him into a different direction, but I haven't had much luck. And now this. Getting him involved in something like this is like taking an alcoholic on a tour at Hiram Walkers'. I told Cal to find somebody else, but he says Andrew's your best hope."

The smile returned to her face. "There! I've said my piece, and now you know. Anything happens to Andrew and you'll have to answer to me … and it won't just be an 'I told you so'."

Jack started to say yes ma'am, but thought better of it. "Is he still here?"

"Of course he is," Gillian Dempster said, a quizzical look on her face. "He's in his room downstairs. Where else would he be at this time of night?"

"He lives with you?" Jack asked, wondering what kind of a guy would take up residence in the basement of a cop's house.

"Of course he does, Jack. He's only 13. We can't exactly ask him to move out yet."

"Then Andrew is …" Darcy broke in.

"My son. Who did you think I was talking about?"

CHAPTER THIRTY-SIX

About the time Jack and Darcy were pulling up in front of a Calvin Dempster's home in Scarborough, Wolfe was sitting quietly in the Arrivals Lounge at Pearson International Airport. The last flight of the day had just landed, a connecting flight from Russia. Wolfe watched the passengers as they exited customs into the nearly empty terminal. He studied the crowd like a hawk ferreting out prey.

Pavel fussed with the seatbelt buckle, unable to free himself from the contraption until a little girl in the seat next to him reached over and flipped the catch. Pavel tried to play it off as a joke and the youngster giggled like a co-conspirator.

"Good-bye Mister. I hope you like Toronto," the little girl said, like a miniature Canadian ambassador of good will.

"Sure, sure. I will. You be good girl for your Mommy. You hold her hand. It's a big, scary place, the city," Pavel said in a thick Russian accent, meaning every word.

"I will. Bye," the little girl called over her shoulder.

Wolfe had arrived at the airport about three hours earlier and spent the first hour assessing the layout. That done, he settled himself into an uncomfortable airport lounge chair and waited. His right thumb subconsciously tested the edge of the blade he planned to use tonight. Not a standard weapon, but effective none the less.

The man Wolfe waited for was the last off the plane, just ahead of the flight crew. He carried only a small attaché case. His cheap suit was rumpled from having been slept in and his hair was still wet from being slicked back a few minutes before landing. His red eyes attested to the fact he hadn't slept well. Wolfe sat facing away from the arrivals portal and watched the man in the mirror formed by the terminal's plate glass window and the pitch black of the night outside. He didn't try to conceal his interest, and shook his head at the others carelessness. The man had no idea that he was being watched.

The traveler made his way to the front of the airport. Wolfe following a discreet distance behind. They stepped through the automatic doors to the outside only seconds apart. The attaché case banged against the man's leg. Wolfe noted wryly there wasn't a chain attached to this one. Before hailing a taxi the traveler set his brief case on the ground and rounded his shoulders to reach an itch high on his left shoulder. When he straightened up he dropped his arms at his sides and stretched vigorously, trying to work out all of the kinks. When he did Wolfe stepped up silently behind the man, an American Express card in his strong hand, one side of the card sharpened to a razor's edge. *Never leave home without it.*

Pavel followed the small crowd out towards the waiting taxis and limousines. Having never been at Pearson before, he looked around with the wonder of a little child. He was bumped roughly by someone evidently in much more of a hurry than himself, the alcohol emanating from the man's breath failing to excuse the lack of an apology. The Big City! Standing on the concrete apron that ringed the entrance to the airport, Pavel felt like a lamb being led to slaughter.

Wolfe flattened himself to the man's back and with lightening speed brought the card up to the traveler's neck with his right hand while his left hand pulled the man's chin up exposing the jugular. The man didn't even try to resist. Wolfe leaned his full body weight into the man and whispered in his ear, "You're dead."

Before he had a chance to draw the card across the man's throat, however, Wolfe felt his wrist locked in a vice-like grip and a sharp pinprick on the left side of his groin. Pressed up against the man's back like he was, Wolfe could feel the man's face twist into a vicious grin.

"No lad … you are." The pain in Wolfe's groin increased just slightly before the man relaxed his grip and pulled the card carefully out of Wolfe's hand. When the traveler stepped away and turned around, Wolfe looked down in amazement at the six-inch plastic knife, similar to the one he carried in his belt, partially hidden in the traveler's hand and coat sleeve.

The man had a shit-eating grin on his face. "Nice to see you, Johnny … or what do I call you now?"

"Wolfe." The mercenary grinned, touching a finger to his groin to see if there was any blood.

"Wolfe, is it? Appropriate … except for the fact your instincts are shot." The traveler scratched his 'itch' again and the plastic knife was back in a sheath sewn into the lining of his jacket.

"Up yours you old goat," Wolfe replied. "You would have been dead if I'd wanted you that way."

"Not true, lad, not true. You followed me like a bull at Pamplona. I had the knife in my hand before you made your move. You would have been gutted like a perch and I … I would have been scratched at best."

The two men shook hands and then hugged briefly, slapping each other roughly on the back. The traveler picked up his case while Wolfe motioned for the limousine.

Pavel had heard stories of the crime rate in big cities and believed every word of them. He'd seen some things in his Mother Russia he'd never forget, but he'd heard that the US was even worse, and to him, Canada was just another part of the United States.

He watched in fascination the exchange between the two strangers, certain he was about to witness his first murder. *And only in the city a few minutes! Wouldn't that give Katherine something to think about. Call me paranoid! Ha!*

When the two men hugged, Pavel was relieved and a little disappointed. A part of him would have liked his worst fears confirmed. It would prove that what he felt every time he stepped out of his home wasn't abnormal. It was rational and logical and ... sane.

He looked around for Katherine. She was supposed to pick him up. How could she abandon him in the middle of an angry mob? His fear and anger melted away when Katherine pulled her silver BMW in shortly after the limousine carrying the two men pulled out. She looked tired and anxious, but to Pavel Katherine also looked like a guardian angel.

"Traveling in style these days are we now, Johnny?" the traveler said, patting the leather seat of the Lincoln.

"Only the best for you, Patrick, only the best." Wolfe found himself subconsciously picking up the other man's brogue in his own speech.

"You're a liar and a thief my friend, but I like your style," the other man said, looking around the interior of the big Towncar.

This time there wasn't any plastic on the floor and the only thing in the champagne cooler was ice and a few bottles of ale.

"So, what are you getting me into this time, Johnny?"

"I need a demolitions man, Patrick. I realize it's short notice but ..."

The two men spent the next several hours talking about a plan that would change both of their lives forever.

After securing the CPU prototypes in a massive vault in the basement at ComTech, Katherine took Pavel directly to his hotel. The Hilton Suites in Markham is a luxury hotel located basically in the middle of nowhere. It was perfect for someone who didn't like being exposed to one person he didn't know, let alone the millions of people that live and work in downtown Toronto. Katherine could tell Pavel was anxious to get behind a door, any door, and lock out the world. *If I let him*, Katherine thought, *he would have stayed in the vault with the CPUs until it was time for the board meeting.*

"So many people," Pavel said, as if reading her mind. Katherine looked around her at the dark, mostly deserted streets. "And more to come, yes?" Pavel asked, a little shake in his voice.

Katherine wasn't sure what he meant. "I'm sorry?"

"More people. More people will come to Toronto to celebrate your Canada Day? Lots of tourists like me come to the city, yes?"

Katherine almost laughed out loud at the thought of Pavel thinking of himself as a tourist, including himself in the July 1st celebrations. She looked over at Pavel and gave him a reassuring smile.

"Don't worry, Pav. Just as many people leave the city on Canada Day. Maybe more. Sometimes it's like a ghost town around here. You'll be fine … I promise."

Katherine couldn't help but feel sympathy for her friend, and a little sad. She also couldn't help but wonder if perhaps this time he was right, if his fears were completely justified. She decided to change the subject.

"We need to talk about the project before the board meeting," she said, as they pulled into the parking lot in front of the hotel.

Pavel's head bobbed in agreement, but Katherine knew him well enough to know that all he wanted to do was get his room key and lock out the world.

"We do," he said. "We do, but not tonight Katerina … if that's okay? It's been a long flight and I'm tired. Like Russian bear, I need to hibernate."

His words were light, but Katherine knew him well enough to know he was near the end of his rope and that she shouldn't push.

"Our darlings are locked away in your beautiful, shiny vault, and now … now I would like to be locked away in mine," he said, glancing at the hotel. "We talk later, yes? When I've had chance to rest, I can tell you everything. I promise, everything can wait."

Katherine wasn't so sure.

CHAPTER THIRTY-SEVEN

"If you could give this to Andrew, I'd really appreciate it," Jack said, holding up a copy of the crossword.

"You can give it to him yourself if you want. He's still up. But before you do …" She held her hand out to Jack. "What is it?"

"A crossword."

Gillian Dempster looked at Jack with a *'Don't give me that shit'* scowl on her face.

"We think it's a code to get him into the computer Cal brought home," Darcy said.

"It's important," Jack added.

"I know, life or death."

Gillian Dempster stopped suddenly, as if realizing what she'd just said. Jack watched the look on Darcy's face. It didn't take a mind reader to know what both women were thinking.

"I'm sorry. Cal told me what happened. What you did."

Darcy didn't have to say anything. The look on her face said it all.

"You have nothing to feel bad about, Hon." Gillian Dempster continued. "You did what you had to do. Don't lose sleep over a man like that."

Jack could see Darcy was caught off guard by the woman's warmth and sincerity. The words were simple, but spoken with such understanding and compassion that Darcy's eyes began to fill with tears.

Gillian Dempster switched gears quickly, turning back to Jack. "It's just that I don't need any more phone calls from the U of T asking me to get Andrew to stop changing the grad student's marks from A's to F's."

"He did that?" Darcy asked.

"And he hacked into the Department of National Defence and requisitioned a CF18 fighter jet for Cal's birthday."

Darcy wiped her eyes quickly and started to laugh. The moment had passed.

"You sure it's okay," Jack asked, indicating the basement stairs with a tilt of his head. "We don't want to keep him up past his bedtime."

"It's past my bedtime, not his," Gillian Dempster said without humor.

"Andrew has trouble sleeping. I think it's because his mind is always going. Right now he's either reading a textbook on quantum physics or an Archie comic. If he's having a real hard time sleeping he could be flipping through recipes."

Jack looked at her with raised eyebrows.

"What can I say? The boy loves to cook. I think it's because cooking is a lot like chemistry. Follow the proper steps and you get something delicious. Screw up and I spend a week scraping goose liver off the ceiling."

Jack was relieved to see Darcy's smile broaden.

"That ever happen?" She asked.

"More than once. That's why we don't let him use the blender anymore. Every once in a while he does the dumbest things. No common sense whatsoever."

"Gets that from his father?" Darcy guessed.

"You got it, Hon. Now you're starting to see the light. I knew I was going to like you right from the start."

Gillian's bright smile faded a bit as she became serious.

"Jack, when I said Andrew's different, that wasn't just a mother talking. He is. Sometimes he's so smart it scares the hell out of me. Last year he entered the Gauss Mathematics Contest. He finished in the top three percentile," she said, her mother's face showing both pride and awe.

"In the country?" Darcy asked, incredulous.

"In the world, Hon," Gillian Dempster said. "Want to meet the little genius?"

"I'll wait up here," Darcy said.

Jack followed Gillian down a short flight of stairs. At the bottom she knocked on the door and pushed it open without waiting for a response. Jack wasn't sure what to expect, but he pictured a neat laboratory setting with shelves full of textbooks along one wall and white boards filled with complicated mathematical calculations. What he found was just about the opposite.

Andrew Dempster was sprawled face down on a double bed amongst an assortment of gym socks, comic books, video game cases, and dishes from his bedtime snack. An eclectic mix of posters adorned the walls— everything from the Toronto Blue Jays to Wiz Khalifa to Stephen Hawking. A long board leaned against the wall behind the door. There were models and robots and dinosaurs scattered throughout the room, and an acoustic guitar in the corner. The laptop from the Vaughan Road apartment sat on a desk surrounded by a number of other computers, some of them partially disassembled.

Andrew didn't turn around. "Mom! After a knock you're supposed to wait until someone says come in. That's the way it works. You knock, I say come in, you open the door. I didn't say come in."

Gillian Dempster cleared her throat in that certain way that only mothers can do. The one that says, *Want to try that again before I ground you for life?*

Andrew must have heard it a few times in the past. His head snapped around like she'd used a cattle prod on his buttocks. By the time Jack could nod in greeting, Andrew was standing beside his bed, smoothing his pajamas, and stammering out an apology.

"Sorry," he said, looking quickly at his mom and then down at the floor. "Sorry."

"Andrew, I'd like you to meet Detective Sergeant Wright."

"Nice to meet you, Andrew," Jack said.

"Nice to meet you, sir," Andrew said, giving Jack's hand a firm shake. His parents were obviously raising him right.

The second thing Jack noticed about Andrew was that he was tall, about 5'10," and rail thin, only about 135 pounds. The first thing he noticed about him was that he was oriental. Jack looked quickly at Gillian Dempster without really meaning to, a look of surprise obvious on his face.

"Oh, you noticed, eh?" She said, a smile lighting up her face. "Yup, Calvin and I are adopted."

"I'm going upstairs to spend some time with the brains of your operation," Gillian Dempster continued. Then, turning to Andrew and said, "Try not to let him talk you into anything that'll get you arrested again, okay Sweetie?"

"Yes, Mom."

When the door closed behind her, Jack walked over to the guitar and looked at Andrew. "May I?"

Andrew nodded. "You play?"

"I fiddle," Jack confessed. "My Dad use to collect guitars. I still have his '48 Martin Double Ought 18."

Andrew whistled. "Sweet. Small guitar with a big sound."

"You got it," Jack agreed. "I wish I could do it justice. All I can manage is D, G, E and the occasional F."

"I hate F," Andrew said.

"Everybody hates F," Jack said with a chuckle. "Maybe I'll bring it by sometime and you can show me what you can do."

Andrew nodded.

"In the meantime, your Dad tell you what we're looking for on that thing?" Jack asked, indicating the laptop.

"Dates, times, names, places, anything and everything I can find."

"Any luck?"

Andrew looked embarrassed. "No, sir. Sorry. The security programs are amazing. This thing's locked up tight."

"Maybe this will help," Jack said, handing Andrew the crossword.

"What is it?" Andrew asked.

"If we're lucky ... a key."

CHAPTER THIRTY-EIGHT

"She's quite a lady," Darcy offered.

"Hmm." Jack wasn't listening. His mind was spinning with the possibilities contained in the squares of a crossword puzzle.

"She's obviously crazy about Calvin, despite what she says."

"Hmm," Jack said again.

"It's possible she's part of the robbery plot," Darcy said quietly.

"Uh-huh."

"Some day I'd like to bear your children."

"Hmm, that would be— What?!" Jack spun around to look into her face and almost bounced the Impala off a parked car. "What did you say?!"

Darcy laughed and turned back to face the front. "Relax Detective, I have no designs on your bachelorhood. You were a million miles away. Nice to have you back."

Jack laughed, albeit shakily.

"Sorry. I was just thinking about the crossword. I didn't mean to ignore you."

"That's okay, I'm used to it. Miro does it all the time."

"Boyfriend?" Jack asked.

"Cat," Darcy answered "The main man in my life."

"But I thought ..." Jack began and then stopped.

"What?"

"Nothing. Disregard. Just a little confusion on my part."

She sat and stared at him without saying a word. Waiting.

Jack quickly changed the subject. "I know it's late but, if you'd like we could grab a cup of coffee. I know a place that's not too far and they never close. The coffee's pretty good and it's dirt cheap."

Darcy looked at the side of his face as Jack stared straight ahead and waited for her answer. She liked what she saw—a caring, sensitive face, a face you could trust. He had a reputation for making the toughest criminals crack like walnuts, and Darcy was beginning to see why.

"I'd like that," she said after a minute. "I don't think I could sleep now if I tried."

"Coffee it is. Sit back and enjoy the ride, M'lady."

Darcy smiled and did just that. Neither one said a word until Jack pulled the cruiser into the lane that led to the back of his property.

"And just where do you think you're taking me, Detective?" Darcy asked with a wry smile on her face.

"I told you … not far, it never closes, and it's cheap. What more can you ask for?"

"Your castle I presume?" Darcy was only half kidding. In the dark the three storey Victorian architecture was impressive. The few lights that Jack left on highlighted the stained and leaded glass windows.

"You presume right, although I wouldn't call it a castle. Neither would you if you saw it in the light of day. It needs a lot of work."

"It's huge."

"Not really."

"You ever live in a bachelor apartment?" Darcy asked under her breath. And then a little louder, "So who do you have to kill to live like this?"

"Actually, it was my wife's before she passed away".

"Oh God, Jack, I'm so sorry. I didn't mean …"

Jack was already holding up his hands. "It's okay. It was a long time ago. Something we can save for another time, if that's okay?"

"Of course. Shit, Jack, I'm sorry. God, I feel like such a …"

"Darcy, forget it," Jack said. "You didn't know. Come on, the coffee's on the inside and if we stay out here too long we'll wake up Mrs. Leishaman. She'll end up calling the cops on us."

"Seriously?"

"Every time I bring home a new woman, she calls the cops. I think she's jealous," he said, obviously trying to alleviate Darcy's discomfort.

"So how many women have you brought home in the dead of night?"

"Including you?" He asked.

Darcy nodded, looking up at him, feeling goose bumps raise on her arms in the cooling night air.

"One," he said with a chuckle, and moved to open the back door for her.

The heavy oak door jammed as usual and Jack had to step in close beside her to kick the brass plate that protected the bottom. As he did, his cologne lightly filled in the space between them, making her head swim just a little. He stood still for a second, very close, looking down at her, his face illuminated by a light shining through the beveled glass windows at the side of the door. His hazel eyes were more green than brown and seemed to hold an invitation. Neither of them moved for what seemed like a very long time. Finally, without taking her eyes from his, she managed to break the spell.

"Is it stuck?"

"What?" He asked.

"The door," she said, still staring into his eyes. "Is it stuck?"

Jack cleared his throat. "Yeah ... yes, sorry about that. Damned humidity."

He kicked door again and stepped back. He clicked on the light in the kitchen and threw his coat on one of the shaker pegs that lined the wall.

"Jack, my God, it's ..."

The kitchen alone was almost half the size of her entire apartment, and the white of the cupboards and brilliance of the stainless steel appliances shone in the half-light.

"It's ..."

"Like it?" Jack asked,

"Are you insane? How could I not? I mean it's ... gorgeous!"

"I'm glad you approve. But trust me, the rest of the house is a little ... tired. I'll give you the five cent tour."

With that Darcy was almost bowled over by a rocketing little bundle of fur. Darcy wasn't exactly sure what was attacking her at first, but she was glad that it was friendly. Charlie's whole back end was wagging so hard she thought the little dog might dislocate something.

"Charlie!" Jack scolded, "Is that any way to treat a guest?" Charlie made two turns around Jack's legs, leaping and nipping at his hands in excitement, and then shot back to Darcy who had crouched down. She started to scratch behind his ears and down his back. That stopped him dead in his tracks.

"That's Charlie, The Dumpster Dog."

"Dumpster Dog?"

"Long story. I'll tell you later. Let me show you around and then we can get that coffee. Don't worry about him," Jack said, inclining his head towards the little dog. "You couldn't get rid of him now if you tried."

True to Jack's words Charlie followed them around from room to room on the short tour until they found themselves back in the kitchen.

"Regular or decaf?" Jack asked.

"Decaf, definitively. I've got to sleep sometime tonight."

Darcy listened to Jack make the coffee and set out a plate of cookies while she poked around the kitchen and checked out Mrs. Leishman's back yard. She could just make out the garden through the huge window on the back wall.

"My mother would have loved this kitchen," Darcy said.

"Mine too, I think," Jack said. "She passed away before Caroline and I moved in, but I think she would have approved. She loved to bake."

"As for the rest of the house ..." Jack shrugged and left it at that.

"Are you doing the work yourself?"

Jack nodded. "Can you tell? That's why it's taking so long. I should have it done just in time to move into a nursing home."

"That soon?" Darcy kidded.

"Easy there, Tiger. I'm not *that* old."

"How old *are* you?" Darcy asked.

"Old enough to know not to answer that question."

"Wow!" Darcy said with a giggle. "That old?"

"Smartass!"

They sat across from each other at the kitchen table, Darcy absentmindedly scratching Charlie who was sprawled upside-down on her lap. She wanted to ask Jack about Caroline, but decided against it. Instead, she reached across the table and brushed some errant cookie crumbs off Jack's face. It was a strangely intimate gesture, but for some reason it felt perfectly natural.

"God, where did you learn your table manners, in a barn?"

"As a matter of fact, yes."

Having decided to stay away from business for a while, their conversation veered into the personal, with Jack doing most of the talking. Jack became unusually candid about his past and the road he traveled to get to the present. He talked about everything, Darcy noticed, except his wife.

He talked about growing up on a farm north of Cobourg, where the woods at the back of their century-old farmhouse provided a limitless array of natural mysteries to be solved. He talked about losing his mother to cancer. Jack remembered her as a beautiful lady who filled his head with riddles and their country kitchen with the scent of ginger or chocolate or cinnamon, depending on the nearest holiday.

He talked about losing his father when the man buried himself in his Toronto law practice and all but abandoned Jack. When his father returned to the farm on weekends, he spent his time badgering Jack about his schoolwork or lack of friends. The rift that started between father and son after their mutual loss widened with time until it became a chasm that couldn't be bridged.

Jack took care of the farm, read countless mysteries, studied psychology, and watched as his father replaced his loss with both the tangibles and intangibles that accompany a successful career. Jack's father collected a lot of different things over the years, including guitars, motorcycles, power and a reputation for being single-mindedly ruthless.

After three hours it was obvious that neither wanted the conversation to end, despite the need for sleep. Darcy focused on the positive.

"The farm sounds beautiful, Jack. How far is it?"

"About two hours, but not a bad drive. Nice country. All I have left is a few acres and an old barn we converted into a house. I haven't been there in years."

"I'd love to see it some time. I'm a city girl, born and bred."

"Well, maybe we could take a drive up some day, I mean after all of this is over."

"Detective Wright, are you asking me out on our third date?" Darcy said.

"Well, I—"

Darcy stopped teasing when she realized Jack was feeling uncomfortable for the first time in hours.

"I'd love to Jack … really. Just say the word."

The two sat quietly for a few minutes without feeling the need to speak. Darcy let her gaze drift around the room until she came back to Jack who was staring off into space. Hating to do it, but knowing it had to end sometime, Darcy finally said, "It's past two o'clock. No wonder I'm so tired. I think I better head home."

Jack didn't argue, but he didn't move either.

"No sense in you driving me home. You wouldn't get back before the roosters start to crow, or whatever they do in your world."

"I couldn't agree more."

"I'll call a cab."

"Not a chance."

"Jack, you just said—"

"You're not taking a cab home alone at this hour. No way."

"That's sweet, Jack, but I'm a cop, remember?" For some reason she was amused by his chivalry. "I can take care of myself."

"Uh-uh. Sorry."

"But—"

"You'll just have to stay here."

Darcy was surprised by the backward invitation. She affected her best southern belle accent. "Suh, I'll have you know that I am *not* that kind of a girl!"

Jack smiled. "Good, cause I'm too tired to even think about being that kind of a boy. I've got three spare bedrooms. The cats get one and

Charlie gets the other, but I'll give you first pick. You can bolt the door and put a chair under the handle if you want, but I guarantee you your virtue will be safe in the Wright household tonight."

"Jack, that's nice but—"

"No buts," he said, with a bow. "You, madam, shall be our guest." Charlie woofed his assent.

Darcy was too tired to argue and the thought of being able to crawl into bed without driving anywhere was too alluring to fight. She looked from Jack to Charlie and back to Jack. Both of them had the same expectant look on their faces. She had to laugh.

"All right, all right, I'll stay."

Jack's smile broadened. Charlie licked her hand. Darcy stood with a stretch and said, "Lead on MacDuff, I'm exhausted."

Jack got her settled in the front bedroom with a pair of his pajamas and a stack of clean towels. Darcy looked around the room. It definitely needed updating, but the four-poster bed looked like something out of a magazine.

Darcy pulled back the down duvet on the bed and went into the bathroom to change. She put on the pajama top but decided against the bottoms. The duvet would be warm enough. She looked in the drawer of the old dry sink Jack used as a vanity and found just about everything she needed. Soap, toothpaste, a new toothbrush, a hairbrush … *Jeez, this place has everything. I wonder how many guests he really has stay over?*

Before she could snuggle into bed, she heard a light rap on the bedroom door. She checked her appearance in the full-length mirror. The pajama top was too big for her, but it did little to hide her figure. Her long silky legs were visible from mid-thigh down, just the start of a tan making them look brown in the dim light. The cotton clung to her slim hips and outlined the swell of her full breasts. Her heart skipped a beat as she opened the door a crack. Before Jack could say anything, Charlie pushed his way through and leapt up on to the bed. He sat facing Darcy and wagged his whole rear end in anticipation. Darcy opened the door wider affecting a disappointed look.

"I thought you said I'd be safe from marauding males?"

It took Jack a second to answer and Darcy felt a twinge of excitement and pleasure. She could tell that he was trying not to stare.

"I said *I* was too tired to give you any trouble. I can't answer for the rest of the males in this place."

"I think that one's breaking the house rules," she said, looking over at Charlie.

"Come on Charlie, give the nice lady some privacy." Charlie lay down on the bed with his head on his front paws and stared at the two of them with big, sorrowful brown eyes.

"Traitor," Jack said.

Darcy laughed and turned back to Jack. "It's okay, I don't mind the company."

"I just wanted to make sure you found everything you needed. There's a new toothbrush in the drawer and—"

"Not anymore," Darcy said, and smiled up at him. "Minty fresh."

For someone so astute at reading body language, Jack seemed to miss an awful lot. She took a half step forward, tilted her head further back and closed her eyes. Darcy didn't think she could make the invitation any clearer.

She felt him move closer, felt him hesitate, felt the heat off his body, felt her desire growing. Jack took her face gently in both of his hands and she sighed softly. She felt his lips press tenderly against her forehead in a lingering kiss before he stepped back and closed the door.

"Good night," he said, as it clicked shut behind him.

Darcy stared at the back of the door for a full minute, unsure of what had just happened.

"Good night," she said, feeling ridiculous, but she was too tired to doing anything other than crawl under the covers and snuggle up to Charlie. He licked her face once and burrowed deep into her neck.

"What do you make of that?" Darcy asked the furry little bundle and got his patented 'Hrumph' in reply. "You know I'm not going to sleep a wink, don't you?" she said.

A few seconds later, with the lamp still on and Charlie just getting comfortable, her breathing became deeper and all of the muscles in her body relaxed. For the first time in a week she slept without dreaming of moon faces and gun barrels.

CHAPTER THIRTY-NINE

"Why me, Johnny?"

The two men sat at a makeshift table. The top was a scrap sheet of plywood. The chairs were two discarded packing crates, remnants of a previous tenant.

Sunshine streamed in through an open window and slashed across Patrick Morgan's features like futuristic war paint. It was the only direct light in the loft. The rest diffused through windows covered with the same soot and grime that clung to the outside of the building.

"What do you mean?"

"What I said. Why me? Why not somebody else? Somebody closer? It must have cost you a pretty penny to finance the travel arrangements. I haven't flown that much in years." The flight was anything but direct.

Patrick Morgan was ten years older than Wolfe, although the difference looked to be more like twenty. His red hair was just long enough to be disheveled most of the time. He was forever using his fingers to brush it back. He carried about forty extra pounds on a 5'10" frame, but most of it was in his back and shoulders. His five o'clock shadow was almost pure white.

The lines on Morgan's weathered face bore testimony to the life he'd lived. His ruddy complexion was one part heritage, one part environment, and one part Irish whiskey, although he never allowed his drinking to interfere with his work. The few pints in the limo last night would be all he'd have until the job was complete. He picked up the metal field cup of luke-warm tea and watched Wolfe over the rim as he took a sip. He lit another cigarette and blew the smoke in the direction of the open window.

"You were available," Wolfe said. "And you're an unknown quantity over here."

"Why hire somebody at all? Why not do the job yourself?" Morgan seemed to have an agenda.

"This one's complicated. Too many other things to worry about. I don't want to be fucking around with C4 if something starts to go south."

"Like when Denis got himself killed?"

Morgan watched for a reaction, but Wolfe didn't bat an eye.

"You heard about that?"

"Hard not to. We're a small fraternity."

"Denis was stupid," Wolfe said.

"From what I hear, Denis was working with an amateur. Who picked the team?"

Wolfe's cold, gray eyes flashed briefly.

"Nobody's perfect, Patrick," Wolfe said simply.

Morgan pressed on, knowing full well he was crossing into dangerous territory.

"You used to be, Johnny," Morgan said, looking deep into the other man's eyes.

"If you're slipping in your old age ..."

Wolfe let out a long, slow breath.

"Oscar brought Ricco on board," he said. "To keep an eye on me, I imagine. Part of the deal. I had no say. Not if I wanted the job and, believe me, I want the job." Wolfe rubbed his fingers and thumb together in the universal sign for money.

So, how much?"

"Your cut?"

Patrick bobbed his head once.

"Two hundred thousand, as promised, plus bonus."

"How big of a bonus would we be looking at?"

"Hard to say. I'm working out a few options but trust me, you won't be disappointed."

Wolfe could feel Morgan's eyes on him as he walked away to inspect the supplies he'd purchased to replace what the ETF had seized. The Irishman didn't say anything for a minute, apparently lost in his own thoughts as if wrestling with a decision. Wolfe didn't try to convince Morgan one way or other. He knew the man well enough to know that if he decided to be a part of the operation, he'd see it through to the end. If he decided to take a pass, he probably wouldn't be there when Wolfe turned around.

Wolfe ran his hands along an oily cloth tarpaulin that covered a number of wooden crates stacked neatly to the left of the massive freight elevator. It was an oddly affectionate gesture, like what a car buff might do to a Lamborghini at the auto show. Wolfe threw back one corner of the heavy canvas and inspected the various packing containers, the yellow print vibrant against the dark green. Military codes and warning labels were stenciled along each side of every crate. Wolfe closed his eyes and breathed deeply the heavy smell of mildew and machine oil.

"Right, then," Morgan finally said. "No time for mourning the dearly departed. No rest for the wicked. What's the craig on t'job?"

Wolfe managed a genuine smile. Patrick Morgan was in.

"Simple, really. Oscar is going to put something into a vault; something she'd prefer didn't remain there for too long."

"Oscar's a doll?" Patrick asked, his eyebrows arching up his forehead.

"An amateur, but not stupid," Wolfe said. "She planned the whole thing."

"You've got me planking it, Johnny. I'm not much for working with amateurs," Morgan said.

"Relax. I've gone over the plan. It's not bad. Needs a little work, but then what doesn't? And besides, there's room for improvisation."

"The options you mentioned?"

"Exactly."

"Options that could benefit you greatly, I presume."

"And you, Patrick."

"But it's her company we'll be hitting?" Morgan asked. "Riddle me this then. Why doesn't she just make the withdrawal herself, or better yet, not put whatever it is in there in the first place?"

"She didn't let me in on that part," Wolfe lied. "All I know is they've got to be stolen and there can't be any connection to her. None. That's where we come in."

"That's why the precious code names?" Morgan guessed.

"And all the rest of the bullshit she's put me through. It's got to look like the real deal. Security breached, safe blown, maximum destruction."

"Collateral damage?" Morgan asked.

Wolfe nodded. "Has to be, otherwise it looks too clean. Somebody always has to die, Patrick, you know that."

"I do, but does Oscar?"

"She will," Wolfe said.

"So what's the something we'll be liberating for the lass?"

"Computer processors," Wolfe said.

"Computer processors. Fek off. Ye serious? Why the hell doesn't she just go to a store?"

"You can't pick these up at Future Shop, Patrick.

"Special?"

"Beyond special, if they do what she says they can do. Should put Apple and IBM right of business. Worth billions, literally."

"You think she's tellin' de truth?"

Wolfe had played with the answer to that question for a month now, and finally decided the answer had to be yes. Why else would she go through with all of this? She was desperate to hang on to her ownership of the company. What she didn't realize is that, in the end, she'd be the one who was owned.

To Patrick he said simply, "Doesn't matter. The job's cash up front. It's only the bonus that's in question."

"Does she know your 'istory? About your past employers?"

"She didn't ask for references, if that's what you're getting at," Wolfe said "Good."

Wolfe looked at Morgan, knowing he had more to say.

"Hard to convince them to write a letter of recommendation, given all of them are dead."

CHAPTER FORTY

Darcy woke to sunshine streaming in through lace curtains on the bedroom window. An antique china dish filled with potpourri, warming in the sun on a walnut table by the window, infused the room with the scent of sweet pea and lavender. The room held a dream-like quality. For a few seconds she didn't know where she was. Confusing her further was the fact that there was a warm body pressed up against her back. She hadn't felt that in over a year and a half, except when Miro … Charlie struggled out from underneath the duvet and gave her face a lick.

"Oh no you don't, buddy boy. You, my friend, have morning breath."

Darcy flung back the covers on top of the little dog and struggled out of the warm bed. The mattress was old and deep and tried to pull her back in. She stretched languidly and padded softly to the bathroom. Fifteen minutes later, with her face flushed from the shower and her thick, damp hair combed back into a ponytail, Darcy emerged a new woman. She felt refreshed and … what? She didn't stop to explore the feeling any further.

Charlie followed her like a shadow as she made her way down the stairs. At the bottom he scampered off on his own in the direction of the kitchen. The aroma of fresh brewed coffee helped her to find her way towards the back of the big old house. She pushed her way through the swinging door, but before she could say something smart, a man the size of a small mountain who was standing with his back to her fiddling with the coffee machine, beat her to it.

"About time you got your fat ass out of bed. I know you need your beauty sleep, but this is ridicu—"

He turned with two steaming mugs in his beefy hands.

"—lous."

Ken hesitated, but only for a split second.

"There's something different about you, Jack. I can't put my finger on it. How much beauty sleep *did* you get?"

Darcy smiled and stepped further into the room. She could feel herself blushing.

"Darcy Caldwell."

Instead of shaking her outstretched hand, Ken handed her one of the mugs.

"Ken Kotwa. I hope you take cream and sugar."

"Not usually, but I think I can make an exception, just this once."

Darcy and Ken shared the relative quiet of the kitchen as they sipped their coffees. Ken broke the companionable silence every minute or so with a question.

"You related to Stats?" Ken asked.

"His niece. He raised me."

Silence.

"You call him Stats?"

"Everybody calls him Stats."

Silence.

"What's his real name."

"Clarence."

Silence.

"Parents?"

Mom's dead. Dad didn't stick around."

Silence.

"Married?"

Darcy held up her left hand. No ring.

More silence.

"Boy friend?"

Darcy shook her head, but she could feel the blood rising up in her cheeks again.

Silence.

"You and Jack?"

This time it was Darcy's turn to hesitate for a split second.

"Friends."

Silence.

"Pets?" Ken asked, dropping a Timbit that was gobbled up before it hit the floor.

"Cat."

Charlie gave a low growl as if to show his disapproval.

A few seconds later Jack pushed through the swinging door and made his way into the kitchen like a man in a trance. He was in desperate need of a shave and a coffee. His eyes were half closed. His dark hair was tousled and flattened to one side of his head. He wore faded jeans and a white cable knit sweater that looked like it had seen better days. To Darcy he couldn't have looked sexier.

"Ouch! Not exactly a morning person, is he?" Darcy said, looking at Ken. The two of them started laughing.

Jack raised his hand and started to offer a rebuttal, but must have thought better of it, which only made the other two laugh harder.

"Just the way I like my men," Darcy chuckled, "barefoot and in the kitchen."

Jack ignored her completely this time and poured himself a cup of coffee. He leaned against the edge of the butcher block counter top, gazing out into the back yard.

"And quiet," Darcy added for good measure.

Jack held the pottery mug directly under his nose and breathed deeply. He took a sip and set the cup down so that he could drag his hands back through his hair. The effect wasn't positive. Darcy watched him with obvious delight, and shared another snicker with Ken.

"So what stories has this giant pain in the ass been telling you about me?" Jack asked.

"Listen to him, will you?" Ken interrupted, before Darcy could answer. "As if we have nothing better to talk about than him."

"Actually, your name never came up," Darcy confirmed.

Jack's retort was cut off by the telephone ringing. He slumped off into the living room to take the call. He was back in less than a minute. Nothing about him looked sleepy anymore.

"What?" Darcy asked.

"That was Calvin. Andrew's into the hard drive."

Darcy thought Jack might hug her, and a part of her definitely wanted him to, but instead he turned to Ken.

"Can you drop Darcy at home on your way to work? I have to get out to Calvin's before Andrew has to—"

"Whoa! Back the taxi up. I'm coming with you."

Jack shook his head. "I have to talk to Andrew before school, and you told me you have an appointment with Dr. Cohen this morning?"

"Not nice to keep the force shrink waiting," Ken said.

He turned to fiddle with the coffee maker when Darcy gave him a 'Don't piss me off' look. It was Karski and the fire escape all over again. She was about to be on the outside looking in.

"Cohen can wait," she said emphatically.

"Not if you want to get back in harness."

Darcy turned to Ken for support.

"Don't pull me into this," he said, with a sheepish grin. "I'm just the taxi driver. You two work it out and let me know what you decide. I'm going to Mrs. Leishman's to see if she did any baking this morning. The old girl's crazy about me. I'll be in the car when you figure it out. In case I don't end up driving you, it was nice meeting you Darcy."

He turned to Jack. "In case you piss her off too badly, it's been nice knowing you."

As the back door closed behind him, Darcy wheeled around to face Jack. Before she could let him have it with both barrels, he stepped forward and took both of her hands in his.

"I'm not trying to cut you out. I promise. I'll give you everything as soon as I can. It's just that ..."

Jack hesitated.

"If there's as much information on that hard drive as Calvin says, I think it's time I kick this upstairs and make it official."

Darcy felt a knot tighten in her stomach.

"If you do that, Jack, they'll take me off this thing in a heartbeat. You know that. No way Karski will let me run with this."

"Karski won't let you run with anything if you don't see the shrink, and I won't let them cut you out. I have a little pull with the brass. I'll make sure you're part of this thing, even if your part stays unofficial."

She looked into Jack's eyes to see if she was being fed a line of bullshit. All she saw was a man who desperately wanted her to know that she could trust him.

"I promise," he said, as if that made all the difference in the world.

"I don't have a good track record with your gender and promises," Darcy said.

But after another minute of staring at him, she decided he was right. She needed to be certified fit for duty, and she didn't want to be around when Jack filled the brass in on their non-investigation.

"All right," she said finally. "But you break that promise and Ken's right … You better pick out a headstone before I find you, because you'll need it."

Before Jack could respond, Darcy continued.

"So who are you going to talk to? Casson?"

Jack shook his head, a serious look on his face. "McAllister."

"The Chief?!"

CHAPTER FORTY-ONE

"What did you come up with? Is the crossword some kind of password?" Jack asked, leaning over Andrew's shoulder.

Calvin sat on the unmade bed without interrupting

"Actually," Andrew said, "I think it's a bunch of passwords. The trouble is there's no pattern. I've got my computer doing a random functions breakdown, but what I got so far was pretty much luck."

"Let's see," Jack said.

"When I put in one down and one across I hit the root directory. I thought I had the whole thing figured out. It was easy ... too easy. But take a look at the files." He pointed to a pile of papers. "I printed off what I could get."

Jack started reading while Andrew continued.

"I tried all the logical combinations after that but all of a sudden nothing's working, and I think I figured out why. Whoever programmed this thing is something else ... a genius. I think when I hacked into the root directory I must have tripped some kind of an internal security system ... something hidden in one of the files. I did a systems analysis before hand and this is what I got."

He handed Jack another, smaller stack of papers.

"What am I looking at?" Jack asked.

"A break down of the file properties, from when I first hacked in and then after I hit the stone wall ... see the difference? Look at the bytes used by each sub-root."

Jack marveled at the mind of the thirteen year-old hunched over the keyboard. All of a sudden Andrew sounded a lot more like thirty than thirteen.

"In both printouts the basic configuration of the hard drive is the same, but the size of each file has increased."

"So you mean ..." Jack took a second to collect his thoughts. "... when you tapped into the first file something was added to the rest?"

"Right," Andrew said.

"Like another password?"

The boy just shrugged.

"What else are you thinking?" Jack asked.

Andrew didn't answer right away. He spun back and forth in his swivel chair, looking once again like a thirteen year-old kid. Digits flashed by on the computer screen behind him. He leaned back and looked up at the manuals on the shelves above his head, and his eyes glazed over for a second.

"If it was me," he began, "and I didn't want somebody to get into my files, I'd put in a tamper switch."

"A tamper switch ... a program that watches out for somebody screwing around with your shit—" Calvin cleared his throat. "—stuff, and then it shuts you out. You know, all of a sudden the door you hacked disappears and you have to start all over again. Try to find another way in."

"Is that what you think happened here?" Jack asked.

Andrew shrugged. "Maybe, but if that's the case it's a pretty complicated program. It protected every file at once ... probably with a different security system."

"What do you mean?" Jack asked, wanting to learn all he could before going to see McAllister.

"If you look at the files it's obvious they've been changed, right? Gotten bigger? But if you look at the data you can tell that they didn't all grow by the same amount."

"The second security program added something to every file, but it added something different to each one. It didn't just install another password. It installed a thousand different passwords. Some small, some big."

Jack asked a question knowing full well that he wasn't going to like the answer.

"Okay Andrew, let's say that you wanted to protect something that was a matter of life and death, something so important that you'd kill to protect it … what then?"

"Simple. After three or four tries by somebody with no business snooping around in the file, I'd have the hard drive erase itself."

Jack looked from Andrew to Calvin and then back to Andrew. The same idea seemed to hit all three of them all at the same time. Jack turned to look at the computer screen just as it buzzed with visual static and then went completely blank. The next systems analysis that Andrew ran on the hard drive flashed a simple message: **(0) FILES FOUND**.

Before Jack left, Andrew tried everything he could to recover the files, but nothing worked. While his fingers flew over the keyboard, Jack and Calvin went through the files he'd printed out. Andrew had managed a few small miracles before the security system on the hard drive decided enough was enough, but it was precious little to go on. Andrew said he'd keep trying, but Jack wasn't holding his breath. He had enough to go to McAllister, if only to give his old friend a heads up in case shit hit the fan. The one thing the Chief of the Toronto Police Service hated more than anything else was to be blindsided..

"You're taking this all the way to the top?" Calvin asked. "What about the chain of command?"

"The chain and I don't get along," Jack said. "Besides, McAllister and I have a history. I'll tell you about it over a beer at Stats when this thing is all over.

"No wings this time," Calvin said with a smile.

"No wings," Jack agreed. "Gill made it clear if I ever do that to her again, she'll take both of us out. You first, of course."

"'Course," Calvin said. "What happens after you talk to McAllister?"

"That depends on what he has to say. If he pitches a fit I'll end up back in harness … if I'm lucky."

"And if not?"

"If not, I need to find out everything I can about this," Jack said, holding up one of the printouts Andrew managed to salvage. It's an installation manual for something called a LaserTech 25.

"What's that?"

"If I'm right, the answer to three of our five W's," Jack said, without any humor.

Calvin gave him a quizzical look.

"The who, what and where."

CHAPTER FORTY-TWO

"So … Jack and the Chief?"

"Long story," Ken said, staring straight ahead.

He and Darcy had been driving along for a few minutes in silence, but the question needed to be asked and, as far as Darcy was concerned, answered. In fact, there were a lot of questions about Jack she'd like answered.

"I have the time." Darcy tried being cute. It usually worked for her. Not this time. Ken didn't even look over.

"Come on, Ken. If I'm going to be involved with Jack—"

"Involved?" Ken asked, raising an eyebrow.

"In the investigation," Darcy clarified. "I deserve to know who I'm dealing with."

Ken wasn't buying it.

"Listen Darcy. You seem like a nice person. Maybe it's best you don't get involved … with Jack or the investigation."

"I'm already involved. I was the second I pulled the trigger. I didn't have a choice then and I don't now."

"About the investigation … maybe. About Jack, you definitely have a choice."

So help me make the right decision. What do I need to know?"

Ken continued staring straight ahead for a very long time. They were driving along Bloor Street approaching Yonge. He seemed to be trying to decide which way to go, what if anything to say and how to say it. When he wheeled into an entrance that led to the cemetery that runs behind the stores on the south side of Bloor, it was as if he was letting the car decide. He pulled off the gravel lane onto the grass, put the car in park and turned his great bulk to face her as best as he could.

If Darcy thought she was about to be on the receiving end of a fatherly talk, she was dead wrong. Ken didn't pull any punches.

"Okay. Here it is, straight from the horse's ass. But before I get into it, I need to ask you a favor and you may not like it."

Darcy sat up a little straighter.

"If what I'm seeing here is what I think I'm seeing, then I'm telling you … asking you to be careful."

Darcy swallowed involuntarily, but didn't look away.

"What do you mean?" she asked.

"Listen, Darcy, I don't want to fence with you. I just want you to promise me if something's starting to gel between you two, you'll take it slow. If, on the other hand, this is just a game for you, just fun, or you think it's a good career move—"

Darcy couldn't believe what she was hearing and her blood ran cold. Before she could let loose, however, Ken held up a meaty hand.

"I'm not saying that's what's happening here. I'm not. I'm just saying *if. If* this is anything other than the real deal, then do yourself and Jack a favor and let it go. Catch the bad guys, make headlines, and walk away."

Darcy didn't know what to say.

"Like I said, you seem nice. I don't think you'd hurt Jack intentionally, and I don't want to see you hurt either. But you have to know … that man and I have been through a lot over the years, and I would kill or die for him, just like he would for me. I won't see him hurt again. Not by you or anyone else. Not in this life. We good so far?" he asked.

Darcy nodded, not trusting herself to speak.

"Jack is damaged goods, Darcy. God knows I love the man, but he is. Pain and guilt will do that to you, and Jack's had enough of both. He's one of the toughest men I've ever met but every man has a breaking point and Jack's was about fifteen years ago."

Darcy waited, not sure where Ken was headed.

"You really don't know what I'm talking about?" He asked.

Darcy shook her head. "I don't, unless you're talking about his wife. He said she passed away a long time ago."

"She didn't just pass away, Darcy. She was murdered—butchered actually—by another cop."

Darcy could literally feel her jaw drop. The shock of Ken's words took her breath away and made her feel like a balloon with a slow leak. She deflated into the car door away from Ken and waited for him to continue.

"I can't believe you don't know anything about this. It was huge news at the time. Papers, radio, television … the works. It went on for weeks. It was a fucking media circus with Jack right in the middle of it."

"I was with the military back then, still in Germany."

Ken looked skeptical. "Even so, I don't know how you missed it."

"This has something to do with The Chief? With McAllister?" Darcy asked.

Ken nodded.

"I don't—"

"Jack and McAllister used to work Homicide together. They were tight, on and off the job."

"Okay," Darcy said.

"Jack was married to Caroline, and she was—" Ken's voice broke for a second. "She was beautiful, inside and out. It was a good marriage. One of the ones you thought, yeah, these guys are really gonna make it."

Darcy looked at Ken. He seemed to be watching the movie of what he was describing.

"I mean, perfect?" Ken scoffed. "Nobody's perfect. But Jack and Caroline were good together. They had their fights, but they were always over small shit. Jack used to joke about how much fun they had making up."

Ken looked at Darcy as if to make sure she was keeping up. She was hanging on his every word.

"Then one night, after a particularly stupid fight—I think it was over potatoes—Caroline went out for a run and never came back."

"What happened?" Darcy asked.

"Ricker."

"Ricker?"

"David Joseph Ricker." Ken spat out the name.

Darcy waited.

"Ricker was assigned to Homicide. A learning opportunity. Must have had a Rabbi somewhere in the force, but nobody ever owned up to it after the fact."

"He was assigned to McAllister," Ken continued. "Spent time with him and Jack on and off duty. That's how he met Caroline."

Darcy could see where the narrative was headed and wanted to stop him, but she couldn't. She needed to see it through to the end.

"Best anyone could figure, he became obsessed. The night Jack and Caroline fought, Ricker must have followed Caroline on her run. He caught up to her in Cedarvale Park. That's where he—"

Ken's voice broke again.

"That's where he beat her and raped her and killed her. The Coroner said it took a long time for her to die."

Darcy was looking out of the side window of the car, wanting to give Ken some semblance of privacy and not wanting him to see her cry. Tears were streaming down her face ... for Ken and for Caroline and especially for Jack.

"Jack never forgave himself. Said if they hadn't fought ... Even after he killed Ricker—"

Darcy spun around. "Jack killed Ricker?"

Ken nodded. "The investigation barely got under way before McAllister got a tip. Somebody fingered Ricker. Gave them everything they needed to be sure. McAllister wanted to wait, do things properly, get a warrant, that sort of thing, but Jack was out for blood. In the end he and McAllister decided to bring Ricker in on their own. I don't know if Jack wanted it to go down like it did, but I don't think he was sorry. It was one of his four-sugar nights."

"What— what happened?"

"Jack and McAllister hit Ricker's place just after midnight. Jack went in the front, McAllister went in the back. Cowboys. They were hoping he was asleep."

"But he wasn't," Darcy guessed.

Ken shook his head.

"Ricker got the drop on McAllister. That's when Jack came around the corner. Ricker turned on Jack and managed to get off a shot. Hit him in the chest. Jack wasn't wearing a vest. The bullet lodged somewhere near his spine. It's still there."

"According to McAllister, Jack fired two at the same time. Hit Ricker in the shoulder and the forehead. McAllister says Jack saved his life and saved the province a shit load in court costs."

Ken seemed finished, literally and figuratively. Neither of them spoke for a long time. Finally Darcy broke the silence.

"So McAllister went on to become Chief and Jack. ..."

"Took a bit of a different path."

Darcy waited, knowing the curtain was about to come down on the final act.

"After the surgery Jack spent about six months on morphine and about four years on scotch. I think you know the rest."

Darcy nodded. "He told me some."

"That's the only part he will talk about. The recovery. Everything else is too painful. That's why I say he's damaged goods, Darcy. I'm not blowing smoke."

Darcy looked at the giant of a man beside her and managed a smile for the first time in an hour. There was no use pretending her feelings for Jack were purely professional. They weren't. She wasn't sure what they were, but they definitely weren't professional. She reached out and squeezed Ken's hand, wanting him to know that she'd heard every word.

"So ... if he follows me home, can I keep him?"

Ken smiled too. "He isn't house broken."

"So what man doesn't need a little work?"

Ken put the unmarked in drive. Darcy leaned back in her seat, more than a little happy to be leaving the quiet of the cemetery to those who had gone before.

CHAPTER FORTY-THREE

With something this big, Jack decided to bypass the usual reporting structure and go straight to the top. The Chief's office was near the back on the 7th floor. McAllister was older than Jack, but you'd never know it. He wasn't tall, but his military bearing and sheer presence in a room made him seem tall. He kept his hair close cropped so it was hard to tell where the blond left off and the gray started. For some reason, whenever Jack saw the man the word 'compact' always sprang to mind. The Chief was lean and athletic, confident and gregarious, and had been a police officer for the better part of 40 years. He was a cop's cop. Jack hoped he'd be able to see what was happening without saying 'Prove it."

McAllister watched the rain hit his window, whipped by gusting winds that made it sound like bacon frying in the pan. The day was cold and gray, a throw back to early April. Yesterday's sunshine was a distant memory.

Jack stood, feeling like a new recruit at the Academy, and waited for the decision. He'd been in the office for more than an hour, giving the facts and answering questions. McAllister's voice floated out from behind the chair like a disembodied spirit.

"Okay, it all sounds perfectly logical to me."

Jack tensed, hearing cynicism in The Chief's voice.

"And your information comes from a confessed felon and a computer you had to break into to read."

Jack hadn't told him that Calvin Dempster's thirteen year-old son was now an accomplice.

"Chief, I realize it sounds a bit …"

"Ludicrous?" McAllister offered.

"Yes … but there's more here than meets the eye. I know my information isn't exactly rock solid, but—"

"You can say that again," McAllister agreed, shaking his head.

"I have a hunch that—"

"A hunch?" The Chief interrupted again.

"Yes sir." There was something about the office itself that he had to respond formally.

"Not many people work on hunches anymore, Jack. The courts don't allow it. They call it profiling."

"I know, but—"

"Don't bother finishing. It isn't that hard to see what's happening here."

Jack held his breath, feeling like a convicted felon waiting to hear his sentence. He was sure it wasn't going to be good. He couldn't have been more wrong.

"It's obvious there's more here than meets the eye. Any case you put together, if and when you catch these guys, is probably going to be tossed but …"

"I don't want any more blood on my streets, and this has the potential to spill a lot of blood," he continued. "Figure this thing out, but continue to do it quietly"

McAllister swung around to face Jack. He wasn't smiling.

"No press releases, no extra man power, and no overtime. The Police Services Board has been chewing on my ass for the better part of a week for spending money like water and I have no idea how we're going to cover the deficit. Makes me look like a bad manager."

"Or a good leader," Jack offered. He and McAllister had often discussed the difference between the two and came to the same conclusion—they'd take a good leader over a great manager any day of the week.

For the first time since Jack walked into the office McAllister smiled.

"I remember what it's like to follow a hunch, Jack. But I also remember every once in a while it got us in a world of hurt."

Jack was too lost in a distant memory to offer a response.

After a minute, the Chief continued, "Run with this one Jack, but keep me in the loop … unofficially." The meeting was obviously over.

"Thanks Mac."

Jack felt comfortable enough now to drop the façade of formality, but something still wasn't quite right. As Jack turned to leave, his mind thinking about the tasks ahead, McAllister swiveled in his chair to resume studying the rain that pelted against his window. Just before Jack's hand reached for the door knob he heard McAllister's voice cut through the room like the low rumble of distant thunder.

"You know how it goes, Jack. I'm a politician now. If you're right, I'm going to steal your thunder and use it to get the Board off my back."

Jack waited, knowing what was coming.

"But if you're wrong, we never had this conversation. Understood?"

"Yes sir."

Jack left the room smiling. All was right with the world.

CHAPTER FORTY-FOUR

As promised, Jack called Darcy as soon as he left McAllister. She was just leaving Dr. Cohen's office and didn't seem in the best mood.

"How did it go?" Jack asked.

"Peachy," Darcy replied. "I think she's my new BFF. We're doing lunch next week."

"Sounds like you two really bonded."

"Don't piss me off, Jack. They haven't taken away my guns … yet."

Jack understood her frustration, having been on the same couch in the past.

"Sorry. Would you shoot me if I told you I know how it feels?"

"Probably, but I can save that for later. What did Andrew come up with? More importantly, what did McAllister say?"

"Why don't we save it until we get together and I can tell you the whole story. Cal's headed over to my place right now. You up for a little strategy session?"

"Really? After what I just went through you're going to make me wait? Seriously?"

"It'll be worth the wait. I promise."

"I've heard that line too many times in the past and you know what?"

"What?"

"It never is. See you in an hour."

By mid-afternoon the three of them were back at the kitchen table in Jack's house on Admiral Road. The files Andrew managed to print were spread out in three loosely organized piles. The first pile consisted of a full brief on a security system called a LaserTech 25, the second the blueprints for a nondescript building, and the third appeared to be a military shopping list.

The pile of papers dealing with the LaserTech 25 was the largest. It contained a full service manual, a wiring diagram, installation instructions, and specification sheets. Infrared sensors, motion detectors, laser electronic eyes, and the monitoring stations were all explained in great detail.

The next pile consisted of only two pages, with sparse computer generated lines that appeared to represent the floor plans for a building. They reminded Jack of the Gestalt pictures he studied in university. Given there were no descriptive markings of any kind on the plans, the blueprints could have represented any one of a thousand buildings in Toronto, anything from the Ontario Science Center to the Monkey House at the Toronto Zoo.

The last few sheets of paper detailed a list of men and equipment. It looked like a checklist for the Navy Seals— personnel, communications, small weapons issue, light machine gun detail, explosive supplies; everything necessary to start a small war.

Despite the intriguing nature of the material, the first thing Calvin and Darcy wanted to know was what McAllister had to say.

"He said go for it."

Calvin and Darcy looked at Jack to see if he was joking. Surprise was written all over their faces. Finally Calvin broke the spell.

"You're kidding."

Jack shook his head. "I'm not."

"No shit?"

"No shit," Jack said. "It's an official investigation, sort of.'"

"What do you mean 'sort of'?" Darcy asked.

"If we're right," Jack said, "and we nail these guys, McAllister gets to ride the glory train."

"I could just about script that press conference," Calvin said.

"And if we're wrong?" Darcy asked. "Or if shit hits the fan?"

"No problem," Jack said, grinning. "McAllister and I never had that conversation, the investigation was done without authorization, and I'm on my own."

"We're on our own," Calvin corrected.

Jack shook his head. "He doesn't know anything about you two, and I want to keep it that way. He okayed a small investigation. No extra people, no overtime. Besides, I think I better take it from here. Things are going to heat up for you over at Guns and Gangs, Cal, and Darcy, you start days what … day after tomorrow? Besides, if Karski ever found out you were involved in this he'd go ballistic."

This brought a storm of protest from both Darcy and Calvin. The yelling got so loud Charlie abandoned his post at Darcy's ankles and headed out for parts unknown.

Jack finally held up his hands in mock surrender.

"Okay, I give up, but your part has to stay unofficial."

"No problem," Calvin said.

"No problem," Darcy agreed.

"Well, it might be for you Darcy. You're back with the ETF in a couple of days. That won't leave you much time for doing any leg work on this, and that's what it's going to take … a lot of leg work."

"I've got twelve weeks of vacation saved up. Karski's been bugging me to take some time, even before the … shooting."

Her hesitation was only for a split second. Jack noticed, but chose to ignore it. That decision would come back to haunt him later.

"So what's the first step?" Calvin asked.

"Coffee?" Jack looked from one to the other. Both nodded in unison.

Jack laughed, and set about putting a pot on to brew. When it was done, and everyone had a steaming cup close at hand, Darcy brought them back to the task at hand.

"So what's the plan?"

"The first thing we need to figure out is where. Darcy, you get the needle in the hay stack. The blueprints. They give you damned little to go on—just corridors and rooms.—but maybe if you ask the right people they'll see something we don't. You could try City Hall, the

Planning Department or the Building Department. Check the library, architectural firms, design schools, the works. Anything you can think of. If it's a relatively new building maybe somebody will recognize the floor plan. It's a lot of running around and a long shot for sure, but …"

"No sweat. I have a contact at the university, a professor of architecture, maybe he can help me out."

"If that turns out to be a dead end, you could get on to the RCMP and the DND. See if they're having any luck with a photo of Denis Brousseau. If you get one we can put it on the wire and ask for information and known associates. The investigation's official now."

"Sort of," Darcy said.

Jack smiled, but let it go.

"What about me?" Calvin asked.

"We have to figure out if they're still planning to go through with it."

"Supplies?" Calvin asked.

"You got it," Jack said. "Unless these guys have an arsenal at their disposal, they'll need to buy some new shit."

"If they go for the same stuff, it should cause a ripple on the street," Calvin agreed.

"That's another thing," Jack said. "The list on the computer doesn't exactly fit what was seized at the apartment. There's no mention of M72's. And why go to the expense of buying Uzis when Mac 10s will do the same job?"

Darcy remained quiet in the background.

"And there seems to be a lot more C4 listed than we found," Calvin noticed. "Do you think there's more of that stuff floating around out there?"

"It's possible," Jack conceded, "if they bought that much, but it might just be a mistake. Maybe they didn't need as much as they first thought."

"Or maybe whoever put that list together doesn't know what he's talking about," Darcy said.

Jack turned to look at Darcy who was staring out the window into the back yard.

"What makes you say that?" Jack asked.

"It makes sense. Maybe this guy, Oscar … maybe he's just an idea man. Maybe he doesn't know what it takes to pull a job like this, but he wants to look like he does, so he puts together a list of men and equipment after surfing the internet or reading a book. Maybe this list was written before he hired the people who are actually going to do the job."

"Wolfe," Jack said.

Darcy nodded.

"And when Wolfe starts looking at the job he realizes there's way too much C4."

"And maybe he likes having the firepower of a few M72's," Calvin said.

"All I know," Darcy said, "is that whoever made this list up is no professional."

Jack's eyes narrowed as he began to see the truth. "But whoever bought the stuff we seized is."

"Is what?" Calvin asked.

"A professional," Jack said.

"A professional what?"

"You said it yourself, Darcy … about Tinker. You said he looked like he'd been under fire his whole life. He was calm and controlled. A real professional. Who else would have a preference for a certain gun, one that he feels comfortable with, one he knows? And who else would know how much C4 it takes for a specific job, or feel comfortable having rocket launchers around … just in case."

"A professional soldier," Calvin said, putting in words what they were all thinking. "Oscar's hired mercenaries to carry out a jewelry heist!"

"It looks that way," Jack agreed.

"It's the only thing that makes sense." Calvin started to pace back and forth. "Oscar gets the idea to pull a robbery and hires Wolfe. Wolfe hires Ricco and Tinker …"

"And God knows who else," Darcy added.

"The whole thing is set up via the computer so that no one knows the ringleader. You were right, Jack. The hard drive *is* the key."

"Or was," Jack said.

"God help the people they plan on robbing," Darcy said. "Mercenaries are only good for one thing."

"What about you, Jack? What's on your agenda?"

"I want to talk to one of our sketch artists, work up a composite of the guy I saw over at The Don. I'll pass it by Ricco. If he ID's the sketch as Wolfe, I'll send it out, tell the guys on the street to keep their eyes open."

"Why not just go with the one Ricco gave us?" Calvin asked.

"I haven't had a chance to look at Ricco's sketch yet, so maybe we'll come up with two different views of the same guy. If not, if this guy's a chameleon, having two sketches could be an advantage."

"And then what?" Calvin asked. "We sit around and hope to get lucky? Even if your sketch is bang-on, the chances of one of our people seeing this guy aren't very good."

"I know, but it's all we have. That, and I have an appointment with a Mr. Benjamin Thurlow in about an hour."

"And he is?" Darcy asked.

"The president of the company that manufactures the LaserTech 25. From what I can see from these," Jack said, tapping the largest pile of papers on the table, "it's a pretty sophisticated piece of equipment. Leading edge stuff. There can't be a lot of places using it. If we can get a client list, maybe we can figure out which one of them has something worth stealing … like a fortune in gems. Or maybe we can match the blueprints to one of the buildings protected by a LaserTech."

"And if not? What then?" Calvin asked.

"We're back to square one and it becomes a waiting game."

"Waiting for something to break or for the robbery to be committed?" Darcy asked.

There was no humor in Jack's answer.

"Yes."

CHAPTER FOURTY-FIVE

"What you're asking for is highly confidential." Benjamin Thurlow, the president of LaserTech Security Inc., peered over top of reading glasses that perched precariously on the tip of his thin, sharp nose. His pinched features reminded Jack of an underfed ferret.

"I understand that, Mr. Thurlow, and under normal circumstances I wouldn't even consider approaching you with—"

"Without a search warrant?" Thurlow interrupted.

"—with such a request if it wasn't extremely important," Jack continued. "And we're working against a deadline that could have serious consequences for one of your clients. If we could get a list—"

"From what you've told me, Detective, you're not even sure one of my clients is involved. And I can assure you if one is, the LaserTech 25 is the most sophisticated security system in the world. It's virtually unassailable."

"I'm sure that's true in most cases, Mr. Thurlow, but given the expertise of the criminals involved—"

"Detective, we're not talking about your bargain basement burglar alarm here. These systems are state of the art."

"I understand, but—"

Benjamin Thurlow spent the next few minutes describing the virtues of the LaserTech 25, explaining how it was virtually impossible to beat the system. Jack felt like part of the audience at a sales conference.

"Very impressive, Mr. Thurlow," Jack said. "But my concern is that if somebody knew how the system works, it's possible ..."

Thurlow stiffened. "All of my people are carefully screened. If you're suggesting that one of my employees—"

"Not at all, sir. What I'm getting at is that, through trade journals or technical manuals, someone might have figured out a way to beat the system."

"Impossible."

"Why?"

Their conversation was momentarily interrupted by Thurlow's secretary who stepped into the office after a sharp knock.

"Coffee or tea, gentlemen?"

She was tall, well into her sixties, and impeccably dressed in a smartly tailored suit of lavender and cream. Her snow white hair was cut very short. She seemed the epitome of efficiency. When both men declined and she left the room, Thurlow picked up the discussion where they'd left off.

"There are no trade journals and our installation and service manuals are carefully monitored."

"Well, perhaps the designer ..." Jack ventured.

Benjamin Thurlow smiled, but his eyes belied the fact that he was anything but amused.

"I'm the designer, Detective Wright. The LaserTech 25 Security System is my creation. It was a solo effort. I spent five years developing the project."

"What about the actual engineering of the system?" Jack asked. "All of the components must be purchased from outside agencies."

"That's true, but simply having knowledge of the individual components wouldn't allow anyone to fathom the system as a whole."

"But—"

"Frankly, Detective, I'm getting a little bit offended by this conversation. The imputation that our products or people are somehow flawed ..."

"I'm sorry, Mr. Thurlow. I didn't mean to insult you or the company." Jack leaned forward in his chair. "It's just that we have credible Intel that a person or company using the LaserTech 25 is about to be the target of a major assault."

"It all sounds so military," Thurlow scoffed. "I mean really, how do you know this isn't some kind of an elaborate hoax."

"There's nothing about the case that suggests a hoax, Mr. Thurlow. All I'm asking is—"

"All you're asking, Detective Wright, is that I break client confidentiality to assist you with a crime that hasn't been committed yet, and one that may never happen. My business is based on the concept of trust. I trust my customers to pay their bills, and they trust me not to divulge any of their secrets. I take that trust very seriously."

"I understand the need for confidentiality and I promise I'll respect your clients' privacy. I guarantee the list will be destroyed at the end of the investigation."

"I'm sorry. It's quite impossible."

"Mr. Thurlow, you're in the field of security. Your company is paid to protect the property of your clients. I'm only trying to help you do that."

"Detective, I *am* protecting my clients … from you."

"I hope your clients see it that way when they find out you had a chance to step in and you did nothing? If there's a possibility that one of them may be the target …"

Thurlow's face flushed. "Don't threaten me, Detective. Nothing you've said so far has convinced me that any of my clients are in any danger at all."

"It's not a threat, Mr. Thurlow. If you don't—"

"I'm sorry, Detective Wright, I can't help you." Benjamin Thurlow stood as he spoke and moved toward the door. "Without a warrant I'm not at liberty to provide you with any information … even if I was so inclined."

"Mr. Thurlow, I wish you'd at least consider the request and—"

"I'm afraid that's impossible, Detective. Good day."

The interview was over.

Jack was so angry he didn't hear the footsteps following him down the hall. When the elevator doors slid open, he felt a push in the middle of his back that forced him into the lift. As the doors slid shut with barely an audile whisper, Jack spun around, fists clenched, and found himself starring down into eyes that were the same shade of lavender as the suit worn by the woman in front of him.

"Sorry to push, Detective, but I thought you might stand there forever," the woman said. She pressed the button for the parking garage. "I wanted to talk to you, but I didn't want it to become the topic of office gossip." Her tone, like her manner, was no-nonsense.

"I'm sorry," Jack began, "you're Mr. Thurlow's—"

"I'm Virginia Lloyd-Kendall. Lloyd's my maiden name and I should have left well enough alone," she said, as if that explained her whole life.

Jack liked her immediately. He was about to like her a lot more. Before he could introduce himself, however, Virginia continued in a business-like fashion that suggested the agenda had already been set.

"I'll walk you to your car. It will give us a chance to get acquainted. You're on P3?"

"Yes. How did—"

"I make it my business to know everything that goes on in the building, Detective Wright. Do you mind if I call you Jack? I find titles to be off-putting, don't you?"

Jack didn't have a chance to respond.

"Good. And please, call me Virginia. I'll feel so much better doing what I'm about to do if it means helping a friend. You understand, don't you, Jack? Of course you do."

"I'm sorry, I'm not really sure—"

"Shh. All in good time, dear."

Virginia Lloyd-Kendall stared at the rapidly descending numbers above the doors. Jack used the time to observe his new friend in the polished steel of the elevator. She was impeccably dressed and from what Jack could tell the jewelry she wore was the real deal. She was what some people would describe as a handsome woman. Jack put her at 65, although she looked younger and was probably older.

When they reached P3, Virginia stepped off the elevator and walked what seemed to be a pre-determined distance along the garage wall before turning to face Jack.

"I believe we're safe here," Virginia said.

"Safe?" Jack said, looking around.

"Cameras, Jack. I'm sure you noticed. There's barely a spot in the building you can go without being front and center on a surveillance camera. After all, dear, we're a security firm."

Jack felt foolish, but Virginia didn't give him time to recover.

She pulled a large white envelope from inside her tailored jacket and handed it to Jack. The logo of LaserTech Security Inc. was printed across the middle on the front.

"I'd be obliged if you destroy the envelope before anyone else sees it. I didn't have anything else to put it in."

Jack instinctively stuffed the envelope inside his own jacket. He felt like a second rate spy in a bad movie.

"Is this—"

"The list you asked Mr. Thurlow for? Of course, dear. I hope you're not disappointed. I'm afraid my social calendar is all booked. This is the best I could do. Consider it a consolation prize."

"How did you—"

"I have my ways, Jack. I make it my business to know everything that goes on around here, and this is a security firm. We have all kinds of gizmos and gadgets to make my life easier. Technology can be a wonderful thing."

Jack was visibly shocked. "You bugged his office?"

"Don't look so surprised, Jack. I just do it to keep myself amused. It's harmless really, and quite simple. I installed it myself."

Jack shook his head in amazement and admiration.

"Why are you helping me?"

"I've worked for this company for more years than I care to remember. I was here long before the name was changed to LaserTech Security by that arrogant little man you met this afternoon."

"Mr. Thurlow."

"University educated, a genius in laser technology, and an egotistical pain in the ass."

Jack was through being surprised by anything Virginia had to say. He waited for her to continue.

"I used to work for the previous owner, Colonel Frank Danagher. He started the company after the war, mainly to give the men from his unit something to do. He was quite a man. Tall. Strong. Dynamic."

Jack watched a fleeting smile pass over Virginia's face.

"We supplied bodyguards to executives, royalty and some of the biggest stars in Hollywood. I met Bob Redford several times. It was always the people that mattered. It wasn't a matter of technology and gadgets. Frank always said he'd rather be guarded by one loyal man with half a brain than by all the computers in the world."

"But LaserTech Security is a leader in the field of high tech," Jack said. "What happened?"

"Progress." Virginia shrugged. "With the advent of cameras and monitors, motion detectors and infrared sensors, one man could do the work of twenty. The company went public back in the eighties, with share holders, quarterly reports—"

"And a Board of Directors," Jack finished for her.

"Precisely, my dear. I knew you were bright the second I laid eyes on you. Frank resisted the Board's call for modernization for a while and tried to protect his people. The Board finally got fed up and replaced him in his own company. It killed him, literally. He died of a massive coronary six months later."

"And you stayed on?"

"I had to. I had nowhere else to go. And besides, Frank created a lot of trust and loyalty among our clients, and I guess I feel a little responsible for them. The last bastion of warmth in a cold business, if you will."

"So you make sure that Benjamin Thurlow doesn't completely lose touch with the real world by using his own technology to keep him in check?"

"Apropos, don't you think?" She said. Virginia dropped her hand on his. Her touch was warm and light. She looked up at him and held his gaze for a few seconds.

"When you find what you're looking for, I'll hear from you?"

It was phrased as a question but Jack was smart enough to know it was anything but. Virginia walked quickly back to the elevator without waiting for an answer.

CHAPTER FORTY-SIX

After leaving LaserTech and stopping at the Don Jail to show his sketch to Ricco, Jack sent out copies of the two composites of Wolfe to every officer on the force. McAllister said no 'official' media releases. He never said anything about an internal bulletin.

Within an hour, photocopies of the composites had started to leak out to the press. Wolfe wasn't the only one with sources inside the department.

As tempting as it was, none of the legitimate media outlets did anything with them. The tabloids, however, were a different story. They cared about selling newspapers, not about the truth. The banner headline in one of the sleazier papers, printed in huge boldface type read, ***Killer on the Loose!***

"Well, it's not a great likeness," Morgan said, leaning back on his bedroll, "but I wouldn't go strolling around the city for a few days."

Unlike Wolfe's part of the loft, Morgan's was cluttered with various pieces of equipment and clothing thrown here and there. The only thing placed with any care was the new 9mm. Beretta, tucked close at hand under the right side of his bedding.

Wolfe stood by the open window in a shaft of sunlight studying the pictures. His source at the department had identified the author of both. The first wasn't a surprise. He expected Ricco to fold. But the second one was something else. For such a brief encounter, the detail was damned accurate.

Who are you, Detective Wright, and why so interested in the stories of a two bit criminal like Ricco?

Wolfe could feel Morgan staring at him. "What have you got in mind, Johnny? You're starting to make me nervous."

In answer, Wolfe flipped open his phone and punched in a number. The phone was picked up almost immediately.

"Records, Postma."

"Hey. Can you talk?"

"Yeah, sure, just let me …" Wolfe could hear the squeak of chair wheels as Officer Postma moved to a different location. "Yeah, go ahead. It's cool."

"Good. Listen, just wanted to say thanks for the sketch. My Editor loved it."

"No problem. Thanks for contributing to my favorite charity."

Wolfe put on a chuckle that sounded phony, even to him, but Postma didn't seem to notice.

"Just remember to forget where you got it, okay?"

"Done," Wolfe replied. And then, "By the way, meant to ask you. What can you tell me about a guy named Wright— Jack Wright— works Hold-up? I want to do a sidebar on him. Human interest piece."

"What do you need?"

Wolfe smiled into the handset.

"Everything."

CHAPTER FORTY-SEVEN

Katherine and Pavel sat at a small dining room table in one corner of his elegant suite, the wreckage of a room-service gourmet brunch scattered between them. She'd been unable to convince him to venture out even as far as the restaurant on the main floor, which was just as well. It would have been a waste. Katherine did little more than push a few olives around her plate with a fork and drink cup after cup of the rich hotel coffee.

"So, our presentation ... your Board of Directors ... is small, no?"

"A handful of old men, Pavel. Nothing to worry about," Katherine said.

"Then why are *you* worried?"

"I'm sorry?" She said, refilling their glasses with Perrier from a bottle wrapped in a linen towel. Pavel stopped her in mid pour and forced her to look at him.

"Katerina, I've known you what ... twenty years?" His smile was kind, but sad. "You think I can't tell when something is bothering you?"

Katherine said nothing.

"You don't look at me, your mind is somewhere else, and you don't eat your lunch," Pavel said. "You love smoked salmon, but today you don't touch. Why?"

Katherine forced herself to look directly into his eyes.

"I'm fine, really. There's just so much going on." Katherine hesitated. "So much I have to tell you ... and I don't know where to start."

"Beginning," Pavel said, his smile brightening. "Or ending. Lots of stories in Russia start at the end. It doesn't matter so much as long as you start. Trust me."

"I do trust you … and you trusted me. That's the problem," Katherine said. "You shouldn't have."

Pavel looked at her without speaking. With a furrowed brow and his head cocked to one side, he reminded Katherine of a confused Labrador retriever.

"I brought you over here on false pretenses," she said finally.

"False—"

"I lied."

"We're not making presentation to Board?" Pavel asked.

"Oh, we are," Katherine said. "Just not for the reasons you think."

"I don't understand." Pavel took Katherine's hand and pulled her gently over to the couch, patting the cushion as he sat. "It's me, Pavel. Sit. Talk."

Katherine looked into his soulful brown eyes and wished she could be anywhere else, rather than sitting there about to break the heart of her only friend.

"You said we had to make presentation to Board, to show them our progress so the funding continues, yes? That's why I had to bring processors. The Board has to see we're not wasting the money. That's what you said."

"I—"

Katherine couldn't find the words. How could she tell him the truth? He knew nothing of the contract or what lay ahead. She stared at her hands and hated herself on so many levels, but mostly for being such a coward. He deserved the truth, to know that he was right after all, that the world was a dangerous place and that everyone – without exception – was only in it for their own gain, even the people you loved and trusted the most. She needed to just say it, destroy his faith and expectations, and get him back on a plane to Russia. But it was Pavel who broke the silence.

"But that's not what we're going to do."

Something in his voice made her look up at him. He wasn't asking a question, he was making a statement. There was something in his inflection that sounded a lot like cockiness. And the smile on his face …

"We're going to do something much, much better," he continued, patting her hand affectionately. "We're going to show them just how well their money was spent. So no more worries. Eat your salmon. I have surprise."

Now it was Katherine's turn to look confused.

"I don't understand, Pavel, what are you talking about?"

"Your Board," Pavel said. "They want proof, yes? Proof their money is well invested?"

"Yes, but—"

"Then we give them proof," Pavel said, a look of pride replacing the cockiness.

"I still don't—"

"The processors, Katerina. We give them the processors … and your wonderful programs. What more proof do they need?"

"But Pavel, they don't work. That's why I've had to—you don't understand.'

"No, Katerina, you don't understand," he said, a smile breaking across his whole face. "That's what I've been trying to tell you. Why I agreed to come all the way over here to see you. That's my surprise. I've stabilized the compound. The processors work!"

CHAPTER FORTY-EIGHT

Once the shock wore off, Katherine opened up and let it all out. She spent the next two hours pacing and talking until there was nothing left to say. She told Pavel about the contract, about The Plan, about Wolfe, and about the police raid that started things on a downward spiral. She explained why she needed him to come to Canada, and why she was now desperate for him to leave. She said she'd make it up to him somehow, but right now he had to go. It wasn't safe.

Throughout it all Pavel sat in silence, too stunned to speak. He'd come to Canada to see Katherine and to share his wonderful news. He'd even hoped he might finally be able to tell her how he really felt about her. Now everything was in tatters. He felt deflated, unable to speak and unable to listen to another word. He couldn't bring himself to look at her. In the end, when it was obvious Katherine had nothing more to say, he simply picked up the phone and asked the Concierge to connect him to Aeroflot.

When Katherine left, he didn't say good-bye. He didn't say anything. There was nothing left to say. He didn't want her to make it up to him. He didn't want anything from her. She could have the processors that were locked away in her shiny vault. He wanted nothing more to do with them or her, ever.

An hour later Katherine was back in her office, her elbows pressed into the mirrored surface of her desk, her face buried in her hands. A glass of water and a bottle of Imetrix, a powerful headache medication, were the only things in reach. For a brief second Katherine couldn't decide whether to take one or the whole bottle. The thought passed quickly. She pressed the intercom button.

"Jane, do I have anything urgent on the books? Anything we can't reschedule?"

"Another migraine?" Jane guessed. Even through the speaker Katherine could tell Jane was very thoughtfully softening her voice.

"As usual. Please tell me you can work some magic and get me out of here."

Jane hesitated and Katherine's heart sank. "I'm guessing that's a no."

"Detective Sergeant Wright with the Toronto Police Hold-Up Squad called while you were at lunch. He asked for a few minutes. I couldn't get a hold of you and he said it was important. I made it tentative. He'll be here any minute, but I can put him off. Do you want me to reschedule? Katherine?"

"Ms. Sharpe? I'm Jack Wright." Jack refrained from using his official title. He found it much easier to build a rapport if people could forget he was a police officer, even for a few minutes.

"Jack Wright, Detective Sergeant, Toronto Police Service, Hold-up Squad," she said, reading from the card he'd given her secretary. "To what do I owe the pleasure?"

"I'm—"

"Please, have a seat," she said, pointing to a chair.

"Thank you. I appreciate you taking the time."

"My pleasure. I'd like to help the police if I can, but I have to say, I'm a little confused. We've never had a hold-up at ComTech. I can't even imagine what that would be like. How can I help?"

Jack waited a second before responding to collect his thoughts and to do what he did best … observe. Katherine Sharpe was on the right side of 40, tall, slim and very attractive. Her ash blond hair was bobbed in a stylish cut that framed a long face. Her green eyes were a vibrant contradiction to her pale skin. She seemed comfortable and at ease, a successful woman very much at home in her element and with herself.

"Actually, I'm hoping to find out about your company."

"Of course," Katherine responded brightly. "What do you need to know?"

"Information regarding what you produce and if there's something special you're working on right now."

"Everything we produce is special, Detective, that's how we stay in business," Katherine said with a mischievous grin, "But I take it that's not what you're after."

"Not exactly." Jack laughed, but then pressed on. "I understand you're the owner of the company, but you're also in charge of Research & Development."

"That's what they tell me," Katherine laughed, "but sometimes I wonder."

"Is there anything *extra* special on the go right now?" Jack chose his words carefully.

"Do you mind if I ask why you need to know?" Katherine inquired.

Jack decided to lay his cards on the table. He had a good feeling about this woman, and it seemed highly unlikely she would be involved in a plan to rob her own company. He'd have to admit later that it wasn't one of his better judgments.

"We're investigating the possibility that ComTech might be the target of a robbery in the near future."

"Seriously?" Katherine seemed genuinely shocked.

"It's a possibility," Jack said. "One of many we're running down."

"Okay, but what would make ComTech a target? What are they after?"

"That's what I was hoping you could tell me." Jack didn't elaborate.

"Well, we deal in computer technology, hardware and software. I suppose computers—the hardware—is worth stealing, but most of that is stored off site. Is the robbery supposed to take place here, or at one of our warehouses?"

"We don't know."

"When's it supposed to happen?"

"We don't know that either," Jack admitted.

Katherine Sharpe leaned back into the soft leather of the couch, a smile playing at the corner of her mouth.

"Is this some kind of a joke, Detective?"

"I realize it sounds a little absurd, but I'm afraid I'm serious. We have reliable information that someone who installed a LaserTech 25 is being targeted for a robbery. We don't know when and we don't know who, but the list of people who use that particular system is pretty small."

"Which only leaves one question," Katherine said. "What's a LaserTech 25?"

Jack wasn't sure if she was being serious or not, so he waited.

"I'm sorry, Detective. I have absolutely no idea what you're talking about. What is it?"

Katherine's smile was dazzling and her green eyes sparkled with good humor.

"It's a very expensive security system manufactured here in Toronto," Jack said.

"Oh, that explains it," Katherine said. "It also explains some of the checks I've signed since Brad Mikstas came on board."

Jack waited for her to explain.

"Brad Mikstas is our new head of security. We hired him about a year ago. I leave anything to do with security up to him. He came highly recommended, but as I recall, he also came with a wish list a mile long."

"If you don't mind me asking, Katherine, if there's nothing worth stealing at ComTech, why all the security?"

Katherine shook her head. Her expression became serious.

"It's not that we have nothing of value here, Detective. I didn't mean to give you that impression at all. We do. Some of the schematics and programs we have locked away in the vault would be worth millions to a competitor. It's just there's nothing particularly interesting happening right now. We have big plans for the future, but they're a long way off. There's nothing really earth shattering on the horizon. I wish there was, but there really isn't. And I wish I could help you more, but I really can't."

"No problem," Jack replied. "Like I said, we have to check out every possibility."

"Maybe you should speak with Brad. He might be more helpful," Katherine said. "I could set it up for you today if you'd like. If nothing else, he may be able to help you cross us off the list."

"I'd appreciate that," Jack said. "But before I go let me ask you one more question. Do you use any precious metals or crystals in your manufacturing, something someone might mistake for jewels?"

While Jack was meeting with Brad Mikstas, Katherine Sharpe was in her washroom trying not to throw up. Everything was going to hell. The Plan was coming undone at the seams.

How did the police find out about ComTech? Wolfe is the only other person who knows the whole plan and he wouldn't say anything to anybody. Which means they must have hacked the hard drive … but how? Nobody alive could defeat those security programs.

But even as the thought occurred to her, she knew it wasn't true. Where there's a will, there's a way.

Think, damn it! If they only broke into some of the files, what else do they know? What's their next move? More importantly, what's my next move? The CPUs work. We did what I said we would. The deadline is null and void. I don't need to steal anything now. It was all for nothing.

The irony of the situation pounded into her brain again and again, like the dull thud of heavy surf against the shore. She felt like flotsam caught in between two rocks. It was time to take back control, and there was only one way to do that. *But how in the hell do you fire someone like Wolfe?*

CHAPTER FORTY-NINE

"What's this?" Calvin asked, when Jack dropped a number of folders on the table. They were back in the kitchen of Jack's house on Admiral Road.

"These," Jack corrected.

"Okay, these. What are these? You an English teacher now?" Calvin shot back. Darcy chuckled in the corner.

"These," Jack said, with a pointed look at Darcy, "are companies currently using the LaserTech 25. If I'm right, one of them is the target."

Calvin and Darcy moved in for a closer look.

"You mean LaserTech just handed over the list? No warrant?"

"Not exactly. I'll tell you about it later."

"Who did you have to kill?" Darcy asked with a smile.

"Nobody," Jack said, "I just turned on the old Wright charm."

"No, really," Darcy said. "Who did you have to kill?"

"Listen, Caldwell—"

"So what's the next step?" Calvin interrupted

Jack looked at Calvin and then back at Darcy, who stuck her tongue out at him. Jack chose to ignore it.

"Before we get to that, what have you come up with?" Jack asked.

"Just this, and I don't think you're gonna like it," Calvin said, handing a manila envelope to Jack.

"It's the service record of Denis Brousseau, Royal Canadian Air Force, complete with photo. Two years as a regular grunt. Went on to specialize in demolitions. Dishonorably discharged 22nd July, 1994 for

209

reportedly blowing up his commander's quarters. Apparently he didn't like being turned down for a spot on JTF2."

"JTF2?" Jack asked.

"Joint Task Force Two," Darcy said. "The Canadian version of Delta Force."

"The psyche test tripped him up," Calvin said. "They dropped him from the list and about a week later, eight buildings on his base mysteriously disappeared in a cloud of smoke. The case against him wasn't solid, mostly rumors and speculation, but when they offered him the discharge instead of a court martial, he jumped at it and disappeared."

Jack pulled an 8x10 glossy out of the envelope and looked at the face of a very young Tinker. "Any known associates?"

"A few," Calvin said. "But all of them are dead or missing. Hazards of the job."

"Well, at least we know we're dealing with professionals. Good work, Cal."

"Uh … actually it was Darcy."

Jack looked at Darcy with feigned admiration, and Darcy countered by holding out her hand. "You may kiss my ring."

"You can kiss my—"

Calvin cleared his throat. "Moving right along. Which one of these do you want me to start with?"

Jack slapped Darcy's still extended hand out of the way playfully and turned his attention back to the folders on the desk.

"There are nine. Grab three each."

"Only nine?" Calvin asked.

"The system is state of the art, brand new, and very expensive. They've only installed nine systems in the Greater Toronto Area."

"How can they stay in business when they only sell nine systems in a year?"

"Nine in the GTA. Their clientele is mostly international," Jack said.

"That, and the price tag is astronomical," Jack added, flipping open a price list and dropping it in front of Calvin. "The figure circled is their basic system."

Calvin whistled.

"Any of the nine deal in jewels?" Darcy asked.

"A couple. You guys take a look and tell me what you think. Try and get an appointment with someone near the top, but be very careful what you say and to who."

"Whom," Darcy corrected.

Jack gave her a look.

"Well you started it," she said innocently.

"We've got to remember that somebody on the inside of one of these companies could be dirty, probably is."

Darcy and Calvin both nodded.

"Are you guys up for a dinner meeting day after tomorrow? That'll give you two days to do some digging. I can warm up the barbecue and we can meet back here at … say … seven, seven thirty?"

Both nodded again in unison. Jack shook his head as he walked out the door. It was like working with the Bobsy Twins.

CHAPTER FIFTY

"We have to talk."

Wolfe had given her a number in case of an emergency. He was pretty sure what she had to say wouldn't qualify.

"I'm listening," Wolfe said, casually flipping a knife at a packing crate some twenty feet away, scoring a perfect hit in an 'O' stenciled on the side. Morgan pulled the knife from the case he was using as a seat. He tossed it underhand back to Wolfe who caught it by the blade without cutting himself.

"Not on the phone. We have to meet."

"I thought that was against the rules," Wolfe said, sarcastically.

"Things have changed."

"How so?"

"For god's sake, didn't you see the papers?! Your face is all over the front page."

"You mean the tabloids? No big deal. I just won't go out dancing for a while."

"I'm not joking."

"Neither am I. Let's move on. What else is on your mind?"

"I told you, not on the phone. We have to meet in person, somewhere safe."

"That's impossible now. Too dangerous ... for me."

"Then you can forget the whole thing."

That got Wolfe's attention. There was a note of determination in the woman's voice. He stopped his arm in mid throw and sat up.

"Come again?"

"I said either we meet now or you can forget the whole thing."

"Okay," Wolfe said, deciding to hear her out. "What did you have in mind?"

"I don't understand you, Johnny. Why bring her here?"

"What do you think I should do, Patrick? Walk around until some cop digs his head out of his ass long enough to recognize me from the tabloids?"

"I still don't like it. There are always options."

Unlike Morgan, Wolfe didn't see any viable alternatives. It was a risk, no doubt, but one he could handle quickly and quietly.

"She's a woman, Patrick," he said, as if that said it all.

"Then why deal with her at all? Why not steal the processors now and be done with it? Sell them to the highest bidder."

Being someone who never learned to share his toys, Wolfe wasn't about to tell Patrick about what was really at stake. Instead, he told him just enough to shut him up.

"She's the only one who knows when the merchandise will be in place," Wolfe said. "Without her we could move too soon. Besides, she has the security codes for the main building and access to the vault. Without her we'd have to bypass the security system and blow the safe. Not on my agenda this time around."

Patrick didn't ask for more information than was necessary to do the job, and Wolfe didn't offer.

"So we need her?"

Wolfe shrugged, "For now."

CHAPTER FIFTY-ONE

Katherine parked her car near the address Wolfe gave her, across from the dreary facade of an abandoned slaughterhouse. Convincing Wolfe to meet in person had seemed like a small victory. Now she wasn't so sure. She was glad she took the precautions she did, one of which was loaded and tucked into the side pocket of her purse.

The air felt damp and heavy, despite the fact that it was almost nine in the evening. Nothing moved. There wasn't enough breeze to rustle the trash along the gutter. The building in front of her was dark and forbidding, like the task ahead. Everything she had and everything she wanted for the future was riding on her ability to get Wolfe to see reason. They couldn't possibly go through with it now – that would be insane – and they didn't have to. She'd pay him well just to walk away. It was the best thing for everyone involved. He had to see that.

She walked up a short flight of stairs to get to the loading bay. The battered steel man-door next to the big roll-up was unlocked, as Wolfe said it would be. Katherine pushed it open. Steel on steel screamed, shattering the still night air.

Katherine was immediately hit with the smell of urine and decay. She felt her stomach lurch. She wanted to leave, but she wasn't about to back down now. She'd been in worse places in her life, literally and metaphorically. Wolfe was just one more man in a long list of men she'd had to handle, one way or another. She took a last breath of fresh air before plunging into the darkness.

Katherine's heart was beating like a trip hammer, but she squared her shoulders and pressed on. The building was dank and fetid. The scurrying and scampering of very little feet rustled all around her. When her eyes adjusted to the dark she could see the gaping hole of the elevator against the far wall. She ducked beneath the jagged pipes of the safety gate and stepped tentatively into the car. When she rocked the brass handle backward, as Wolfe had instructed, the platform dropped a foot before a hidden mechanism caught and started it moving slowly upwards. She felt like an actor being raised from the bowels of the theater, about to take center stage, not sure if she was supposed to be in a comedy or a tragedy.

The ancient motor on the service elevator cranked to life. It sounded worse now than it had when he'd first arrived. Wolfe turned to Morgan.

"You'd better make yourself scarce. I don't want Oscar to see you."

"Or me her?" Morgan said.

"The golden goose," Wolfe said, shrugging his shoulders with his palms upraised.

"You don't trust anyone, do you Johnny?"

"No. Get out of here. There's a trap door over by the far wall. It leads to an old conveyor system. Take the fire escape to the street."

"I was wondering about something like that," Morgan said. "Never known you to lock yourself in without a way out. How much time do you need?"

"An hour, no more. See if you can find a copy of The Star."

"Starting a scrapbook?" The heavy trap door fell into place behind Patrick, cutting him off in mid-chuckle.

Wolfe slipped into the shadows as the elevator groaned to a stop about two feet below where it should have.

Katherine climbed out of the elevator. A Coleman lamp to her left gave off enough of a glow to see where not to put her hands. When she straightened up she found herself face to face with Wolfe, not more than a foot away. He seemed to come out of nowhere. She stared up into his gray eyes. They looked black in the dim light. The sheer power of the man took her breath away. Her mind jumped back twenty years to another man she'd come to fear and eventually hate. Her hand instinctively brushed the bulge in the side pocket of her purse like a child stroking a beloved stuffed animal for comfort.

Before she could lose her nerve, Katherine said what she came to say. She told him about the CPUs, about Pavel's success, and about how they no longer needed to steal anything. She told him it was over, that his services were no longer required.

Wolfe sat passively staring off into space and Katherine wondered if he was listening at all. As it turned out, Wolfe had listened to every word she said. As it turned out, she'd said too much.

"So Pavel's here ... and he knows everything?"

Katherine realized her mistake, but it was too late and there was no point in trying to lie. Instead she said nothing. Check!

"When you prove to Sumner the CPUs work, you'll own 49 percent of a company worth billions. Not bad."

She looked into his face and could just make out the start of a grin. It reminded her of the wolf in a Grimm's fairy tale. Mistake number two. Check!

"I'll pay you what I promised" she said finally. "But it's got to stop now."

Wolfe didn't seem to be listening anymore.

"But what if Sumner thinks the CPUs don't work? Our operation nullifies the performance guarantees as planned and you still own half. To Sumner it would appear to be worth much less than it is. What happens then?"

Wolfe answered his own question. "Standard shotgun clause. One of you buys the other out? In this case, you buy Sumner out at a reasonable price, I arrange the financing, and *we* own one hundred percent of a company worth billions. Even better."

Katherine was too shocked to speak. The idea was absurd. She had no intention of owning anything with this lunatic. But she realized her third mistake might just be a fatal one. She should never have under-estimated the man. He wasn't merely a hired gun, and he was completely insane. Checkmate!

CHAPTER FIFTY-TWO

"It's not over," he said, as if the decision was his to make. "We go ahead as planned. You do exactly what I say and we both end up with more than you ever dreamed."

Katherine stared at him, trying to understand what just happened. A paradigm shift seemed to have taken place in the shadows around them. Their roles had somehow reversed. She could feel her tenuous grasp on the situation slipping away. A flutter of panic started in the pit of her stomach. She needed to make him understand she was still in charge.

"We're done," she said. "The police already suspect ComTech's a target. I just spent an hour trying to convince a detective he was wrong. If I have to, I'll go to the police myself. Tell them everything. It's over. Can't you see that?"

"No, it's not." His words came out like a growl, more feral than human. "You need to finish what you started."

As if to emphasize the point, Wolfe pointed a .9 mm Browning High Power at her forehead. Katherine's bladder almost let go, but she managed to hold it together.

"I'm not going through with it. Without me, you haven't got a chance."

Wolfe pulled the hammer back on the pistol. The snap was so loud in the still of the loft Katherine wondered for a second if the gun had gone off. When she realized she was still standing she gritted her teeth and stared him down. She refused to let him see the fear that threatened to break out in a scream.

"Go ahead. Then it really will be over … for both of us. You'll get nothing and the police will know everything about you."

Wolfe's eyes narrowed. He waited for her to continue. Katherine took a deep breath.

"If I don't make it back to ComTech tonight, a computer in my office will e-mail every police department, TV station and newspaper in the country—a complete file on you and the plan. Pictures,videos from our surveillance system, everything."

She could see both surprise and anger in his eyes, but there was something else. Something that looked a lot like admiration.

"Very nice," he said, tucking the pistol in the waistband at the back of his pants.

"I'll pay you what I owe you," she said. "But it's over."

"The detective who came to see you this afternoon, what's his name?"

"What? That's not—"

"The name?" Something in the way he asked made Katherine answer without further argument.

"Wright."

Wolfe nodded in recognition. "What did he say?"

"He knew about our security system. He asked if we were developing anything special."

"What did you tell him?"

"That we weren't but—"

"Anything else?"

"Isn't that enough?" Katherine said. "He wanted to know what we do, if we use gold or precious gems. He said they had a reliable source. For Christ's sake, Ricco's been spilling his guts. They've got the hard drive. If they've hacked into that they have everything. It's over, can't you see that? If you kill me the computer will finish the job. Just go away. Keep the money I gave you already. I'll send you more. I promise. But it's got to stop!"

"So you're willing to take your chances telling them about the robbery?"

Katherine didn't answer.

"Are you willing to spend the rest of your life in jail for conspiracy to commit murder?"

"What?" The question was part shock, part wariness. Her voice shook.

"Life in prison. Are you willing to spend twenty-five years in a cell?"

"What are you talking about?" She said.

Katherine wasn't sure where he was going, but she had no doubt she was about to find out.

"There's a body buried in a swamp north of the city. It's the body of a young man you and your Russian friend hired. He was murdered." Wolfe described the death of the young courier in detail.

"I didn't—"

"No. Of course not. But that's not what I'll tell the cops … via long distance. Are you willing to take the chance they'll believe you had nothing to do with it? You planned to rob your own company to rip off the majority share holders. You hired mercenaries to help you do it. You think the cops will have a hard time believing you arranged to kill a courier when something went wrong? Give your fucking head a shake, Katherine. They'll be all over it. They like to close cases and this one's wrapped up like a Christmas present. You'll spend the rest of your life in jail and I'll be long gone."

When Katherine found her voice all she could manage was "No." It wasn't much more than a whisper.

"You couldn't even pass a polygraph because, let's face it, you *are* guilty."

"Not of murder," Katherine managed.

"That's how the courts will see it."

"You bastard!" Her voice was barely audible.

Wolfe covered the ten feet separating them without seeming to move a muscle. She barely had a chance to drop her right hand into the pocket of her purse before his fist shot out and gripped her by the throat, lifting her until the tips of her toes were barely scraping the worn plank floor. He tightened his grip until she knew she was about to pass out. His breath in her face smelled as rank as the building.

Wolfe released his grip and dropped her to the floor.

Katherine lay with her face in the dust for a moment, gasping for air. Tiny electrons of light burst around her as her brain tried to adjust to the rush of blood and oxygen. Wolfe stood above her with a look of utter contempt on his face. When her brain cleared and she could trust herself to stand, she snatched the Smith & Wesson 640 out of her purse and pointed it directly at his heart. It was a meaty little five-shot revolver that packed a hell of a punch.

"I'll kill you if I have to," she said with finality.

"I don't think you have what it takes."

"You'd be surprised," she said, her voice calm and controlled despite the pain in her throat.

Wolfe cocked his head to the side and looked at her as if seeing her for the first time.

"Maybe," he said.

The next thing she knew she was back on the floor and Wolfe was pointing her shiny little revolver at her. She didn't even see him move. Her ears were ringing and her right arm hung uselessly at her side. She wasn't sure if it was broken or not.

"I'm tired of fucking with you," he snarled. "If you even think about crossing me again I'll be your worst fucking nightmare. Do you understand?"

Katherine didn't answer.

He reached behind her and yanked on her hair so that her head was pulled back and her neck exposed.

"If you try to go to the police I'll know it before you even finish the phone call. If you tell anyone about me you'll spend the rest of your *very* short life behind bars, wondering when I'm going to kill you. Now listen very fucking carefully. You're going to go back to the office and disable that program. Then ..."

CHAPTER FIFTY-THREE

"Any luck?" Jack asked.

"Not much. You?"

"The same. What about Cal?" Darcy sounded tired, but she looked beautiful. Jack pushed the thought aside so he could concentrate on business.

"He's not coming up with much either. One possibility," Jack said, "but not a definite standout."

They were standing at the rear of the station after a long day of shaking the bushes.

"Well, if we're sticking with jewelry as the theme two of mine fit the profile, The Diamond Exchange and Morrison's On Bloor, but I don't like either of them as a target."

"Why?"

Darcy shrugged. "The Diamond Exchange people didn't want to even open the door for me, but they told me it's business as usual, there's nothing special going on. Morrison's is basically a mom & pop operation. They only installed the system because it was almost free. LaserTech needed a test market."

Jack dragged his hands back through his hair and closed his eyes. He knew he was missing something, but he couldn't nail it down. Something somebody said, or the way they said it.

"You have something better?" Darcy asked, breaking into his thoughts.

"No. That's the problem. With an operation this well organized the target should stand out like a sore thumb."

"But it doesn't."

"Not even close."

"Maybe that's what these guys are counting on, or maybe Ricco was full of shit."

"Maybe," Jack conceded. "But I don't think so. I think he was telling the truth."

"Maybe we don't have a full list of companies using the LaserTech 25?"

Jack shook his head, a wry smile on his face. "You didn't meet Virginia Lloyd-Kendall. I'm sure she was very thorough. What else have you got?"

"Maybe one of the people using the system is lying."

"That's the only thing that makes sense," Jack said.

"I was kidding. We're trying to stop a robbery," Darcy said with surprise. "Why would they lie to us?"

"Human nature. Everyone lies to the cops. You know that."

"There has to be more to it."

"I'm sure there is, but I have trouble thinking on an empty stomach. You up for a little dinner?"

"Our third date? Tongues will start to wag."

"Don't start that again, Caldwell. I'm tired and you're just not that cute."

Two hours later they were sitting in the screened in porch just off the deck at Jack's house. The smell of lilacs from Mrs. Leishman's garden perfumed the air all around them. The remnants of a light supper— French bread, Brie, grapes, and pate de cognac—were scattered on a wrought iron table between them. A nice bottle of cabernet sauvignon made it easy for them to forget about business for a while.

"So you're like your dad."

"I'm nothing like my father."

"From what you've told me, you are."

"How so, Doctor Freud?" Jack asked.

"Well, for one thing, you're a collector like he was."

"Oh?"

"Sure. Your father collected guitars and old motorcycles. You collect strays and mysteries."

"My father was a workaholic."

"When was the last time you took a vacation?" Darcy asked.

Jack ignored the question and divvied up the last of the wine.

"He also pushed people away. He preferred to be alone," Jack said.

Darcy raised her eyebrows and looked around. The unspoken question was unmistakable.

"I don't prefer to be alone. I just can't find anybody that'll put up with me for more than a few hours."

"Keep looking," Darcy said. "There's a sucker born every minute."

She leaned back into the wicker loveseat and tucked her feet up under her. The night air was chilly so late in the evening. She was wearing the same cable knit sweater Jack wore when he made his appearance at breakfast the other day. It was at least four sizes too big. She was full, a bit light headed, and she felt like talking. Apparently, so did Jack. "What about you?"

"What about me?"

"I've told you my whole life story and you haven't told me a thing about you. Quid pro quo."

"Nothing to tell, really," Darcy said, looking into her glass of wine.

"I doubt that," Jack said.

"Why?"

"You used the word 'really'. It's a qualifier. Means there's a lot to tell, but you don't feel like talking about it. Staring at your glass is a way of creating distance from the source of your discomfort. In this case … me. Am I close?"

"Maybe," Darcy said. "Or maybe I really am just that boring."

"You're anything but boring."

Darcy looked up at Jack. His smile, illuminated in the candlelight, made him look kind and strong and sensitive and sexy, all at the same time. She hoped to hell it wasn't just a trick of the light.

"What do you want to know?"

"Anything you want to tell me," Jack said.

Darcy decided to give Jack a Reader's Digest version of the Reader's Digest version.

"Born and raised in the Beaches, mother and father divorced when I was eight, Mom died of cancer two years later, Dad stuck around long enough to dump me on Uncle Clarence and Aunt Delores, and they raised me as their own until I was old enough to run away and join the army."

"Why the army?" Jack asked.

"The circus wasn't in town," Darcy said.

"I spent ten years in," she continued, "most of it as an MP, traveled the world and came home when Aunt Delores passed away. I worked in the bar for a while and kept an eye on my uncle. I eventually applied for the police, got accepted and the rest, as they say, is history."

"Wow, impressive. You told me your whole life story in two breaths and managed to reveal absolutely nothing. I could have gotten that out of your file at work."

"Did you?"

"What?"

"Check my file."

"Yeah, but it was boring."

Darcy threw a grape at him.

"How about something personal?" Jack said.

"Such as?"

"Boyfriends?"

"I approve of the concept, but the practical application seems unworkable."

"Meaning?"

"They all suck," Darcy said.

"Maybe you're setting your standards too high."

"Or maybe I just haven't found Mr. Right."

It was Jack's turn to look at Darcy with raised eyebrows.

"I mean, Right. Capital 'R'. Not 'W'. Not you, Wright. Not—oh fuck, you know what I mean."

Jack started laughing. Darcy joined him a few seconds later. When the laughter petered out, Jack became serious.

"So, nobody special?"

Darcy hesitated, unsure of how much to say.

"There was," she said, "But things didn't work out the way I thought."

Jack leaned forward, but didn't interrupt.

"I dated this guy for a long time, even let him move in. Miro didn't approve. Turns out he's a better judge of men than I am."

Jack waited.

"About two weeks after he moved in things changed. He didn't like the way I dressed, my friends, my job. I put up with it for a while because …" Darcy shrugged, "I was in love, right?"

Jack nodded.

"But then it got physical." After a long silence, Darcy continued with a little prodding from Jack.

"What happened?"

"One night he went too far and I— I don't know. One minute he's grabbing me by the throat and the next thing I know he's bleeding all over the kitchen floor."

"Knife?" Jack guessed.

"Wine," Darcy said. "I was making Coq au vin. I grabbed the first thing I could find. Turned out to be a bottle of Pinot Gris. Twenty-seven stitches later he's arrested, the chicken's burned, Miro is happy, and I'm single."

After an appropriate silence, Darcy was relieved when Jack changed the subject.

"So I collect strays?" he asked.

"Sure. Hobbs, and Flynn, Charlie … me." She smiled shyly, and looked at him from beneath her bangs.

"Is that what you are?" He teased. "I was beginning to wonder."

He was sitting across from her in what he claimed to be his favorite chair. It too was wicker, well broken in, and just the right height for him to rest his feet on the coffee table if he had a mind to. Apparently he had a mind to.

They sat in silence for quite a while, neither wanting or needing to say anything. The whole room had an air of contentment. Michael Bublé crooned quietly in the background, and every few minutes a gentle breeze brought new smells from the garden to do battle with the lilac. Charlie raised his head off Darcy's lap and gave a 'woof' before being lulled back to sleep by her hand gently stroking his head.

Mrs. Leishman didn't see the man standing statue-still in the shadows at the side of the house. If she had, she wouldn't have lived to tell. Wolfe watched the old woman drag a wheeled garbage can to the sidewalk, cussing under her breath when it stuck on a rut in the driveway. He didn't make a sound, didn't move a muscle, didn't breathe. A lightweight balaclava hid his face. Dressed entirely in black he was all but invisible.

As the old lady walked stiffly back in the direction of the carriage house, Wolfe exhaled silently.

"What are you thinking about?" Darcy asked.

The candles on the table had almost burned down to the holders. Jack had felt a little silly lighting them, but he was glad he did. Their soft glow seemed to bring the world down to just the two of them.

"Nothing really."

"Really? Come on. You were about a million miles away. What were you thinking?"

"Actually, I was only about 100 miles away as the crow flies."

Darcy gave him a quizzical look.

"I was thinking about the farm, or what's left of it. Just a converted barn and some scrub pasture. I haven't been in ages. When my father died, I couldn't seem to let it go. It was never really my home, but in some ways, it's the closet thing I have."

Darcy leaned forward but didn't interrupt.

"I was just thinking that I'd like to go back sometime … and that it might be nice to have some company."

"If you can find somebody that'll put up with you for more than a few hours?" Darcy teased.

But Jack was in a serious mood now. "I was kind of thinking that you and I … that maybe we could—"

Charlie let out a bark that all but stopped Darcy's heart and scrabbled off her lap. He ran to the window, whining incessantly, while his little body shook from head to toe.

"He must need to go out," Jack said.

"Either that, or he was testing my pace maker," Darcy laughed, clutching her chest.

Jack didn't get a chance to finish the invitation.

Mrs. Leishman's cocker spaniel could be heard taking up the call to arms with a few barks of his own. The old lady opened the antique screen door and let it close with a soft bump behind the little brown and white body of her pride and joy, Butterscotch. The dog bounded off the back porch steps and nosed around in the grass for a few seconds before setting off on a mission to mark as much territory as possible. Wolfe watched him out of the corner of one eye, not wanting to risk detection by turning his head. The dog chased a firefly half way up a small cherry tree in the garden before focusing on a cricket by a chair near the fence. *Stupid mutt!*

Wolfe slowly cocked his arm and aimed a razor-sharp Kershaw throwing knife at the little dog's chest. Luckily for Butterscotch, something two doors down knocked over a garbage can and sent the little dog yipping in a whole new direction. Wolfe lowered his arm and exhaled a breath, but held tight to the Kershaw, just in case.

"What was that?" Darcy asked.

"What?" Jack was gathering up the remnants of the meal.

"I thought I heard something outside."

Suspecting one of the neighborhood pests at the garbage again, Jack wasn't too concerned. "I'll take a look when I see to His Majesty."

"I'll get the rest," Darcy said, "you make sure the kingdom is safe."

"M'Lady." Jack bowed.

When he entered the kitchen, Charlie stood with his front paws on the windowsill, staring out into the blackness and shaking like a leaf.

"What is it, Charlie? What do you see?"

The little dog whined.

"What's the matter, buddy? Is there a cat in your yard?'

Charlie whined again, more insistently this time.

"What's the matter with him?" Darcy asked, pushing the door to the kitchen open with her shapely hip.

"I don't know, but I think I better take a look. There's something out there he doesn't like."

Jack opened the closet and pulled out a heavy teak walking stick from its depths. He sheathed it in an imaginary scabbard and bowed once more to Darcy.

"Not to fear, M'Lady, I'm off to protect the realm."

"Do be careful, sir." Darcy tossed him a dishtowel as a token of her favor.

"Adieu," Jack said, bowing. As the screen closed behind him, he could just make out Darcy's last words.

"You're an ass."

Wolfe watched the performance without seeing the humor. He held the Kershaw by the blade. He'd been patient, but enough was enough.

Jack walked to the gravel driveway and looked between the houses, past the invisible form of Wolfe who was wedged into the shadows by the chimney. Jack stood stock-still and listened, but there was nothing. After a moment he turned and started to walk back towards the kitchen. It was a target Wolfe couldn't resist. He stepped silently from the shadow and cocked his throwing arm back behind his head.

Darcy finished scraping most of the remains of their meal into the garbage can. When she offered Charlie a mouthwatering tidbit of pate and the little dog didn't even look around, she knew that something was wrong. She opened the door and Charlie was between her legs in a second, barking furiously and charging around the corner onto the driveway.

Wolfe was thrown off by the little bundle of fur hurtling along the driveway like a miniature locomotive. The mercenary bolted the length of the drive and disappeared among the cars parked along the boulevard. Jack didn't even hear his assailant until Charlie shot past him like a rocket. After a short chase both man and dog stopped at the edge of the property, unsure of which way to go. Charlie wouldn't stop barking until Jack squatted down and shushed him, gently patting the back of his head. Jack listened to hear footsteps or ragged breathing but he couldn't hear either, despite the fact that he was less than ten feet away from a man who wanted him dead.

"What do you think? Peeping Tom? Burglar? What?"

"Probably a burglar. Not much to peep at around here."

"Jack, no jokes. Did you get a look at him?"

"No." Jack became serious when he saw the look on her face. "It happened too fast. I didn't even know he was there until His Majesty went ballistic."

Charlie raised his head from where he was sitting and accepted an affectionate scratch behind the ears. Darcy and Jack were standing in the foyer at the front of the house. Charlie was staying very close to his master, almost as if he realized how close he'd come to losing him.

"Did you see what he was wearing?"

"All I saw was a shadow, tall and slim. And fast. The guy could move."

"So what do you think?" Darcy asked again.

Jack moved closer and took her hands in his. "I think it might not be safe for you to go home tonight," he said.

They were only a few inches apart, and Darcy didn't move away, but Jack could tell something wasn't quite right. He leaned down and kissed her gently on the forehead. She melted into his arms and rested her head against his chest. He turned her face gently up to his and kissed her softly on the lips. The kiss lasted for a long, delicious moment. "Thank you," she said, "for dinner and … everything."

Jack smiled and kissed her again, more ardently this time, sliding his hands up her neck to cradle her face. He felt her lips part for a brief moment, and then felt her pull away slowly. He looked down at her, his hands still tangled in her silky hair.

"The guest bedroom's still made up, you know. I'll even give you Charlie to protect you against things that go bump in the night. I really don't like the idea of you going home by yourself. We're not sure who that guy was and …"

Darcy brushed the back of her hand along his cheek. "I appreciate that, but I'll be fine. I'm a big girl. Besides, Miro needs me, and you don't ever want to get on the bad side of a twenty pound cat."

She kissed him once on the cheek, and then walked quickly down the front steps to her car. As she drove slowly along the street, Jack couldn't help but feel a kind of pleasant emptiness. He would have been thrilled to know that Darcy was feeling exactly the same thing. Thrilled, and a little scared.

Wolfe found Morgan leaning back on his bedroll, a newspaper in his lap, the Beretta close at hand.

"Well, lad, how did the *recce* go?"

"Good, but it could have gone better. I had a chance to take out Wright tonight but the neighborhood was crawling with dogs. Does everybody in this country own a fucking dog?"

Morgan laughed and turned back to the paper. "Never rush a job, Johnny. Stick to the plan. Tomorrow night. Neat, clean, quick. The cops won't know what hit them. Is it still a go?"

Wolfe turned and flicked his wrist. The Kershaw buried itself two inches into the rough wooden beam along the far wall. The point pierced the forehead of a recruit picture of Jack Wright, taken directly from his personnel file at headquarters and delivered by courier this afternoon.

"Fucking right it's a go!"

CHAPTER FIFTY-FOUR

Jack spent most of Thursday putting out fires and in meetings that had nothing to do with the case. After work he stopped in at the club for a black belt class. Darcy followed up every lead she could and then hit the ETF training facility for a quick workout. Thankfully, the gym was deserted. Calvin spent most of the day doing what he did best—listening. Today he heard plenty.

He got to Jack's a little before seven, and found Darcy and Ken on the back deck enjoying a 'non-prescription remedy for what ails you', as Ken put it. Sitting in comfortable deck chairs, the two looked like old friends after a hard day of lawn bowling.

"Don't mind me," Ken said. "I'm just here as window dressing. Can I get you a drink? The laird and master should be here any time."

"Are we off duty?" Calvin asked.

"I don't know about you, but I'm on vacation," Darcy said. "Doesn't your shift end at 4:00?"

"That's when they stopped paying me. What are we having?"

"The lady is having Chablis and I'm enjoying our host's fifteen year-old single malt. What's yours?"

"Do you have anything a little less up market?" Calvin asked.

"One beer, coming up," Ken replied.

"Cretin," Darcy teased.

"Make that two," Jack said, walking around the corner.

"Two Cretins it is," Ken said, and disappeared into the kitchen. All three laughed.

"Now I know where all my liquor goes."

Jack shook hands with Calvin and then turned to Darcy. It was an awkward moment, but Ken saved them by appearing with two Cameron's Auburn Ales.

"Two of Toronto's finest for two of Toronto's Finest," Ken said.

"What service!" Calvin exclaimed.

"Yes. The staff tend to work harder when they get caught dipping into the master's supply of scotch."

"I won't dignify that remark with a response," Ken said.

After some small talk, Ken moved into the kitchen to prepare his world famous Greek pasta salad. He left the other three to get down to business.

"What's the word, Cal? Any luck?"

"A little, but I'm not sure if it's good or bad." Calvin dropped a manila envelope in front of Jack. "That snap was taken in Northern Iraq, April 1991."

"US Marines?" Darcy guessed.

"Mercenaries," Calvin said. "The guy that took the picture is Arnie, one of my C.I.s. He lives out of a bottle down by Cherry Beach, but he used to be with this bunch 'in country'. He says he was logistics, but I think he must have done some of the real work."

"Which was?" Darcy asked.

"Killing," Calvin said simply. "These guys were hired to help put down the Kurdish uprising. They were tasked with taking out the leaders. Apparently they were damned good at it."

Jack stared at the photograph of ten heavily armed men standing around the bodies of several people. At least two of the victims were women, bound and naked, lying in the dirt at the feet of the smiling men. When Darcy looked over his shoulder, Jack could feel her whole body stiffen.

"Recognize the guy on the left?" Calvin asked.

"Tinker," Darcy whispered.

Calvin nodded. "Look four from the right. Look familiar?"

Jack was slow to answer. "It could be. It's hard to tell. The photograph's grainy as hell."

"When I showed the sketches to Arnie he remembered the guy right away," Calvin said, shaking his head. "Amazing. The guy's fried his brain so much that he can't remember his name, but he remembers twenty years ago like it was yesterday."

"What did he say?" Jack asked.

"Plenty, some of it garbage, but what I *did* get is that to these guys killing wasn't just a way to make money. It was fun."

"And your friend says this is our guy?" Jack asked.

"Didn't even hesitate," Calvin said

"Did he give you a name?"

"Niles," Calvin answered, "Not sure if it's a first name or a last name."

Jack nodded, "Something to go on."

They talked on about what it all meant until Ken called them in for supper. He'd been busy—steaks on the barbecue, pasta salad, baked potatoes, and fresh strawberries for dessert. It wasn't a feast, but from the way Calvin and Darcy fussed, it might as well have been.

Jack watched Darcy help Ken clear the dishes into the kitchen, and overheard her ask, "So, do I get the recipe for the pasta salad?"

Ken shook his head. "Old family secret. You don't get that until I know you can be trusted."

"She'll have it out of him by the time the coffee's ready," Jack said, winking at Calvin. "He's a push over when it comes to beautiful women."

Ken started to offer a retort, but Darcy interjected.

"Don't bother, Ken. He's just jealous."

As darkness fell over the neighborhood, a lone figure jogged along Admiral Road in gray sweats, a headband and plain white running shoes. On his back he carried a small knapsack. The shoes were old and road weary. The shirt was faded light in most places except for the dark stain where it was plastered to his chest by sweat. His breathing was labored and he looked like he was using up the last of his reserves. At the end of Jack's driveway he stumbled and almost fell, pulling himself up just before hitting the sidewalk. Exhausted, the solitary runner leaned against the back of the dark blue Chev Impala parked at the end of the gravel drive. He doubled over to ease a stitch in his side. When he straightened back up the slight bulge at his ankle had disappeared, and a small red light glowed out of sight against the gas tank of Jack's unmarked police car.

CHAPTER FIFTY-FIVE

Pavel sat on the couch in his luxury suite in Markham staring at the drapes that closed him off from the rest of the world. The television was off and the book he'd brought with him lay unopened on the bedside table. He felt confused and empty and very much alone. The excitement of sharing his success with Katherine had been replaced by a feeling of betrayal far more powerful than anything he'd felt in his life.

His suitcases, packed five minutes after Katherine left, lay on the unused double bed in his hotel room. If he could have, he would have left right then, but flights to Russia weren't exactly leaving Toronto every hour. Instead, he sat on the couch and waited for time to pass.

Katherine tried to call several times, once from the lobby, asking him to give her a chance to explain, but Pavel didn't want to hear it. He didn't want to listen to her excuses, to hear her try to justify something that was beyond his comprehension. Nothing she had to say could alleviate the pain of losing not only his friend and partner, but also the woman he thought he loved. He told her to leave and to never call again. He wanted nothing more to do with it or her, for the rest of his life. He got his wish.

When Katherine pulled out of the parking lot and onto Warden Avenue she barely glanced at the white panel van parked near a service entrance at the back of the hotel. Even if she noticed it, she probably wouldn't have recognized it as the same one parked at the end of the visitor's parking lot when she left ComTech. The van and its driver, Patrick Morgan, were both by design, unremarkable. The bomb hidden in a pail in the back of the van, on the other hand, was designed to be very memorable.

CHAPTER FIFTY-SIX

When the time was right Ken pulled himself out of his chair.

"Before you professionals get back down to business, I think I'll retire to Bedlam, otherwise known as the Kotwa household. I was only invited as domestic help anyway."

"You weren't invited at all," Jack shot back. "You never are. You just show up … like junk mail."

"Charming, isn't he? Good to see you, Cal. Officer Caldwell, always a pleasure."

"Good to see you too," Calvin responded.

"Night, Ken," Darcy said, as Ken disappeared around the corner. "Thanks for the recipe," she called after him.

"Told you," Jack said to Calvin, and then addressed his two remaining partners.

"Night cap or coffee?"

Calvin held up his hand. "Coffee for me thanks, I have to drive."

"Me too," Darcy said.

Jack tried not to show his disappointment at Darcy's response. "So, where are we?"

"About the same place we were last week," Calvin said. "The *when* is anybody's guess and we still don't know the *where*. None of the companies I checked out look like a good possibility."

"So that leaves us with The Diamond Exchange, Morrison's, and the computer place," Darcy offered.

"I don't think much of Morrison's," Jack said. "Not from what you told me earlier, Darcy."

"The Diamond Exchange then?" Calvin asked. "Ricco said the target was gems."

"Maybe," Jack said. "But the timing isn't right. Christmas is their busy time."

"That, and the floor plan we have doesn't fit the layout," Darcy said.

"What about ComTech? Are computers worth the risk?"

Jack shrugged. "The floor plan is pretty vague and I didn't get to see much past the reception area. The place is huge."

"If they're working on something special …" Calvin said.

"But they're not," Darcy interrupted. "Jack talked to the head of R&D."

"Yes they are," Jack stated flatly.

Darcy looked confused. "But I thought she said—"

"She lied," Jack said. "I'm not sure why, but she started lying the second I walked through the door."

At the end of the street, within sight of Jack's house, Admiral Road meets Lowther Avenue in a T-junction. Beyond a quaint sitting area, the lights of the Royal Naval Club could be seen in the distance. Wolfe found the small park a convenient place to wait. Close, but not too close to the target.

The running gear, a knapsack, and a pair of latex gloves were gone. The lightweight clothing that he now wore was wrinkled, but otherwise nondescript . It was just dark enough to make him all but invisible to the casual observer, but not dark enough to look suspicious. He sat on one of the benches in the shadow of a crab apple tree.

"Whoa, you better explain. We're trying to save the company from being hit, and they're lying to us? That doesn't make sense."

"It does if they're more worried about industrial espionage than a robbery."

"I don't follow," Calvin said. "First off, how do you know she was lying?"

"And why didn't you tell me sooner?" Darcy sounded hurt.

"Sometimes it takes a while to be certain," Jack began, and then turned to Darcy. "That's why I didn't say anything."

"So you know because …?" Calvin asked.

"It's a combination of things. Her body language, what she said, and what she didn't say. People like to tell the truth. It makes them feel good. When they don't or can't, they use qualifiers. They leave blanks in a statement, or cover up time lapses with things like 'the next thing I knew'. They don't lie, they just don't tell the whole truth."

"And nothing but the truth," Calvin said.

"And you think that's what Katherine Sharpe was doing?" Darcy asked.

"She was trying *not* to lie to me," Jack said, "and doing a really lousy job of it. They're definitely working on something interesting."

"So you think maybe ComTech is the target?"

"I didn't say that. The only thing I know for sure is that the Director of R&D wasn't completely honest with me. There could be a dozen legitimate reasons why. Maybe she just doesn't like cops."

"Or maybe the Wright charm isn't all it's cracked up to be," Darcy offered.

"On that note, unless there's more business, I better get my tired ass home. Gill's had the kids all day and she gets kinda cranky if I don't at least make an appearance. Thanks for the grub."

"Hang on a second, Cal. I've got to move the cruiser. I'm parked behind you." Jack started to fight his way out of a very comfortable chaise lounge.

"Don't worry about it. Toss me the keys. I'll put it on the street and leave them on top of the visor. I know it's a lousy neighborhood, but it should be safe for a little while. Besides, you'd just have to move it again for Darcy," he said, with a wink.

Calvin reached out and took Darcy's hand. "See you tomorrow, Beautiful. Don't keep the big guy up too late."

When he realized what he'd said, the look on his face was priceless.

"I didn't— What I meant to say was—" Calvin gave up. "Ah, forget it. Later."

Jack and Darcy were laughing so hard it was almost impossible to say goodbye.

"See you, Cal." Jack tossed him the keys.

"Good night, Calvin," Darcy said, and winked to let him know that he was off the hook. "Say hi to Gill for me."

Calvin waved a hand over his head without saying another word and headed for the front of the house.

From his vantage point, when the door opened and the interior light in the Chevy winked on, Wolfe could just make out the figure of a man sliding in behind the wheel. He waited until the sound of the engine reached him before pushing the top button on a small remote control. The light on the device attached to the gas tank turned from red to green.

The car backed into the street facing north. Wolfe had hoped that Wright would come south, as close to his location as possible, so that he could watch Wright die. When the reverse lights on the unmarked cruiser winked out and the car started to move ahead, Wolfe shrugged and pushed a second button on the remote control.

It took a split second for the signal to reach the car. When it did, a detonator activated four ounces of C4, which in turn vaporized the gasoline in the cruiser's fuel tank. The resulting explosion blew out the windows up and down the street and sent a fireball reaching past the top branches on the majestic oak in front of Jack's house. The fire burned for half an hour despite the quick response of the local fire brigade. Calvin Dempster never knew what hit him.

CHAPTER FIFTY-SEVEN

The strobe lights on a dozen emergency vehicles played across the brick facades of the houses up and down Admiral Road. No one thought to turn them off. For some reason even the bystanders felt better with them illuminating the scene. It was as if their presence meant that everything was all right; that the cavalry had arrived. But everything was *not* all right. And for Gillian Dempster and her two children, everything would not be all right ever again. Ambulance crews and the fire brigade worked gingerly around the body of the husband and father who wouldn't be coming home.

Few of the onlookers moved from the spots they'd staked out. Even after the fire was extinguished, the show was far from over. What was left of the car, securely covered by a heavy canvass tarpaulin, was being carefully winched onto the back of a flatbed tow truck. Calvin's body, burned beyond recognition, remained in the front seat further covered from view by an orange sheet from the back of an ambulance. It would take many tedious, heartbreaking hours of work to extricate his remains from the burned out shell of the car. The Coroner had come and gone. The last of the television crews were packing up.

Jack stood with his arms folded across his chest, his bandaged hands tucked painfully under his arms. He clenched and unclenched his fists, welcoming the pain, knowing that it was only a precursor of what was to follow. The first and second-degree burns would heal. The hair would grow back. The guilt would probably never leave. It was already starting to gnaw at his insides.

Darcy slid up to where Jack stood on the front lawn watching the activity to make sure that it was all done right. He watched the EMS crews attending to the body. He watched a burly tow truck operator struggle to find a part on the vehicle strong enough to hold the winch cable. He watched the firemen rolling hoses so that the water spilled out along the gutter and ran down towards the park. He watched one Ident technician package and label various scraps of evidence, while another one photographed and measured every inch of the area. He watched the lights.

He watched his own personal hell unfold before his eyes. He didn't turn at Darcy's touch. He didn't have it in him. He didn't have anything in him at all. Darcy stood beside him with her arm around his waist and leaned her head onto his shoulder.

"You couldn't have done anything."

Jack didn't say anything. For a few minutes Darcy just stood beside him, apparently needing to feel him close as much as he needed to feel her arms around him. Finally she spoke again.

"One of the guys thinks it might have been gang related."

When Jack responded his words were calm and deliberate.

"It wasn't gang related, and it wasn't meant for Calvin. You and I both know that." He looked her directly in the eyes hoping to see some argument, but there wasn't any.

An Ident Officer approached them holding up a small plastic bag like an offering, his white contamination suit sticking to his back despite the coolness of the night. The bag held the charred remains of a diode and a few short wires.

"What have you got, Terry?"

"Electrics. Part of the police radio or …"

"A detonator?"

"That'd be my guess. Listen Jack, I'm sorry about Cal. We crossed paths a lot over the years. He was first rate, you know? If there's anything I can do to help …"

"Just make sure we don't miss anything. I mean—"

"You got it, Jack. If this guy left a spare breath, I'll find it. I promise."

"Thanks, Terry."

Jack turned back to watch the car being chained down to the flatbed, as if missing a part of the process would ruin any hopes of catching the bastard that set it in motion. When the bed of the tow truck was lowered back into position the whole scene took on the appearance of a macabre parade with the burned out unmarked as its main float. The high-powered halogen spotlights used to help investigate the scene snapped off leaving only a few strobes to fight the darkness.

Jack finally found the strength to put his arm around Darcy and was surprised to see she was gone. She was asking questions of the few neighbors who remained, something he should have been doing. He walked over to her as she finished up with a woman from a few doors down the street.

"Nobody saw anything before the explosion."

"I'm not surprised."

"Jack ..." But it was obvious she had no idea what to say.

"It wasn't gang related," Jack said again, fighting his way through some pretty rough waters.

"And it wasn't meant for Cal. It was him." Jack stated it flatly. "That bomb was meant for me, which means he's done his homework. He knows where I live. He knows what I drive. He—" Jack looked around the crowd searching for a face.

"Terry!" His voice carried along the street startling a few of the onlookers. The white clad technician hurried over, eager to help.

"Terry, you've seen enough of these things. What are we dealing with?"

"I can't be sure, Jack, but—"

"I don't need you to be sure. I just want your best guess." Jack felt a sense of purpose, something that wasn't there a few minutes ago.

"I won't hold you to it." Jack continued. "Just give me something to go on."

"Small explosive device on the gas tank. What did you have, half a tank?"

"A little less. Maybe just over a quarter."

"Yeah, that sounds about right. It wasn't a pipe bomb or dynamite. I'm guessing C4. Blew the gas tank. It wasn't wired into the ignition. Maybe a timer."

"Not a timer. This guy had to make sure I was in the car. He couldn't have known when I'd be leaving."

"You think this was meant for you?"

Jack ignored the question. "A remote?"

Terry nodded.

"How far could somebody be from the bomb and still set it off?"

"Reliably? That all depends on the transmitter. He could be anywhere from two feet to two miles, although if I were him, I'd take the second option."

Jack was in the middle of a thought and it seemed to him that Darcy must have been reading his mind.

"Jack, if this guy was using a remote control, he'd have to be close enough to see the car, but far enough away to mistake Calvin ... for you. That wouldn't be that hard in the dark."

Terry moved off to continue processing the scene. Jack stood looking around at the faces in the crowd. They were still gathered along the street. Most wouldn't leave until the show was completely over. Jack started thinking out loud again.

"What's this guy like?"

"Who?'

"Wolfe. What does he do?"

Darcy didn't answer.

"Calvin said it, and I should have listened ... he kills and he enjoys it."

Jack continued to look around at the faces in the crowd, studying each one for a few seconds before moving on to the next. Most of the people were from the neighborhood. Their faces showed a mixture of fear, concern, and a hint of relief—relief that it wasn't them, that they were still alive to repair their windows and carry on with their lives.

There were still a few media types angling around behind the yellow police lines, trying to get the best shot. The firemen left were milling about, their hoses packed and the cleanup all but complete. The tow truck carrying the now tarped shell of a police car was just pulling away, second in the parade to an ambulance with no patient on board.

Jack moved to the edge of his property and stepped up on a low stone wall that separated his yard from the one next door. No one paid him any attention. He looked up the street, watching the tail lights of the flatbed disappear around the corner. He looked down towards the park and watched a few of the bystanders leaving towards whatever life they'd interrupted. Nothing caught his eye until one of the girls walking on the far sidewalk jumped back from a tree about half way to the park. He watched as she quickened her pace and hurried towards the safety of somewhere else. Jack stepped off the wall and moved back towards Darcy. He didn't look back at the huge oak down the street. He didn't want to give anything away.

"Are you armed?"

She clued in quickly and nodded. "Why?"

"I think he's here." Jack was glad to see Darcy resist the urge to look around.

"Where?"

"Half way down the street to the south, far side, behind the oak tree."

"Did you see him?"

"No, but I think he's been watching this whole mess."

"Why?"

"I don't know. Call it gut instinct."

"Call for back-up?" Darcy asked.

Jack shook his head. "There isn't time. Here's what I want you to do …"

Darcy made her way as casually as possible across the street, past the last of the stragglers, trying to blend into the scenery as much as possible. When she was out of sight she sprinted between two houses towards the lane that ran behind them parallel to the street. She watched Jack move across and speak to the fire captain for a second before turning south and walking quickly towards the park, keeping the trunk of the big tree between him and whatever was on the far side.

Darcy unsnapped the .38 from an ankle holster and looked for a gate in the high wooden fence that backed the property. Unable to find one quickly, she tucked the gun into the waistband of her jeans and jumped for the top of the fence. She swung her leg up and over the top, landing on the far side with barely a sound. Her first step in the darkness, however, found a discarded pop bottle that went spinning down the alley like an oriental wind chime. The noise that echoed off the tin garages along the laneway seemed deafening in the darkness.

Jack slowed his pace as he neared the tree, the massive girth of the trunk hiding the far side from view. Unarmed, he leaned on the trunk of the oak trying to decide what to do. After a second he reached in his pocket and quietly removed his key ring, a tricky maneuver given the bandage on his hand. Tossing the keys to one side of the tree, he dashed around the other. The yard was empty. There was no one there.

He shook his head at his own foolishness. *Some gut instinct! Paranoia more like it.* He sighed as he bent over to pick up his keys. A split second later a 9mm. round from a silenced pistol took a fair sized chunk out of the tree just above his head. Jack dropped to the ground automatically and rolled to cover off to his right. A second shot thudded into the front porch next to him. A splinter of wood sliced a cut just above his right temple. Nobody on the street heard the shots. Jack had to warn Darcy.

"Gun!" He shouted it at the top of his lungs, hoping to hell she'd hear him.

He chanced a quick look and saw a tall, thin figure racing for the back alley. The dark clothing made him all but impossible to see. Jack ducked low and sprinted towards the back fence in a blind rage. Years of police training disappeared in a heartbeat. He was pursuing an armed man into an unknown area without a weapon of his own. He should have disengaged. He should have called for back-up. He should have used his head. He didn't do any of the three.

The man who killed Calvin was just about at the alley and about to get away. Jack poured on a burst of speed just as Wolfe leaped for the top of the fence. Jack managed to grab a hold of one pant leg, but slammed painfully into the decorative wooden planks. The fence, years old and obviously neglected, buckled under the impact spilling both men into the alley in a tangle of spongy boards and rotting fence posts.

Wolfe's 9mm. clattered out of sight across the lane, but he was first on his feet, like a cat ready to pounce. He snatched up a plank and swung it at Jack catching him squarely across the back and shoulders. The rotten board disintegrated upon contact. Jack shook off the blow and dove at his assailant, forgetting everything he'd ever learned in karate. All he wanted to do was to get his hands around Wolfe's throat and choke the life out of him. He out-weighed the man by at least thirty pounds. The fight was short and to the point.

Wolfe hadn't forgotten a thing. He read the situation perfectly and allowed Jack to almost reach his neck before blocking the chokehold and opening Jack up like a book. A vicious jab to the solar plexus and an elbow to the jaw sent the detective spinning around like a marionette. A split second later a knife-hand strike tossed Jack across the alley and up against the front of one of the garages. Jack's head hit first and a thousand stars careened around the darkness in front of his eyes. The noise of skull on tin sounded like another small explosion in the neighborhood. Jack dropped to the ground only semi-conscious.

Dogs barked. Yard lights snapped open on both sides of the lane. Angry voices shouted at the periphery of the darkness. Above the cacophony Darcy's voice split the night.

"Police! Don't move!"

Wolfe stopped in mid-step and turned to face his new opponent.

She stood in a modified Weaver stance in the middle of the alley about forty feet to the north. Body angled slightly, both hands gripping a revolver out in front of her, left elbow cocked, right elbow straight and locked. Both eyes were open as she sighted down the short barrel of what looked like a Smith & Wesson. Wolfe spread his arms out to the side and opened his palms to show that he wasn't armed. He smiled and didn't say a word. The barrel of the gun wasn't wavering. He watched her eyes for just the right moment. When she looked over at Jack to make sure he was all right, Wolfe simply stepped sideways into a gateway through a hedge at the side of the garage.

Darcy saw the move and shifted the pistol over to lead her target. She didn't take the shot. She hesitated for a split second and he was gone. That hesitation would haunt her until the day she died.

CHAPTER FIFTY-EIGHT

"What happened?"

Wolfe didn't say anything right away. He sat on one of the packing crates in the loft staring off into space. His mind was racing through the night's misadventure.

"He's still alive, then?" Morgan was more than a little surprised.

It took a second for Wolfe to come back to the present. "He is, his partner isn't."

Morgan nodded. "So you killed a cop, you just killed the wrong one?"

"Is that what passes for humor in your world?" Wolfe's eyes flashed with malevolence.

"There's nothing funny about it, lad. I was just stating the obvious. The police are going to blanket this town looking for a cop killer. We won't be able to move."

"Oh, it's worse than that," Wolfe said with a sardonic smile. "They're going to blanket this town, all right, but they're going to be looking for *me*."

It was almost three o'clock in the morning before Jack was able to shut the front door for the last time. The evidence had been collected and was already stored for examination the next day. Statements could wait until the morning. Homicide detectives were canvassing the street talking to anyone who might have seen anything. Chief McAllister had a press conference scheduled for seven o'clock in the morning. The case was being given the utmost priority.

Like any police force, The Toronto Police Service hates to lose one of their own. Unfortunately, out of necessity, they were getting good at it. Plans for a massive police funeral were already in the works. Gillian and her children were being taken care of by a group of officers and civilians who specialize in providing comfort and support at a time like this. Jack would call on her when things calmed down a bit, but he had no idea what to say. I'm sorry just wouldn't cut it.

Jack sat across from Darcy at the kitchen table wondering if he looked as bad as she did. He could imagine he looked worse. The clock above the doorway sounded like a metronome. Full cups of coffee sat like a barrier between them, cold and forgotten. Jack broke the silence.

"You okay?"

Darcy was slow to answer. "Yeah … you?"

Jack reached out to take her hand. The bandages covering his knuckles were already badly in need of changing. The dirt and blood from the fight, and the purulence from the burns, made them look like something out of a civil war movie. Darcy picked up a first aid kit left by one of the firemen.

"Those bandages need changing. You'll get infected."

Jack looked the bandages she put on earlier and smiled. "You're not much of a medic." If he was trying for comic relief, it backfired miserably.

"Not much of a cop either," Darcy said quietly, rummaging around looking for the scissors.

"What's that supposed to mean?"

Darcy looked at him for a good long minute and then dropped her eyes. Jack could see a mixture of emotions pent up just below the surface. Something had to give.

"Darcy?"

"I froze, damn it! I hesitated. I didn't take the shot."

Her words came out in a rush and the tears were quick to follow.

"I had him, Jack. I had him right there. But he didn't have anything. I couldn't see a gun. He killed Calvin. I should have blown his fucking head off. You were on the ground. I looked at you. I knew he was going to move. I saw it coming. I still had him. I could have taken the shot, but I didn't. I let him just walk away. Why didn't I take the shot, Jack? Why the fuck didn't I take it?"

She broke down into deep, sorrowful sobs and Jack knew nothing he could say would help. He held her tight and rocked back and forth, until the tears were all gone and her sobs turned to sniffles. She held on with a fierceness that told him this wasn't just about a missed opportunity. Jack pushed the pain of losing a new friend into another part of his mind. He had his own demons to excise, but that would come later ... much later.

After putting Darcy to bed in the spare room, Jack sat on the back deck with a glass of scotch, trying not to think of the 'what ifs' and 'if onlys'. He sipped at the drink and stared at the light in a house three blocks away. He was still there when Darcy woke him up a few hours later.

"Hey." She shook his shoulder.

"Hmph." He smacked his lips together and tried to remember why he felt so awful. A full glass of scotch, sans ice, was on the table beside him, so it couldn't be that. It didn't take long to remember. *Hello world, welcome to my nightmare.*

Darcy handed him a glass of orange juice. He watched her carefully as she sat on the side of a chaise lounge across from him. Her dark hair was damp from the shower and pulled back into a loose bun. After a sip he was able to articulate in more than grunts. "Thanks. You look better."

"Don't be fooled. It's all an illusion, but about last night, thanks for listening. I guess I came off pretty bad, eh?"

"Darcy, what happened in that alley, it could have happened to anybody."

"It could have, Jack, but it didn't. Anyway listen," she said, obviously uncomfortable. "We can talk about it later. Right now, we've got an appointment at Homicide, and then I want to talk to Karski."

"Hey, if you're going to talk to him about what I think, do yourself a favor and wait for a few days."

She smiled at him, but there was something sad and resigned in the way she did it.

"I appreciate what you're saying, Jack, but ..." She tried a smile again and this time she almost brought it off.

"Well then do *me* a favor, will you, and wait on it for a few days. When this is all over we can talk."

Darcy stared at the wall for a minute before giving him an answer.

"Okay, but it won't change anything, Jack. I am going to talk to Karski and I am going to quit the ETF. You can't hesitate on that team, not even for a second. If you do, you'll end up getting somebody killed. I couldn't live with that. I just couldn't."

Katherine was still slightly drunk from the night before. After leaving Wolfe in his den she'd cracked the seal on a very expensive bottle of Russian vodka. An empty bottle now stood on the counter in her kitchen. Unfortunately the vodka hadn't solved her problems.

She was behind the wheel of her BMW threading her way through early morning traffic. Usually she didn't mind the drive to the office. This morning, however, it seemed unbearable. Her head pounded to the rhythm of some ancient dirge. Her stomach lurched crazily with the stop and go of the cars around her. The windows were down full and the AC was turned up high, but it didn't help.

The stereo in her car seemed to be part of a conspiracy that involved construction crews, large trucks, and small motorcycles. The everyday noises of the city were amplified by the remnants of vodka still in her system. The shouting and honking and opera seemed to combine into a type of noise that was so thick she could almost touch it. Katherine reached for the power switch on the stereo, but stopped as the Italian soprano was replaced by the soothing tones of an FM announcer.

And now what's making news in your world.

Two separate bomb blasts overnight leave two dead, one injured and a lot of questions unanswered. Timothy Corbey has this report.

Police this morning are sifting through the carnage left in the wake of two separate explosions that occurred simultaneously last night at 11:15 leaving two men, one of them a police Sergeant, dead. It's not immediately clear if the two bombs are connected, but police are investigating that possibility.

The first explosion occurred on Admiral Road in the Annex, where it is believed that a pipe bomb was used to destroy an unmarked police cruiser killing Sergeant Calvin Dempster of the Guns & Gangs Unit. Police sources are suggesting this may be gang-related violence considering the nature of the officer's work, however, at this time it is not clear whether or not Dempster was the intended victim. There is speculation the bomb was actually intended for Detective Sergeant Jack Wright. Sources say the bomb was actually placed on his car while it was parked in front of his house. The police are not releasing any details at this time.

The second explosion occurred at the same time at the Toronto Hilton in Markham, north of the city, killing one man and injuring a second. It appears a bomb placed on the door handle of one of the suites exploded when the guest responded to a knock, killing one man and injuring another guest staying in the room across the hall. The second man was treated at hospital and released a short time later.

Very little information is available about the man killed in the blast, although a York Regional Police spokesperson confirmed he was a Russian national who came to Canada very recently on business. Reporting live from the Toronto Hilton Suites and Conference Center in Markham, I'm Timothy Corbey.'

The news cast continued, but Katherine wasn't listening. Her world suddenly became a giant kaleidoscope, twisting and fragmenting all around her, so much so that she didn't see the red light. Car horns blared angrily as she barreled through the intersection, barely missing a cab going the other way. When she realized what was happening she turned off the road and pulled into a vacant lot. She managed to fight her way out of the seatbelt and stumble to the front of the car before throwing up everything she had inside of her, which wasn't much. For some reason the only thing she could think was that she was going to be late for work for the first time in her life.

Dark clouds boiled on the horizon promising a late afternoon thunderstorm. The air on the top floor of the old factory was already taking on the heaviness that usually precedes a good blow. It took Morgan's eyes a few minutes to adjust to the gloom after returning from a corner shop with two cups of coffee and a box of donuts. He found

Wolfe in a quiet, thoughtful, dangerous mood. He set the food on a packing crate and pulled up a second one for himself.

"Stop your thinking for a few minutes lad, and come join me for a bite," he said, holding up the box.

Wolfe took a coffee but ignored the donuts. The two men sipped in quiet contemplation until Morgan broke the silence.

"So what now? Damage control … or do we take another look at this thing and see if it's worth doing?"

"Oh, it's worth doing, Patrick. But there's a few loose ends that need to be taken care of before it's a go."

"Such as … the two cops that saw you in the alley? Wright and the other one?"

Wolfe shook his head. "It's too late for preventative medicine. The only thing those two can do now is to identify me, and unless the police are completely incompetent, they'll know who I am by the end of the day. Once they print the pistol …" Wolfe shrugged.

"And that doesn't worry you?"

"It was inevitable. By the time they figure it out I'll be long gone, a ghost."

"If not Wright, then who?"

Wolfe's eyes narrowed. "Actually, I was thinking about Mr. Ricco."

"Why bother with him? He can't do any more than he's already done."

"Maybe," Wolfe agreed. "But you know me, Patrick. I hate to leave loose ends."

A clap of thunder rumbled in the distance as if applauding the decision, and Wolfe set about preparing for the task ahead.

Jack and Darcy made it to the precinct a little before seven, just in time for the Chief's press conference. They avoided the media circus by entering through the prisoner sally port. The drive in gave them a chance to talk about the case.

"What I don't understand is how this guy knows where I live and what I drive?"

"Drove," Darcy corrected, without humor.

"Drove," Jack agreed. "In fact, how did he know about me at all?"

"You said it last night, he's done his homework."

"That doesn't wash. Only a few people knew about the investigation. How did he link me to the case, and why is he so worried he'd risk killing a cop?"

"Maybe he wasn't that worried," Darcy said. "Maybe killing for him is just that easy. You crossed his path once too often."

"If that's the case, he's even more dangerous than we thought. And that still doesn't answer the main question. Where did he get his information?"

"There's only two possibilities; either these people have somebody feeding them information from the inside, or you've touched a raw nerve somewhere."

"Maybe it's both," Jack said.

Darcy looked at Jack but he was a million miles away. She couldn't tell if the mystery was getting any clearer.

CHAPTER FIFTY-NINE

"Katherine?" It was Jane's voice on the intercom.

Katherine didn't react. She was sitting behind her desk with her head cradled in her crossed arms on the green felt blotter, wondering if she looked as bad as she felt.

"Katherine?"

"Yes?" Her voice was barely audible. Jane's was sympathetic.

"I'm sorry to bother you but there's a man at security asking to see you. He says he's your cousin. He said it's urgent."

"What? Who?"

"Probably a reporter about—about Mr. Milanovich. They'll say anything. Do you want Security to get rid of him?"

"Did he give his name?"

"Wolfgang, but I've never heard you mention—"

Wolfe! Katherine had to struggle to make her brain work through the fog.

"No! No, that's okay, Jane. My mind's not working right. I've been expecting him. Just stall him for a second so I can splash some water on my face, please."

"Of course, Katherine. Are you all right? Can I get you anything?"

"No, thanks, Jane. I'll be fine. Just give me a few seconds."

"Sure, Katherine, and uhm …"

Katherine could feel her grip on reality slipping, like a climber hanging over the edge of a deadly precipice, her fingertips wedged in a crevice. It was getting harder to hold on.

"I just wanted to let you know that everything's been taken care of. The Russian Embassy is making arrangements to have the—to have Mr. Milanovich repatriated. His funeral will be next week. I sent flowers to his mother and the embassy staff let her know we'll be taking care of all costs. She asked them to say thank you for all you've done."

Katherine felt one hand slip from the crevice.

Morgan hunched over the make shift table, working quickly in the poor light, molding and shaping the off-white putty. His hands worked of their own accord, while his mind was elsewhere. That's one of the nice things about C4, it's a very forgiving medium that can't be accidentally triggered. It has to be intentionally detonated.

The timers themselves were ready, lined along the far edge of the plywood tabletop with the wires disconnected from the detonators. The digital quartz stopwatches glowed orange in the dim light of the loft. Each device was a mirror image of the one beside it—neat, compact, precise. Only the time on the LCD's showed any difference from one to another. There were eight in total; four primary and four reserve.

Two of the reserves were attached to larger shape charges, set to explode long after the dust had settled from the first, when investigators were still combing through the debris. They were designed to tear the heart out of the Toronto Police Service and obliterate any trace evidence. The idea didn't seem to bother Morgan in the least.

Katherine stepped back into her office from the washroom as the main door closed behind Wolfe. Neither one of them said anything for what seemed like a very long time until Katherine broke the silence. Wolfe had to strain to hear her.

"Why Pavel?"

"You know the answer to that, Oscar."

Katherine shook her head, but there was no conviction in the movement. Wolfe could almost feel the remorse tearing her apart. He watched her carefully, studied her. What he saw was familiar—the slack muscles, the monotone voice, the thousand yard stare, the onset of combat fatigue. He'd seen it before. The look of someone who'd been pushed past the limits of their endurance. Wolfe used it like a weapon.

"What do you see when you look in the mirror?"

Katherine didn't answer.

"There's your answer. It's you. You're the reason behind everything. You're why I'm here, why Tinker's dead, why Ricco has to die. You're the reason we had to kill Pavel. If you hadn't told him our secrets ..." Wolfe held out his hands and shrugged his shoulders. His tone was reasonable, almost soothing.

"Why can't you just go away?" Katherine sounded almost sleepy. "I'll pay—"

"Too late for that, but the hard part will be over soon. Sooner than you planned."

"What do you mean?" Something seemed to stir behind her sleepy eyes, but Wolfe chose to ignore it.

"I mean the date's been moved ahead. It's happening tonight, that's why I'm here. It's time to go."

Morgan carefully stored the explosives in the bottom tray of three identical blue toolboxes that had been suitably scuffed and banged around to look old. He replaced the top trays and stacked the boxes neatly beside the gaping mouth of the freight elevator. The rest of the supplies were carefully packed and arranged at the far end of the lift.

His work complete, Morgan began to pace. He didn't like waiting. *This will be my last job. I'm getting too old for this.* He raised a flask of scotch in a toast and took a sip, something he'd never done before on a job.

"To success." He capped the silver flask and put it back in his pocket for later.

"Go?" Katherine's voice was tentative, searching.

"Go," he said. "Until this thing is over, you and I are going to be like Siamese twins. Get your things. We've got a schedule to keep."

A light came back into Katherine's eyes. It was the last spark of resistance.

"I can't just leave. I won't."

"You don't have a choice. We're leaving ... now."

"No!" The spark grew just a little. "I'm not leaving. I can have security here in seconds."

"Please." Wolfe gestured to the phone. Katherine didn't move.

"Please," Wolfe said it again, almost cordially. "Call."

Wolfe withdrew an H&K .9 mm pistol from one pocket of his suit coat and a vented silencer from the other. His movements weren't hurried. He calmly started screwing the threaded end of the silencer onto the barrel of the handgun. His eyes never left hers. He watched the spark grow into a flame.

"Go ahead ... kill me." She swallowed involuntarily. "It's what you're going to do anyway. Go ahead. I don't care anymore."

"Don't be stupid. This isn't for you." He paused to make sure the silencer fit properly.

"One way or another, you're coming with me. You're a big part of my future. This," he held up the pistol, "is for that lovely young thing in your outer office, and for anyone else you choose to call, so go ahead, start dialing."

The spark in Katherine's eyes fizzled and died. She got up from where she'd been sitting and walked towards the door like a zombie.

"I need to use the ..." she pointed at the washroom.

Wolfe nodded but stepped in ahead of her and took a quick look around. Nothing she could use to hurt herself, no intercom, no phone. He nodded again and stood aside to let her in. She looked like she was about to throw up.

"Leave the door open a crack."

Katherine didn't try to protest. She pushed the door until it was almost closed and then stepped over to the sink. She turned the cold water on full and watched the door in the mirror. When she was sure Wolfe wasn't looking she stepped quickly to the wastebasket and dug under the garbage. She pulled out the cell phone she'd put there when she'd found out Wolfe was on his way up. It seemed like a good idea at the time. It seemed like an even better one now.

She turned the water off and got down on her knees by the toilet. She pushed two fingers down her throat and retched into the basin as loudly as she could. She flushed the toilet once and dialed the number on Jack's card. As the water swirled in front of her eyes she heard the line click and the start of a message.

'I'm sorry. All of our operators are—"

"Shit!"

She hung up and dialed again, flushing the toilet at the same time. This time the line was picked up on the third ring.

"Robbery, Turpin."

"Detective Wright, please. It's urgent."

"Nope. Sorry. You got me. Take it or leave it."

"You don't understand." She covered the mouthpiece with her hand and turned the water back on in the sink. "This is an emergency. I have to speak with Detective Wright."

"Oh, well ..." Turpin said, taking another bite of his sandwich. "If it's an emergency, let me see what I can do. Nope, you still got me. What can I do for you lady?"

Leaning back in one of the few desk chairs in the office strong enough to take his weight, Dick Turpin listened with a self-satisfied smile on his face. He heard 'Tell Detective Wright that it's happening tonight' before the line went dead in his hand. He looked around, shrugged, and threw the receiver on the desk. Reaching for a scratch pad, he spoke to no one in particular.

"I'll be sure to tell him it's tonight, lady. Wouldn't want him to miss a date. Fucking social secretary's all I am. Shit."

Without dropping his feet, Turpin scribbled a quick note and sailed it in the direction of Jack's desk. The note fell about two feet short of the mark and floated aimlessly under a rolling file. He took another huge bite of his pastrami sandwich while he studied the ceiling tiles and thought about nothing in particular.

Katherine felt the cold steel of the silencer press into the soft spot just behind her ear. Wolfe reached around and pushed the End button on the phone.

"That was stupid. Who were you talking to?"

Before she could answer Wolfe jabbed her in the kidney with a vicious punch that dropped her to the marble floor. He reached down and wrapped his free hand in her hair, yanking her savagely to her feet. Katherine was shaking, partially from the blow and partially from fear.

"Who were you talking to?"

"I was trying to call— "He yanked her hair again. "—the police."

"Ah yes, Detective Wright, I presume. Did you get through?"

"No." Katherine shook her head.

Wolfe punched her in the other kidney, but this time she didn't go down. She sucked in a breath and held it.

"I … I left a message that it was tonight. That's all I got out before-"

He punched her again and dropped her to the floor. Taking the phone, he smashed it on the edge of the counter, sending a shower of plastic bits in every direction.

"Clean yourself up. We leave in three minutes. If you try anything else, I'll kill everyone I see on the way out of this building. And you better pray to God Wright never gets that message."

CHAPTER SIXTY

After writing out statements, Jack and Darcy left Homicide and made their way back to Jack's office. Composite sketches of Wolfe, updated since the last encounter, were already being distributed as a suspect wanted in the murder of Sergeant Calvin Dempster.

The morning papers had the sketches plastered across their front pages under banner headlines. The net was beginning to tighten. Jack was expecting fingerprints and the service photo of John Stephen Niles to arrive at any moment. The prints on the gun were clear and detailed. The chance of a match, if one existed, was good. There was no question in Jack's mind that Niles, Wolfe, and the man he'd seen at the prison were one and the same. But there were still too many unanswered questions. Would the robbery still go down? If so, when and where? Who was Oscar? Where was Wolfe? Jack had a lot of ideas, but none he could organize into a logical theory.

"That was strange, being on the other side of the interview." Darcy said.

"I know what you mean," Jack replied. "I've done a thousand 'will says', but I've never had my statement taken by a cop."

"Imagine if you were actually guilty of something."

Jack shook his head and smiled. "Innocent as a newborn babe."

"Yeah, right."

"It's good to see you smile." Jack let his hand touch hers for a brief second.

"You too." Darcy turned serious again, "but it doesn't change the way I feel. I'm still going to have that talk with Karski."

"I know."

They walked the rest of the way in silence. Inside the office things were hopping. Even though Ken Kotwa was handling the murder investigation, solving the LaserTech case meant nailing the bastard who killed one of their own. Nothing got a higher priority than that.

"Any word from the military, Jesse?"

"Nothing Jack. They put a rush on it, but—"

"Call them back. Light a fire under someone's ass. What about the gun?"

"Tommy's got that one," the young officer said, picking up the phone to call the DND for the third time that morning.

"Tommy?"

"Browning .9mm. The serial number's been filed off. We may be able to raise it through metal density tests from the stamp, but it'll take time. There's a good set of fingertips, but so far AFIS hasn't come up with a match."

"It may not," Jack said. "If this guy's as good as I think there may not be any prints out there to match. That's why we need that file from the military. If it's Niles, his service record may be the only hope we have for a positive ID. Who's got forensics?"

"That's me." One of the uniforms brought in as extra manpower put up his hand. He was young, eager and obviously nervous. "Parnell, sir. Jim Parnell."

"Okay Jim. What have you got?"

"CFS says the bomb was remote controlled. Standard transmitter/receiver unit. The diodes are generic and used in just about every Japanese toy on the market. The explosive was military—C4 plastique. They're doing hair and fiber analysis on some clothing that was found in a couple of trashcans in the area, but they say that won't help unless we have a suspect in custody. Oh, and a guy named Terry says you owe him lunch."

Jack gave the young man a nod. "Good work. Keep that up and we'll give you Dick's job … as soon as we figure out what that is."

"What about the other explosion? The one in Markham?"

"Nothing to connect the two yet. York Region say it was a fancy pipe bomb— black powder and shrapnel—hung on the door handle and triggered by movement. No C4, no remote, no detonator. It looks like a coincidence."

Jack looked around the room feeling a little uncomfortable. It was like everyone there was waiting for him to say some words of wisdom. He didn't have any.

"I don't believe in coincidences. Keep at it," was all he could manage.

Darcy signaled him from the corner with a cup of fresh coffee. Jack felt like a very old man as he made his way across the room.

"You buying?" Jack asked.

"Yeah," Darcy said.

"Cream, four sugars, heavy on the inspiration."

"You look tired."

"Thanks, that wasn't exactly the kind of inspiration I had in mind."

"Need some help?" Darcy asked.

"I could use a crystal ball. I'm not having much luck predicting the future."

"Then stop trying. Concentrate on the past."

"What do you mean?"

"Take a step back, Jack. You're too involved right now. Go back to the start, walk through it. What happened? What do you know for sure? What do you think you know?"

"Maybe you're right."

"I'm always right. Get used to it. Step into my office." Darcy pulled up a chair at the nearest desk and the two sat down facing each other. "So go back to the start and tell me everything."

When he was done reviewing the events of the past five days, Jack's head ached but things didn't seem any clearer. He looked around the room at the flurry of activity. The serious faces attested to the nature of the case. Doors banged with the various comings and goings, telephones rang, voices shouted, and keyboards clicked incessantly. A white board on the far wall held all of the pertinent data in neatly ordered columns. A second one held pictures placed on a loosely ordered family tree.

At the top was a question mark beside the name OSCAR. The room seemed like a newspaper office just before a deadline.

"What about Ricco?" Darcy asked. "Is he worth talking to again? Maybe he knows more than he's telling."

"I don't think so. He tried to pretend he was holding out but …"

"Is he safe?" Darcy asked. "Maybe that's where you touched the raw nerve. If Ricco does know more …"

"I thought about that," Jack said, "but I can't see Niles being crazy enough to go back to The Don. Every police officer and jail guard in the city has his picture. He'd have to be insane. Besides, Stan Jacobs said he'd baby-sit Ricco personally."

"Your friend?"

Jack nodded, rubbing his temples trying to relieve the throbbing.

"Okay, what about Oscar?"

"I don't know. I've been trying to figure that one out from the start. I've been trying to get inside this guy's head, but I can't seem to do it. Is he on the inside? Is he just somebody with a good idea?"

"An incredibly careful somebody."

"No argument. The guy's a little too careful, almost paranoid. I don't think he's a professional."

"What makes you so sure Oscar's a 'he'?"

Jack was too caught off guard to respond.

"I'm serious, Jack. Right from the start we've made the assumption we're dealing with a *guy* named Oscar. What if it's a woman?"

Jack nodded his head slowly, a thought starting to take shape and coalesce with a few others than had been banging around in the back of his mind. Before he could organize them or put them into words, however, his cell phone rang. Given its size, it took Jack a second to dig it out of his pocket. Darcy laughed.

"I'm buying you a new one for Christmas," she said.

Jack gave her a sardonic smile and answered it.

"Jack Wright."

"Jack?" The voice on the other end of the phone was tremulous. "It's Gillian."

Jack's heart sank. The guilt he'd been repressing washed over him like a tsunami. He should have visited already, or at least called, but he'd had no idea what to say. The idea that it should be him lying in the morgue instead of Calvin didn't exactly inspire conversation.

"Gill, I—"

Darcy was looking at him and reached out to take his hand, apparently not caring that everyone in the room was watching.

"I'm glad you called. Both Darcy and I want to see you, to tell you how sorry we are about Cal. I don't even know where to begin. I should have been there already, but—if there's anything …"

Jack could hear a stuttering intake of breath and knew that Gillian was crying. There's nothing more devastating to a person's resolve to be strong than a sympathetic voice. Jack waited until Gillian could regain control. Finally she continued.

"No, we're fine, Jack … honestly. Everyone's been amazing. Chief McAllister's made sure of that. The only thing I need—that Andrew needs," she said, "is for you to find out who did this … and let Andrew help. If not, I'm afraid Andrew may never stop," she finished.

"Stop?" Jack said. "Stop what?"

"Blaming himself."

Jack was thunderstruck. "Gill, what—that's crazy."

"I know, but that's the thing about guilt," Gillian interjected. "It doesn't have to make sense to tear you apart. He's been in his room with that computer since he found out. He thinks if he'd cracked the hard drive earlier that Calvin wouldn't—that his Dad would still be alive."

"Gill, that's—"

"I know. I know, Jack, but he's obsessed. He needs to feel like he's a part of it, you know. He wants to make it right. It may be the only way he'll ever move on. Will you talk to him?""

The anguish in Gillian Dempster's voice was like a knife slicing into Jack's heart.

"Of course." Was all he could manage.

While Gillian Dempster went to get her son, Jack tried to think of something to say. He didn't need to worry. Andrew obviously wasn't in the mood to listen.

"Sergeant Wright? Okay, so the first thing I found is a date. July 1ˢᵗ. Nothing else in the file, just the date. July 1ˢᵗ. Does that sound important?"

Andrew sounded excited, almost manic. Jack could tell he was desperate to come up with something that would help.

"Absolutely. That could be our 'when'. That's excellent. What else have you got?"

"I don't know. Maybe something, maybe nothing. A couple of small files. I—I kind of ignored them to get at the big stuff. Maybe I shouldn't have … I don't know."

There was a pause on the other end of the line before Andrew could continue.

"Anyway, they were still in the cache when I went back in. They weren't wiped out with the rest of the files. I took another look at them and hacked in pretty quick. It was easy, maybe a little too easy, you know? The language is different and the security codes are nowhere near as complicated. It doesn't even look like it was written by the same person programmer."

"That's good, Andrew. Really good. What's in the file?"

"It a phone list. Fifteen names and numbers, and then some dollar amounts next to the names. You want to see it?"

"You know it."

"You got a fax machine?"

"Yes." Jack gave him the number.

"Go stand by it. It should start coming through in about thirty seconds."

"Good work, Andrew. Excellent. This is a huge help. Your Dad would be proud."

Jack wasn't sure if he should have said the last part, if the pain was too raw, or if it was what Andrew needed to hear. As it turned out, it was probably a little of both. Jack heard a quiet 'Thanks' before the connection was broken.

The fax machine in the office started chattering in less than the thirty seconds promised. Jack picked up the sheet and scanned the names. When he got to the second last name on the list his stomach dropped to the floor. He grabbed his jacket and bolted for the door calling back over his shoulder.

"Darcy! Call the Don Jail. Talk to the Warden, nobody else. Tell him to isolate Ricco, now! I'll explain later. I need a cruiser ... who's got keys?!"

Tommy threw his from the far side of the room. "1640. In the back, far right."

"Jack, what—"

Before she could form the question, the office door rebounded off the wall and slammed shut behind Jack, leaving only the sound of his footsteps pounding down the hall. Darcy picked up the fax sheet from where Jack had dropped it and looked at the list. The second last name was familiar.

'Stan Jacobs DJ 555-8197'

CHAPTER SIXTY-ONE

The fully-marked cruiser was an older model Chev Caprice with an LT1 Corvette engine and police suspension. It was meant to be driven at speeds well in excess of 100 miles per hour. For the first part of his trip Jack was lucky to get it up to ten. Lunch hour traffic had the city streets snarled. Every time a lane cleared even slightly, the big car surged forward like a jungle cat lunging at prey. Jack muscled through a number of tight squeezes that barely left enough room for the stripes on the side of the car. Finally traffic in front of him opened up and Jack hammered the accelerator praying to God he wasn't too late.

As the line of prisoners moved along toward the dining hall, all eyes looked straight ahead. Dressed in identical coveralls the color of orange sherbet, few of the men took notice of a small knot of prisoners that was beginning to bunch up around inmate #66719. The guards, too, seemed oblivious to the disorder in the ranks.

The men in the knot of inmates all seemed to inhale at the same time just before the first punch was thrown. A loud shout, the blow, and then swift and violent retaliation. The man was much more solid than his thin frame suggested. He swung a fist that caught his attacker under the jaw. The man staggered, but came back at him almost immediately.

The prisoners crowded around the two combatants and began shouting encouragement. An emergency siren split the air, whistles blew, doors slammed shut, and bolts shot home automatically. The din became deafening, magnified by the stone and steel. A number of guards came running with batons and mace, their police boots echoing along the tiers, adding to the commotion. Other officers moved in an orderly fashion to lock down the corridor.

Prisoner #66719 landed several more good shots before his assailant took his feet out from under him. He hit the cold cement with a dull thud that signaled the end of any serious resistance.

"Detective Sergeant Wright, TPS. I need to see one of your prisoners right away. Somebody from my office called ahead." Jack released the 'Call' button on the intercom at the side of the Don Jail sally port.

"Hold on." The intercom went dead and stayed that way for what seemed like an eternity. A red light on the camera above the door blinked in slow motion. Jack swore under his breath at the delay.

After what seemed like an eternity, Jack was buzzed in. He shoved his pistol and extra mags in a security locker, and stepped between two heavy steel doors. As one large door slid shut behind him and locked with an ominous *snap*, a uniformed guard gave him the once over before opening a second steel door in front that allowed access to the intake rooms. The prison itself lay behind still more doors and gates and heavy-meshed screens.

"Business or pleasure, Sarge?"

Jack ignored the comment. "I need to see one of your inmates right now. Ricco. Vincent Ricco."

"Sorry, Sir," the guard said, obviously realizing it was no time to joke. Do you have a number? It'll be faster."

Before members of the tactical squad managed to split the ring of inmates, one of the men knelt in close to the fallen man and punched him square on the nose just hard enough to start a torrent of blood flowing. The two men nodded at each other and then allowed themselves to be pulled away by the guards. They continued to yell invectives and made a show of trying to continue the clash, but everyone watching knew it was over. Inmate #66719 tried to staunch the blood with his sleeve, and thought of the cigarettes and the ounce of Colombian that would be hidden in his room by the time he got out of solitary. He smiled to himself behind his bloodied shirtsleeve and thought, *Hell, I'd have done it for the grass alone.*

Further back in the line, seconds after the first shouts began, Vincent Ricco was grabbed by strong hands and pushed through a door that should have been locked. It led to a maintenance tunnel barely wide enough for two men to stand abreast. It hadn't been opened in years, but the newly oiled hinges allowed the heavy steel door to swing inward without a sound. The diversion created by the fight worked as intended. None of the guards noticed a thing.

The tunnel, which wound through the bowels of the ancient institution, had conduit running parallel to the floor some ten feet above the floor—the plumbing, electrical, and mechanical systems that feed the prison. Emergency lights were situated along the wall every thirty feet leaving areas of pitch blackness in between yellow cones of light. It looked like a surreal subway tunnel without tracks.

Ricco knew he was in serious shit before the door slammed shut behind the two men who had dragged him into the tunnel. His instincts for survival kicked in. Doubling over he grabbed the larger of the two men by the crotch and twisted viciously eliciting a yell that echoed the length of the tunnel. Swinging back up immediately he caught the second man full in the face with the back of his head and sent him sprawling backwards into the door.

Dazed himself, Ricco managed to break the grip of the giant man who was struggling to hang on despite the attack on his manhood. Ricco stumbled forward and then sprinted into the darkness with no idea where he was running. He was a survivor, and the little voice in his head was screaming "Run!"

Jack and the guard looked at each other when the first faint whistle reached the desk area. When the siren erupted the two other guards in the room reacted in a practiced manner that suggested trouble was common. Jack stood back and watched them slap switches and yank levers in what appeared to be random acts of recklessness. In reality everything was being done by the book. Video monitors were scanned and recordings started.

Jack watched a bank of video screens and tried to make sense out of the chaos. The screens showed four different angles of the area. The scenes flipped from view to view every few seconds making it difficult to concentrate on any one person. One of the guards pushed a button and stopped the cameras from scanning. In the transfer hall Jack watched as a large group of prisoners crowded around the two main combatants. Jack checked the grainy black and white image for a glimpse of Ricco. Nothing.

He watched as the guards moved like a well-oiled machine to separate the fighters. He was impressed with their efficiency, but a little surprised at how quickly order was restored. As if on cue, the prisoners stepped back in line and watched passively as the two principals were cuffed and escorted away without incident. The prisoners all looked down and remained silent. Something just wasn't right. Jack felt a sense of dread start somewhere in the pit of his stomach and spread slowly upward.

A thin trail of blood flowed into the two-day growth of stubble on Griffin's upper lip as he stepped back through the unlocked door and joined the line of prisoners. He swore softly at himself for underestimating Ricco. The little prick was tougher than he seemed. Having grayed-out for a second from the vicious head butt, he woke up just in time to see the broad back of his friend, Juju, lumbering into the darkness. Juju was bent slightly at the waist and hissing like an angry tom. Further down the tunnel he could hear the retreating footsteps of Juju's quarry slapping blindly against the cement.

Juju was too stubborn to give up and too stupid to understand the consequences. He'd spent his whole life doing what other people told him to do without question. That was what had landed him in jail in the first place. Today he was doing what Griffin told him to do, and Griffin knew nothing was going to stop him.

CHAPTER SIXTY-TWO

Jack spent most of the afternoon at the prison answering questions, looking for answers and providing a 'will state'. In the end there was little that was absolutely certain except the fact that Ricco was dead and Juju had no chance of making parole in September.

The search for the missing inmates started shortly after the rest were locked down and counted. The tactical squad found Juju sitting beside the very still, very twisted body of Ricco. Juju smiled when one of the guards confirmed that his neck was broken. Juju always did what he was told, and that's what he'd been told. *Break his freakin' neck.*

Stan Jacobs booked off sick about an hour before the fight started. He hadn't been heard from since. A 'uniform' sent around to the house reported that there was no answer when he knocked on the door and no signs of life. Jacobs was now wanted for questioning as a Person of Interest in a First Degree Murder investigation.

While Jack was busy at The Don, Wolfe and Morgan were carefully packing two stolen white panel vans. Magnetic signs now decked the side panels identifying the vehicles as part of a maintenance company. The license plates had been replaced with ones switched the night before from vans of the same color, make, and model year.

Katherine was sitting on one of the packing crates on the top floor of the warehouse, all but ignored by the three men studying blueprints at the makeshift table. She hadn't uttered a word since being taken up by

Wolfe. There was no indication that she even knew what was happening. She was like a marionette with all of her strings cut.

The three men arrived the night before on different flights from three different cities. They spoke in low tones, pointing out problem areas and possible escape routes. It was obvious from the way they worked they were professionals. The first string was in place.

"There's one thing I don't understand," Darcy said. Her voice on the other end of the phone sounded a million miles away.

"God, I wish there was only *one* thing I didn't understand," he said.

"The list with Stan's name, it was in the computer?" Darcy sounded skeptical.

"Andrew got it off the hard drive. That's why I went tearing out of the office. I had this crazy notion that I could actually do something right on this case."

"Stop blaming yourself, Jack. You had no way of knowing Stan Jacobs was dirty. How could you? He was your friend, not a suspect. You can't be on all the time. Give yourself a break."

"It doesn't matter. I should have been more careful with Ricco. I should have put him in segregation."

"It wouldn't have mattered. Jacobs could have gotten to him anywhere. Wolfe and the men at the prison killed Ricco, not you."

Jack didn't argue. Darcy was right, but like Gillian Dempster said, guilt doesn't have to make sense.

"So what is it about the list you don't understand?" Jack finally asked.

"It was on the computer before Ricco was arrested, right? How could Oscar have known he could use Stan Jacobs?"

"I don't know. I've been trying to figure that out."

"And how did Andrew break the code?" Darcy asked. "I thought it was impossible, that the files were wiped clean."

"There were a couple of files that weren't protected. They didn't get deleted. And according to Andrew the programming was different, the codes were different. Everything was a lot simpler, which means Oscar didn't write them."

"So who did? Wolfe?"

"It makes sense. I'm starting to get a feel for this guy and it fits. He's done this type of job so often he knows what to expect. He plans for every possible contingency. And according to the list he isn't afraid to pay well for the right kind of help. When the game's over he burns all of his bridges."

"Only in this case you think he wanted us to take care of that for him."

Jack didn't answer right away.

"So this is a list of what, informants?" Darcy asked.

"Maybe, or maybe just a list of possible informants. Not every one of them has a dollar figure beside the name. I think Wolfe tried to think of every angle, and then did his homework. He found the people who could help him out, no matter what happened. Stan Jacobs couldn't possibly have been a help until after somebody was caught, which means Wolfe is either psychic or incredibly meticulous."

"Maybe someone getting caught was part of the plan," Darcy offered.

"If that's the case, this guy's a little *too* good," Jack said.

"I didn't get a good look," Darcy said, "Was there a dollar figure next to Stan Jacobs' name?"

"There wasn't," Jack said, "but I'm guessing there is now."

CHAPTER SIXTY-THREE

"Tell me something, Johnny, now that the gang's all here, if you weren't planning on using him, why bring Ricco on board in the first place? Why hire that kind of liability?"

"Oh, he's far from a liability, Patrick. In fact, he's worked out just fine."

"Oh come now, lad. You can't tell me that you planned all of this to happen?"

"All of it? No." Wolfe smiled, but didn't elaborate. He continued to throw blankets and tools on top of the supplies in a way that looked disorganized enough to be natural. When he was done he stepped out and slammed the rear doors shut.

"Let's go upstairs. We've got a lot to go over before tonight."

"Have you had anything to eat today?" Jack asked.

"Not much, how about you?" Darcy sounded more than just a little tired.

"Nada. Think Uncle Clarence could whip us up a little food for thought?"

"I think I could talk him into it. What time?"

Jack checked his watch. "How about 7:30. I have to go see a lady about a little white lie."

"Sounds interesting."

"Something you said. I hope you're wrong, but everything seems to point in the same direction. I'll tell you about it when I gets to Stats."

It was six o'clock by the time Jack pulled into the Visitor's Parking in front of an impressive building. The brand new green facade of ComTech shone like an emerald in the late afternoon sun. With any luck, Katherine Sharpe was a workaholic. If not, he'd have to catch her in the morning. The 1st of July was still a few days away.

There wasn't another car in the lot, but Jack guessed most of the executives parked underground. As if to prove his theory a brand new Cadillac nosed its way up the steep ramp that led down to the garage. It hesitated at the top for a second and then roared off in a cloud of dust. Although the buildings were complete and the grounds around them totally landscaped, the road in front of the building had yet to be paved.

Jack tried one of two revolving doors set in the middle of the ultra-modern six-storey building. The first three floors of blue/green glass towered above the cement walk like the outer walls of a 21st century castle, while the last three receded back from the street like oversized steps. The revolving door didn't budge when he pushed on the stainless steel handle, but Jack could make out a security guard waving him to a secondary door to the left marked 'Emergency Only'.

The guard was young, with flaming red hair and a pale complexion. The freckles that covered his face did little to hide a touch of acne. The shine on his boots would have made a West Point cadet proud, and his uniform was pressed so the creases were perfectly straight and razor sharp. Jack put him at no more than twenty, probably a college student with a new summer job. His smile was friendly and eager to please. A polished brass nametag identified him as 'Ernie'. "Can I help?"

"I hope so. Detective Sergeant Wright, Toronto Police." Jack flipped open his shield and was impressed when the young man took a second to study the warrant card rather than just accepting the tin at face value. "I was hoping to speak with Ms. Sharpe if she's still here."

"I'm not sure if there's anybody left upstairs, sir, but I can try her office for you." He continued chatting as he paged through a corporate listing of names and extensions. "We're just in the middle of shift change so I don't know who's come and who's gone."

Jack leaned on the chest high green marble counter and watched the three video monitors on the desk flip from view to view.

"Here it is, 6120. Do you want me to tell her you're here?"

"No. I'd rather surprise her. Tell her there's an old friend here to see her."

Jack watched the video monitors and listened to the one sided conversation. After a second the young guard covered the mouthpiece and turned to face Jack.

"Her secretary says Ms. Sharpe left work this morning. Would you like to speak to her?" Ernie held the phone out to Jack.

"Miss Symmons, it's Detective Wright, we met a few days ago? I realize it's late but … Yes, very important. Thanks, I appreciate that. No, if I get lost I'm sure Ernie can point me in the right direction."

Jack handed the phone back to Ernie who was all business.

"If there's anything you need while you're here, get someone to ring the desk."

Jack smiled and turned to go, but then turned back.

"Actually, there is something you can tell me. Is Brad Mikstas working tonight, or is he strictly nine to five?"

"The Boss? No sir, he hardly ever works nine to five. Likes to make snap inspections. He's not in right now, but I was given a heads up that he's coming in later. That's why I'm cleaning," Ernie said, with a chuckle.

"Strict boss?" Jack asked.

Ernie was dead serious. "You know it. Ex-military and tough as nails. He expects everything to be perfect."

Jack gave the young guard the once over. "I think you'll pass."

Ernie straightened his back, smiled broadly, and snapped off an impressive salute.

"Thank you, sir."

"Carry on, soldier."

Five minutes later Jack was on the sixth floor. Jane was straightening up her desk before leaving for the day. She looked tired, but smiled when she saw Jack.

"Detective Wright, you just caught me."

"You're working late. Is this the norm?"

"Only when I have a day like I've had today. How can I help you? You said it was important? Is Katherine all right?"

Jack nodded. "Actually, I was hoping to talk to her, but the guard on the front desk told me she left this morning?"

"Yes, I'm afraid so. There's been a death in her family. I'm not sure when she'll be back. Is there anything that I can help you with?"

"I was hoping to make an appointment to meet with her as soon as possible, but if you're not sure when she'll be back ... was it a close family member?"

"I'm not sure. She didn't say. She did seem pretty upset when she left, though."

Jane must have realized she was being a little too candid and stopped talking. Jack waited an awkward moment and then cleared his throat.

"Please give her my condolences, and ask her to call me when she feels up to it. She has my number. It's very important."

"I'll see that she gets the message."

"Thank you." Jack walked to the door and then turned with his hand on the brass knob. "By the way, did she get a call this morning from one of her family or ...?"

Jane answered without thinking. "No actually, her cousin came to the office. Is this part of your investigation, Detective?"

Jack ignored the question. Bells and whistles were starting to ring quietly in the back of his head.

"Male or female?"

"I'm sorry?"

"Her cousin. Man or woman?"

"A man, but I don't really see what—"

The bells and whistles got a little louder.

"Can you describe him by any chance, or did he leave a name?"

Jack could see the hesitation in her eyes.

"Really, Detective Wright, I don't see how—"

"It's important. I think Ms. Sharpe may be in trouble and I want to help. Do you remember anything in particular about him? Anything at all?"

"I—" Jane hesitated. "I don't remember much about him, really. He was tall and thin and well dressed."

"Do you remember his name?"

She nodded. "It's hard to forget a name like that. You don't meet many people in Toronto named Wolfgang."

CHAPTER SIXTY-FOUR

Darcy made it to Stats about fifteen minutes before Jack, and took up a stool at the far end of the bar. It was the same stool she'd used for more than half of her life, but tonight she couldn't get comfortable. She wanted to talk to Jack about what she'd learned since he rushed out of the office. Instead, she sat at the bar letting her coffee get cold and chatting with the waitress whenever there was a lull in the action.

Darcy laughed at something the girl said and turned back to the bar just in time to catch an update on the evening news. A perfectly coifed newscaster was giving the latest on the two bombings.

'Police are still investigating the murder of 50 year old Detective Calvin Dempster of the Guns & Gangs Unit. This afternoon, investigators confirmed a connection between the bombing that killed one of their own and the recent fatal police shooting of a suspected gunrunner. Police are asking anyone with information on the whereabouts of this man to contact them as soon as possible, or to contact Crime Stoppers. The composite sketch shown here was made from eyewitness accounts taken on the night of the bombing. The man, classified only as a 'Person of Interest', was seen in the area of the explosion and is wanted for questioning.

In other news, the investigation continues into another explosion that claimed the life of one man and injured a second. No connection has been made between the two bombings, although police have not ruled out the possibility they are related. The second explosion occurred shortly after the first killing 43 year old Pavel Milanovich, a Russian Physicist in Canada on a work visa. A spokesman for ComTech Dynamic Industries, the victim's employer, said everyone at the company is deeply saddened by the loss and their thoughts and prayers go out to the Milanovich's family back home in Russia. Anyone with any information is asked to contact The York Regional Police Service.' Reporting live …

Darcy didn't hear Cathy asking her if she wanted something to eat. All she could hear was the pounding in her ears. *ComTech Dynamic Industries! That was one of the companies on the list. Jack was there three days ago. That was the woman that … Jack said he had to see someone about a little white lie'.*

Darcy bolted for the front door. She had to find Jack right away. She did. The door caught him squarely in the chest when she burst through it, almost sending him flat on his ass.

"Jesus woman, what are you doing? You almost killed me!"

Darcy was breathless with excitement. "Jack, the news. The second bombing. I know what the target is! The guy was connected to—"

"ComTech Dynamic Industries," Jack said, rubbing his chest. "I know."

"You heard the news?"

Jack shook his head.

"Then how—"

"I just came from ComTech."

"But if that's the target then I was right. Oscar's—"

"—a woman named Katherine Sharpe."

Darcy hit him in the shoulder with a closed fist. "Would you let me finish a fucking sentence?!"

"Would you stop beating me to a bloody pulp? Come on back inside. We've got a lot to talk about and I'm starving."

"Are you nuts?! Jack, we've got it. We know when and we know where and now who, right?"

Jack turned serious.

"No question. I just spoke with her secretary. She said a man named Wolfgang collected her boss this morning about 11:00. She identified Wolfe from the composite sketch I showed her."

"So what are we going to do?"

"Well, I don't know about you," Jack smiled, "but I'm gonna have the special. Your uncle does a mean prime rib."

CHAPTER SIXTY-FIVE

The two stolen vans moved through the city on separate routes leading to the same location. It was 9:30 in the evening. The last of the meager daylight was disappearing quickly. The roads seemed deserted in comparison to the traffic on them both times they'd driven them during their practice runs.

Wolfe was in the front passenger seat of one of the vans, while Morgan rode shotgun in the second. All five of the mercenaries were identically dressed in white company coveralls over dark military fatigues. The coveralls would be shed once they were inside. Underneath, each man wore a Toronto Police Service ETF uniform—just in case.

Wolfe tested the digitally encrypted walkie-talkies.

"Delta One from Alpha One."

"Delta One—go."

"Radio check."

"10-4 Alpha One, you're coming in 10-2, confirm."

"10-4 Delta One, 10-2, out."

Wolfe insisted the two teams use basic military radio procedure, including the primary Ten Codes. Wolfe and his driver were Alpha One and Alpha Two. Morgan and his team were Delta One, Delta Two, and Delta Three.

The vans met up near the Langstaff exit of the 400, a major highway that runs north from Toronto, and headed east towards Concord. Morgan's driver, Delta Two, moved in behind the lead van from an access road. The timing was perfect. The two vans moved as one until they reached the construction zone in front of the complex.

There was no need for any communication between the vehicles at that point. The men involved had worked together on several other jobs over the years. Each one knew his assignment without being told. The planning and preparation were behind them. There was nothing left but the execution.

CHAPTER SIXTY-SIX

"What's her background?"

"As far as I can tell she has no record. Not even a parking ticket. It doesn't make sense."

"So what do we know about her?" Darcy asked.

"41, single, no children. Lives in Forest Hill just off St. Clair. No boyfriend, no siblings, and both of her parents are dead. Hard working blue-collar family. Her father died when she was young. She was raised by her mother and a step-father."

"So how does that translate into criminal mastermind?"

"It doesn't," Jack said.

"What's her D.O.B.? I've got a friend who can do an off-line search for me."

"Twelve, August, '71."

While Darcy typed a quick text, Jack continued. "According to her secretary, Katherine Sharpe is brilliant, graduated top of her class at MIT and started ComTech shortly after graduation. That was fifteen years ago. Impressive for somebody so young."

"Okay," Darcy wasn't convinced. "So she's got the brains, but what about the motive? She must be making a pretty good buck. What's her reason?"

Jack shrugged. "Power, fame ... maybe just for kicks. It wouldn't be the first time somebody did something like this because they could."

"Maybe, but what are they after? Computers? Seems like a lot of work for the money. It's obviously not jewels, unless they use them in the production somehow?"

"No, I asked about that."

"So Ricco was lying?"

"I don't think so," Jack said. "He was telling the truth, or what he thought was the truth."

"You lost me."

"I think Wolfe hired Ricco as a fall guy, just in case. That would explain why he had Stan Jacobs lined up before anyone was caught. I think Ricco was told it was a jewelry heist because Wolfe knew if it went south he'd sing like a canary."

"Which is exactly what happened."

"I wouldn't be surprised if Wolfe planned this whole damned thing."

"You think this guy's that good?"

"Oh, I think he's a hell of a lot better than 'good'."

The restaurant and bar were beginning to fill up with a good crowd of the regulars. The NBA finals were playing on most of the televisions, and the noise level rose and fell with the level of excitement in the game. Jack and Darcy ignored it all. The waitress removed their plates and quickly wiped down the table between them.

"Can I get you anything else?"

"Just the bill, thanks Cathy," Jack said.

Cathy looked at Darcy and rolled her eyes.

"Stats' number one rule," Darcy explained. "Family eats free."

"God, if your uncle had adopted me ten years ago, I would have saved a fortune."

"What would you do with a fortune?" Darcy teased.

"Retire and let somebody else bang his head against a brick wall."

"I don't believe that for a second," Darcy said. 'You'd miss it too much."

"You think so?"

"I know so. You'd miss the people, you'd miss the excitement, mostly you'd miss the challenge. You live to unravel mysteries. It's why you get up in the morning."

"I get up because Charlie needs to go out."

"Without it you wouldn't know what to do with yourself. You'd rather die than retire."

"Hopefully both are a long way off," Jack said.

He was a little uncomfortable and pleasantly surprised that Darcy had pegged him so quickly.

"What about you? What would you do with all the money in the world?"

Darcy was quiet for a long time.

"I don't know. There are a lot of people I'd like to help … a lot of things I'd like to do. I love my job, but … if you asked me that a week ago … I think the first thing I'd do now is take a month off at a spa. Spend some time thinking about the future. Career, kids, life, you name it. Pretty corny, eh? Do I look like June Cleaver to you?"

Jack reached across the table without thinking and took her hand in his. She didn't pull away.

"Not corny at all," he said. "As for how you look … you look like the most beautiful woman I've ever seen."

Darcy interlaced her fingers with his. One of the guys from the precinct noticed and pointed it out to a fellow officer with a tilt of his head. There would be a new rumor floating around the 56th by morning.

CHAPTER SIXTY-SEVEN

The stolen vans pulled into the visitor's parking lot in front of the complex and moved to the far end of the building. With no moon and the streetlights in the construction zone not yet installed, the world outside of the glass fortress was pitch black. Wolfe lifted the small radio and, looking at his watch, gave one final instruction.

"Alpha One. On my mark everyone set your watches to 22:15."

"Mark. Go!"

Ernie wasn't aware he had company until he heard a knock at the front and looked up to see the president of the company, Ms. Sharpe, standing by the small emergency door. He grabbed a set of keys off the marble desk and punched in a code to disable the perimeter alarm before walking quickly to the door shaking his head in commiseration. He wasn't the only one working late. He could make out the figure of a second person standing behind Katherine Sharpe, but he didn't think anything of it until he pulled the door open and saw the silenced barrel of a pistol pointed at his head. Complacency, even at 20, can be a bitch.

Wolfe pushed past Katherine and pressed the Beretta up against the guard's forehead.

"Back up. Move."

The young man did as he was told, the color draining from his already pale face. He stopped when his back hit a door behind the desk.

It lead to a small room that housed the security sensor controls and the video recorders.

"Open it," Wolfe said, indicating the door with the barrel of his gun.

The guard reached behind and searched frantically for the door knob. The click of the lock and the *snap* of the 9mm. round happened at almost the same time. The hollow-point round caught the young man in the middle of forehead, expanding on impact. He was dead before he hit the floor.

Any spark of resistance left in Katherine died with Ernie. To Wolfe it was like watching the candle on a cake being blown out by a strong breath. Her eyes glazed over as a last defense to a world that she just couldn't handle.

Katherine would have hit the floor at about the same time as Ernie if not for Morgan. He'd followed in closely behind Wolfe and was there to catch her as her legs buckled. He put his arm around her waist and pulled her towards the elevator. He held onto her gently, like a father leading his sleepy child to bed. Katherine moved like an automaton, a scream stuck somewhere deep in her throat and silent tears flowing down her cheeks.

Delta Two moved into the first elevator that arrived and held it for Morgan. Katherine was left to lean against the cold brushed steel of the foyer walls. The two men took the elevator down two floors to prepare for the work ahead. When the doors to the second elevator slid open Alpha Two steered Katherine into the lift. Wolfe stepped in right behind him and pushed the button for the sixth floor.

CHAPTER SIXTY-EIGHT

Darcy pulled her hand away before Jack did, a blush turning her cheeks crimson.

"Where do we go from here?"

"What do you mean?" Jack was enjoying the fact Darcy was uncomfortable.

"I mean with the case. What now? Do we just wait until the 1st and hope they stick to the schedule? I mean, we're not even sure the date Andrew found is right, although it certainly makes sense."

"I don't follow."

"Canada Day," Darcy said, as if that explained everything.

Jack waited.

"Do you know how many gun calls the Comcenter gets on a night when there are fireworks. People all over the city call in to report gunshots and bombings. The ETF gets called out on a regular basis for nothing. Response times are way down."

"For something like this a delay of even a few minutes could mean all the difference in the world," Jack said. Wolfe seemed to have thought of every advantage.

"Assuming it is the First of July, that only gives us a little over a week to figure this thing out."

Jack shook his head and turned serious. "I'll see about setting up surveillance in the morning."

"On ComTech?"

"And Katherine Sharpe. Maybe we can pick up Wolfe before anybody else gets hurt."

Darcy dropped her eyes to the table and Jack thought he knew why. Darcy still blamed herself for letting Wolfe slip away. He changed the subject.

"I'd also like to talk to Karski, have him take a look at the building. Maybe he can figure out a weakness so we can anticipate how these guys might try to hit the place."

"What about warning the company itself? Shouldn't we tell somebody, maybe the CEO or someone on the Board?"

"Not until we figure out exactly who's involved. If we go in there and sound the alarm, Wolfe may go to ground, and that's one bastard that I definitely want to meet again." His last words were low and ominous.

"So we leave the company completely in the dark?" Darcy asked.

"Not completely," Jack said. "I'll have a talk with Brad Mikstas, the Director of Security. Feel him out. I'm willing to bet he's not involved. If he was, they wouldn't need to make this a military operation."

"Makes sense. When did you want to speak to him?"

"You feel up to a little overtime?"

"Paid?" Darcy joked.

"In your dreams."

The ride to the ComTech building in Concord was made in relative silence until Darcy's Blackberry buzzed softly.

"Uh-oh. In-coming," Darcy said.

"What is it?"

"Shelly, my friend from Intel."

"Ours?" Jack said.

Darcy shook her head. "Don't ask."

Jack waited while Darcy scrolled down the message from her mysterious friend. A low whistle confirmed she'd found something interesting.

"What?" Jack asked.

"Well, Ms. Sharpe, isn't exactly Snow White. She's got a record as a Young Offender."

"For what, truancy?"

The smile froze on his face when Darcy answered.

"Murder."

CHAPTER SIXTY-NINE

"What?!"

Jack waited impatiently while she finished reading the text. After what seemed like a millennium, Darcy filled him in.

"Apparently she hit her step-father over the head with a baseball bat while he was sitting in his La-Z-Boy drinking beer and watching the hockey game. The report said she hit him numerous times. That's the word they used ... *numerous.*"

Normally Jack would have made a quip about her not being a Leafs fan, but he was too stunned to say anything.

"She was charged with Second Degree Murder. Defense introduced a whack of evidence at the Prelim pointing to years of sexual abuse by the accused. Katherine was only fourteen at the time. The Crown elected not to proceed. Apparently they felt there was no prospect of a conviction."

"You think?" Jack said.

After a long silence, Darcy switched to something else that was obviously bothering her.

"If Mikstas is part of this, we're screwed."

"I talked to him on Tuesday. I'd give odds he wouldn't step out of line for anything in the world. He oozes integrity. A company man, through and through."

"I hope you're right."

"So do I," Jack said. "My track record hasn't exactly been stellar lately."

CHAPTER SEVENTY

When the doors of the elevator slid open on the second basement level, Morgan couldn't resist the temptation.

"2B or not 2B," he said quietly. His partner looked at him blankly and then turned to face the open door.

The two men hesitated long enough to make sure no one was walking the corridor. As far as they knew there were three remaining security guards on duty, all of them armed.

Once satisfied, they moved quickly across a wide hallway and into a mechanical room that housed the boilers and a host of other massive machines. There were dials and switches and valves everywhere, all clearly marked. *How convenient,* Morgan thought.

Morgan and his partner stripped off their white coveralls to reveal the gray fatigues. Each man wore a small 9mm Uzi sub-machine gun on a harness under the shoulder, along with extra clips, and a lightweight Kevlar vest. Morgan was carrying a blue toolbox in each hand. He moved to the back of the room to set a two-hour time delay charge on the gas main. That done, he moved over to the panels that handled the hundreds of telephone lines that serviced the building.

Delta Two went to work on the door of the cubicle that held the central processor for the LaserTech 25. He unpacked an array of sophisticated tools from the top tray of his toolbox. He organized them carefully before beginning his assault on the lock. One of the few faults of Benjamin Sharpe's system was that the cubicle itself wasn't alarmed.

The LaserTech 25 wasn't designed to protect against an assault from within.

Alpha Two stepped off the elevator first when it reached the sixth floor, the Uzi held out in front of him just below eye level. Both sets of coveralls were rolled in a ball in the corner of the lift. He backed up against the far wall and checked in both directions before signaling for the other two to join him. The EXIT signs at either end of the corridor were the only things clearly visible in the dim emergency lighting.

Katherine stumbled into the hallway with Wolfe holding her arm in one hand and the silenced Beretta in the other. He half pushed, half dragged her in the direction of the executive offices, gripping her upper arm hard enough to leave a bruise. He moved quickly and confidently in the darkness, like a cat on a familiar path.

"Which one is Sumner's?"

Katherine looked up at him, a look of confusion in her eyes. Wolfe slapped her across the face with just enough force to clear the cobwebs.

Before she could answer, however, the door to the office behind them opened and the hallway was immediately bathed in light. Ted Sumner stood just to the left with his hand on the light switch. Brad Mikstas stood in the doorway with his body bladed sideways to the door, a nickel-plated Colt Python .357 Magnum pointed directly at the back of Wolfe's head.

CHAPTER SEVENTY-ONE

"No need for that, Mr. Wolfe. Have your friend step into the light … nice and easy.."

Katherine was never more happy or relieved to see anyone in her life. The elation didn't last long.

"Alpha One this is Delta Three. You have two visitors approaching the front door. They look unfriendly, compris?"

A brief burst of static followed Delta Three's transmission.

"If you don't mind, Mr. Sumner, I need to answer that. We may have a problem."

Mikstas didn't move and Sumner didn't answer quickly enough to suit Wolfe.

"Mr. Sumner, I'm here to do you a favor. Tell him to put down the gun. I thought we had an understanding?"

"We do, Mr. Wolfe, but Brad here is a very cautious individual. You put away your weapon, and have your friend lower the machine gun, I'm sure everyone will feel a lot better."

Wolfe nodded at Alpha Two at the same time he holstered the Beretta. He pulled the radio off his belt, without waiting for permission from Sumner, and answered the call.

"Delta Three, Alpha One. Maintain your position. Alpha Two will intercept. Acknowledge."

"Delta Three. 10-4."

Wolfe nodded at Alpha Two who moved quickly toward the elevators without looking back. Mikstas started to object, but Sumner cut him off.

"I trust he'll handle the situation as we discussed?" Sumner asked.

"No one gets hurt," Mikstas barked. "That's the deal, right? No rough stuff with any of my people!"

Katherine looked from one man to the next without seeming to recognize any of them. She was too shocked and confused to even begin to understand what was happening. She started to giggle hysterically when Brad told Wolfe that no one was to be hurt. She could still see Ernie, his eyes open and lifeless. Mikstas lowered the gun and stepped back. Sumner reached out to guide Katherine into the well-lit office.

"You don't look well, Katherine. Come in and sit down." The concern in his voice added to the surreal atmosphere as she felt herself pushed gently down onto the couch.

"Confused, Katherine? There's no need to be," Sumner said.

Standing at a bar in the corner, pouring a healthy shot of scotch into three crystal tumblers, he spoke over his shoulder

"Really, it's a simple business transaction. Right, Mr. Wolfe?"

Wolfe raised his glass in a toast.

"You see, Katherine, you hired Mr. Wolfe to do a job. You hired him to steal something that rightfully belongs to the company, which therefore belongs to me."

Katherine didn't acknowledge the glass in front of her or Sumner's words. Sumner carried on anyway, obviously enjoying the spotlight.

"Being a businessman, Mr. Wolfe realized the folly of your plan and came to me with a very interesting proposition. You were going to pay him five hundred thousand dollars to steal the new processors. He offered to give me the details of your adventure and convince you to hand over your programs on artificial intelligence for one million. Given the market value of something like this, how could I refuse?"

Sumner unsnapped the clasps on a thick legal-sized briefcase and flipped up the lid so Wolfe could inspect the neat stacks of well-worn bills. Wolfe nodded and Sumner closed the attaché case again and laid it on the desk.

"In the end," Sumner continued, "you agree to sign over your portion of the company to avoid prosecution, my investors and I get what's rightfully ours, and my friend Mr. Wolfe here will be one million dollars richer. Isn't that right, Mr. Wolfe?"

"Except for one thing, Ted," Wolfe said. "I'm not your friend."

Mikstas turned to the bar with a smile that froze on his lips when he caught a reflection in the mirror. Wolfe drew the Beretta and fired two shots into the back of the Security Director's head before the man could turn away from the image of his own death. He crashed into the shelves and dropped to the floor in a shower of glass and blood and scotch.

Katherine's scream seemed to go on forever, in perfect harmony with the breaking glass.

CHAPTER SEVENTY-TWO

Jack pulled the unmarked Chevy into the visitor's parking in front of the main doors at ComTech Dynamic Industries. Two white vans were parked at the far end of the lot in the shadow of an adjacent building.

The front foyer was brightly lit behind the glass facade and Jack was a little surprised to see there was no one behind the marble desk. Something didn't feel right.

"I wonder where my friend Ernie is?"

"Who?" Darcy asked.

"The kid I told you about. That young security guard. I didn't take him for the type to go AWOL."

"Probably had to use the washroom. Even Renfrew of the Mounties had to pee on the odd occasion."

Jack wasn't in a joking mood. Something was definitely wrong.

"What about those vans at the far end of the parking lot?"

Darcy nodded, seeming to pick up on the vibrations Jack was giving off.

"I saw them. Looks like some kind of a cleaning company, but I can't make out the name."

"Solitarus Cleaning and Maintenance," Jack said, squinting to bring the picture into focus.

"Good eyes," Darcy said. "What do you think?"

"It's a damned strange place to park if you're doing a late night cleaning job."

"A long way to carry your mop and bucket," Darcy agreed.

Jack looked at the trees and then back to the vans.

"How's your Latin?" Jack asked.

Darcy gave him a quizzical look.

"Solitarus. It means singular ... or lone."

"Lone Wolf. You don't think—"

"There's somebody in that first van," Jack interrupted.

"How—"

"Cigarette," Jack said simply. "There's a glow in the cab of that first van. I think we better go find Ernie. Keep an eye on that van and watch your ass."

They tried not to look conspicuous as they approached the front doors of the building. "What's the game plan?" Darcy asked.

"First, we find out what happened to Ernie, then we call in the Cavalry. I'd rather be wrong and look stupid than—"

They were walking past the small door marked 'For Emergency Use Only' when Jack suddenly stopped talking. He could just make out the toe of one very shiny boot poking out from behind the green marble counter.

"What's wrong?"

"Time to call in the Cavalry."

"What is it?"

"Ernie. It's going down tonight. Shit, I should have seen this coming. We need backup now."

"Call from inside?"

Jack shook his head. "If they're smart, they've already cut the phone lines."

"Cell?"

"In the car. Dead battery," Jack said.

"Christmas," Darcy said without humor, reaching for her Blackberry. "Shit!"

"What?'

"No signal."

Jack was too pumped to give her a smart ass reply.

"Use the car radio, but watch out for our friend in the van. Walk over like you forgot something in the car. Here, take the keys. I'll watch from here. If he makes a move, get the hell out of there. If you have to split, just hit the horn. I'll be right behind you. I don't plan on being a dead hero."

"No? What do you plan, Mr. Wayne?"

"Smart ass!"

Jack pushed on the small door and found it unlocked. He looked at Darcy and shrugged.

"I have to check on Ernie. I won't go past the front desk until you get inside, I promise. Once we know backup's on the way, we'll take it one step at a time."

"Don't break that promise. You get yourself killed, I'll never speak to you again."

With that she walked off in the direction of the unmarked patting her pockets and trying to look perplexed. Jack couldn't help thinking it was a good thing she became a cop instead of an actress. Delta Three keyed his handset in the darkness and relayed another message to Wolfe.

Darcy tried to watch the van out of the corner of her eye, but it wasn't easy. She didn't see any movement, but then her eyes weren't as good as Jack's. She couldn't even see the cigarette. She brushed her hand across the pistol under her jacket as she moved towards the Chevy. It seemed like an awfully long walk.

When she got to the side of the car she made a show of searching for her keys and slipped the pistol from her shoulder holster. She used her left hand to unlock the door, holding the pistol in her right. Sliding in behind the wheel, she dropped her weapon on the passenger seat so she could operate the police radio. She realized her mistake right away, but it was too late. The inside of the car smelled like an ashtray. She could tell how sharp the blade was by the feel of it against her throat. Everything happened so fast that she didn't even have a chance to scream.

CHAPTER SEVENTY-THREE

Jack watched Darcy until she was almost at the car, then drew his pistol and moved quickly through the door. There was no sense in being coy. He extended both arms out in front of him and swung the Glock from side to side. The big gun did very little to boost his sense of security. The bright lights and lack of cover made it seem like being in a bad dream, the one where you suddenly realize you're naked in a public place.

He sidestepped along the front of the building until he could see behind the security desk. Ernie's body was face down on the cold marble floor, lying in a pool of blood.

Jack moved quickly over to the desk, covering the door behind and the bank of elevators to the left. He kept glancing at the building's front wall of glass, expecting it to implode at any second. He crouched behind the desk with his back to a set of drawers, and pushed on the service door to the security room. The door moved easily and swung flat against the wall with barely a sound. The light in the small room revealed smashed video equipment and cut wires, but no bad guys.

Disregarding his own safety, Jack moved to the body of the young guard and felt for a carotid pulse. As expected, there wasn't one. He moved around the desk in a crouch covering the elevators and then swung his attention to the set of double doors that led to the first floor main office. He used the mirrored front facade to watch the far side of the foyer, trying to ignore the fear in his own reflection.

Jack checked the front door every few seconds, expecting to see Darcy at any moment. He was so focused on the two areas of possible danger that he didn't notice the number above the far elevator start to descend from six. The lift stopped briefly on four and then continued downward. When the bell signaled its arrival, Jack swung around to cover the doors as they slid open and put six pounds of pressure on an eight-pound trigger. He eased off and relaxed a bit when he saw a security guard step from the lift.

CHAPTER SEVENT-FOUR

"Jesus Christ!"

Sumner dove on the floor when the shots were fired and covered his head with his arms as if he expected the ceiling to collapse. Katherine stopped screaming at the sound of his voice and buried her face in the couch. The only sound from Mikstas was the air slowly escaping from his lungs, like a bicycle tire with a bad leak. Wolfe turned his flat gray eyes on Sumner and slowly brought the Beretta around so the sights rested on the bridge of his nose.

"There's been a change of plans, Mr. Sumner. You're experiencing what they call a hostile takeover."

The corner of Wolfe's mouth curled into a grin, but his eyes never changed.

"Stand up, please."

Sumner didn't move. Wolfe fired a shot into the desk about six inches from Sumner's head.

"Stand up!"

Sumner did as he was told, using the desk to pull himself up. He was shaking so badly his legs could barely support his weight.

"Now ... let's get a few things straight. Ms. Sharpe hired me to do a job. I intend to carry it out. You have the power to make my job easy or hard depending on your level of cooperation. I, on the other hand, have the power to make your death easy or hard, depending on that same cooperation. Understand?"

"You're fucking insane! We had a deal. I kept my end. If you think I'm going to pay you one cent more—" Sumner used the anger to hide his fear.

Wolfe snapped off a quick shot that tore through the shoulder pad in Sumner's jacket. A puddle of urine started to stain the carpet at the executive's feet.

"Am I getting through to you yet, Ted?" Wolfe asked, almost cordially. "The deal we had is null and void. It's a whole new ball game. Time to start renegotiating. What you're bargaining for now is how quickly you die. Slow and painful or quick and easy. Personally, I don't care one way or the other."

Sumner's eyes grew wide with fear and he tried to speak, but Wolfe couldn't make out a coherent word.

"Good," Wolfe said. "I can see we have an understanding. Now, given Katherine's present state, I need your security pass and the combination for the vault downstairs."

Sumner was still leaning on the desk and shaking badly, but he looked at Wolfe from under hooded eyes and found his voice. "You're insane. Go fuck yourself."

Wolfe's smile broadened considerably.

"I admire that kind of courage, Ted, but—"

Wolfe snapped off two incredibly fast shots hitting Sumner in the right hand and left foot. The silencer on the Beretta was beginning to clog from repeated use, but it didn't matter. The gunshots were muffled by Sumner's screams. Katherine buried her face deeper in the couch and covered her head.

Sumner dropped to the ground, blood now mixing with the puddle of urine at his feet. There was no more defiance. He was sobbing like a child and rocking to ease the pain. The tears were cascading down his face and his nose was free flowing. Wolfe didn't waste any more time. He pressed Sumner's head down with the barrel of the gun and increased the pressure on the trigger slowly.

"The combination."

"Stop it!" Katherine screamed. She was standing by the couch with a wild look in her eyes. Her hair was disheveled and her eyes bloodshot from too many tears. "Stop it! Leave him alone! I'll give you what you want."

Wolfe eased up on the trigger and smiled in her direction.

"Now," Wolfe said simply.

Katherine quickly scribbled a series of numbers and letters on a piece of paper from Sumner's desk and handed it to Wolfe. Wolfe scanned the scrap of paper, and then looked deeply into Katherine's eyes, taking his time. When he was sure Katherine had given him the real combination, he spoke quietly to Sumner without looking down.

"You know the contract you have with Katherine, Ted?"

Sumner didn't respond.

"Ever hear of a shotgun clause?"

Wolfe squeezed the trigger and fired one shot into the back of Theodore Sumner's head. He watched as the breath rolled out of Katherine in a low groan. She sank down into the soft leather of the couch just as Wolfe's radio crackled to life.

CHAPTER SEVENTY-FIVE

The security guard, an older man, tall and thin with a fringe of gray hair, took a tentative step off the elevator and stopped. He turned to look at Jack crouched behind the desk and seemed to smile, but something was wrong. Jack found out what when the man pitched face forward on the floor. The back quarter of his head was completely gone.

Before Jack could react, a figure dressed in a gray uniform exploded from the lift. It's amazing how the human mind works ... or doesn't. Jack stood frozen in place for a second, wondering why a member of the ETF would kill a guard.

The man squeezed off a well-aimed burst of automatic weapon fire as he ran to his left. Jack ducked as his mirror image, a few feet to the right, shattered into a thousand pieces. The mercenary, realizing his mistake, tried again, but Jack was already returning fire. His first two shots went wild, but the third one caught Alpha Two in the right shoulder spinning him in a complete circle along the wall.

The mercenary stayed on his feet, but wasn't able to raise the weapon with his shattered right arm. Jack fired again catching him dead center in the chest, but it seemed to have no effect.

When Alpha Two switched the weapon to his left hand Jack fired two more quick shots, this time aimed at his assailant's head. One of them hit home, slamming the man back into the brushed steel. Jack covered the mercenary with his pistol as the man slid down the wall into a sitting position leaving a trail of bright red on the spotless wall.

It took everything Jack had to remember his training. He kept his Glock out in front of him, sweeping it from side to side to cover the front door, the elevator, the office doors, and the body of the mercenary. He moved carefully, sidestepping like a crab to keep his back to a wall. When he got to the body of his attacker he stepped on the barrel of the Uzi. He didn't bother to check for a pulse this time, but reached down further and felt the man's chest, finding what he expected—Kevlar.

He started to move to the front door to check on Darcy when the radio on the dead man's belt stopped him in his tracks. The volume was turned down low but the words seemed to echo in the empty foyer.

"Alpha One this is Delta Two."

"Delta Two, go."

"I have one of our unexpected guests with me—a female—and we have one male gate crasher in the main floor ballroom. Any requests for the band?"

Wolfe was tired of the charade. It was time for plain English. "Kill her!"

"Already done."

"Then sit tight. We'll take care of the other one. Make sure there's no interference from outside. Acknowledge."

"Acknowledged. Out."

Jack stared at the radio for what seemed like a very long time. For a second he wasn't sure he was going to be able to stay on his feet. He rested his head against the wall and squeezed his eyes shut. *Darcy.* He tried to think about procedure but for a second he couldn't remember a thing he'd been taught. Then his mind began to focus on one thing. *Wolfe!*

The far elevator hummed as it started to move down. Jack dropped the clip from his pistol and inserted a new one. A tactical reload. His training was coming back.

CHAPTER SEVENTY-SIX

"You heard the man, Cheri. I have no choice. As far as he knows, you're already dead." Delta Three shook his head. "What a waste."

Before Darcy knew what was happening, her assailant stepped from the car and reached back in through the open door to press a pistol to the side of her head. The man moved like a cat, quick and graceful. He was slightly taller than Darcy and quite a bit heavier. She watched him out of the corner of her eye, gauging him, watching for any mistake. So far, he hadn't made one.

When she'd slipped behind the wheel of the unmarked he'd wasted no time in pressing a knife to her throat. When she tried to scream he pressed the double-edged blade hard up under her chin drawing blood in two places. He'd already disabled the police radio and searched the rest of the car for weapons. She had no idea how he managed to get to the cruiser without being seen, but he was batting a thousand.

He nestled the pistol into the notch behind her ear and pulled her from the car. He wasn't rough about it and she didn't resist. It would have been pointless.

"Now what?" She tried to keep her tone casual, but her heart was racing like a thoroughbred.

"Between the vans, Cheri. Be nice and I promise it will be quick. If not …"

Delta Three pushed her hard up against the far van, her face against the cold metal, her arms out at her sides. Standing behind her, he let her feel the knife in his left hand caress the back of her neck before he tucked the pistol back into the holster at his waist. His movements were now slow and sensual. He ran the knife down the side of her face and then back to the front of her neck. He pulled her head back roughly by the hair, leaned in close and licked the back of her neck.

"Nice," he said. "Very nice." His breath held the acrid stench of stale tobacco.

He kept the knife hard against her jugular as he slipped his right hand slowly up from her stomach to her right breast, continuing to kiss and lick the side of her neck. He rubbed the breast lightly at first, then harder and more aggressively, pinching her nipple painfully through the thin fabric of her bra.

Darcy closed her eyes and tried to concentrate. She pushed back against him and felt his hardness press into her buttocks. When he didn't react, she pushed herself a little further from the van.

The man slipped his hand inside her bra and hefted her full, round breast. She pushed back a little harder and could hear the man's breathing become shorter.

"That's right, Cheri. Don't fight it."

He leaned into her and rubbed himself up against the back of her leg. He took his hand from her breast and moved it down to the crotch of her jeans. She could feel him smile against her neck. His smile didn't last long.

She was standing about two feet from the van now, and leaning backwards. Her arms were still out to her sides posing no threat at all. She was submitting completely, or so it seemed.

The second he moved his hand on its downward journey, Darcy felt the knife in his left hand shift ever so slightly. She moved with the practiced grace that could only come from years of hand to hand combat training. Everything happened at once. She scraped the sole of her shoe down the front of his shin to give him something to think about. At the same time, her left hand came up and slapped the elbow of the arm holding the knife. She turned her head to protect her throat and grabbed the knife hand with her right. The cuts she received on her throat and hand would heal in a matter of days.

Darcy moved with the kind of speed born out of desperation. She knew she couldn't beat him in a protracted battle. She had to win, and win fast. She brought both feet up against the side of the panel van and pushed backwards with all of her strength. Delta Three slammed back against the second van hard enough to lose his breath. Darcy stepped under his arm and twisted his knife hand savagely back so the blade was facing his stomach. She moved in and brought her knee hard against the nerve that runs along the outside of the leg. At the same time, she pushed as hard as she could upward on the hand holding the knife.

The viciousness of the attack and her attacker's own momentum allowed the razor sharp stiletto to easily pierce the bulletproof vest. The six-inch blade missed the sternum by an inch and all but bisected the mercenary's heart. He was dead before his head hit the pavement. Darcy didn't wait to check for a pulse.

CHAPTER SEVENTY-SEVEN

The elevator stopped on five.

The radio in his hand buzzed before Wolfe's voice came across so crisp and clear that for a second Jack thought the man might be standing right behind him.

"Alpha Two."

No response.

"Alpha Two, come in!"

Again, no response. There was a longer pause this time, punctuated by soft static.

"Alpha One to all units. Alpha Two isn't responding. 10-3. Go to plan Baker."

The elevator started to move again. When it stopped on the main floor and the doors began to open, Jack didn't wait. He fired three shots into the car, one of them through the door as it was sliding back, before realizing the lift was empty. He shook his head, knowing he'd just been tested … and failed.

The elevator to his right hummed to life. Jack stepped back so that he could get a good angle into the car when it stopped, but it continued past the ground floor, stopping on 2B. Jack swore under his breath, and for a moment he wasn't sure what to do. He looked around at the three dead bodies. The first floor of ComTech looked like a war zone. He tried not to think of Darcy.

Shaking it off, he moved quickly to the security desk and lifted the phone just to be sure. As expected, the lines were dead. He opened drawers and emptied baskets looking for a pass card or a set of keys. He couldn't find anything that looked like it might help. He ran to the older guard and rolled the man onto his back. Jack unclipped the guard's photo ID card from his breast pocket and felt the unusual thickness—a security pass card. He unhooked a set of four large keys from a holder on the guard's belt.

Jack moved over to the body of the mercenary. Putting the Glock back in his holster he unsnapped the Uzi from its harness. Familiar with how the weapon worked, he cleared the breach to make sure it wasn't jammed. He inserted a new magazine, chambered a round, and pocketed two extra clips. He was still trying to push thoughts of Darcy aside as he moved through the double doors that led to the office beyond.

Darcy pulled the semi-automatic out of the holster on the back of her assailant's belt and checked the vans just to be sure. When she pulled back the sliding door on the first van she found herself staring at a small arsenal. Three M72 rocket launchers were extended and uncapped, and ready for action. There were a number of large caliber fully automatic rifles—AK47's—and two extra Uzis with several spare magazines. The second van held much the same. *These guys are ready for anything!*

Darcy grabbed the keys out of both vans and tossed them into the ditch on the far side of the road. Before heading for the complex she took a pair of side cutters from the floor of one of the vans and snipped the valve stem off of the front tires on both vehicles. The vans sagged sadly on the rims. *So much for a getaway car.*

CHAPTER SEVENTY-EIGHT

Wolfe stepped off the elevator and moved confidently down the hall with Katherine in tow. She didn't resist. She stumbled along beside him like a sleepwalker, apparently not caring that he was holding her tight enough to leave a bruise on her arm. He could tell she was numb, mentally and physically. Beyond that, Wolfe barely gave her a second thought. She was nothing more than a minor annoyance that had to be carted around, like a little sister on a first date.

He walked a convoluted path through the bowels of the complex without making a wrong turn. He'd studied the blueprints for days. Fourteen minutes and eleven seconds had elapsed since they'd entered the front of the building. Time was running out and unforeseen complications were beginning to worry him.

He found Morgan just beginning to lay the charge on the huge vault at the end of the wide hall. The holes were already drilled in the case hardened steel. The drill itself lay smoking on the floor just off to the left.

The door to the vault was seven feet high and reportedly just about as thick. Morgan was obviously being careful not to damage the hydraulics that allowed the door to swing outward. If he screwed that up they'd never be able to open the vault.

"You're behind schedule." At the sound of his voice the older man spun around and pointed his Berretta at Wolfe's head. "Relax," Wolfe said.

Beads of sweat on Morgan's forehead formed small streams that ran down the side of his face. His shirt was soaked. He turned back to his work.

"Luis had trouble with the alarm system. Fucked up my timing. I'm almost done."

"Here, this might help." Wolfe handed him the slip of paper with a long series of numbers scribbled across the top.

"He gave it up?" Morgan asked, not all that surprised

"She did, with a little convincing." Wolfe shrugged, pushing Katherine against the wall beside the vault. She stayed perfectly still like a life size poseable doll.

"Is the alarm on the vault still active?"

"That's what you wanted, isn't it?" Morgan asked.

Wolfe nodded.

"Then that's what you get. When this door opens the monitoring station will get a main transgression alarm. When the guards don't answer, they'll send in the troops."

"Response time?"

"Four minutes if there's a car in the area, eight minutes if there isn't. Either way, lad, we'll be long gone. If anyone shows up earlier, Jean Paul can earn his pay. What about Alpha Two?"

"He was sent to take care of a visitor on the main level."

"He didn't respond when you called."

Wolfe nodded again. "We could have trouble there."

"Meaning?"

"We improvise. When you open the vault I'll take the package and clear out. We meet back at the loft in 30 minutes. Don't be late, I won't wait."

"And me?"

"You stay with Carlos and finish the job. Set off the charges and get the hell out of here. Make sure there's no loose ends."

"While you're high and dry? I'm not sure I like that idea."

Wolfe tossed him the brief case he was carrying in his left hand.

"I didn't think you would. Consider it a bonus for the added risk."

Morgan unsnapped the clasps and flipped up the top of the attaché to reveal the tightly banded stacks of money. He looked up at Wolfe and winked.

"That ought to just about cover it, Johnny." His face clouded over when he looked at Katherine standing next to the corridor wall. "What about her?"

Again, Wolfe didn't hesitate.

"Kill her."

CHAPTER SEVENTY-NINE

Jack slid the guard's ID through a card swipe. He stepped through the first set of doors and looked to get his bearings and to find something to prop open the door. If Darcy *did* manage to call for backup before ... they'd need a way in.

Stuffing a wastebasket between the door and the jamb, he moved quickly to the far end of a large room crowded with desks and filing cabinets. Small emergency lamps set high near the top of the ten-foot walls provided the only light. An EXIT sign glowed eerily above a door in the far corner. Jack moved as fast as he dared.

He held his breath and pushed on the crash bar, easing the door open so he could check the stairwell. He listened for almost a full minute before moving forward. Sliding his back along the wall, he used his foot to search for each stair. He held the Uzi in one hand. Several of the emergency lights were either smashed out or missing, leaving uneven pockets of light every few floors up and down the full height of the building. The lights for the basement levels were out.

At the bottom of the stairwell a red light glowed in the pitch black. It danced and swooped like a firefly in sync with the blood pounding behind his eyes. He swiped the card and the light changed to green. The lock snapped open with a crack that sounded like a rifle shot.

The space beyond was clean and brightly lit. Jack checked the safety on the Uzi, flipped the switch to full auto, and began picking his way through the labyrinth of rooms and corridors. Somewhere at the end of the maze was a man that he very much wanted to kill.

If Darcy had been a few steps faster she would have heard the lock snap at the bottom of the stairwell. She was following the path that Jack was marking, unsure of what she'd find. The dead bodies in the lobby told their own macabre story. If she was right, Jack had broken his promise and moved beyond the foyer on his own. If she was wrong ...

An alarm sounded when she stepped into the corridor at the bottom of the stairwell. At first she thought that she must have triggered the security system, but quickly dismissed that idea. The alarm was ringing very faintly in a distant part of the basement.

She moved in the direction of the sound. Her movements were methodical and practiced. The volume of the siren seemed to increase with each step. She kept to the center of the wide hall staying away from the concrete walls. Missed shots tend to hug walls and floors. She watched every door and looked into every open room. Despite the care she was taking she almost missed the gray clad figure in a room at the end of the corridor.

He was dressed exactly the same as the man she'd just killed in the parking lot. Crouched down with his back facing the door, he was working on something Darcy couldn't quite make out. She used the noise of the alarm to cover her steps and moved up behind him, looking quickly around the room to make sure they were alone. She pressed the Berretta to the back of his head.

CHAPTER EIGHTY

Once Morgan keyed in the combination for the main vault it took Wolfe less than a minute to breach the secondary safe and retrieve the case containing the CPUs. The alarm was deafening in the enclosed space. Wolfe walked past the pair without so much as a glance at Katherine, the titanium case swinging in his left hand. Just before turning the corner he looked back at Morgan and nodded.

He took the elevator up to the second floor and walked the full length of the building to an emergency stairwell at the west end. When he stepped into the open air, the night was cool and quiet. The external alarm on the building had been disconnected long before the vault was opened.

Jack froze in mid-stride when the alarm suddenly stopped. Despite the ringing in his ears he could hear a voice just around the corner. A man with a heavy Irish brogue seemed to be chatting away to no one in particular.

"To be sure, I wish I didn't have to do this, lass, but ..."

Jack stepped around the corner with the Uzi at eye level, the trigger partially depressed. A man was standing at the end of a short hallway beside an open vault the size of a transport truck, a large semi-automatic pistol pressed to the forehead of Katherine Sharpe. A second corridor ran off to the west behind him. The man didn't appear to know he was there until Jack barked out a command.

"Police! Don't move!"

The man spun around behind Katherine and wrapped his left arm in front of her throat. He pushed his pistol hard up against the side of her head, using her body as a shield. Katherine didn't try to resist. The man looked quickly down the corridor to his left and then back at Jack.

For a moment it was as if time stood still. Nobody moved. The two men stood staring at each other from about thirty feet apart. Finally, the man relaxed his grip and gave Jack a roguish grin.

"Ah ... Detective Wright, I'd wager."

Jack didn't respond.

Morgan continued, "We haven't had the pleasure, but I've heard a lot about you."

"Drop the weapon."

"I think we should talk about this, lad."

"Drop the weapon. Do it now!" Jack increased the pressure on the trigger.

"I don't think so, Detective."

"Drop the fucking gun ... now!"

"I think it would be better for everyone here if you'd lower *your* gun ... and listen. Believe me, you'll want to hear what I have to say."

Something in the man's words made Jack relax the pressure just a hair.

"Good lad, very smart." The man kept the pistol pressed against Katherine's head. "I'll make this quick and simple. This corridor is lined with explosives. Very powerful. Had to make it look like we broke in, didn't we? There's one charge right behind me on the door. It's kind of redundant now but ..." Morgan shrugged.

"What's your point?"

"Point being," Morgan said, raising his left hand and pressing a button on the remote hidden in his palm, "We have slightly less than three minutes to resolve this situation amicably before it becomes a moot point."

Jack didn't say anything at all. He'd missed the detonator. He didn't want to miss anything else. He watched the man's eyes, the way he held the weapon, the way he stood ... everything.

"I'm not bluffing, Detective. I assure you."

The words were calm and convincing, but Jack waited. The seconds ticked by.

"I'm open to suggestions," Morgan said, his grin fading slightly.

"Okay," Jack said. "Here's a suggestion, drop the weapon, turn around, put your hands out to you sides, and walk back towards me … slowly."

"Not funny, and not very productive."

The smile disappeared from the mercenary's face. Beads of sweat stood out on his forehead like raindrops. He licked his lips. Jack took it all in and waited, knowing whoever spoke first would lose.

"We haven't time for games, lad."

"I hate games," Jack said. "You have one choice and about a minute and a half to make it. I'm willing to wait."

Jack could see the sweat starting to run down the side of the mercenary's face. The older man's gun hand became unsteady. He didn't need to be an expert in body language to see the bravado cracking.

The man's voice rose ever so slightly when he spoke. "Then I guess we're all going to hell together."

Jack couldn't resist the opening. "You first."

The man swung the gun toward Jack and fired a quick shot that missed by at least a foot. Jack was already moving to his right, but before he could bring his front sight back up on target a gunshot echoed from the west hall. The man did a slow pirouette to face down the second corridor. A strange look crossed his face like a shadow. He let go of Katherine and started to raise the Beretta. Before it got past his waist a second and third shot snapped his head back and sent him crashing against the door of the huge vault. When Darcy stepped from around the corner Jack was too stunned to move.

CHAPTER EIGHTY-ONE

Wolfe made it to within fifty feet of the vans before he realized that something was seriously wrong. The front of both vehicles sagged listlessly on the rims of the flattened tires. Another few steps put him adjacent to the space between them where the lifeless body of Delta Three still lay. Wolfe changed directions without a moment's hesitation. He found the car and the sleeping guard a few minutes later.

It took the dozing guard a few seconds to remember he was on duty and sitting in a security car at the back of an office complex adjacent to ComTech. It took another few seconds to realize that it was a gun pressed up against his left temple. Wolfe opened the door and moved back. He motioned for the guard to step out. The middle aged man, soft and still confused, had to work to get it right. His legs had gone to sleep while he napped.

"I need a car. Any objections?"

The guard shook his head without uttering a sound. He moved back with his hands in the air.

"Good," Wolfe said. "Turn around and count to one hundred out loud. When you're done, you can call the police. Understand?"

The guard turned around and faced the building as he was told. "Y—yes sir. One."

Wolfe fired one round into the base of the guard's skull.

"Two."

CHAPTER EIGHTY-TWO

Jack's first thought was to grab Darcy in a bear hug, but there was not time. "I thought you were dead," he said instead.

"So did I. I'll explain later. We haven't got much time."

"I know. This whole place is set to blow." Jack said.

"You know about the C4?"

"We were just discussing it," Jack said with a tilt of his head at the body. "Which way?"

"Back the way I came," Darcy answered. "I diffused the two charges my friend pointed out. He's a little tied up right now, out of harm's way."

Jack had no idea what she talking about, but there was no time for an explanation. The LED on the timer by the vault read 00:32. They both grabbed Katherine by an arm and started to run. She was like a dead weight. Between the two of them they half dragged, half carried her the length of the hall.

"The stairs!" Jack said.

The first explosion shook the building. The second and third explosions followed one on top of the other. The fourth and fifth were indistinguishable, one from the other. A noise like a freight train rushing through a tunnel rumbled at them from the far side of the complex. A fireball filled the corridor a split second after Jack slammed the heavy steel door closed behind them. The fire door buckled but held despite the proximity of the last blast.

The three of them lay for a few minutes in a jumble under the bottom flight of cement steps. By the time they tumbled out into fresh air through a side emergency door a few minutes later, the faint sounds of a fire siren could be heard in the distance. They collapsed onto the cool green of the newly laid sod that surrounded the complex.

Jack looked at Darcy. "You all right?"

"Yeah … you?"

"Yeah."

"What about her?" Darcy asked, indicating Katherine with her chin.

"I don't think she even knows where she is. What about Wolfe?"

"I didn't see him. You?"

"No, but I heard him on the radio," Jack said. "That's why I thought you were dead."

"Then he's still around."

"I don't think so." Jack was shaking his head.

"He's got to be. I flattened the tires on the vans. Our car's still here."

"That wouldn't stop him. He probably had this all figured into the plan."

"So he's gone?"

Jack didn't know what to say. The three of them sat on the damp grass and listened to the emergency vehicles getting closer.

"He spells it with an 'e', you know?"

It took Jack a second to realize who was speaking. Katherine was sitting a few feet away, her knees tucked up to her chest, her arms hugging them tightly, a funny, incongruous smile on her face.

"Wolfe. He spells it with an 'e', like Nero, but he's more like the animal. He should spell it without the 'e'." Her voice had a dreamy quality to it, like a child not yet awake.

"Ms. Sharpe?"

She turned to look at Jack.

"Katherine … it's Jack Wright. Do you remember me?"

She nodded.

"Katherine, he's getting away. I need to stop him. Do you know where he's going?"

She nodded again. Her eyes seemed to be clearer and brighter.

"He's a wolf. He's going back to his lair."

CHAPTER EIGHTY-THREE

When the service elevator started down from the fifth floor with a groan and a brief shriek of metal on metal, Wolfe barely gave it a second thought, other than to be surprised that Morgan was on time for once in his life. The echo of the ancient lift hitting the stops at the first floor vibrated up through the beams of the old building. Wolfe smiled at the thought that he only had to make one more trip down on the dilapidated hoist. The motor whined in protest as the elevator started back up.

"When we get to the top, stay on the elevator and stay down. Christ, I can't believe this."

Katherine was standing by the large brass operator's handle of the lift. Jack was sorry she'd ever come out of her stupor. Once she started talking on the ride over, it was almost impossible to get her to stop. She filled in a few holes, but it was on her terms. She wouldn't give them an address, just directions, and she also refused to be left downstairs when they arrived.

"I know where he is. You take me with you or you can search the whole building from top to bottom."

Jack watched her carefully for a second. The earlier weakness was replaced with a stubbornness that showed in how she stood and the way she set her jaw. Jack couldn't take the time to reason with her. Now, on the ride up, he was sorry he didn't at least try.

"If shit hits the fan, find something solid and get behind it. Darcy will have the troops here in no time. All I want to do is make sure he can't use the elevator as a road block."

"I started this mess. I'm going to see it through, one way or another," she said, and then looked at Jack with pleading eyes. "Can you stop him?"

"One way or another," Jack said.

"I never meant for any of this to happen. Nobody was supposed to get hurt. I—"

"I know. Just stay down and stay quiet. It's going to be all right." But even as he said it, Jack knew it was a lie.

Darcy sprinted the short distance to the phone booth across the street without breaking a sweat. That didn't happen until she lifted the receiver and the handset came up without a cable attached. Neither she nor Jack had a working cell phone. His was dead and the screen on hers must have shattered when they landed in a heap under the stairs after the final explosion.

Darcy looked around the darkened streets quickly for another pay phone. Nothing. *Shit! No pay phone, no back up.*

CHAPTER EIGHTY-FOUR

Wolfe worked quickly to re-pack the CPUs and discs containing the artificial intelligence programs in a different case, along with cash and a set of false ID, one of several he'd use over the next few days.

When the elevator ground to a halt on the fifth floor, Wolfe didn't bother to turn around. Complacency can be a bitch.

"Nice of you to be on time. Grab your kit, Patrick, we leave in five minutes."

"I don't think so."

Before the words were out of Jack's mouth Wolfe was moving. The elevator had stopped three feet below the proper level and Jack used the bulwark that it formed as cover. Wolfe dodged to his right and then rolled to his left. His reflexes were razor sharp. He brought the Uzi up with his left hand and fired blind into the mouth of the lift. 9mm rounds ricocheted off the metal wall at the back of the elevator narrowly missing both Jack and Katherine.

Jack fired off a burst from the Uzi, emptying a clip in seconds. Pieces of hardwood floor splintered up behind Wolfe as he ran and then dove out of sight around a corner. Katherine lay curled in a ball at the other end of the big lift. Jack wasn't sure if she'd been hit by a stray round. As he was just about to check, the loft was plunged into sudden darkness. The elevator dropped slightly as the power to the big motor was cut. Wolfe must have reached the fuse box.

Darcy looked up at a rusted fire escape that snaked up the back of the old factory and couldn't help being consumed by an overwhelming sense of déjà vu. The night was rife with similarities, but it was the differences that really mattered. This time the operation was strictly ad lib. There wasn't time to plan anything. She wasn't working as part of a well-trained team. She had no communications and no body armor. More importantly, there was no time for caution and no room for hesitation.

The first burst of automatic weapon fire pushed any doubts aside. She didn't think, she reacted. Her feet barely touched the steps as she raced from landing to landing in the pitch black. The only lights in the building glowed dimly through the dirt covered windows on the fifth floor. When she got to the top landing she slammed her back against the blackened bricks, holding the Berretta in both hands, cocked and ready. The closest window was ten feet away and too high to get a look inside. As she wondered what to do next, the lights winked out.

Darcy waited for half a second to catch her breath, and then pulled on the fire door handle. It didn't budge. Another burst of gunfire echoed around the interior of the top floor. Darcy stepped back against the railing and emptied half a clip from her High Power at the lock. When she pulled on the handle again her heart sank. The door held firm.

CHAPTER EIGHTY-FIVE

The elevator wasn't safe. That was the one thing Jack knew for sure. Neither he nor Katherine had been hit in the exchange of gunfire, but only by the grace of God. Jack didn't want to give Wolfe another chance. He moved to the far side of the lift so that he could whisper.

"We have to move."

Katherine was shaking like a leaf.

"When I fire, get the hell out of this thing. Go to the right and get down behind something heavy."

Katherine nodded.

"Watch the top grate when you roll out. Don't stand up right away. Keep low when you run. Got it?"

Jack squinted out into the darkness. The loft was a mosaic of shapes and shadows.

"There." Jack pointed Katherine in the right direction. "You're going to be all right. I'll be right behind you. Get ready." He took a deep breath. "Go."

Jack squeezed off most of a magazine in short bursts as he backed up along the lip of the elevator. He fired blind, hoping to draw Wolfe out. It didn't work. The shots weren't answered by anything more than an echo.

When the gun jammed Jack didn't bother trying to clear it. He dropped the Uzi to the floor of the elevator and grabbed the Glock from his shoulder holster. He rolled up and out of the lift, covering the area that he'd just strafed. When he tried to straighten up he was caught with a kick to the solar plexus that sent him crashing to the floor and his pistol spinning off into the blackness. With his eyes adjusting to the dim light Jack could just make out Wolfe standing over him with a silenced Beretta in his left hand. The pistol was pointed at the center of Jack's head.

"You've been a major pain in my ass, Detective Wright. No more."

It was at that moment the rounds from Darcy's pistol slammed through the thin metal of the fire door. The added security bolts, however, held fast. Wolfe reacted instinctively to the sound of gunfire and pulled the Beretta up to cover the door. Jack didn't hesitate. It was the only chance he was going to get. He hooked one foot around Wolfe's ankle and drove the heel of his other foot as hard as he could into the mercenary's stomach. The kick dropped Wolfe to the floor. Jack could hear Wolfe's pistol clatter off into the same black void that had swallowed his own.

Jack and Wolfe both rolled to their feet and squared off like prizefighters at the end of fifteen rounds. Wolfe moved in quickly but Jack caught him with a solid right cross and an uppercut that stood him up on his heels. Wolfe shook off the punches and blocked the next two with ease. When Jack tried a kick to the mid-section, Wolfe caught it and used Jack's leg as a lever to slam him back into the wall beside the elevator. Jack struggled for breath after he felt it explode out of his chest. Before he could recover Wolfe spun him around and threw him up against a solid wooden post with a sickening thud. Jack knew without a doubt that he wasn't going to win this fight.

CHAPTER EIGHTY-SIX

Darcy kicked at the door, knowing it was useless. The door was set in a solid frame and hinged to swing out. She could hear the sounds of a struggle inside, and for a minute she had no idea what to do. The frustration was maddening. She had to find another way in.

She played her MiniMag through the rusted grating of the fire escape. The penlight picked out another recessed doorway one floor below. It was her only hope. She lunged down the stairs, jumping the last six feet, and hauled on the door with every ounce of strength she possessed. The door wasn't locked. She had to grab the railing with both hands to keep from tumbling backwards into space.

The fourth floor was a duplicate of the fifth, except that most of the antique machinery was still in place. The bright light of the MiniMag made it seem as if Darcy had stepped back in time. Dust and cobwebs were everywhere. Darcy played the small flashlight around the room looking for a set of stairs but couldn't see one anywhere. Packing crates and barrels were piled throughout the room and along the walls. Dust swirled into the beam of the flashlight as she moved over and around the debris. She could hear the muted sounds of a fight one floor above and knew time was running out.

She swept the MiniMag across a huge conveyor system that climbed to the ceiling, passed it once, and then came back. Something was different—out of place. The cobwebs above the conveyor were gone. The dust. There were brush marks and one distinct footprint in the dust.

Somebody had used the conveyor like a slide to get down from the top floor. She held the small penlight in her mouth and started to climb.

Jack sidestepped around the huge wooden post, using it to buy time. Wolfe picked up a crate and swung it at Jack with everything he had. The wood shattered against the support a few inches away from Jack's head. Jack rolled to his left and came back up in a defensive stance.

Wolfe moved in with his right hand out and his body angled back to the left. Jack couldn't see what he was holding in his other hand, but he didn't have to, he was sure it was a knife. He was right. Wolfe lunged and the blade cut deeply into Jack's forearm when he tried to block the attack.

Jack could hear Nina's voice in his head. … *stick to the basics … for heavens sake forget about a spinning backwards anything … we live in the real world …* He was desperate and nothing about the present situation seemed remotely 'real'. Jack dropped to one knee and spun his leg out backwards in a desperate attempt to stop his attacker. It arced through the air at the perfect height, 6 inches off the floor, fast and smooth.

At the top of the conveyor Darcy pocketed the Mini-Mag, pushed the trap door aside, and slipped through silently. She could make out the two men battling on the far side of the loft, but she couldn't tell who was who. She moved forward in a low duck walk, praying she wasn't too late.

Sensei Nina Mariko was right. *She was always right.* Wolfe saw the kick coming and countered with ease. The foot sweep missed and Wolfe stepped in, dropping his full weight on the side of Jack's knee. Ligaments and tendons tore, and the joint disintegrated from the impact of Wolfe's foot. Jack screamed in pain and crashed to the hardwood, holding his mangled knee in both hands.

Wolfe moved in and picked Jack off the floor, his clenched fists gripping him by the collar of his shirt, the knife still in his left hand. Jack tried to balance on one leg but the pain from his shattered knee made his head swim. He was on the near side of unconscious. Even so, he could feel the keen edge of the blade Wolfe was pressing hard against his jugular. The mercenary held him so that their faces were less than an inch apart.

"You shouldn't have fucked with me."

Darcy was less than thirty feet away but the two men were so close they appeared to be one. She couldn't get a clear shot. *Move, damn it!* She was afraid of hitting Jack, but she had to do something.

"John Stephen Niles!"

At the sound of his name Wolfe spun around like he'd been slapped, but even so the move wasn't enough to give Darcy a clear shot. The tritium sights on her pistol glowed spectrally in the dark and she silently begged one of them to move … just a bit. Darcy added another pound on the trigger of her Beretta.

The gunshot sounded like an explosion in the empty loft and caught everyone by surprise. For a split second Darcy thought she'd shot unintentionally. The echo bounced around the loft like a crazy ricochet. Jack looked to his right and saw Katherine standing about ten feet away with his Glock held in her trembling hands.

A dark red stain began to form on the front and back of Wolfe's shoulder, just to the left of where his Kevlar vest stopped. He staggered back, staring down at the wound in disbelief. Jack sagged against the wall to the left of the elevator.

Darcy didn't hesitate. She fired two rounds dead center of the chest. The force of the 9mm. hollow points knocked Wolfe off his feet and sent him tumbling backwards into the service elevator. He disappeared over the lip and dropped the three feet with a dull thud. Darcy forgot her training and started towards Jack who was struggling to sit up against the wall. The mistake almost cost her life.

Wolfe reappeared with Jack's discarded Uzi in his weak left hand, racking the action to clear the jam with his right. Katherine Sharpe fired another shot, but this one was wildly off target. Wolfe ignored her and brought his weapon around to Darcy who realized her error and was sighting in for a headshot. He leaned forward on the floor of the loft to steady himself, and squeezed off a single round. His injured shoulder caused him to jerk the trigger and the bullet passed by Darcy's head with less than an inch to spare.

Jack didn't give him a chance to fire again. He reached into the elevator and grabbed the brass operator's lever giving it a violent jerk to the 'Down' position. With the power cut the dilapidated lift dropped six feet before the emergency stops had a chance to catch. The upper safety gate, twisted and jagged metal that looked so much like teeth in a misshapen mouth, caught Wolfe midway down the back and pinned him to the floor. The elevator dropped out from beneath his feet as two spears of tubular steel punctured his heart and crushed his spine. Darcy moved in quickly to kick the Uzi away, but there wasn't any need. Wolfe was dead.

CHAPTER EIGHTY-SEVEN

Darcy moved over to Jack—half walking, half crawling—fumbling for the penlight in her jacket pocket. Her hands were starting to shake but she was still fairly much in control. There would be lots of time to break down later. When she saw the blood pouring from the cut on his forearm, she put the MiniMag in her mouth and began tearing strips of cloth from her shirttail to use as bandages.

"Ou ta ell aught ou t ight?"

Jack grinned through the pain. "What?"

Darcy took the flashlight out of her mouth.

"Who the hell taught you to fight? They should have their license revoked."

"I won, didn't I?"

"In your dreams. You fight like my grandmother. Hell, my grandmother could kick your ass."

"Come from a long line of bad-assed women, do you?" Jack winced in pain.

Darcy ignored him, glad he could still make jokes.

"Does this hurt?"

She tightened the bandage around his arm to try and stem the bleeding, and then ripped another strip from her shirt.

"No, but if you keep tearing off pieces your shirt this could get interesting."

"Again, in your dreams. Just be a good boy and bleed quietly."

Jack reached up and touched her cheek with his good hand. There was just enough light in the loft for Darcy to see everything she needed to know. She leaned over and kissed him softly, quickly, and then pulled back.

"You're a mess, but you'll live."

"Check on Katherine, will you?"

Darcy swung the small flashlight in Katherine's direction and found her standing in the same spot, the Glock still clutched in her trembling hands. Even at a distance it was easy to see she was in serious trouble. When the light struck her she reacted as if she'd been burned.

"Katherine?"

She was staring at Wolfe until Jack spoke. When he did, her head snapped around like a whip. She looked like a deer caught in the headlights. Her eyes seemed to look right through Jack.

"Katherine, you're all right now. It's over. It's all over."

Jack spoke in soothing tones but Katherine didn't seem to hear. Her head snapped back to Wolfe and then to Darcy. Katherine's hands were trembling and she was shaking like a leaf. When she suddenly stopped shaking Jack knew they were in trouble.

Jack tried to stand before the gun even started to move. He made it part way up the wall before the pain sent him crashing back to the floor.

"Katherine, don't!"

She brought the gun up under her own chin and pushed it into the soft flesh at her throat. Her finger was on the trigger. Her hand was as steady as a rock now. Jack knew she'd made her decision. Her finger squeezed the trigger slowly.

"Katherine, listen to me."

She squeezed the trigger a little more.

"It's not worth it, Katherine."

Jack could see the recessed hammer of the Glock extend past the frame of the gun as she squeezed a little harder. He had to find the key. *What did she say in the car? What was she talking about? What started this whole thing?*

"Katherine, if you do it, they'll win." He could see her hesitate. "They'll get everything, and in two years you'll just be a bad memory."

He tried to keep his voice low and calm.

"They win, Katherine."

"Not Sumner," she said, as if in a dream.

Jack exhaled slowly. The first step was to get them talking.

"No, not Sumner."

"Wolfe killed him." Her eyes shifted over to the body of the mercenary.

"I know."

"They'll take it away from me anyway."

"They might," Jack conceded, "but they will for sure if you're dead." He couldn't lie to her now. Building trust was everything and she would see through a lie in a second.

"They'll take it away and I'll spend the rest of my life in jail."

"Katherine, you didn't mean for any of this to happen. I *know* that."

"It doesn't matter."

Her hands were starting to shake again, so much so that Jack was afraid the gun might go off by accident. Despite his injured leg he leaned forward and tapped Darcy on the shoulder. She understood. She started to move slowly forward.

"It does matter, Katherine. You never intended to hurt anyone. Hold on to that and use it."

"It's too late. It just— I never—" The tears started to fall. Her hands could barely hold the gun.

"Katherine, what's on the hard drive? Look at me. Look at me!"

She pulled her eyes away from Wolfe.

Jack tried again. "What's on the hard drive?"

It took Katherine a second to realize what Jack was talking about. "Everything."

"The whole plan?"

"Everything."

"Did you plan to kill anyone?"

"No!" The tears were flowing like a small stream down her face.

"Then start from there."

"It's too late."

"It's only too late if you pull that trigger. You can't fight if you're dead. Don't do it, Katherine If you do it they win. It's what they'd want you to do. Take your finger off the trigger."

Darcy moved slowly forward with her hand out.

"Katherine, give me the gun. Let us help you … please."

Darcy reached out further and gently pulled the barrel out from underneath Katherine's chin. When she did Katherine slumped to the floor and curled into a fetal position, emotionally spent. Darcy dropped the magazine out of the Glock and cleared the round from the chamber. She handed the weapon to Jack and sat down to hold Katherine. Amongst the dust and the blood and the broken boards she held her like a mother cradling her child, rocking back and forth and whispering softly.

"Shh. Shh. It'll be all right. It's going to be all right. Shh."

Jack leaned his head back against the wall and wondered if anything would ever be all right for her ever again. The pain in his leg brought him back to all the things still ahead.

CHAPTER EIGHTY-EIGHT

A police funeral is something that has to be experienced to be fully appreciated. There are no words to describe, no way to really explain what it's like to take part in something so moving, so powerful. It has to be lived.

For everyone in attendance it means something different. For the thousands upon thousands of uniformed officers who travel, sometimes great distances, to be a part of it, who stand and march and cry as one, it means the chance to say goodbye to a fallen brother. It's an opportunity for a group of men and women who share a calling to also share their emotions and fears and grief as if they were one body, rather than ten thousand individuals. And for some, for those who truly understand that the difference between life and death is a single breath, it's a chance to offer a prayer of thanks they're not the one being honored on that day.

For the public who line the parade route, who silently offer their admiration and respect, it's a chance to say thank you to someone they didn't know and who they might well have derided just the day before. It's a chance to touch something special, to be an intimate part of something that is at once both tragic and magical.

For the family, it's a chance to both give and receive the support that everyone desperately needs at such a terrible time in life. It's a chance to say publicly what you used to say only in private; to say I love you, to say I'll miss you, to say you are and always will be my life, to say thank you for sharing my world if just for a brief time ... a chance to say good-bye. Gillian Dempster said that and so much more, with the class and decorum and strength that Jack knew she'd find. For one brief shining moment she shared Calvin with the world, and in that same moment had him returned to her whole and complete and alive.

For some, like Jack and Andrew, it was a time to say I'm sorry, to make amends for something they did or didn't do, and for which they would carry a guilt they shouldn't own but might never excise.

As the parade moved down University Avenue in the heart of downtown Toronto, Darcy pushed Jack in a wheelchair as just another member of a fraternity that tripped slightly when one of their own fell. He refused to be singled out or accommodated, much as he'd refused to see the orthopedic surgeon until after they'd laid Calvin to rest. There'd be time for that later. There was no way Jack was going to miss the opportunity to pay his respects to his friend and colleague, and nobody, including Darcy, tried to change his mind.

Jack stayed until the end of the massive reception. He was never more than a few feet away from Darcy and Calvin's family, both offering support and drawing strength. It wasn't until emotional exhaustion and the medications that were masking his physical pain finally overwhelmed him that he allowed Darcy to take him back to the hospital. The healing had begun.

CHAPTER EIGHTY-NINE

Darcy struggled out from under a thick duvet, careful not to wake Jack. The wrought iron bed frame creaked as she shifted her weight and stepped into the pink bunny slippers she'd brought with her to the farm. Jack had teased her mercilessly, but only until she'd threatened to make him cook his own meals. With a full length cast on his left leg and a bandage on his right arm, she knew he was helpless, if not hopeless.

She opened the wide French doors and walked out onto a balcony that looked out over the pasture to the south. Three of the neighbor's horses were munching placidly below on the new grass. The main house, a 150 year-old renovated barn with a three-storey glass wall and steel spiral staircase, was still a little musty from being closed up for so long. Darcy didn't care. She hoped they'd stay long enough to get it well and truly aired out. Decisions about the future—hers, his and theirs—could wait. If Darcy had her way those decisions would be put off indefinitely and they'd never leave. It was beautiful beyond words.

The barn sat on a twenty acre parcel of land in Hamilton Township on a road that could have been featured in a tourist brochure. A mist on the fields was just starting to lift, and somewhere in the distance a mourning dove called to its mate.

Darcy sat in an oversized wicker chair with a cup of coffee and watched the horses move languidly from tuft of grass to tuft of grass. When she heard Jack stir, she padded softly back into the main room and called upstairs.

"Good morning, Sleepy."

Jack 'hrumphed' and tried to turn over, until he remembered the cast on his leg.

"Oh, it's Grumpy this morning. I never know which one of the seven dwarfs I'm going to wake up beside."

"Doesn't say much for your morals, does it woman?"

"Be nice or I won't bring you your fresh-squeezed orange juice," she said, rounding the last of the spiral steps.

"Fresh squeezed, you're kidding!"

"Actually, yes. It's from concentrate. Take it or leave it."

Jack took the glass and finished the juice in one go. "Smart ass!"

"Thank you," she said, swishing away from the bed with her robe pulled taut over her firm buttocks.

Jack reached out and grabbed the robe before she could escape, and pulled her back down onto the bed. Their lips met in a passionate kiss as Jack's hands found their way inside the silk negligee that Darcy wore under her robe. It was difficult to make love with a cast on … but not impossible. They'd found that out over the past three days. Darcy reached down and found Jack already hard.

"I take back what I said about you being lazy. You're up early this morning."

Jack pulled her over on top of him and entered her with ease. They were a perfect fit. He kissed her again, deeply and more fervently than before. They made love with the slow burning passion of those who know there's no need to rush.

They'd come to the farm shortly after Jack was discharged from the hospital, to get away, to convalesce, and to get to know each other better. Jack was on sick leave while Darcy had been granted a six-week leave of absence. The only person who knew where they were was Ken. So far he'd called at least once a day, just to make sure everything was okay.

After making love they sat on the balcony in the old wicker furniture, Jack with his leg propped up on an antique cedar chest. Darcy watched for clouds in a clear blue sky while Jack sifted through a packet of information forwarded by Ken.

"Is that the case brief?" Darcy asked.

Jack nodded, "Uh-huh."

"What's going to happen to her, Jack?"

"I don't know. She's being held at a psychiatric facility for evaluation."

"Do you think they'll try an insanity plea?"

"Not likely, and if they did it wouldn't fly. She's incredibly intelligent and as sane as you or me. I think when she gets better she'll put up one hell of a fight."

"You sound like you almost admire the woman."

"I do, in some ways."

Darcy gave him a look that said it all.

"I know, I know. She broke the law but—"

"But?!"

"You should read through some of this stuff. Especially this," Jack said, holding up a computer printout the size of a small coffee table book.

"What is it?"

"The whole plan, from start to finish. Everything. How it started, where she found Wolfe, the code names, everything."

"I thought the hard drive was erased."

Jack shook his head. "Just programmed to look that way. Katherine told me how to get it if I promised to hand everything over to the defense."

Jack was lost in thought for a few seconds and then, "The damned thing started out as a mental exercise to blow off steam."

"It's too bad it didn't end there," Darcy said. And then after a minute, "So what set it off?"

"I don't think it was set off so much as it just snowballed," Jack replied. "It only really got rolling when she hired Wolfe."

"Now there's a piece of work," Darcy said, shuddering involuntarily.

"Yep. He's what brought it from the world of fantasy to the world of reality. Once he was on board there was no turning back."

"Maybe she didn't want to turn back."

"Maybe," Jack said, "Maybe not. Don't get me wrong, I'm not trying to defend her, I'm just trying to understand. Sumner and his crew had a lot to do with it. A few of the files read like a diary. He was an asshole."

"So she was right to steal the CPUs?"

Jack shrugged. "That's what her lawyers are going to say in civil court."

"There's a civil case?"

"You surprised?"

Darcy shook her head.

"The programs for Artificial Intelligence are all hers, but they're no good without the speed of the new processors. The processors belong to the Milanovich family, the company and God knows who. It'll be tied up in litigation for years."

"Probably," Darcy agreed. "That's if the company survives to carry on the fight. There was a lot of damage from the explosions."

"Would have been a lot more if they didn't get to those secondary charges. Karski said the bomb squad diffused them with about five minutes to spare."

"In any case," Jack continued, "the insurance company doesn't want to pay up because an officer of the corporation was involved. They say it makes the policy null and void."

"Typical," Darcy said.

Jack's thoughts wandered unbidden to Stan Jacobs, who was still missing. There were so many unanswered questions. Rumors and speculation. Another mystery to solve.

Darcy brought him back to the here and now. "So, was she a victim or a criminal mastermind?"

"Who knows," Jack said. "I guess it depends on what end of the microscope you look through."

Darcy pulled herself up out of her comfortable chair and gathered up the case file. She moved his cast gently aside and lifted the lid of the cedar chest, dumped the papers into the bottom and closed the lid. She walked Jack back through the open French doors to the wrought iron bed and pushed him down just hard enough to let him know she meant business.

"Can we make a deal?" She asked, helping him to swing his cast up onto the duvet.

"What kind of a deal?"

She propped a few pillows up behind him before answering.

"One, when you get back on your feet, you let me teach you how to fight. I don't want you hanging around Nina Mariko when we get back to the city."

Jack smiled. "My, aren't we possessive. And who have you been talking to?"

"Ken and I had a little chat," Darcy said coyly.

"Ken is going to find himself sans friend," Jack replied.

"And two, you're here to recuperate. For the next six weeks promise me you'll rest and we won't talk anymore about bombs and plots and computers and greed."

"And if I agree, what do I get out of the deal?"

Darcy leaned over and kissed him, gently at first and then more insistently. She moved his robe aside and straddled his hips, being careful not to jostle his cast. She held his wrists above his head and kissed the tip of his nose.

"One, I let you live," she teased.

"And two?" He brought his hands down to caress her hips.

"Give me a minute," she said. "Something'll pop up."

"Smart ass."

The End